The Imam

The Imam

A Novel
By
Harvey Havel

First Amendment Press International Company
uncut. unedited. quality literature

Published by First Amendment Press International Company
New Jersey, USA

First Amendment Press International Company, and the portrayal of
colonial, bell-waving man are registered trademarks.

Publisher's Cataloging-in-Publication
(Provided by Quality Books, Inc.)

Havel, Harvey.
    The Imam : a novel / Harvey Havel. -- 1 st ed.
    p. cm.
    ISBN: 0-9670081-7-4

    1. Imams (Shiites)-- Fiction   2. Shiites
-- Fiction   I. Title.

PS3558.A779I43 2000   813'.54
                        QBI99-1203

FIRST PRINTING

For My Father

An Apology...................................i-viii
Book One...1-174
Book Two......................................175-226
Book Three....................................227-266
Book Four.....................................267-320
Book Five.....................................321-386
Diagrams to Books Three and Four.....387-414
Glossary..I-VIII
Acknowledgments

Book One

"The more we strive to account for such events in history rationally, the more irrational and incomprehensible do they become to us." - Leo Tolstoy

Chapter One
FATIMA AND SHABBIR
11th of Jumaada al-THanny 1416
(November 5, 1995)

Fatima's cloth left her shoulder blades exposed to the Pakistani sun. A red cloth ran to her knees, her legs and feet caked in mud. She lived in the slums, a wide area stretching several miles in all directions at the base of brown hills. Up in the hills she banged on doors. Many doors had been slammed in her face. She became conditioned to the response. While she searched for homes to clean, she carried a sweeper made of straw that she tied with a string to her waist. The sweeper dragged on the dust covering the roads.

Within Fatima lurked a maze of non-sequitur memories. She went to bed within the shelters of the slums below. There the children played in mud, and men brewed tea over fires.

She made efforts to dream of pleasant things, but after a rough day of searching for houses to clean, she lay in the darkness of her small hovel, hearing the cries of children. She thought of the houses on the hills: the carpeting, the stairs, and the voices of the housewives explaining how there was nothing to clean. Some of these women sympathized. They poured shining coins upon her.

She vowed to own a house where the food would be plentiful. She would throw extravagant parties for important people. She thought Allah would grant this if she worked hard. She had seen others in the slums praying, some without prayer cloths, some without stiff, brimless caps. She assumed Allah was with her when she roamed.

She had a different approach to this Allah who lifted the sun during sultry Lahorian days. No need to kneel. She looked up like a child to a father. She opened her eyes to the sky as though in dialogue. She assumed Allah looked into her eyes. Allah may have heard these wishes to end her bad dreams, but surreal nightmares made her perspire until dawn.

The day provided for one meal. She was accustomed to a soggy bowl of rice boiling over a candle. If she received a cleaning assignment, she was set for a week. Although this did not satisfy her, she concluded this was Allah's way of speaking. Sometimes she became bitter with Allah. She believed Allah should take pride in his successes but also accept his failures. Allah, she thought, had his hands full and replied with either terrible dreams or bags of rice.

The houses on the hill took pleasure in watching the slum expand, filling every corner of the city. The slum dwellers below looked up at the houses on the hill and prayed for fortunes to be reversed. Each day Fatima noticed transients in the area. Quite rarely would they ever leave, for once they entered, they found it hard to leave, and many looked for an easy escape. The children from their hovels crept up to the thoroughfares, tapping on windows and following housewives with handbags. Some of these children visited Fatima in her hovel. The children would bounce on her. Fatima would twist the children from her back.

Bringing hard currency into the slums was dangerous. Even rice was not safe. Fatima kept the bags of rice by her head. The slums never emptied out. Fatima was an exception. Five miles of land were packed into a chain of ashen cardboard. The naked children cruised the outskirts as well, prancing about and laughing until sucked in by its magnetism. The children born within the slums would die within the slums. The shantytown crept towards the hills.

From the suburbs on a hilltop, Fatima watched her village below and occasionally ran into a friend, also a cleaning woman. The residential areas were large enough for both to support themselves meagerly. Her friend's name was Shamima. She was shorter, skinnier, and older. She had a flat chest and thin legs. Fatima knew Shamima was not spending wisely.

"You make more than I do," said Fatima. "You seem to be getting lucky, but you're withering away," as they overlooked the slums.

"All of us must make room for others," replied Shamima.

"What's that supposed to mean? You don't have any children. You never told me anything about children."

"I have children, but they are not necessarily my own," said Shamima.

"And you spend on them? There is nothing here. I made two bags of rice this week, and you make more than that. I'm not in the best of health, but at least I'm healthy."

"I give most of what I earn to the children. If I lose out, then so be it."

"And what forces you to do this?"

"Allah does. He is asking me to give, and so I give."

"You should be the recipient, not the provider. I knew there was something wrong. I knew it. You should be thinking of yourself."

"You are too young to understand. Give it time, and you will see."

"I see it now. You're starving. You give charity foolishly. It was never meant for that."

"Look there," as Shamima pointed to a group of naked children. "The only thing lost in our poverty is the innocence. If I don't help preserve it, who will?"

"Leave that to the mullahs in their mosques," said Fatima.

They gazed upon the frolicking children.

Shamima whispered: "There is joy in life. Joy is everywhere, but only if we look at it right. The damaged sky and the white sun, the dark slums, and the stray animals. Beauty can be everywhere if we just take the plunge and look at it as an entity which Allah has blessed. Never separate parts. It's whole and complete."

Fatima caught sight of the far hill girdled by cement walls. She put her arm around her friend.

Fatima then went along one of the residential roads. She took the higher ground and Shamima the lower. The hills carried many servants in lieu of housewives. More cleaning women canvassed the Eastern side. The Western side was more lucrative. The residential hills circled the slums.

Fatima drifted far West towards the highest point. She came to a row of houses she had not passed before. The long row called itself Drakni Drive. A calmness stalked the streets. A few cars passed and crickets shrilled. This hidden row had to pay off. Yet the first house intimidated her.

The door was left open. Entering and getting caught could involve the police. She entered apprehensively. She called for a servant. She crossed a lawn of dying flowers. She entered a living room with two sofas. Plants filled empty spaces and lent a fullness Fatima admired. A threshold led to a pantry. She walked carefully, looking at photographs of the Himalayas. She made sure not to disturb anything.

All the homes she had cleaned were stocked with Qu'rans. This home, however, did not carry the item. In the pantry a small island stood in the middle. Affixed to the ceiling a rack of utensils. She went through the cabinets stocked with fifty pound bags of rice. Surely the owners would not mind her taking just one. She could handle one bag if she went West and then straight down. No one on these routes would find it strange. With one big bag she could eat three bowls a day. She could spend time on the hill and contemplate. Instead she closed the door. 'Rich bastards. Life is not fair,' she thought. 'Joy? Where? In the struggle for rice?' And she walked away.

The road was a welcoming sight, and she vowed never to enter another unlocked home. Drakni Drive was full of rejection. At each door a servant answered. They were refined and kindly. Rejection, however, was still rejection, no matter how calm the servants were. With each rejection came more rejection.

She maintained her anger through the next gate. A long leather strap with three gold bells was nailed to it. She gave it a pull. A bald old man answered. He smiled and stepped into the road.

"And what can I help you with?" he asked.

He was being sincere, and might as well be. The house was one of the oldest. She disliked servants. Apparently few peddlers knocked on this door. The walls of the house were not as high as the others.

"I am a poor woman, and my children are hungry," said Fatima. "Let me clean your home."

"We have no money here. We can only give food," said the servant.

"No money?"

"No money. My offer stands. I can prepare very good food."

Fatima had never taken a meal. She was not hungry but followed him into the house. No pictures on the walls, no religious hangings. Very dark and cool.

"What is your name?" asked the servant.

"Fatima."

"My name is Shrika. I take care of this place, but sometimes I welcome people who want to help. It's a small house, yes, but I could use a break."

The servant led her to an empty room.

"Why don't you start here," he said.

"But this room is clean," said Fatima.

"Generally it is clean, but there is a lot of dust. You won't be needing your sweeper. There is a duster in there. Should you need me, I'll be in the kitchen. Don't be afraid to walk into the rooms. They all need dusting."

The cleaning took two minutes. Hardly any dust. She ate every morsel of the curried lamb the servant cooked for her. She expected to eat outside. Instead she ate at the kitchen table. The portions were large, and Fatima sighed mid-way through the plate.

"How is it?" asked Shrika.

"Delicious, really it is."

"Work well earned. You are from the lower sections I take it?"

"Yes. Right in the middle."

"I see. You came looking for work?"

"This is my first time on Drakni Drive. I've never been this far up before. It's really quite nice around these parts."

"Yes, Allah has blessed us with peace up here. I haven't been down that way for some time."

"You're not missing anything. It just goes on."

"Oh I know what goes on. Many years ago I was born down there."

The servant made it to the hills, and Fatima's surprise turned into frustration. Too many wanted it too badly. She delved into her food.

"As I recall," said Shrika, "we were all trying to make it to these hills. Some make it. The key is in our respect for the All Mighty. He alone is the master."

The shabbiness of the house deceived her. Many could sleep comfortably in its spacious rooms.. Fatima took a scoop of rice and lamb gravy and shoved it in her mouth. She wanted to take some back.

"That was really good," she said.

"Would you like some more?"

"Okay, but tell me one thing. You can't be this nice to every peddler. Finding a servant like you is rare."

"Finding a cleaning woman like you is rare too."

"And why is that?"

"You are so young and full of life. A bit dirty, but we can live with that. You must be a smart one, yes?"

"Smart enough to read, but there are many smarter than I."

"You deserved this plate of food, and I myself am having a good day. No one is home, and why not do something for Allah's children. He takes a special liking to you. He thinks about you always. Never forget that he is always watching out for you, but at the same time watching over you."

'Rubbish. Absolute rubbish,' she thought. 'The old get religious.'

She folded her arms thinking that this servant had to be thankful for his luck. But luck did make him kind to others.

They heard the door. Shrika dropped his plate in the sink and brought out a wet rag.

"Don't tell her you've been cleaning here," he whispered. "Say you are my niece. What is your name?"

The footsteps became louder, and Fatima readied herself. She assumed the old man had been planning for such an interruption.

"Who is this?" asked the housewife, startling both of them.

"I thought you were coming later tonight, madam," said Shrika.

"I cut my trip short," she said.

"This is Fatima," said Shrika. "She is my niece."

"You never spoke to us about a niece! What a surprise! Let me look at her."

Fatima gave her a quick smile, making sure not to utter a word.

"My name is Sakina," said the housewife. "So where have you been hiding her?" she asked Shrika.

"She lives in the lower sections. She has been here a few times before. You popped in at the right time," as he piled more food onto Fatima's plate.

"Hold on," said Sakina, "why are you people eating now of all times? Hold off till dinner. It'll be ready soon. Shabbir will also be back."

"Fatima has to be going," said Shrika.

"Nonsense. Are you still hungry?"

Fatima returned a shy smile.

"You see. She'd rather stay."

"It's not that simple, madam. You see they are expecting her for a very important dinner at home. I have to get her back on time, or else she'll miss it."

"Oh very well then," she sighed. "But just to let you know, even though Shrika is our servant, he is also part of our family. So please stay once in a while. Shabbir and I would be glad to have you."

Fatima followed Shrika to the front gate. She decided to visit the home again, hopefully when the housewife was present. But for now, she had had enough food. She was bloated.

The sun moved to its highest point. The hills were much cooler than the slums. Fatima had only walked but a few feet on Drakni Drive when she noticed a man coming towards her. He was a young, tall man. She moved to the other side of the road.

"Hey, I saw you coming out of our house," said the man from across the road.

"So what is it to you?" asked Fatima.

"I seemed to have missed you. I'm Shabbir Hussein. I am owner of the house. Did you get any cleaning work done? We usually discourage peddlers. I'm surprised our servant let you in."

"I am a cleaning woman, but I am also your servant's niece," said Fatima.

"So that's it. Shrika never told us about a niece. Where do you live?"

"The lower sections."

"I see. Did you meet my wife?"

"Sakina is a very charming woman. She wanted me to stay for dinner, but I'm in a rush."

"I see. Well, I hope you stop by sometime," he said.

As Fatima approached the lower sections, the old shacks were open for business. Goats explored the vegetation. The merchants worked in small shops. Fatima caught some of the merchants holding their brooms and studying her. She had grown used to it. They kept their gaze as she walked towards the denser part of the slums. Small smoke stacks filled the sky with dull smog. The slums melted into the haze of the horizon. The elderly slum-dwellers slept. Children leaned against posts and ran their fingers into the dirt. Some slept in the nude. Mothers sewed. Workers banged on pieces of metal. A gang of children accumulated behind her.

She often took the children to the hills. The children raged with curiosity, but then lost interest, only wanting to play in the open spaces. The line for water extended to the foothills. Young men filled tin pails. She left the children and walked faster into the thickness. The trail pinched. She tripped over a dead pair of legs. Akbir's men were probably responsible, she thought, running through the slums with their guns. They had not moved into Fatima's territory yet, but she heard talk of their arrival. Many slum-dwellers were warning each other. Some of them purchased cheap pistols to protect themselves. No one had to worry if they paid Akbir's men, but the price was often steep.

As the shacks grew warped, she thought she'd visit another friend, Mama Khadija. Fatima normally passed through her neighborhood on her way to the South. She had neglected to pay her a visit for some time and sensed her concern. She came upon her shelter in the middle of a long row. A heap of trash had been piled in front of the entrance, to deter strangers.

Mama Khadija was short and round, and her slow, heavy gait and white hair were reminders of her final days. But Fatima did not heed these signs. Her features were a tribute to longevity. In a crackling voice, Mama Khadija bid her welcome and led her through a tapering hallway. A torn sleeping cloth lay on the dirt. At each corner candles were lit, flooding the walls with shadows. The floor had been swept, and a bowl of water simmered over a flame. Fatima did not want to journey to the South just yet.

Mama Khadija sifted through her clothing and found a small piece of cloth. She spread it over the floor with Fatima's help. Fatima performed lengthy salaams which added to their comfort.

"Come my child, I'm making some tea," she said. "You're just in time."

"Sorry for not coming sooner. I have been busy, and today I have been blessed with a home up in the hills. One of the servants took kindly to me."

"A servant? I don't believe it," said Mama Khadija with a chuckle. "So now our little devil will start saying prayers."

Fatima spotted a fat roach crawling on the wall.

"Leave it be," said Mama Khadija. "I've become used to them. Even creatures so ugly must endure the blessings of life."

The water came to a boil, and Mama Khadija used a hand clamp to lift the pot. She poured the water into dusty cups weighted with shards of black tea. Fatima noticed her concentration at the expense of her shaking hands. Much of the boiled water spilled into the dirt.

"Don't let the hills get to your head," said Mama Khadija. "You have a long life ahead of you, and you are still growing. Hardships will come and go. The triumph in life is found in dealing with these hardships. Even the roaches know how to deal with good fortune."

"I'm going again tomorrow," said Fatima sipping her tea. "These hill dwellers are different. The servant feels guilty. All these stocks of food packed in cupboards and closets, you wouldn't believe it. The servant used to live down here."

"Many start out from down here. Naturally they feel responsible to help someone like you. It's not guilt. It's their way of giving something back. You are still so young, and your intelligence makes you dangerous. You have no understanding as to what this scheme is about. Take your friend, ah, what's her name? Older than you? Skinny?"

"Shamima."

"You should take after this woman. She prays daily, five times, even though she's hard at work. She brings food for the children..."

"I don't neglect the children."

"Of course you don't. But all you do is play with them and take them around like some gang leader. The children need food most of all. And since you are old enough now, you must give some of it to the children."

"No one gave me food when I was a child. My mother sent me into the roads. I earned my food."

"And when your mother left?"

"I earned it."

"Don't be foolish. My sister and I gathered up food for you children. So many had to go without. But since my sister and your mother were close, my sister always put rice into your hovel.

"You see it takes other human beings to put Allah's will into practice. You cannot do it alone. No one can do it alone. Even the people on the hill can't do it alone. They have problems too. There are so many levels to this grand house, and it takes time, and many prayers, before we can all eat in one dining room."

"You talk so strangely sometimes," said Fatima. "We all have to eat, and in our dreams we can play on that field, where everyone is happy and each is given a ten pound bag to start their trek through this unknown hell. But suddenly we want to feed mouths. We see this as the vision, and we pray for it to happen, but it never happens. Time we can spend working hard in the hills turns into many wasteful afternoons hoping the stuff will fall from the sky. We have to help our own, but not at the expense of ourselves. Shamima just wants the dream to come true, so she gives the children rice as payment to Allah."

"At least you admit Allah needs to be paid."

"No. For me I earned it, and I never worshipped."

Mama Khadija doused the fire. A vent added more light and also a breeze which blew out two candles. A murky effect resulted, and Mama Khadija found matchsticks.

"You should wait before you go back there."

"Why?They invited me back, even the man of the house."

"Don't be impatient. If you go back too soon, or go back too many times, they will not accept you. Wait a few days, and they will be glad to see you. Visit too often and they will be sick of you. Just stretch it out a bit, so that it lasts longer. Go on with your general routine. Use their home as back up."

"I'm going tomorrow. They want me back."

"This servant let you in. It is a sign from the All Mighty. He is looking after you, but he wants you to look after others in that same way. We reap what we sow, and you are doing all of the reaping just as the smallest stems sprout."

"If I get bad dreams tonight, I will not go. Satisfied?"

"Very stubborn. Are you still having those dreams?"

"Once in a while. I will find my mother again."

"You must not think of the past too much. Try not to. Your mother would want peace for you. I know in my heart she does. She will always be remembered as a strong woman who stood up to Akbir's men."

"There is talk of Akbir moving into the South," said Fatima. "Many will not take his extortion."

"May Allah bless them. Did you see already the damage Akbir has done? They say he murdered nearly fifteen in this area. Many are unburied. I'm helping with a group tomorrow."

"Did he really burn down our whole place? I remember some of it."

"How many times do you want me to tell you? I'm not going to remind you of those times. There are too many fragments in you already. Let them go. Your mother is dead. Look ahead. Never look back. You are young. You are making your own way. Let them go and think only about how you must live."

"I don't want the same thing to happen again. I myself stepped over a body on my way here. It will happen again in the South."

"Live with me then. They at least have the decency to ignore an old woman."

"Yes, but once they see me, they will demand rupees. Maybe I should get a gun?"

"Absolutely not. You will get a prayer cloth and pray before you get such a wicked instrument. All these guns do is hurt. We need things that will help."

"And I suppose getting your house torched by Akbir's men and praying to the All Mighty is the solution?"

"I don't know what the solution is. Buying a gun only inflicts harm on others. And that doesn't sound right."

"That's not good enough. I'm trading some rice for a nice old gun. You of all people should be encouraging me. You lost your only son. I can never understand how you people just sit there on your sajjadas and pray for things to get better, when what you really need is to shout so loud that all these low-down huts can hear the complaints against Allah. Sure he does some good, some of the time, and for those times Allah ought to receive thanks, but not too much. He'll turn on you in your sleep the next minute."

While walking along the narrow trail, Fatima glanced at the booths where many stuffed tobacco leaves in their lower lips and then spit their residue into the dirt; all of them were boys she had once played with. Growing had separated them. They were a pack of wolves now. She caught them smiling and whispering. They no longer flattered her. She searched for Hassan the Trader.

Hassan was not well-known to the South, but many knew he dealt in things illegal. Most of Hassan's business was conducted at night, and the news of Akbir's men must have kept him busy. Fatima abandoned this search and walked faster through the narrow alleys to her hovel.

Fatima could not remember her dreams when she awoke the next morning. A spike of sunlight made its way as far as the rice bags piled in the corner. She crawled out and adjusted to the light. She checked her neighbor for the time and news. Her neighbor wore a skull cap and recited verses. He said Akbir's men were now in the area. They pulled people out of their hovels in the early morning. No one was hurt. All of them had to pay for protection. The neighbor was certain he was next. From under a cloth he uncovered a small pistol. He purchased it from Hassan The Trader who had moved his operations to this area on alert.

"I have prepared myself," said the old man. "I have the right to protect myself against these common killers and thieves."

He suggested the same for Fatima who was awestruck by the pistol. The old man held it delicately.

"You're gonna have to grow up quick," he said. "There are no rules in here. This place is too full. We are cramped. There is no such thing as quiet anymore. You must protect yourself."

In the afternoon she approached a silent Drakni Drive. A hot breeze swept across the vacant road. She remembered Mama Khadija's words, but could not wait. The opportunity was too timely to pass up. She expected a warm welcome. She forgot the servant's name but remembered his balding head and squinting eyes. She did not plan on the servant's tenderness. The housewife would easily sniff her out. The servant could have spilled the truth, but Fatima thought this too risky for the servant.

Shabbir Hussein, the same man she had met on the road, opened the gate. Fatima tightened her cloth.

"I'm sorry, but your uncle isn't home," he said.

"I guess it was stupid of me to travel all this way."

"But how could you have phoned? There are no telephones in the lower sections."

"You're right."

"Come. I will prepare some food for you. It's okay, no one is here. Shrika should be back soon."

He led her to the kitchen where he searched through the cupboards. He dumped a cold stew into a bowl.

"We don't have much at the moment. My wife will be back later."

"And where is Uncle Shrika?"

"Running some errands. Sometimes he takes a long time. He should be back. I'm curious what brought you here again."

"You people invited me back."

"Simple enough," as he moved to the table. "It seems you'll be sticking around for a while. Your reunion with your uncle was very surprising for us. We rarely have visitors, but we do get peddlers here. I take it you engage in that sort of work, not to be rude. Consider yourself welcome here."

"Believe me, I'm not making this a habit."

"Just relax and enjoy the food," smiled Shabbir, lightly touching her shoulder. "I didn't mean to hint at anything. Guests are the things we need around here. I get so bored in this old house."

The bowl dropped on its way to the table.

"No, please, I'll get it," said Shabbir.

Fatima, however, jumped at it. The mess was larger than expected. She cleaned most of it.

"That should be fine, really," said Shabbir, "and I thank you. Now if I could just find something to cook..."

Fatima stopped him as he searched.

"Don't worry about the food," she said. "It's no problem. I'll come back when my uncle is here."

"No, no," said Shabbir. "At least have a drink."

He took out the Rooh Afza from the cupboard. He prepared the glasses. She gulped down the sweet, rose-colored water.

"Take your time, unless you are in some kind of hurry."

"I'm in no hurry to get back," she said.

"And why would you be? The lower sections is no place for a beautiful young woman."

"I would like to live up here in the hills one day, but until then, the slums are my home, and I belong there."

"I think you belong in a home. A decent home, where you can cook and clean and look after the children, perhaps children of your own one day. You've got so much time. You're still very young. Keep working, and Allah shall give you his bounty."

"Allah?"

"Yes. He watches over young women. He is the protector of them. Women keep the family strong. You must wait your turn. The angel Mik'ail will find you. He will tell the All Mighty how hard you work without a husband. Allah will look fondly upon this at first, but he will want you to marry. The prophet has said that the best woman protects the rights of the husband and keeps her chastity while the husband is absent."

"And what of the husband?"

"We are to behave modestly. We are the caretakers."

"So I do nothing?"

"It depends. If your husband says so, then you must. But if you wish to tackle other lofty goals, then you are free to do so, as long as your duties to the family are maintained."

"In other words I do nothing but stay in the home?"

"What else is there for a woman to do? You're not in some high society. This is the life chosen for us."

"Allah is guiding me differently."

"Do you give thanks for this guidance?"

"When my luck is good, I do. When my luck is bad, I don't."

"That sounds convenient. But you know what you practice is not Islam. It shall send you to the fire."

"It is Islam in the purest sense," retorted Fatima. "While all of you are too busy following the scriptures, I'm submitting to the good which Allah has placed within us all. I know the difference between good and bad. I eliminate the bad and submit to the good."

"Much too simple..."

"...which is better than complex."

"You go for simplicity, eh?" said Shabbir. "It's good that you come up with your own ideas. It points to your ingenuity. But sooner or later you will realize that praising Allah and doing his will are not simple things. It requires a constant focus. Allah has his hands in all things, and in order to secure a place in the after-life, you must submit to His will. You are not following others. Others are submitting to Him as he has prescribed in the Qu'ran."

"I don't believe in an after-life," said Fatima. "There is only one life, and this is it. We live to exist. Allah guides us through this one life, and then we are devoured by the soil."

"And you call yourself a Muslim? This is not from the Qu'ran."

"One does not have to read the Qu'ran to be a Muslim."

"Then what are the requirements?"

"Only to practice the good. Islam was made from that point."

"You seem too young to be speaking with such conviction," said Shabbir after a moment. "Take it from someone who has been around longer. You need to investigate Islam."

"Okay. I'll visit that vast library we have in the slums."

"I didn't mean it that way..."

"And you don't look so old and wise yourself."

"I'm hardly old, and I'm nowhere near to being wise..."

"Spend some time in the slums, and you can see for yourself where my ideas originate. Many in the slums fool themselves too, but I have risen above it. You should see the nobility in the lives we lead."

"Is this an invitation?"

"Call it what you like."

"Very well then. I accept. I have never been down to the lower sections before."

"That comes as no surprise. People in the hills are so detached and blind."

"If that were the case, I think your Uncle Shrika would not be working with us."

She agreed to take him to the slums on the condition he change into something more ragged and impoverished. Shabbir said it would be a learning experience, an adventure to submerge himself in the activities of the poor. He did convince her of his devotion to the All Mighty and his skepticism towards her ideas. He changed clothing but still looked like a resident of the hills. Such was the worst combination of clothing he could find.

She led him to the road which rolled to the lower sections. The houses were replaced with broken shacks inches apart from each other.

Fatima sucked her teeth as the men on the stoops cracked jokes. Both were aware of how odd they looked together. Fatima put out her hand. He clasped it for a minute or two, then let go as the sweat in their palms mixed.

They walked side by side down the trail. They arrived at the mangled huts. Naked children ran about. Perplexed by his frown, she again hung onto his hand, clammy and familiar in the slow sunset. Fatima felt him shaking, and she gripped tighter.

They did not talk as they did before. The rodents in the trail nibbled at each other. He asked to return to the hills, but Fatima ignored him. Faces peered from the shelters. The trail narrowed. Prayers began on the early side, and old men in torn and soiled robes kissed the mud.

The children grabbed at Shabbir's arms and ankles.

"Oh they're harmless," giggled Fatima.

"I've seen enough," he said.

The thickness of night soon covered the area. He followed her to Mama Khadija's. Fatima asked him to wait a few shacks down. The blaze of bonfires cropped up in all directions.

Fatima found Mama Khadija boiling water for tea.

"I brought someone from the hills," announced Fatima.

"Here? But why?"

"He wanted a tour, so I thought I'd give him one."

"That's foolish. These parts can be dangerous."

"He's a man. He'll be fine."

"A man, you say?"

"Yes, and he's handsome too."

"It's not a good idea to bring someone from the hills down here."

"And why not? Most men on the hill never see this place."

"Most of us living in the slums never see a man from the hills, although we know his territory. You just left him out there?"

"I just thought of dropping by first."

"Why don't you bring him in? He must miss all those pounds of precious tea he has in the hills. I'm preparing another cup for him."

"Let me get him then."

As she untangled herself from the garbage protecting the hovel, she saw a group of men walking towards Shabbir. Their rags were not long enough to cover their legs. The men looked over Shabbir suspiciously and then moved on.

"Oh thank Allah," said Fatima.

"What for?" asked Mama Khadija.

"Wait, they're turning back."

"Who's turning back?"

"Those men. I better get him."

"No!" shouted Mama Khadija who grabbed her by the arm.

"Let go of me! I have to get him!"

"Those are Akbir's men. Lay low."

"I can't. I have to get him."

Mama Khadija held her waist so she could not move and gripped her mouth so she could not yell.

The din of the area tapered off. The wind whipped the alley like the faint whispers of children who peeked at the event from their hovels. Heavy and broken speech of the men surrounded Shabbir. A deep scar cut the face of the shortest of the three who rubbed the sleeve of Shabbir's kurta between thumb and forefinger. Fatima saw Shabbir pulling back his arm. The short one would not let go. He held Shabbir's wrist and uttered vulgarities. The other bandits laughed when Shabbir resisted. The short one drove a tight fist into Shabbir's gut. Shabbir coughed, fell to the ground, and curled in a ball. The three of them ripped away his kurta. Only his trousers were left which they tore from his waist. Shabbir kicked at them. A blow landed on the chest the tallest one. They then pulled Shabbir by the collar and throttled the side of his head. Shabbir slackened as the men yanked his trousers free and waved them like a captured flag.

After the men vanished into the trail, Fatima was set free. She fought her way through a circle of curious children carrying torches to see the beaten face of Shabbir Hussein. Fatima called for spare cloth and a cold rag to tame the ghastly puffiness. She embraced him and kissed him as he stood. She held the cold rag over his face and covered his body with the spare cloth. The cold rag hid what the children were trying to see: a trickle of blood from his nose and a reddish bulge over his eye.

Fatima cried as her crying perhaps suspended the earth. Without resting at Mama Khadija's, they both hurried South in the dark. They arrived safely at Fatima's hovel on the South side of the slum area.

"And where am I supposed to sleep?" asked Shabbir.

"There is enough room for two. I'll move all of this stuff out of the way."

"And that, I take it, is the mattress?"

Candles glowed from the other huts. Slum-dwellers wandered through the pathways, stepping over bodies, some sleeping, some dead. The wind scattered debris over rooftops and within alleys. They crawled into the hovel, shutting out stray rubbish.

"I can hardly fit in here," said Shabbir.

"It's made for one, but sometimes I have guests, like my friend Shamima. We can sleep fine. How's your head?"

"You leave me out there like a package of meat, and then blubber away with your apologies. Your friend must have had a time of it watching the assault. This place is a nightmare, and I've never before wished so hard for tomorrow. The perfect stalking ground for Iblis, and the perfect breeding ground for insects and bacteria. What a contribution to mankind: an abundance of sewage for miles! Can't these people do anything? They beg on the hills, they sleep in the roads. Don't get me wrong, it's tough all over. Just existing takes effort, but these people don't give a damn about helping anyone, especially you. Look where it got you: in the sewage pit of life. Pakistan Zindabad! and long live this cesspool and all of your good-natured and noble people. Try prayer. At least it will make you useful."

"People like you know nothing better," she reacted bitterly. "You know nothing of it. You sit up on the hill and fear it, but you don't know why. You have no idea how hard we work. You just suck the life out of us and keep us here, and then you complain and cut us down, as though we are nothing, as though we don't do anything. We'll be strong eventually, and when we are, they'll be an end to this, and there will be an end to so much excess on the hills. You take so many things for granted. Find your own way back. It would be fitting of you never made it out of here."

She pushed him out of the hovel and closed him out by sliding a piece of cardboard over the entrance. She thought there was truth to what he said but was too angry to let him inside. She left him alone on the trail and mused how he would now fit in with the slum dwellers, for one night at least. Yet something shook within her, and her eyes welled up. Beyond the cardboard she heard the litter swirling. She tried to sleep, but within a few minutes she felt his hand reach between the cardboard slats. She slapped at his arm.

"Hear me," he said. "I've been out here for Allah knows how long. I know you're awake. I can't take it anymore. I'm sorry for what I said. I was angry with how things worked out. I never meant those things. I know how hard you people work, and I know how we're wrong. I was angry and beaten by bandits, but I'm not angry anymore. When people are angry, they say things they don't mean."

"Get on your way," said Fatima in the darkness.

"I don't know how to get out of here. I've never been down here. I can't sleep here. This is ridiculous. Please, I did not mean those things."

"You're just saying that because you need a place to sleep."

"I was so very shocked. You can't blame me. I was beaten up. Look at my face. Here is your proof. I am half-naked here. This whole area is a result of some economic deprivation, some sort of injustice spanning the centuries. It would be humiliating of me to believe the things I said. You have to believe me. Allah is my witness, and if you believe what you said about people in the hills, then you'll have to take me in to show how much better you are. I'll die out here."

"No you won't."

"Then I'll come close. There are strange men out here."

"They won't bother you."

"I'm asking for the last time."

"And what will you do? You'll sleep in the gutter and head home in the morning."

"Just let me in. I don't want to be out here."

"I should let Akbir's men kick you around some more. Nothing but a bum of the hills. You don't deserve to be let in."

"Look at the insect bites on my arms. I'm scratching myself."

She slid the cardboard, and Shabbir Hussein crawled inside. They fumbled through the darkness, arms and legs touching. They exchanged groans. He continued to scratch his arms through the long night.

"Shhh. Enough scratching," she whispered after tacitly forgiving him.

"I have to."

"Shhh," as she rubbed her palm over the bumps. "I'm so sorry," she whispered, "sorry about your face, sorry about your arms and legs. Sorry it has come to this."

She caressed him for a while in the darkness. Her hands moved from his arms and chest to his swollen face and lips. His lips were much softer than her own. The kindness and the comfort of her hands took control until suddenly he rolled on top of her.

"What are you doing," she asked.

"I don't know," he replied.

Chapter Two
SHABBIR RETURNS TO THE HILLS
13th of Jumaada al-THaany 1416
(November 7, 1995)

The morning came with more sweat. Shabbir's bites itched again. He found distaste in the morning. Through the spaces of cardboard he could see the slum-dwellers walking, yelling, and selling things on the trail. Fatima confusedly awoke and begged him to sleep longer.

"I can't," he whispered. "My family worries for me."

"A few more minutes," she said, "just a few more."

"I can't. The trail is already crowded. I have missed my prayers."

"Then go if you must," she said.

"How do I get out of here?"

"When will I see you again?"

"How do I get out of here? My family must be worried, I can't stand it when they worry."

"Who?"

"My wife and my daughter, even your uncle."

"He's not really my uncle."

"Not your uncle? Shrika would never lie to us."

"I don't want to get him in trouble, but just so the truth is known, he is not my uncle."

"I can't believe Shrika would lie to us."

"So you're just taking off, is that it?"

"What more do you want?"

"How quickly you forget."

"I have a wife and child. There is no way I can see you again. With the exception of fifteen minutes, the visit was a nightmare. I have to find my way out."

"By the time you get home, you'll want to come back."

"Nothing happened last night."

Shabbir Hussein found his way back to the hills, asking slum dwellers for directions along the way. His damaged face blended in, but he had no money to buy clothes. Out of fear he wrapped some cloth around his head.

He arrived at Drakni Drive an hour later. Shrika would not let go of his knees. Sakina, holding their daughter, came to the courtyard to see his swollen face. They were loaded with questions. Shabbir had plenty of time to concoct answers. His wife did not pry right away. She instead prepared an ice bag and led him to a warm bath. He reeked of slum odor. Sakina was careful not to come too close. In the tub, she fired questions at him. The police had been called. She was not satisfied with his explanations. She said he acted stupidly preaching the faith to the poor.

"We cannot afford to wait," said Shabbir at lunchtime. "Allah has put the power in me to help them. It is my job and my duty, and Allah sent me visions to get to the slums and contribute. When Allah calls, I cannot wait to tell my wife and child where He has sent me."

"Allah be praised!" cried Shrika.

"No! At that moment I had to leave my home, and notice how he chose a time when all three of you were out of the house. Notice how I come back with nothing but bruises and filthy garments. It was Allah's lesson, teaching me how the slums are growing out of control. So many down there transgress against the faith, and many wept on my shoulder and asked me to pray for them. Many down there are living a life of sin, but some I've changed. I said to them: 'Adopt the view of Allah's followers and praise the Creator. He alone is watching over you. And with it I can promise you salvation and glory."

"Allah be praised!" cried Shrika.

"I was speaking to a whole bunch of them in the dust right outside those shacks, and after I finished my sermon, they all held my knees. They promised they would give praise to Allah and follow the writings in the Qu'ran. It was truly an amazing sight.

"Never before have I felt so endeared to the poor of our city. But I stayed there too long. I had been preaching the whole night through, and when it came time to journey back to the hills, I was jumped by three youths. I didn't bring any money. They just ripped my clothes off, and when I tried to defend myself, I got this swollen face. It was a sign from Allah that there are enemies of the faith, and that I should keep on my toes."

"Allah be praised!" shouted Shrika.

"Indeed!" replied Shabbir who munched on a chicken bone.

"It was foolish of you," Sakina said. "You could have been killed."

"Allah is watching over me and protecting me. I had faith nothing too drastic would happen. You as my wife should have a bit more faith."

"Just don't do it again," countered Sakina.

Chapter Three
FATIMA RETURNS
9th of Rajab 1416
(December 2, 1995)

Fatima inspected her swollen belly in the creases of sunlight which glowed through her small hovel. She had been told by Mama Khadija that she carried a child. Through the tender months of feeding herself extra rice borrowed from her friends, she sometimes stopped her cleaning work and took walks above the slum area. She imagined living in a household with servants of her own and giving her child a place and home on the hills. She knew the key to this arrangement rested with the father of the child. Even though she banged on the gate of the Drakni Drive home for a week straight, Shrika would not let her in. Her belly grew, and she cursed the father and how he rolled on top of her in the middle of the night and imposed what she never wanted to offer.

Fatima's life had been rearranged, but not the father's life. She could feel the resentment sweep through her like a hot flush of wind funneling through a slum trail. She reluctantly thought that with patience and a bit of persistence she could get the father to accept responsibility for the child, even though the balding servant shut her out.

Sometimes she sat on a cool spot overlooking the slums, hung her head, and wept with anger and bitterness. Then she would see something beyond her anger. The father presented an opportunity. Maybe he would miraculously change his attitude, and the servant would change his mind, and all would be well under Allah, and the boy or girl would have a father and food to eat.

She caught herself imagining too much. She spotted a small child along the road following a man from the hills. She wondered what possessed such a child. All children dreamt, she thought, and children and adults connected in their capacity to dream.

Banging on the Drakni Drive home became a routine of constant rejection. She undertook the extra work for the small child growing within her.

She rang the bells at the Drakni Drive home just after midday prayers. Shrika slammed the door on her again. This time, however, she refused his answer. She tugged at the bells repeatedly.

"What is it that you want?" seethed Shrika.

"To speak to Shabbir," said Fatima.

"What could you possibly want with him?"

"We have personal business to discuss."

"Haven't you caused enough trouble for me?"

"I don't mean to cause you trouble. I just want a word with him."

"You can't, do you hear me? You can't. Now get out of here before I call the authorities."

"I'm not leaving until I see him. Something is happening, and it's his fault!"

Shrika slammed the door, but she still tugged at the bells. Shrika returned shortly and with a strong heave ripped the bells from the door. He led Fatima through the wide courtyard. He showed her to Shabbir's bedroom.

"Oh dear Allah, what has happened to you?" she asked.of Shabbir.

Shabbir's health had deteriorated. He had grown thin and pale. He lay in bed supinely like a living corpse, hands to his sides.

"I might ask the same of you," he said weakly. "I got your message the last time, and I guess that wasn't enough. I do admire your tenacity."

"I have to be. I have been treated so rudely by your servant. They think I'm invisible, when I'm carrying your child."

"How do you know it's my child?" he asked.

"You are the first person I've ever been with. The only person."

"Come closer to me."

She noticed the darkness, the grungy smell, the bed with layers of sheets, his sunken cheeks where the swelling had been. She sat beside him.

"Please, take it off," said Shabbir.

"Take what off?"

"Your cloth. Take it off."

She thought it unusual but untucked the red cloth and then sat on his tired waist. His hands ran gently over her full stomach.

"I will support this child of ours," he said. "It is an important child. Your belly is beginning to show. Plump and firm. We are blessed with this child."

Fatima envisioned her child in the hills with his father, and she a second wife. The reminders of slum living would be flushed. She arched her back while sitting on his waist, letting his hands free.

"Take me as your wife," she whispered. "It's the only way. The slums are no place for a child."

"Can you tell it's a son?"

"What difference does it make?"

"I need a son from you."

"Then you shall have one."

"I feel my son inside you. It's living inside you."

"And we should be married then?"

"I don't want to make commitments. I am very ill."
    She kissed him, sure she had caught a vulnerable point. She tucked her
cloth into her chest and left Shabbir's home. She said nothing to Shrika on her
way out.

Chapter Four
THE PLAN
15th of Jumaada al-awal 1417
(September 28, 1996)

    Syedna Tariq Bengaliwala, surrounded by his bodyguards, began the
prayers within the Al–Azim mosque. He led two thousand believers in
prostration towards Mecca. The high tones from the muezzin's voice calling
everyone to prayer overwhelmed even the bodyguards. Their duty to pray
without restraints overrode their duty to guard Tariq with the closest attention.
    They bowed their heads to the ground and kissed their prayer cloths in
unison. Blank faces and moving lips, aligned in neat rows and columns,
matched the muezzin's accelerated pace. Engraved within the four marble
walls surrounding the mosque were the flowing verses of the Qu'ran. The high
dome of heavy white marble reverberated the strong sentiments of the
muezzin's song. Its clarity pressed the believers to pray harder.
    Tariq prayed for the mujlis to end. He thought it useful to encourage
Allah to make room in his tight schedule. A shift had been willed in the social
order of the religion. Praying for patience seemed quite useless. He had done
so a number of times while touring through the Indian provinces of
Maharashtra and Kashmir.
    The Imam was dying a slow, cruel death outside the Indian borders. He
must have selected a son as a successor, but even something as simple as that
could not be counted on. The prayers alleviated his struggling. Surely Tariq
had faith in them and never gave up his praying during every spare moment of
the crisis. But the timing was off. The Imam was dying as he barely shed his
youth.
    Tariq first met The Imam in Delhi four years ago: A tall, muscular
young man with a fine beard of black. Instead of introducing himself through
the traditional salaams, this young Imam gave him a firm handshake and a
relentless look of confidence. His eyes neither shook nor retreated as they
melted into Tariq's own. His bold talk of strengthening the faith while
promoting the highest unity among the believers ignited a stream of fantastic
thoughts. Tariq felt young and jubilant around him. As a young man, Tariq had
these same dreams of a powerful Islam. Within this young Imam he found

renewed hope of thwarting the false pride ballooning within the Western heathens. Every minute counted. Tariq muttered the last verses of prayer and faced the followers. With a nod of Tariq's head the muezzin yelled through the microphones "Syedna Tariq Bengaliwala." The believers stood and answered "Zindabad!" With this shouting of "Long Live!" and then with Tariq's name volleying back and forth, he grew sick of these faceless men in the front and women in the back crying with fierce devotion. The muezzin calmed them for Tariq's sermon.

With a rehearsed patience he stood before hungry eyes and open ears as they settled on the marble floor. He turned towards the archway beyond which stood a wall of bright sunlight. Shielding his eyes, however, he hurried through it with his bodyguards. Surprised and confused that Tariq neglected his sermon, the muezzin rallied the crowd again. The residue of their chants played in Tariq's ears like some captured melody.

Outside the military personnel in khaki green with long rifles slung around their shoulders linked hands to keep Tariq's path clear. Some of the smaller children snuck underneath their wall of held hands and pestered the bodyguards. Tariq had seen this too many times before. He ordered Vasilla, his most able bodyguard, to remove them from the path. At the threat of Vasilla the children scattered. Vasilla caught one of them under the shoulders and deposited her gently within the swaying crowd.

Suddenly Tariq stopped cold. With reluctant eyes he looked to the right and left. They chanted "Zindabad!" for him with such resonance that it rung in his ears. The bodyguards braced themselves. He held his chest with his right hand and raised his left into the air, bent at the elbow, a salute blessing the entire throng of believers. To this show of attention the crowd roared. Their sway undulated. The massive crowd of brown faces and shining caps swirled and blurred, their arms waving in the air. Tariq closed his eyes to absorb their chanting. Through every pore it filled his body. He accepted this paltry reward for his life–long task of touring from mosque to mosque, using trained bows and memorized verses.

And their cheers in his vast but disciplined mind elevated him to a higher plane: to the Bridge of Destiny upon which he treads through delicate rose petals. A dense mist envelopes him, soothing and relieving his worldly anxieties. His garments fall to the floor, and the graying hairs on his body flush away. His wrinkles and blemishes disappear. On his face a beatific smile as the mist vanishes and reveals an infinite-garden with trees, their trunks of gold and their branches of pearl, ruby, and emerald bearing thick, ripe fruit. In the distance he makes out a vast pond with its water as white as milk and an overwhelming scent of musk. On its banks sit fat and fleshy fowl whose necks are as long as camels' necks. Not far from the pond a vast tent made of pearl. A chorus of seventy–two Houris from within the tent break the silence. Without garments they sing:

We are immortal.
We shall never die.
We are born to enjoy comfort,
hence shall never know hardship.
We are born of good cheer,
hence shall never be unhappy.
Blessed be the man to whom we belong
And he is for us.

From the seventh plane of heaven the angel Israfil descends and sings a variety of songs praising Allah's name. The naked Houris and the birds from the adjacent bushes mix with harmony. Suddenly more angels descend from their lofty stories, all with pleasing, resounding voices. The garden is alive with the sight and sound of celestial creatures joined in celebration.

Tariq opened his eyes to a determined crowd struggling to get closer to him. "Quickly," he told Vasilla as he spotted the white Mercedes with its white curtains. Vasilla held open the door. The crowd enveloped the car shouting "Zindabad!" with the same force. Sick of it all, Tariq closed his eyes to erase the sight. He caught cheeks and noses pressed upon the glass. With a quick swipe of his hand he jarred the side curtain. He looked up front. The windshield became a portrait of pressed hands through which he could make out a group of women begging for blessings.

"Run them over if you have to. We're getting late!"

He heard the engine rev as people flew aside like cattle. The beating on the roof and the chanting ended as they broke through the gates of the Al–Azim mosque.

Vasilla progressed through the populated roads of Bombay, closer towards Sahar Airport. They could see another flock of believers waiting for the bavasaab. Vasilla parked away from the main terminal and took a rickshaw into the vortex of noise and tumult. Tariq wanted to enter incognito, but Vasilla found he would have to push the Indian authorities.

"You have to realize sirs, the bavasaab needs to board with the greatest speed, without the slightest delay," said Vasilla. "He is on a very important assignment."

The guards traded a series of crooked grins.

"We can't leave like that," said one of them. "We have to go through High Command. It will take some time."

Vasilla reached into his pocket and revealed a thick wad of one–hundred rupee notes.

"In other words gentlemen, we need your help. Come quickly."

The men followed.

When they arrived at the car, Tariq was perturbed by the delay. He examined their ranks stitched to their epaulets, their name tags, their berets tilted to the side. Tariq bumped into one of their suspicious faces. He chose to refrain from any insulting comments which might have eaten more time.

His eyes then jumped to the jumbo jets he loved as a child. At the age of four the expansive wings, the gusting engines, and the bulging front lend majesty to an object his father finds mundane. The emblem on the tail and the lettering across the vast hulk of steel add a divine splendor. It looms beyond human creation; not a toy, but a joy ride at speeds all too rare. He cries for a window seat. They pass the other machines idle at their gates. He waves to them and enters a mysterious pause. Then the might, the thrust, the rush tugging him across the runway. He whispers goodbye as he embraces an old truth: there is more hope in the journey than its destination.

At the age of fifty this still held true. Tariq's destination was now confined to the vast crowds draped in their white kurtas and capped with stiff topees. Through each town the same scene: brown faces hypnotized, shouting comments of praise, always in submission. He dreamt of someday ending his tenure as bavasaab, shedding his uniform of Allah, freeing himself of all the mess. Or perhaps charging the cheering crowd, grabbing one of the believers by the shoulders, shaking him and shouting: "Just stop it. Hold your tongue. Save it for your creator! Save it. The day will come when you truly need your voice, and you will not have a chord left."

His plane waited. He ended his study of the mud-packed huts along the runway. As their van approached the tarmac, he couldn't help but feel anxious. He detected a field of energy trapped at his fingertips and clenched his fists to rid himself of it. He wanted them to move faster. Some of this tension rubbed off on Vasilla who egged on the driver.

"Since we will not have time when we get down, we thank you men now for this great service," said Vasilla to the Indian guards. "The bavasaab shall surely remember you in his prayers."

They ignored Vasilla's clumsy words. They drove past the main terminal. The flight crew waited below the airplane.

"May Allah be praised. We are so happy to have you on this flight. We know that it will pleasant. We can assure you peace and tranquillity."

Tariq snuggled into his first class seat. He absorbed the occasional twangs of the sitar and the hollow thumps of the tubla. The air conditioners hadn't been started. Although they tried not to disturb his peace, the flight crew crept by him one by one to get a quick look at the man whose photograph hung proudly in millions of Middle Eastern homes: a thick, flaxen beard of white flowing to his chest, his head covered by a thick turban, the irises of his large brown eyes surrounded by a white milky haze, and his heavy bifocals. He did not heed their stares. They looked innocent to him, like the small children at Al-Azim. He continued reading the Ou'ran with an air of righteousness. But between the heavy lines his mind wandered to the spacious city of Lahore and its hillside. The Imam waited for him, his urgent message sent a few hours ago.

He was served a gosh of some sort, a curried meat under brown gravy and green chilies. He delved into it. Upon descent Tariq caught the layout of Lahore with its buildings low to the ground. From a high altitude it looked like any other Pakistani city. He could not distinguish the automobiles on the roads but could make out the bland patchwork of agricultural territories.

He watched his bodyguards in the middle seats lapping at their food. They had been attending him for several years, selected from a small pool of experienced candidates. They accompanied him from mosque to mosque, ignorant of his business.

He forbade his advisors from joining him on the Indian tour. All matters regarding the faith were decided by him alone. Only Tariq communicated with the Imam. The Imam could summon Tariq upon whim. Tariq, however, was forbidden to call on him except in the gravest of circumstances.

The Imam sent him a series of letters four years back. The letters never said much and tapered off after a few months. These letters still befuddled him. The Imam's wife, Sakina, had a baby daughter, not a son. At the time The Imam ruled out the next best alternative: to take a string of wives to conceive a male child. He cited the monogamy of the Prophet Muhammad towards his first wife, Khadija. Tariq ground his teeth at this.

Tariq hadn't heard from him since and resumed full command of the Organization without his guidance. Although the Imam's sickness was unfortunate and untimely, it would soon leave Tariq with full authority over the Organization and the order of clerics until a new Imam could be raised.

Tariq would have his hands full. The religion was being trampled by the loose values of the West, and at the same time the glorious Qu'ran was being portrayed as a handbook for towel-headed zealots holding the world hostage with terror and persecution. While most Westerners mocked Islam, the intellectuals labeled the faith a mystery to mankind, pervasive yet much too controlling for developed cultures.

Although Tariq felt it a necessity to sow seeds of Islam in the West, he also believed in unifying more the faith in the Middle East. He yearned to make it as strong as in the days of the Prophet, when the believers prayed the required five times a day, the women fully covered their charms, the children fulfilled the duties of Islam prior to other goals.

He gazed upon the mackerel sky from his airplane window. The formations wouldn't catch him if he dove. Neither would the spirits of his forefathers. Upon his graduation from Al-Karim University in Cairo, Tariq committed himself to their traditionalist dogma. Islam was not in a popularity contest. The few who strictly submitted were preferred to the many who half-heartedly followed. Strong and wealthy Westerners lacked moral rectitude. They became nothing but fuel for the fire.

Tariq's grandfather ran the Organization with similar philosophies. How Tariq remembered him! His grandfather worked with the Imam over issues of policy, interpretation of the holy scriptures, and educational initiatives. The current Imam didn't do any of this. Tariq neither knew his position on important matters nor the ways he spent the Organization's allowances. The Imam was unable to communicate, a recluse who might have been straying from the straight. But Tariq would never dare question the Imam's authority, faith, and wisdom. It had never been done.

Still Tariq could get away with it if he wanted to. The Organization had to believe every word Tariq said. Even if the Imam did come out of hiding over a disagreement with Tariq, the believers would hang the Imam as a heretic in a public square. Without Tariq's formal recognition, the Imam never existed. Tariq could betray the Imam at any moment and get away with it. But Tariq believed he would swallow fire in the next life if he ever betrayed him. He remained the weaker partner in a relationship solidified by Allah. Both were stuck with each other.

In his seat these thoughts stayed with him. He had no recourse but to wait and read the Qu'ran. It helped hinder his cycles of worry. He had memorized the whole of it as a young child. His reading was only a review. He could pick its verses from memory like wild flowers. But he was reminded of the Prophet's advice: give up reading when the concentration wanes. He closed the leather-bound book and brought it from his forehead to his lips. He could see the detailed features of Lahore stretched below him. Not as crowded as Bombay.

The low pressure in the cabin made his ears ache. "In the name of Allah," he uttered as the plane touched the ground. A small security team escorted Tariq and his bodyguards to an alternate exit which circumvented the bustling terminal. Another curtained Mercedes awaited them. As Tariq slipped into the white leather seat, he felt the sun's heat penetrating the windshield. He tapped on the window desperately and mouthed to Vasilla to hurry.

A strange pain in Tariq's head spread to his stomach. It moved beyond nausea and crawled up his throat. His head burned as Vasilla started the car.

"Vasilla, the air conditioning."

A dry heat poured from the vents.

"Just drive, Vasilla, Drive!"

With his handkerchief he wiped the sweat from his brow and mumbled: "I seek refuge in Allah from the accursed

Satan's touch, pride, and poetry.

I seek refuge in the Lord of the Dawn,

From the evil which it has created,

From the evil of the sorceresses who blow knots

And from the evil of the envier.

I seek refuge in the Lord of Mankind,

From the evil of the slinking whisperer,

Who whispers in the hearts of men,

From among the Jinn and Mankind."

He was oblivious to the rumble of the road.

"What's wrong sir?"

"Oh Vasilla, just drive."

His stomach turned and ground.

"Allah there is no God but He, the Living, the Eternal."

He closed his eyes as they drove through the inanimate streets of Lahore. The blurs of the eroded buildings fluttered by.

"Vasilla, stop by the side of the road."

He opened the door. With a short heave and tears in his eyes, the plane food along with several cups of lukewarm tea tumbled out of him. The backlash stained his kurta. Vasilla handed him a pile of silk handkerchiefs and a small cosmetic mirror.

"I do not feel well. Stop by someplace."

Before Vasilla parked in front of the hotel lobby, Tariq removed his turban so no one would recognize him. In the hotel room he washed away the dirt and vomit of the flight and changed into a fresh kurta. He sat on a comfortable double bed facing the balcony. The room gave him a limited view of a busy avenue split down the middle by a lawn of burnt grass. Imported violets and daisies, wilting in the heat, marked the edges of the road. Cars and rickshaws raced past.

His prayers seemed to be coming up blank, as though some spirit snatched them between the heavens and the earth. If Allah knoweth all, the Imam must be dying for a reason. Tariq had no right second-guessing his divine plan. From his handsack he pulled his subha beads tangled from the flight. With care he ran them along his fingers and counted each ivory bead with his thumb while muttering healing words. Between the gathering of clouds growing dark and heavy in his mind, he understood he was being tested. He soon fell asleep with the beads in his hands.

He did not mean to sleep for so long. After hearing Vasilla's thick voice beyond the door, he examined himself in the mirror and remembered the many faces crying at Al–Azim.

He imagined from the four corners of the globe all the Muslims gathering at the mosque of Namira on the ninth day of Dhul Hijja. White tents blanketing the tents of Arafat, pilgrims from all over the world in loin cloth hearing the mighty call of the adhan, stalking rocky terrain, calling the Lord's name. The noon sun rises full in the sky as Tariq introduces the one true Imam of the Shias, the fruit of Ali. The leaders of all sects are present to recognize this one Imam as the closest human being to Allah. The Imam delivers a sermon which washes the sin from their souls and produces tears of joy for their rebirth. His soothing tones of glorious poetry direct the faithful. With a stern voice which ripples down the rocky crags of Arafat, The Imam vows to return each year until his son fills the divine office. In response they raise their hands in the air and rejoice:

Hallowed be Allah, and praise is due to Allah.

There is no God but Allah, Allah is the greatest.

The angels carry their energetic cries to the creator.

Tariq's thoughts raced. He searched for his turban. He had left it in the car. He caught Vasilla lounging on the sofa. Tariq excused his laziness and dashed down the hotel corridor. Vasilla and the other bodyguards caught up. Behind the concierge's desk in the lobby he spotted a large picture of himself in front of a swaying, chanting crowd. No one recognized Tariq, or else he would have been obliged to bless the hotel and all its staff. A feast would have been held in his honor. He would have been bound by courtesy to finish a full meal on his tender stomach and bless the entire feast.

He begged Vasilla to hurry. He gave the address of 116 Drakni Drive. Vasilla shot straight through the heart of Lahore. They ended up in a suburb. A vast hillside overlooked the mangled huts below. An old house with its beige exterior chipping and peeling baked in the sun. A steel entrance gate blocked the view of the property. Vasilla insisted he come for protection, but Tariq waved irritably, forbidding him to leave the car.

The air smelled of disease. The warm breeze lifted Tariq's hoary beard as soft as yarn. The heat from the Lahorian sun wounded his face. A goat from the road vanished from the corner. The gate stood open, and Tariq stepped into a gravel courtyard with shrubs and short trees browning against the sun's intense rays. Stone flags marked the pathway to the oversized door. Tariq kept his eyes fixed to the ground while humming a hymn he learned as a child. A leather tail with three gold bells stitched to it, this same leather tail he had given as a gift many years ago, was missing from the wooden door. He breathed deeply and knocked.

An old, bald servant answered his call. The sun blinded the servant's eyes. He squinted before the taller figure. Shrika looked him over carefully.

"Shrika, it is I, Tariq."

Shrika bent and grasped his knees.

"Oh my holiness, it is you who has finally come. You have answered our prayers. I beg your forgiveness for not recognizing you at once."

"There are no apologies necessary for someone as righteous as you. Come. Show me the way."

Shrika led him into the dark home, and Tariq made sure his faith in Allah had reached its highest point. Even this prodigal Imam deserved that respect.

"Please, your holiness, he is in the bedroom."

"Go tell Vasilla to wait by the front door. He is in the car. Leave the others outside."

"Yes, my holiness."

It was musty, as though the place had not been inhabited for some time. He thought he heard movement behind him but dismissed the premonition as a remainder of his nausea. The walls stood bare. All rested in abeyance, as if time had gathered itself into tiny bits of dust lining the window sills and the low tables. Cushions rested against the walls, neatly laid out, not the slightest wrinkle. A Persian rug lay on the floor beside the cushions trying with its faded thread to revive the home.

One of the doors clicked open at the slightest touch of the handles. An empty room, neatly made. A thin white sheet was stretched over a mattress. Underneath one of the nightstands a gold–plated picture frame lay on its back. With his bony fingers Tariq wiped away a layer of dust reigning on the secular portrait of wrinkled faces. He matched these faces with their names. All former Imams. He understood why they were displayed in such a stale, unglorified manner.

The Imams have never supported glorifying themselves or their clerics, but permitted it only in rare circumstances. As Tariq looked at their simple faces, he was reminded of the enemies of the faith. The Imams were driven underground long ago.

He continued down the hallway. Shrika startled him by slamming the front door. He patted Tariq on the back as they proceeded.

"Come, my holiness. He is in here resting."

They entered a spacious room. Soiled garments were scattered around a large bed. A warped lump outlined the curves of Shabbir Hussein's back.

"But where are Sakina and the baby?" asked Tariq quietly.

"Shabbir has sent them away," said Shrika. "They did not want to leave, but he insisted."

"If that was his wish, then so be it."

Their whispering made Imam Shabbir roll to the side, his eyelids half closed.

"Shrika, you must leave us now," said Imam Shabbir.

Shrika closed the door on his way out. Tariq knelt beside his superior and kissed his knees. Shabbir, now fully awake, held Tariq by the shoulders, cutting short his gestures of reverence.

"So my brother, we see each other after some time, and I guess the All Mighty wishes to take me first," said Shabbir weakly.

"For my sake, don't speak such things," said Tariq. "We need you here, especially now. Islam is sprouting like the first flowers of life. Every day it becomes safer to tell our brethren there is one and only one Imam who exists, that the Imam is alive, that the faith among us never wanes, only grows."

He paused for a few moments while taking in the smells of Shabbir Hussein's decaying body. Tariq breathed through his mouth to avoid the stench. In the darkness he made out Shabbir's face: smooth and thin, high cheek bones, the flesh sticking tightly to his skull. Beads of sweat guarded his dark hair matted upon his brow. As Shabbir swept his hand through his hair, it crumpled like a crow's nest laden with dandruff and bits of lint. Frayed and splintered cuticles from which grew long, yellow fingernails added irritation to his pain.

This was not the same man Tariq had known. Rather it was another creature almost alien, reduced to a sickly shape, thinning into nothing. As he held Shabbir's hand, he mused how he could easily wrap his fingers around his wrists. A round of bitter, hacking coughs reminded him that Imam Shabbir Hussein still lived.

"My dear Shabbir, what has happened to you?"

"You are thirty years my elder. Look at me. You must be looking for something, yes? You answered my call quickly."

"Do you have a son as of yet? I must know. We must plan this out."

"Sit by me, won't you? You make me nervous."

Although they hardly knew each other, they always kept each other in mind. Tariq had spent much time in clandestine council rooms making his positions clear. Western intervention into the strict affairs of the Arabs and the loss of innocent lives in Iraq infested his conscience.

He had high expectations for Shabbir Hussein. There were new issues at stake and tougher conflicts to resolve: clashes between Pakistanis and Somalis, Jamu and Kashmir, the Afghani civil war, war–torn Yugoslavia, renewed raids on Iraq, the emergence of Islamic republics is Central Asia. Muslims fought to preserve the Islamic way of life. Ironically that area of the world which antagonized the faith now bred Muslims. The number of Islamic emigrants and converts multiplied at a tremendous rate.

Although Imam Shabbir remained miserably detached from the Organization, he still sensed the need to take action that would push the proliferation of Islam. Tariq hoped their ideas were running on the same plane.

"Maybe we should bring you out," said Tariq.

"But what would that do to me?"

"Shabbir, you are dying. If I may speak frankly, let the enemies kill you. It will strengthen the unity like never before. I will give you full confirmation in the press and immediate recognition from the Organization. You have no successor. You are ending the line, and perhaps it is meant to be this way. We are in a position of advantage. Christianity and Judaism have lost their clout. Buddhism and Hinduism remain localized. The young Islam has stumbled onto its greatest period. Allah is telling me this in my dreams."

"You are my mouth piece. You do not have the blood of Ali in your veins."

"Of course," said Tariq, "but I still think you should come out. It would unite us at this opportune time."

"And what would my father have said to all this?"

"Surely Imam Khalid would have approved. I am confident the time has come to act."

"Our foothold is not strong enough in the West but is gradually becoming stronger," said Shabbir. "The next Imam must suck up the West with him. He must live there, breathe their air, absorb their culture, understand their weaknesses."

"Move through their governments, tap hidden resources, provide outlets for other Muslims..."

"Precisely. I have not been blind during this short life. We are useless here, for Islam is strong, praised within our very constitutions. We must take other areas, and capture them by sheer numbers under the name of Islam. Do you see the future? Can you see this plan Allah has sent down to me?"

"Certainly, but it is not a new one," said Tariq, realizing how utterly delirious the Imam had become. His words were too fantastic to be taken seriously. Nevertheless, he played along.

"The point is that I have been given these signs. The time to prepare is now. We implant the next Imam in the West. We bring him with his followers back to the East."

"It may not be safe in the West. He will be persecuted. You would have not survived there. Only within these hills have you survived."

"But the next Imam will have the knowledge essential for survival. We shall place men to protect him."

Shabbir then paused for a difficult swallow and said:

"There is a problem I forsee which may unravel our plans. The Imam being of the Western world will not adopt all of our tradition. The West will chew him up and spit him out into a Christian or better yet a Jew!"

"Indeed." said Tariq, stroking his beard for effect. "I'll see to it that he follows the chosen path. Leave this matter to me."

"But will you be alive for so long?"

And then Imam Shabbir Hussein remembered.

"My dear Tariq, there is one thing I have not discussed with you."

Shabbir lay on his back and begged Tariq to come closer.

"We have come far, you and I, in such a short time, although my health does not permit me to go farther."

"I respect you, your judgment, and your wisdom to the highest possible extent."

"As you may or may not know, I have at this time my darling daughter Nisrin whom I care for very much. I must ask you or your son to oversee the her wedding. But I would not have burdened you with such a plan if I were not expecting another child."

"What! Another child? Oh, dear Allah, why didn't you tell me this earlier? I've been worrying for the last two years. I have been planning everything around it..."

Tariq, shocked by this news, noticed Shabbir's swollen eyes and pursed lips.

"...but this is a day of celebration," continued Tariq more mildly, "and I shall make it so throughout the Shia world. Allah has heard our prayers. We are blessed like the dawn. I shall never doubt again. Always, always have faith. And where is Sakina, the blessed Sakina, the mother of the blessed child?"

"I have kept it from you only to protect you," interrupted Shabbir. "This is a very delicate matter.

"Tariq, as an Imam I am not error–free. I do make mistakes, and I pay for them dearly in conscience. Nor are you as my representative invulnerable. Allah has turned my error into a blessing. A cleaning woman named Fatima is carrying my child, the next Imam, Insh'Allah. This Fatima is not married to me. The child will be born out of wedlock, but an important child it remains. You must seek her out; find her in the slums below."

He blew raspy coughs into his pillow.

"Do not look down upon me. We are all striving to reach Allah's heights, and we often fail to some degree. Allah is oft–forgiving and most merciful.

"Sakina must never know of my temptation over the woman. But I shall be forgiven. Our minds are changing, this is for sure. And there is a new Imam waiting in her womb, a poor woman's womb. I can feel it. She's a frightened, innocent creature who must never be labeled an adulteress. I am the one to blame. I have betrayed my loving wife's trust, and you see this weighs upon me, if you only knew how much. Each day I pray and pray for forgiveness. How heavy this weighs on me..."

His words slipped into a series of fast whimpers, followed by a chain of coughs. He tried to resume, but Tariq held his shoulder, slowing his pace.

"It is my wish that you find her as soon as possible. The child is on the way."

The birth of a bastard from the womb of some poor prostitute. These ideas jumped into Tariq's mind, but he quickly rid himself of them. He prayed for a legitimate birth blessed by Allah and for a healthy, male child. He refused to ask where the child was conceived or how the interaction took place; irrelevant questions. The lewd images seeped into focus.

Shabbir could have married her. The young ones somehow stick to their first loves. But pleasure, had it been authorized, need not have thrown Shabbir into complete and deadly transgression.

"Before you say a word, I have asked for forgiveness," resumed Shabbir. "Allah will forgive but will never forget, and as you shall see, Allah shall grant me a son, the next Imam, the true Imam, the twelfth Imam.

"In the mind, my brother, I have toiled, and my family knows of this toil. They see it in my face each time I turn away. I cannot look at them anymore."

Tariq lowered his ears to his lips.

"I have not found it easy. Yes, I have supreme authority, but I have abused it. The Prophet would have spit in my face. The Imams of the future shall never stray from righteousness. My son shall be poised to lead armies, waving the flag of Islam. I dream of such things in and out of sleep. You also see it, don't you? Strong Imams, pious Imams? Imams the world shall follow?

"Wait patiently for this cleaning woman to give birth to the child. If the child is female, expose me to the masses without hesitation. If the child is male, bring him to me. I must bless my son before I leave this earth. Allah's plan is a mystery to us all. Allah has his intentions, and they are perfectly devised."

"Is it our intention to bring your son out?" asked Tariq.

"That is up to you. But do not bring him out unless ultimately necessary. The timing must be better than perfect. He will be advised by you or your son, Khozem, to conceive a male child. But if my prayers are answered, he shall live a long enough life to guide generations of devout Muslims. He shall die in peace knowing that his own male offspring is in the world. He shall preserve the traditions already in place."

"Allah be praised," said Tariq squeezing Shabbir's hand.

"This is my final decree. If Fatima bears a son, from birth you must prepare him. But as with all our timeless leaders, Islam must be revealed to him by Allah's message alone. No one shall force him to pursue the faith. Only apply pressures.

"Put him in the West. Place him with a strong, Shia family of your choosing. They shall raise him under you. Then he shall make visits to the East. Let him learn humble values which are free from vanity. Let him be taught discipline and pious behavior. Marry him well. Reveal to him his destiny only when the time is right. I will be watching from the heavens as our hard work unfolds."

"And if he refuses the faith or resists my pressures?"

"How can he resist? Like his father, he is an Imam. Tell him of his destiny when it's most appropriate. He can't shed his responsibility. The Imams have always done what is right and just. Is he not, after all, the descendant of our Prophet, the fruit of Ali? You will see that he will be better than Imam Khalid. Over time things shall be made known to him."

"You speak with such conviction, as though you know him already. I find it hard not to have faith. You are my sovereign, and I will do as you wish."

"Draft a well designed plan for his life with all your wits intact. See to it my son follows it. Make sure to give him enough room to learn of himself. We must count on you for his success."

"And what of his new representative, my son Khozem?"

"That's your department. The bavasaab and the Imam will have to work together. They must be compatible. This may be difficult, since they shall be living on opposite sides of the globe. Unfamiliar territory. Make the bavasaab

knowledgeable of Western culture. Put Khozem in the West for visits. My plan
is doomed without compatibility."

A bough shook outside the window. Its rattling grew louder than his
voice. Dangling his finger in his beard, Tariq thought he had enough years to
oversee the Imam's development. As Imam Shabbir lay whispering, he grew
anxious. He had much to sort through. Vague instructions cluttered his mind.

Tariq could not leave Shabbir. He lay under moist sheets, moving his
dehydrated lips. He patted the back of his hand and heard the adhan being
called from area mosques. He left his side and went to the car for his prayer
cloth. He still felt nauseated. After returning to Shabbir's bedroom, he made
himself cry. The tears rolled when he dwelled upon Shabbir's mottled dream
induced by long, tortuous days in bed.

The room grew dark, and Imam Shabbir fell asleep. Tariq said a small
prayer for him and blew a quick breath on his brow. He spread his prayer cloth
on the carpet. As he bowed and kissed the ground, he asked Allah for
guidance. Did he really expect to trust a dying man's visions? It was a choice
between the visible and the invisible, the ways of the modern world or a
deathbed hallucination. He suddenly vowed to thrust Islam into a new era of
expansion, strengthening the spirits of those who lived by the laws of Islam,
bent their backs through Hajj, starved through Ramadan, gave zakat, believed
so firmly in the vision of Allah that no power existing or non-existing could
match it. He begged for the well-being of the next Imam, that this Fatima bear
a son to keep the line of Imams perpetuating, that the next representative, his
son Khozem, compliment the Imam's intention to create a new order of Islam,
to bestow upon it more glory than it currently held. Imam Shabbir proved to be
no example, but he had initiated the holy expansion into the West by the grace
of Allah.

And at the same time Tariq understood how preposterous this idea was.
He fought against this sense of absurdity and found for the first time in a very
long time a faith in Shabbir's words, or more likely, the need to believe and the
need to have faith.

Tariq bid salaams to both his right and left. Before he left Imam
Shabbir's side, he tried to say something significant. He tried to be as profound
as possible, as though his prayer would be discovered under a thick weight of
cream-colored pages in some Islamic text, but nothing came. He was rusty. He
thought of the passionate eulogy he would give. A day of fasting and prayer.

As Vasilla gawked from the car, Tariq paced the side street outside the
small house. Tariq had never been to a slum before. He figured they were
rampant with disease, uncleanness, and infection. He sometimes saw them
through the thick plastic windows of airplanes or while moving through the

narrow roads with Vasilla at the wheel. He stopped his pacing. He said to Vasilla:

"You will stay here until you find a cleaning woman who goes by the name of Fatima. She lives in the slums down the hills. I don't have any more information than that. Once you find her, call me immediately in Mecca. Do not approach the woman. Operate discreetly. She must not know someone is looking for her. Don't leave Lahore or don't contact me until you find her. Do I make myself perfectly clear?"

"Yes, my holiness," said Vasilla.

"Do you have enough funds?"

"More than enough, sir."

"Here. Take some more."

Tariq retrieved his traveling sack from the sedan and stuffed one-hundred rupee notes into Vasilla's palm. He left Vasilla standing in the dust. With the remaining bodyguards, he sped towards the Lahorian airport. The next stop was Mecca.

Tariq had waited for the day his son would take over, and that specific day grew closer with each sunset, with each mysterious rising of the pale Arabic moon. Tariq knew Shabbir Hussein's plan would fail if Khozem did not possess the strength and endurance to lead the masses. It would probably fail regardless, but again his urgent need to believe. Tariq was summoned to become the bavasaab at the age of forty. And Khozem was young, perhaps too young to become involved in such a charade. He belonged in Cairo for more training. The university seemed like a safe place to leave him, like the infant who is kept within a crib. But it was time to bring Khozem to his people, even though he was only eighteen. The need to believe.

While Tariq would still lead for the next few years, Khozem would be learning the tricks of inspiring faith and hope within the millions of downtrodden zealots who flocked to the mosques. The world would be Khozem's home as it was Tariq's for the past four decades, except this time the stakes were much higher. The hypothetical expansion into the West lay in the hands of Khozem with this unborn Imam to guide him. Tariq envied his son. He functioned no more than to bring his prized son into the world. He was to be at the center of all that was important. He was privileged enough to stand within the whirlwind of change. Tariq was merely there to preserve the status quo as did his father and great grandfathers before him.

Khozem, however, would move with total power. There would be no holds in securing Islam for the millions in the West who were ever so ignorant of it. The element of surprise would wipe them out. The swelling Islam would spill upon the parched Western society. It will happen surreptitiously, and it will happen all at once.

As Tariq boarded the plane on that hot afternoon amidst the clamor of bodyguards and onlookers, he could not help but think his time had passed. He did not say a word at the airport. His bodyguards did not have the nerve to inquire. As he sat at the front of the plane he muttered a prayer for Khozem. He did not want to be envious of his son's youth. He prayed for Allah to take this jealousy away from him. Two hours had been enough. But words failed him as he entered Afghani air space. Khozem would have to do much of it on his own.

Chapter Five
THE VEIL
16th of Jumaada al-awal 1417
(September 29, 1996)

Khozem glanced about the naked room of the university hall. It seemed stripped of any aesthetic quality. A desk sat menacingly in the corner. A picture of his father stared at him from the wall. A long table with chairs lay towards the front of the room. To Khozem the desk by his father's picture seemed out of place. No one really came here to get any work done. Rather, people sat in judgment of each other in this warm, muggy room, so muggy that the wallpaper perspired and peeled in places.

He took a seat on the first chair nearest to the entrance. Like a cobra he waited for the other professors to arrive. He was usually asked to sit in judgment, and he liked this position of power, so extreme that with the slight nod of the head or a wave of the hand he could expel anyone he wanted. The rest of the professors on the committee would side with him. After all, he was the bavasaab's son, and Allah had placed him in a position to rule however he saw fit. Like waiting for kulfi on a hot summer's day, he waited in the stark room. He was always the first to arrive, which irked him a bit, since he should be the last to arrive for a change. Respect demanded he be the last. But he could not wait and arrived on the early side.

He did not know the person he was expelling today. The other professors on the board were advisors. Khozem would make the final decision, and he would push for expulsion. For the last year he had done nothing but that and got his way each time. The other professors never put up a fight. Some of them rolled their eyes, snoozed in boredom, or played with their thumbs. They left it up to Khozem.

Dr. Fahrrukh was the second to arrive. His corpulent body moved like the sail of a vessel through the open door. His face was formed by globs of sweat and scarred from old acne, making him look like a jolly pineapple. In his white robe and turban he smiled to Khozem before dropping his small notebook and taking a seat.

"So who are we judging today?" asked Dr. Fahrrukh, opening his notebook and glancing about the room.

"I'm not sure," replied Khozem. "I heard it's a man who yelled at a professor over the Verse of the Throne."

"Ah yes. The one who claimed that Islam had too many commands, too much hellfire and damnation. The same man who said the Prophet was an epileptic. If only Allah knew how much I would like to punish these people. I've always had faith in the Verse of the Throne:

Allah! There is no god
But He,– The living,
The Self–subsisting, Supporter of all
No slumber can seize him
Nor sleep. His are all things
In the heavens and on earth.
Who is thee can intercede
In his presence except
As He permitteth? He knoweth
What appeareth to His creatures
As Before or After
Or Behind them.
Nor shall they compass
Aught of His knowledge
Except as He willeth.
His Throne doth extend
Over the heavens
And the earth, and He feeleth
No fatigue in guarding
And preserving them
For he is Most High,
The Supreme (in glory)."

Khozem said the Verse of the Throne with Dr. Fahrrukh, as though they were two children learning nursery rhymes.

"Let there be no compulsion
In religion: Truth stands out
Clear from Error: whoever

Rejects anything worshipped beside Allah
And believes in Allah hath grasped
The most trustworthy
Hand–hold, that never breaks
And knoweth all things.
Allah is the Protector
Of those who have faith:
From the depths of darkness
He leads them forth Into light. Of those
Who reject faith the patrons
Are the idols from light
They will lead them forth
Into the depths of darkness.
They will be Companions
Of the fire, to dwell therein (For ever).

"I get choked up every time I say that," said Dr. Fahrrukh. "Supposedly this man even rejected the Verse of the Throne. He told his instructor that Allah is a narcoleptic, that Islam is a result of both narcolepsy and epilepsy, that without the earth, Allah has no existence. He said when He slumbers, people die accidentally, are thrust into poverty, or begin to fight in wars and kill themselves. I believe this man thinks Allah is not perfect. Did you hear about all of this?"

"How dare someone think that. Allah uses this earth as his footstool. These verses are not to be tampered with. How many times do we have to expel people for it?"

"Expulsion is not such a bad thing."

"No, I guess not. It makes for smaller lines in the lunch room, more books. He can't expect to get away with it."

"I get your meaning," said Dr. Fahrrukh. "I sometimes dream about locking all of these criminals in a sound-proof cage and yelling at them through a tiny speaker within the cage. They hear me, but I can't hear them screaming back."

"What would you yell into the cage?"

"I would turn the volume all the way up and recite my favorite verses. They would hate it so much that they would want to be Jews by the time they got out."

"They would all start kissing the feet of Jews," laughed Khozem.

"That's precisely my point. They would not want to be Muslims anymore. All these criminals would become Jews, and they would flock to the Jewish colony. And because there would be such an influx and infiltration by them, the good, obedient Muslims would take the Jewish colony by force. We could crush the Hebrews one by one. We could lock them both up. The criminals and the Jews together, and this time electrify the sound-proof cage..."

"Stop it. You're killing me," as Khozem burst into laughter.

"No, I'm being quite serious. Sound-proof, electrified cages for all the criminals and the Jews. This will be the wave of the future. I will have the science department set it up for me."

"That's good to hear."

Khozem chuckled as Dr. Farrukh turned the pages of his notebook to a clean sheet. The other professors soon wandered in, telling jokes and laughing. Khozem evil-eyed them for their lateness, and they quickly cut short their laughter and feigned coughing.

There was the hidden rule that the man under judgment could not enter until all the professors on the committee settled in their chairs and were in the mood to hear the plea. None of the professors were in the mood to judge a student today. Khozem, however, tried to get them in the mood. He asked for silence as bits of conversation ended at a polite pause.

"I believe the young man who is making his plea thinks there is too much hellfire and damnation in our holiest of books," began Khozem. "He had an argument with one of his instructors about the Verse of the Throne and called him a 'slimy pig' in his presence. He has called our Prophet an epileptic, and his God a narcoleptic, and I would submit to this board that we expel the individual on the spot for flagrantly misinterpreting the Qu'ran, for it is not about damnation and hellfire. The All Mighty does not slumber while the tragedies of life continue.

Allah did not create Islam through the seizures of his Prophet. Islam is about our full and total submission to Allah, the one and only God. The world is his footstool. It is about beauty, honor, and tradition. The man must learn there are dire consequences for certain actions, so certainly there shall be hellfire for him; hellfire for those whom go against the statutes the Qu'ran clearly outlines.

"No one has the right to comment on the Qu'ran in such a manner, let alone call an instructor directly the lowest form of life. The pig simply is the lowest form of life, am I correct? Let this person sleep with the animals if he likes the word 'pig' so much. Let this person be damned to hellfire for thinking the Qu'ran too impractical and commanding. Let him be expelled; that is my point of view. What do the rest of you think?"

A pause filled the air. The professors squirmed as Dr. Fahrrukh rose from his seat.

"I think I can speak for all of us when I say, you Khozem, are a distinguished credit to our faith. Islam would be weak without you, and when you move on to sit beside Allah in a prime seat of heaven, you're absence will be felt for many generations. We agree with your judgment, but in accordance with Qu'ranic law we must hear the plea. You have thought about this matter fully. We respect what you say and shall implement the full orders for the expulsion of this man."

The other professors smiled and nodded. One of them stood after Dr. Fahrrukh finished.

"Since this man has committed such a vile offense, shouldn't we think about barring his future offspring from entrance into this esteemed university? It would be a just punishment, I should think."

"Hmmm, an original form of punishment," answered Khozem. "We have never come across that one before. But we shall leave the idea open. You never know what this man may turn into. His children may be something worse, in the future of course. In fact, let's not leave the idea open. Let us pursue the idea. We shall ask this man to repent first. Then we will inform him of his expulsion from the university, and then we will tell him his children may never come here either. Tell Shama to mark it down in the files.

"We must remember that Al-Karim is the greatest university on this earth. Allah has sent us here to submit to his will alone. We must not allow those of the criminal mind to take over. Their children are even more of a nuisance to our cause. So let's make him repent, expel him, and then blacklist his children from all our universities, not just this one. Are we all in agreement? Those who are not, please speak now."

No one spoke.

"Then it is final. Let's implement the plan which Allah has so graciously sent down to me. Let the man be banished from our merciful sights. In the long run it will be the best thing for him. Send him in."

Dr. Fahrrukh went outside to fetch the transgressor. In the room Khozem heard nothing but the coughs of the old professors who were gathered there. At the age of eighteen Khozem had no direct connection with these clerics of the academic world. He knew only that he ruled over them. Academics tended to bore him as they were usually quiet around him and had nothing intelligent to offer. He also knew they were scared of his power which pounded like a fist over the small university. The professors were careful not to offend or push him too hard in his studies. He was the bavasaab's son, which made him the most righteous on the planet, aside from his father and the Imam. Khozem was well aware of this. He grew fond of expelling students. Even the professors were under scrutiny. They feared having Khozem in class, as he could have any professor beheaded in Mecca if he pushed for it. But Khozem was not that cold-hearted. He was not a petty tyrant, at least not yet.

Dr. Fahrrukh returned with wide eyes. He was not sure how to tell him.

"Sir, we have a problem, and I'm so very sorry I have to bring this problem to you," said the wide-eyed Dr. Fahrrukh.

The other clerics, donned in white cloaks and turbans, felt lucky they weren't in Dr. Fahrrukh's position.

"What's the problem?" asked Khozem.

"There seems to be a scheduling mix up. It is not my fault, I can assure you. . ."

"What mix up, doctor? Let's get on with it."

"It's Shama's fault. Not mine. I had nothing to do with it. I always knew she was a terrible secretary."

"The problem, doctor. The problem," yelled Khozem.

In the doorway stood a woman. She wore a thick head dress and long black cloak draped to her ankles. A thin black veil blocked her face from view. He hated the sight of her, as women somehow deserved more punishment than men for disobedience. Disobedience was a right reserved for the male alone. But Khozem knew nothing about women. They were not a mystery but more a topic of ignorance, and this woman represented his first contact with the female gender. Sure he had seen them before, roaming about the women's campus in obscurity. But he had never come so close.

He could see only her eyes which were set like the Black Stone, so opaque that they kept the darkest of secrets. Her onyx eyes stared defiantly at him. He needed to know her name but refrained from thoughts so personal. The goal was to punish her, and he would do it severely. He wanted to make an example of her. He could not remember the last time he smiled, but a slow bend grew at the corners of his lips.

"My holiness, this is, umm, Rashida Pendi, first year student of the women's college," said Dr. Fahrrukh. "She is to be judged for the crime of apostasy. Earlier in the day she went yelling through the administrative building about how she has forsaken her faith for something better."

Khozem's grin widened as Dr. Fahrrukh revealed the nature of Rashida's crime. He thought of sending her to Mecca for further punishment. As far as he knew, the price for turning one's back on the religion demanded the strictest penalty: death itself.

Before Khozem said anything, he noticed how she adjusted her veil, making it tighter so it wouldn't fall. Rashida clumsily let the veil slip, and it fell from her face and rested on her shoulder just long enough for Khozem to have a healthy look at her face.

Her smooth dark face evoked a sadness. That fire within Khozem's eyes and his wicked grin stalled into a form of attraction. And she was attractive. Her thin nose curved at the tip, and her thick full lips burst with ideas of the flesh. For that brief, unmolested moment he could behold a woman and relish in her beauty.

She fit the veil back over her face and looked to Dr. Fahrrukh with embarrassment and apology.

Khozem neither heard nor responded to Dr. Fahrrukh's explanation but heard the simple name of Rashida wander through the curving maze of his mind. And his mind seemed to expand in her presence. She conveyed the deep irony that the heart existed not as a function of the mind but as a function of itself.

His vague attempt at exercising some control over the gaping mouths of the old professors grew pointless. He did not notice the interval of silence which smothered the room. He did not notice the heat, the coughs, the buzzing of the lights, or the picture of his father on the wall. He could not tear himself from Rashida's nude face. Khozem continued to stare at her like the child who for the first time sees the face of his mother.

He wanted to speak with her alone. He suddenly wanted to understand her regardless of his reputation for severity. This woman filled him with such an immediate contradiction and inconsistency.

At last Khozem broke from his stare by lifting his hands to his temples as one does when suffering. Such brief moments in the company of this woman was meant to last for lifetimes, he thought, and because Rashida turned away first, he waved with his hand to send her away.

"Expel her, you mean?" asked the sweating Dr. Fahrrukh.

"No," explained Khozem. "Just let her sit in Shama's office for now. I don't want to discuss this as of yet."

"Are you sure, my holiness?"

"Yes," said Khozem calmly. "Take her away. This board shall convene tomorrow."

"But she can't be expected to sit in Shama's office overnight, my holiness."

Khozem again looked at Rashida, but she didn't look back. She only looked at Dr. Fahrrukh in a pleasant patience.

"Fine. Let her go," whispered Khozem while messaging his temples.

"Excuse me, your holiness?"

"I said let her go! Now all of you get out!"

Rashida, as though given some remarkable form of free will, walked briskly out the door.

After the professors left, Khozem paced the room from all angles, his hands behind his back. While recovering from her visage, he began to hurt. He did not know why. He wanted to forget about her, so he recited the Verse of the Throne. But the small prayer did not work. Allah must lurk in women as well. He hit this point like a bat to a ball. Her nudity went against all he had learned.

He turned to his father's portrait on the wall. He wanted to ask him so many things, but found his father only in this black and white photograph. His father had no time for the most important questions, like how to deal with a woman. Rather, the portrait depicted his father catching a revelation.

His confusion pulled him towards a small garden near the large quadrangle. It was a place he had never before been, and the sun, in all of its glory, did not bother him. He was swept by the breeze instead, and after pondering Rashida's features, he found himself among these red flowers in full bloom. The petals seemed delicate enough, so he bent down and smelled what he thought to be a woman's skin, an intriguing scent, as though the flower hid itself from the dull confines of an Islamic society. For some reason these red, sensuous flowers spurred more thoughts of Rashida.

Chapter Six
TARIQ RETURNS TO MECCA
17th of Jumaada al-awal 1417
(September 30, 1996)

Tariq found himself coasting down a bare highway with his two bodyguards in the front cracking open pistachio nuts and drinking warm colas. He had fallen asleep on the plane from Lahore and moved in barren land between Jeddah and Mecca. He had missed both meals on the plane. The road was endless as he watched the car swallowing the blacktop. Every twenty minutes a service station passed with one or two cars idle in a lane of twelve to fifteen separate pumps. These service stations looked distinctly familiar.

He longed to see his wife and son again, but the highway went on for miles. No reason to rush the sure bet of beholding his beloved city as well, carved from the ashen gray mountains that guarded it.

Tan dust and chunks of tough rubble covered the sides of the highway. A fence soon ran along the side and over the low, emerging mountains. He thought it must have taken many pains to get the fence over the hills and back onto the highway. Lots of workers banging their picks into the rock. And they received at the most fifty rials for what they did each day. Hard work counted for little in this land. During the drive from the airport he remembered the men fixing potholes in the road, Indian and Pakistani Muslims in long lines.

Tariq only noticed them out of the mosques. Their old faces with deep lines, for instance. Only at places like airports did he find warmth in the simple, common people, the mother pulling her child by the arm through a difficult customs checkpoint, baggage handlers in slate-blue overalls dragging carts of luggage, strangers standing in boredom. And he glanced into their eyes and knew how these strangers were much like him. Ages ago he used to walk among the commoners. The changes of decades past hit him like the sunshine in the car.

The service stations came more rapidly. Vast spaces on the hills were cluttered with advertisements. Even on the most jagged of mountains large white letters spelled the brand names of audio equipment and wristwatch companies. Tariq reached into his seat pocket and pulled out his Qu'ran. He admired the worn, leather binding. Up front the bodyguards continued snacking, but they also listened to the local radio station which played sweet ghazals and religious chants.

They came upon the security check. Small speed bumps stretched in a simple pattern across the road. Just beyond the checkpoint a large sign, big and bold, read 'Non– Muslims.' This exit led to another highway which avoided the city altogether. A long, candy–caned gate blocked the path as three dark–faced soldiers with thick mustaches approached the vehicle. Their tight black belts held their shirts and trousers in place.

The darkest of them approached the driver and asked for paperwork. Tariq's driver returned a smile to convey this absurdity. The driver merely flashed an identification card permitting their entrance to the divine city. The guard, however, did not let them pass so easily. He demanded the identity of the person in the back seat. Both bodyguards voiced immediate concern and threatened to have him removed from his post. Tariq with his thick bifocals stared back at the guard who popped his head inside. The guard looked too young to know any better. Tariq could have seen this guard as another parasite, nosing his way into higher affairs, but he raised no objection to this intruder, and the guard looked as though he had walked into a woman's boudoir. He apologized for the inconvenience. The driver took this a step further and made him promise never to handle another car in that manner. The dark–faced soldier waved the car through with a quivering smile.

The city slowly came upon them. White–washed apartments sprung along the highway. In the open spaces of desert the sides of white tents flapped. These tents were clustered by two's and three's in tight bunches with cars parked to their sides. While spotting these tents, Tariq remembered his camping days with his father on deep blue Wednesday nights.

His father lacked time for such outings but made exceptions for Tariq. He made sure Tariq was aware of his simple philosophy: to enjoy and respect all of Allah's bounty, both the land and the dark of the sky. While the dark sky served as a barrier to the evil–doers, the stars served as thousands of peepholes for the angels. More than anything, these angels spied on those who sinned, recorded these sins on magic paper, and were rewarded for giving names and records to Allah. So if he remained a good Muslim, then by all means he should bask under the stars. If he had broken into the box of transgressions, then surely he would be discovered. There were no secrets to the open skies, and no one was immune.

Tariq smiled as the tents passed. The rubble of the land resumed. More apartment complexes signified the beginnings of the metropolis. Infertile landscapes transformed into lush lawns. Low homes reflected the intense Arabian sun.

More cars entered the road. There were no exits further down this long strip. There would be no further problems, he thought, for finally he was going home to partake in the Kaa'bah again with all its glory, to be part of his people again, and to see his son again, a miracle to behold, a male to preserve his line for generations.

He longed to feel the embrace of his wife behind closed doors. Every grain of sand surrounding the stretch of road, every deformed rock reminded him of days when life was for the pursuit of Allah exclusively instead of the pursuit of other ambitions. So much hope within this city. He found temporary peace through the ghazals on the radio and beauty while passing under the towering arch upon which a sculpture of an open Qu'ran rested. A most glorious entrance, for once they passed, more advertisements were featured, so many that they filled every space on the black mountainsides. The houses grew more concentrated and abundant with clotheslines and antennae.

The highway narrowed at a series of traffic lights where small trucks and yellow cabs passed in calm patience, the drivers humming the same ghazals. It fascinated Tariq to see a simple intersection.

Another checkpoint. A similar shack by the side of the road. The driver flashed the card and gained admittance without problem. The highway converted into an up-slant with an unbroken barrier down the middle. The city itself had been built upon the hills and was made of low valleys and steep mountains black as flint. The heavy displays in Arabic defined the avenue as more cosmopolitan. The street throbbed with shoppers. A steep incline forced Tariq to move back on his seat, thereby tightening his kurta uncomfortably. He jerked it free of his weight. While doing so he dropped his Qu'ran. 'Don't crack,' he thought, while picking it up and kissing it.

They came to a residential community hidden among tall date trees soaking the sun. Along the road, thick cement walls girdled the properties. Only the rooftops could be distinguished, the second floor of these units like square blocks built upon the first. At the end of the road they confronted a solid iron gate which swung open at the touch of a remote. The home looked like an office building, white–washed with large windows on all sides shielded by blinders. White pillars streamed from the edge of the roof.

He expected someone to be home. Cars moving on the gravel were easily heard from within the home. He even waited in the car for a few moments, but no one came to greet him. He stepped into a warm wind under a clear sky, most of it azure save for the darker borders encroaching on the day.

"In the name of Allah," said Tariq as he entered the home.

He faced a large room with a glossy wooden floor. Towards the East hung a large photograph of himself sitting upon cushions, thumbing his beads, looking into the air. He could not remember the moment his photographer had taken that shot, but he thought it must have been some time ago, for his beard was much shorter, much darker, and his face with fewer wrinkles. This photograph was taken in this very home, in front of close friends and dignitaries of the Arab world. Regardless, those times were less filled with worry. His family had no idea of his worry.

He took off his shoes and spotted the telephone in the far corner of the room. He knew it too early but checked his messages anyway. Vasilla had not called.

At the base of the living room walls thick, white pillows were propped. He dropped his sack by the door and sat behind one of them. He did not want to move, only wanted to rest, which seemed strange since he slept in planes and cars for most of the day. But he ran from those same electrified faces needing to touch him, needing one last blessing. Was this the satisfaction of his work? There had to be something more than the display of himself; more than the traveling salesman of a religion. He closed his eyes and later awoke with the sounds of keys at the door.

A black gown covered her from head to foot. As she removed the cloth, he could not mistake those darkish hazel eyes and flawless brown skin: the same woman he had married almost thirty years ago. He rose to his feet and approached her cautiously, not sure what procedure to use. She looked at him the same way. Tariq held out his hand to her, and Samira bent to receive it. He did the same salaams to her.

"After so long," said Tariq, "my prayers have been answered. Finally I'm home, but I'm not staying for all that long, or at least I don't expect to stay. I know it's unfortunate, but I plan to make the best of it."

Her face fired up, but she kept quiet and climbed the staircase, saving her words by biting her lower lip. She threw off her head–dress and left her veil on the railing.

"You knew the consequences long ago," he continued. "You have always known them, so don't go walking off. You made a commitment to me a long time ago."

"To you, yes," she replied. "Not to your position."

"I came with that, and you knew the consequences. Haven't you gotten used to it by now? It's been thirty-two years. I am the bavasaab. I have to tour these mosques. I may not like it, but it is what I do, and we cannot shy away from it."

Samira moved down the second floor hallway and vanished into the bedroom. Tariq followed reluctantly and paused at the entrance. She removed her black shroud. A multi-colored duppurta came into view. She removed her round glasses and looked into the mirror where she could see Tariq.

"What's most reprehensible," she said primly, "now that I have realized it, is that you have started Khozem down that same road. You've never once thought about me. What about my well-being? Trapped in this room with no one by my side, so much that I can't sleep in it anymore. I have to stay in the guestroom where the bed is small. And not once did you care to call me. Not once. I remember you used to call me all the time from the road. Long conversations we used to have. We didn't want to hang up the phone. And now I see you, no phone call, no nothing, and immediately you tell me that you can't stay...and you expect me to bow my head like the good wife?"

"I do expect you to bow and take it, but this is quite another matter. I get home after many long days on the planes and roads, and I expect nothing but relaxation. Instead I get nagging: 'you're never around,' 'what about this and that.' You think I don't know what's going on? You think I know nothing of loneliness? I've been living it for the past four months. I see it in the eyes of those creatures at the mosques. They have nothing to cling to. The loneliness eats at them day and night, and they unleash it all upon me. And they look at me as the one who can show the All Mighty the suffering they bear. So don't assume I am a novice to loneliness; I play it like an accordian. It's part of me, and I certainly know it better than you do, so look at me.

"Now I have to leave soon, but I'm not letting it spoil the short time I have with you. Put it out of your mind. I'll put it out of mine."

"You make it sound so easy."

"Well, it isn't," as he moved closer to her. "But we're going to try, aren't we?"

"Sure we'll try," said Samira. "Not seeing you has had its effect on me. Khozem, of course, notices it, but he moves along in his studies waiting for the day you will send him in your place. It's the day I dread."

"But why? We'll have more time together. Samira, if you think our family can one day be together as it was, then you are operating under some kind of cruel delusion."

"So tell me about the trip, my darling. You must be tired?" said Samira finally.

"Oh the trip was usual, the same crowds and chanting. It doesn't change much, but for the first time in a while I felt like leaving it, to run into the Organization and say goodbye once and for all."

"But if you left, the direction of the religion would not be yours any longer. It would be up to someone else. Your right to choose a successor would be denied. Where would that leave Khozem?"

"You see, once you're in, it's very hard to find a way out. We're in it until Allah takes us. That or get I shot by some assassin."

"Don't talk like that," snapped Samira.

She checked herself in the mirror. She fiddled with the lipstick and a vial of mascara. Tariq wanted to continue, hopefully to find a way to leave his post.

"How's Khozem?" he asked.

"Just fine. He knows you're arriving today."

"I wonder if he has kept up on current events instead of getting bogged down in study all the time."

Tariq unpacked the light items of kurtas, pants, and handkerchiefs. His collection of skull caps were tightly run over metal bowls to keep their shape. He delved into a bag loaded with books in Arabic: The Hadith and The Sunnah and an unabridged Qu'ran along with two pairs of tangled subha beads and a journal of his own. He placed all of it on the bureau where Samira would put them away later.

Through the oversized window he beheld the Kaa'bah below, surrounded by the mosque where the believers prayed on Persian rugs. In the middle of the grand mosque the black box, the House of Allah. A swarm of densely packed believers circumambulated this black cube and recited-verses. At one of the corners, the black stone. He could see their palms raised high towards that corner. He heared the din of their celebration. As the fat sun set, the marble contours within the tall minurets were illuminated, giving definition to the zigzagging designs and the crescent green pieces marking the tops. The sight hypnotized him.

"So you have a taste of what's to come, eh?" interrupted Samira.

"Yes, I must get down there," as he shut the blinds. "It's as intriguing as the first day I stepped on that cool marble."

"And the Al-Azim visit? I heard it was the largest ever, and there was no violence. It tells us the way our religion is going, don't you think?"

"I don't want to discuss it, Samira."

He moved to the window again and poked through the blinds. It was getting closer to prayer time, and on the street many lay their prayer cloths right where they were standing, some nuzzling as close to the walls of the mosque as possible. He could see Samira biting her lip in the reflection. He wrapped his arms around her wide shoulders. The act felt awkward to both, and Tariq fought the temptation to remove his arms, but he let them rest where they were, wanting to make an impression, so that it would not feel awkward.

"Sometimes I've had enough," said Tariq. "I know I deserve at least a few days of peace and quiet before I start the touring again."

"I know, believe me, I know," said Samira. "It's good that you're home. I've missed you, although not much has happened. I've just grown older."

"We've grown older," corrected Tariq.

"We're having mujlis soon, so you better prepare."

She pulled out a set of fresh clothes. Already the phone rang with invitations to dinners and government functions to which Tariq declined. He told the chambermaid to tell the callers he hadn't arrived yet. The guests would be there soon. Tariq entered the washroom, and with painstaking strokes he cleansed his hands and arms, his nose and mouth. Samira phoned the Custodian of the Holy Mosques of Mecca and Medina. The news had surfaced throughout Mecca that Tariq had arrived safely.

He emerged from the washroom still restless. He wanted Vasilla to call. He did think of him as a tall, brawny clod, but Vasilla had been placed on solitary missions before, and for the most part, they turned out successfully. There were a few exceptions. When Tariq sent him to deliver and guard one of the major emissaries from Syria, Vasilla had lost his way from the airport and ended up in Jeddah surrounded by a mob of unruly Syrians. Just to touch the emissary would have been an honor.

In another incident, Vasilla was sent to apprehend an amilsaab who refused to give part of his mosque's donations to the Organization. Quite a large amount was due. Vasilla showed up at Tariq's home three hours later with the wrong amilsaab and his withdrawn bank account, all cash, in a metal deposit box. The amilsaab complained how Vasilla held him at gunpoint. With soothing words Tariq appeased him and apologized for the confusion. He made Vasilla beg for forgiveness. With respectful words the amilsaab departed but not before urging Tariq to get rid of Vasilla.

Tariq kept him as a favor to Vasilla's poor mother who lived forty miles north of Mecca in the desert sands. He was not much when she begged Tariq to take him. Vasilla was ignorant in the ways of Islam. Given his prominent body, Tariq thought he had potential as one of his personal guards. That was thirteen years ago, and when Tariq found himself unhappy with Vasilla's performance, he recalled the visage of Vasilla's mother with more wrinkles than he could count, dark teeth hanging weakly from her black gums, and those brown eyes so very cloudy and dull. He at once sent Vasilla to the Saudi military for a period of eight years and chose not to teach him the ways of Islam until he came back.

The military hatched a man full of potential, ready for Tariq's personal staff. They had trained him to use weapons with precision and economy, and to sacrifice his own life for the well–being of the bavasaab. After they taught him this, they rammed it into him again like a jackhammer upon a stubborn road. Vasilla came to Tariq with bulky arms and a stiff, protruding chest, dressed in a black suit which concealed a weapon at the side. Within this monstrous package Tariq tried to include the knowledge of the faith. The military didn't do a good enough job, as Tariq expected. In the hotel rooms Tariq forced Vasilla to learn the meaning of the prayers and interpretations of the chapters from the Qu'ran. Although his wits were not his strength, his loyalty was ironclad. He followed Tariq's orders to the slightest detail. The mistakes were big but rare.

Samira reminded him of the bags sprawled to the side of the bed. He looked at his wife and pleaded without words.

"What's wrong?" she asked.

And then again: "Why aren't you getting up?"

"It's not too late to tell our friends to come at another time," replied Tariq. "This may not be the best time. I just got back, and I don t feel too well."

"What's the matter?"

"I'd rather spend time with you, and I must see Khozem immediately. The brothers from the Organization, I can see them anytime."

He wanted to see his son, but the instinct of packing up and leaving weighed heavily on him, such that his own home seemed like an awkward and lonely place. He never expected this to come over him, and once he unpacked, his expectations of his homecoming were drowned. What was the purpose of rest? To see his family, yes. Instead he sat on the edge of the bed and worried about Vasilla. The bags were open and ready to be packed again.

He considered leaving once he saw Khozem. The child of the representative was to be kept away from the family, always in training, the strictest procedures governing his daily routine. Khozem would soon be jumping from city to city, walking among the faithful, never knowing their names, never understanding their troubles, merely a living hope that something will save the righteous eventually.

"Samira, I must call Khozem."

"You can't this week. He's busy with hearings. Just be patient."

Just be patient. And what more was there to do? After an emergency meeting with his council he would be back in the warm car headed towards the airport. He could feel the presence of a crowd thirsting for him.

He performed a second ablution upstairs to rid fatigue. He dressed in clean white garb. The guests had arrived, and he could hear flashes of conversation. He walked downstairs as to make a grand entrance. The mujlis celebrated his return. The visitors arranged themselves in neat rows. Their prayer cloths barely touched. The murmuring ceased as he descended. A pink curtain separated the women from the men. He walked through a path made for him to a shrine of sorts: a comfortable cushion facing the men. Above the cushion hung his photograph. The visitors waited. As they heard the adhan from the Kaa'bah below, their whispers tapered into an eerie silence.

Tariq faced the men who crowded the first floor. Behind the pink shade he discerned the sloping figures of the women. For the time being nothing else mattered but Allah. They shared their prayers at high intensity, their eyes shut while muttering the verses.

After the mujlis, friends and family gathered before a small trail of carpet to kiss Tariq's hand. The gatherers were fed by the image of perfection, that Tariq's son undertook the steps for the eventual ascension to the bavasaab's position, that the son being diligent, intelligent, and faithful followed the father without questioning the reason.

The bodyguards removed the pink curtain, and the women conversed amongst themselves. Their husbands begged Tariq for healing words.

The men who kissed Tariq's hand looked familiar. Tariq recognized them as government officials. He was determined not to talk with anyone but rather bless them all equally, showing no particular favor for or interest in each of their sorrowful tales. With each kiss of the hand, with each salaam, he replied to those who suffered:

"The Night of Power
Is better than a thousand Months.

Therein came down
The angels with the Spirit Gabriel
By Allah's permission,
On every errand: Peace!...
This Until the rise of Morn."

Tariq studied this verse in his younger years at Al–Karim. He remembered that the Night of Power transcends time, for it is Allah's glory. Darkness, therefore, is not ignorant. Darkness, or the Night of Power, has a hand in every affair. And when the Night of Spiritual Darkness is diffused by the morning glory of Allah, a peace and security arises in the soul. The undeniable wasteland of chequered nights and days of this world will be worth less than a dream, for the true believer will behold an eternal morning.

Tariq remembered only this part of the interpretation. The blessing shot out of him like a toy doll upon the pull of a string. After his fifteenth time of comforting a Meccan official whose son was dying of a fever, he became irritated by these faces with familiar lips kissing his hand. With each blessing the importance of their problems diminished. The last man on the long line tumbled to his knees and begged for greater wealth in his textile business.

"I work eighty hours a week and still I am losing my money," cried Tariq's cousin with a trim white beard. "I'm having trouble putting shoes on my teen–ager's feet."

Tariq looked to the ceiling as his cousin spoke. The distant cousin held Tariq's hand and caressed it, but Tariq stared only at the ceiling.

"My holiness, say something. Say anything."

"What do you want me to say?" barked Tariq. "Isn't it obvious what the problem is?"

"No, my holiness. Has Allah forsaken me?"

"First of all, stop whining and squealing in front of me. Just shut up and act like a man for once in your life. Allah has forsaken you thus far in the game, because each time I see you all you do is moan and whine and cry. Haven't you once given thanks for what you already have?"

"But I don't have anything..."

"That's because all you ever think about is your filthy money. You haven't been praying at all, have you? When was the last time you gave zakat? You should stop spending so much time in the shop and get out into the Kaa'bah. No wonder you are cursed. All of you are. Until you commit to Allah you will starve, your wife will seek a more prosperous man, and your sons won't respect you. So get on your feet and do a pilgrimage each day for a month, and if you are still losing your precious money by the time you are finished, then those small pilgrimages were not done to the best of your ability.

Now get up and stop crying and sweating over me. Go out and ask Allah for help, because I am not Allah!"

Tariq raced upstairs. He neither heeded the stares of others nor realized how loud his voice had become. He slammed the door and hoped Samira would come running after him.

In the bedroom Tariq paced with his hands behind his back and occasionally poked through his blinds at the Kaa'bah below until Samira stormed in.

"What is wrong with you?" she asked. "You just yelled at one of your dearest cousins. You're not that tired. I don't like lying to our friends who are here especially to honor your return."

"Then don't lie. Tell them that I'm sick of hearing their stupid little problems."

"Their problems are not stupid, and they certainly are not little. Don't you treat anyone with respect anymore?"

"They are not worthy of it. Each day I hear the same thing, the same whining. Sometimes I think Allah as fallen asleep on the job. And when he falls asleep he makes me clean up his mess."

"Stop talking like that. Allah never sleeps."

"How would you know? All you do is go shopping for the latest dress and gossip with your friends..."

"How dare you!"

"Yes you do. That's all you do. You're no example."

"Don't take your anger out on me. Allah chose you, not me."

"He chose the both of us. Aren't you forgetting that, Samira? He chose us both."

"You are the problem, not I. You're the one leading these people, not I."

"Are you saying I'm not strong enough anymore?"

Tariq sat on the bed. He removed his glasses and rubbed his tired eyes.

"So many things have been happening, Samira."

"Like what? Why don't you tell me?"

"Because you would just gab to your friends about it. What I have to tell you is classified."

"Have I ever told anyone about anything while we were married? No, I haven't. Don't you trust your own wife?"

"When it comes to the business of the faith, I don't trust anyone. Not even you."

"Then remain angry. Soon the reputation you have built will crumble. If you can't trust your own wife, the one who has stood by you for thirty-two hard and lonely years, I guess you can't trust anyone, now can you? You will die a very unhappy man..."

"Must we go through this each time?"

Tariq rose from the bed and took Samira into his arms.

"Of course I can trust you," he whispered. "Allah has sent you so that I can have someone to trust. I would never neglect such a gift."

"So tell me, Tariq."

"This is official business. You must not talk to anyone."

"I know this better than you do."

"Okay. Khozem is to become the bavasaab sooner than I thought. Actually, much sooner than I thought."

"But why? He just started university two years ago. He has at least ten more years to go."

"Don't get hysterical, Samira."

"I'm just surprised. He can't possibly become the bavasaab until his training is over."

"There are exceptions to every rule."

"When does he start?"

"We need to accelerate his training at Al–Karim. He needs to be brought out in less than a year."

"Less than a year? Are you crazy?"

"The business of Islam is not to be confused with insanity my dear."

"But why so soon? He's just a baby."

"A new Imam is on the way, I hope."

"A new Imam! Ah, Sakina is pregnant?"

"Sort of."

"Sort of? What sort of? We should celebrate! A new Imam, finally? Oh Tariq..."

Samira wrapped her hands around his cheeks and kissed his lips. Tariq wanted more.

"I must call Sakina to congratulate her," said Samira.

But, before she could pick up the phone, Tariq slammed the receiver.

"I'll have your hand cut–off," he said. "I told you this is between you and me. You are not to talk to anyone about it, absolutely no one."

"I'm sorry, but I'm so excited. I always knew Sakina and Imam Shabbir had more children on the way. Another Imam! We are truly blessed, truly blessed..."

"Don't get so excited. First of all, we don't know if it's a male or female, and secondly, we have to make sure Khozem is trained as quickly as possible. We must prepare him, even though he'll only be twenty. He has been to Council meetings, so he knows what those are like. Now we have to take him on tour. I don't know if the believers will follow a man so young."

"He is your son. They will follow him as they have followed you."

"I must get him from the university, fast."

"I think he's in judgment hearings. Don't interrupt him now. You know how he loves judging the students. He'll be finished in a few days. Take some time to think about what you're going to say to him."

"I will wait for only a few days, but I need to send the message to him now."

"Let me talk to him. If the message is from you, he'll think it's an emergency, and he won't get to judge all those poor students."

"Then call him tonight, because this is an emergency!"

That night Tariq paced the upstairs bedroom occasionally reviewing some of the Qu'ran. Nothing helped his impatience as he waited to hear from Khozem. As the long evening closed, Samira undressed in front of the mirror. She slowly unbuttoned her blouse and put it away in the walk–in closet. Tariq with the open Qu'ran in his hands watched her from the lounge chair. He had always admired her breasts which were firm and large like ripe pomegranates from the busy Meccan market. Samira removed her bra. In her nudity she approached Tariq. She took his lanky arms and led them around her waist. She kissed his thin, warm lips. She removed his heavy glasses. As they kissed, she moved her nimble hands down the length of his chest.

Slowly she undressed him. She rubbed her palms against his diaphanous chest. She led him to the bed where they hid under cool sheets. As Tariq entered her, she called his name ever so softly and ran her fingernails across his bony back, up and down as though charting the ladder of Jacob or mapping the run between Safi and Marwa. And with all of his feeble might Tariq thrust into her so he could hear his name being called over and over as though they were young again like flowers in bloom.

As the sweat evaporated, and the heat emptied into a stale coldness, their youth escaped as the dream does at the gates of dawn. The old age that had flushed away for that brief moment returned as he rolled over her and breathed freely on his side of the bed. When Samira finally gave up the possibility of a twilight conversation, Tariq was hit by the painful reminder that he was still a servant of Allah, and that his son, Khozem, would be the next in line to suffer as he did.

Chapter Seven
THE TRIAL
17th of Jumaada al-awal 1417
(September 30, 1996)

The rays of a white sun broke through Khozem's window along the quiet quadrangle. The room where he slept was considered the best room on the university campus, even better than all of the professors' rooms, which were half the size. His room was equipped with a large sofa, a Persian rug, an antiquated radio, a large bed, and a small fridge filled with sticky bottles of Rooh–Afza. Pictures of his mother and father were protected within gold–plated picture frames. The heat woke Khozem up in time for morning prayers. He could barely hear the strong, pleasing call of the university crier. In the confusion of half–sleep he gradually discerned the muezzin's call.

Khozem rolled from the bed as he tried to capture remnants of his dream. In his white cotton pajamas, he dizzily stumbled to the bathroom and had a good look in the mirror. He thought about trimming his beard and plucking some of his nose hairs. Rather than rushing to the big mosque on campus, he decided to say prayers in his room. Out of the faucet sputtered a rusty sprinkle. He recited aloud:

"In the name of Allah The Beneficent, the Merciful."

He ran his hands under cold water which broke his drowsiness. With a rough bar of soap he washed his hands up to his wrists and between his fingers three times like a surgeon. He did the same with his mouth, nostrils, face and forehead, arms, ears, head, neck, and feet, each three times. When the remains of sleep and the uncleanness of free dreaming had been abandoned for another morning, he dried himself with a towel and donned his kurta and turban.

He spread his prayer cloth towards Mecca. He tried with great difficulty to concentrate. Each time he prostrated he thought about Rashida and her nude face. He was certain he did not dream of her, but she filled his thoughts before bed and now again while whispering Allah's words. He tried to forget her by reciting the verses more loudly. This helped through the beginning parts of prayer but not through the thick and significant middle. He became anxious to do away with this woman. The more he was interrupted, the louder he prayed.

After a breakfast of fried eggs and dried beef, he adjourned to the university hall and took his seat. Again he was on the early side. He wanted to end the judgment as soon as possible. As he sat alone below the same picture of his father, he hungered for just one more look at Rashida. He wanted to see once more the mystery which lurked behind that black veil.

Dr. Farrukh sailed in and gave hearty salaams to Khozem who did not care for his company. No matter how hard he fought with these involuntary thoughts of her, he could not escape this one woman's face. He kept as silent as a stone wall.

Dr. Farrukh flipped the pages of his small notebook in preparation for the unprecedented hearing. Farrukh even summoned a reporter from the university newspaper. Farrukh told this to Khozem who reluctantly approved. The gaze of the university would be upon them, and Khozem knew he would have to expel her for apostasy, since consistency in judging would have to prevail.

But Khozem went further. He blamed this cloaked Rashida for these odd thoughts and day dreams. Women were never to be seen, and Khozem resented her for dragging him into a troublesome fascination that blocked the routine of prayer and the prompt obligation of expelling each and every student who broke the chain of Islamic tradition. As the minutes passed and the other professors took their seats, Khozem stood, and Dr. Farrukh prepared for heavy notetaking. The young journalist from the university paper was poised to jot Khozem's fierce words.

"Let us not waste time dwelling on a woman," began Khozem. "A crime is a crime whether committed by a man or a woman. I want to send a strong message to that women's college that we will not tolerate any woman who pretends to be as strong and blasphemous as the male. Women were sent down by Allah to provide for the man, not for themselves. They were put here to make our food, wash our clothes, and most importantly bear our offspring and look after our children. This woman has violated her initial purpose.

"A woman must first serve the All Mighty by constant prayer and reading of the Qu'ran. Her second obligation is to her husband, and third to the children. The two sexes shall never exist in equality; the man will lead, and the woman will follow. The woman is meant to serve man. As we all remember the words of the Prophet: 'The best woman is she who, when you see her, you feel pleased, and when you direct her, she obeys. She protects your rights and keeps her chastity when you are absent.'

"This is what we expect from our women, nothing more, nothing less. Committing apostasy is the worst of all crimes.

"In addition to expelling her from Al–Karim, I will also recommend that we ship her to Mecca for additional hearings. She will carry the burden of her crime for the rest of her life, such that living will have been worse than death. Death will not set her free, because she shall be sentenced to the eternal fire for betraying her faith. This shall be the first and last woman we shall ever see in this chamber. Now does anyone have anything to say regarding this matter?"

The other professors kept silent as Dr. Farrukh stood from his chair.

"My holiness," began Dr. Farrukh, "you are certainly correct in pursuing expulsion for this woman who has strayed from the faith. Sending her to Mecca would also be a just punishment. I speak for all when I say that your judgment and wisdom in this matter can be nothing less than a gift bestowed upon you by the All Mighty himself. All women will take this as a warning never to cross the boundaries of being women. I can speak for all of us when I say that we agree with your decision over this woman. Let's expel her and get her on the first plane to Mecca for further judgment by the mutawafs. The quicker, the better."

Khozem noticed the reporter at the far end of the hall writing in a small memo book. At least these words would be recorded, thought Khozem. It would boost Khozem's popularity among his colleagues at the university. His father would be proud.

Dr. Farrukh took his seat, and with a depth in his voice Khozem summoned Rashida to the committee.

Rashida walked calmly through the threshold of the chamber wearing the traditional women's uniform of cloak, headdress, and veil. Khozem could only see her eyes but recalled the intense attractiveness of her face. She wandered in like a shadow that lives and breathes as the sun dives below the flat horizon and permits the darkness to rule over bereft hearts. She stood in front of the seven cold men with her arms at her sides. Khozem could not tear himself away from her black, angelic eyes behind which hid those secrets of a woman damned by Allah and nurtured by another God even more powerful.

Chapter Eight
RASHIDA
17th of Jumaada al-awal 1417
(September 30, 1996)

Rashida had been briefed by the mistress of her dormitory on the protocol of the plea and hearing. She took a quick moment to think of what to say to those men with long beards and curious stares. She searched through her file of close memories of the small university. Men and women were never seen chatting or mingling. They remained within their separate camps: the men on the main campus, the women two miles away on a dust and dirt–ridden land marked by dilapidated shacks and a stench of sewage floating in a nearby stream. The women were occasionally allowed to attend prayer services at the big mosque on the main campus. On these visits Rashida wore her uniform. She became used to it.

She had been accepted early to the university, and at the time she was proud of it, receiving recommendations from two amilsaabs in Cairo and three high school instructors. She made it to the place she had always wanted to study. But things had nagged her, the cloak in particular, which was difficult to draw over herself. She had made it known to her dorm-mates.

"Hey, aren't you girls sick of wearing this thing before going to the main campus? The men do no such thing."

None of the women responded. She asked it again and received dirty looks from all of them, except from the younger ones. She dressed in the cloak anyway and proceeded to the big mosque with the younger ones thinking her brave for questioning the rule.

"Hey, don't you think it crazy that we have to resort to our own women's library and that we can't take any books out from the main library on campus?" she asked everyone in the dormitory one night.

Three women confronted her. The tallest one in the middle was Tazula, and she towered in her cloak over the smaller Rashida.

"Didn't you know the rules before you got here? We do these things for a reason. It is the plan the scriptures have outlined. If you don't like it, you can leave."

"I never expected things to be this strict. It's ridiculous. It's not like this in the city."

"We are not in the city," scowled Tazula. "If you don't like it, you can go back to Cairo. We don't need any of that here. Be loud someplace else."

"I didn't mean to be loud, but the policies here are outdated and unfair. We can't drive to the main campus, we can't take out books from the main library, we have to sit in these insect–infested classrooms, we can't talk to the men..."

"It is not the place for a newcomer to break tradition."

Rashida saw Tazula's bookends nodding in agreement. She remained silent before the three of them turned away grunting. Rashida kept her mouth shut to the entire dormitory. Yet she whispered after lights out to the younger ones close to her bunk. She eventually talked of protest. The younger ones, however, were unsure. They did not want to go against Tazula and her bookends. After a week of Rashida's whispering, one of the younger ones mentioned her talk of protest to Tazula.

On another sultry morning, Rashida awoke to the dorm mistress' assertive voice. She had slept well. She dreamt of piasters on the ground, picking them up with dirty fingers, leading her to the administration building on the main campus: the brown faces, the men in white dress and the women in black cloaks, eagles floating low and crying her name. She had forgotten the rest.

She lay in the bed ashamed, for money was the root of all evil, and in her sleep her soul had been chasing after it. From the above bunk she spotted two short legs dangling. She did not give her bunkmate the usual perky greeting. Her bunkmate took a towel from the cubby hole and headed for the showers. Rashida did the same.

She stepped on perspiring tile while eyeing the other women as streams of water ran down their warm bodies. She admired the body of one of the older ones: a slim stomach and firm breasts catching water from the nozzle. She dared not look for too long. She glanced furtively while picking up the rough soap. The older one left the room, followed by the younger ones in the corner. She was alone suddenly.

The huge bulk of Tazula entered. She found a place in the corner where the younger ones had been. Her two bookends soon followed, checking the temperature of the water with their hands. They talked to each other, but Rashida could not hear them. Rashida soaped herself, her back to the wall. As she rinsed the gritty emulsion from her skin, a towel came full around her neck and jerked her clear from the spray. She screamed, but no one answered. Only the pounding of fists into her delicate face and kicks into her body. The blood mixed with the soap while sliding into the drain.

She wore dark sunglasses after her brief visit to the infirmary.

"Time will heal these bruises, " said the nurse.

She did not listen to her. The nurse applied ointment to her cheeks. Rashida was half–way out the door before the nurse asked how she got the bruises. Rashida remained silent, licking the split in her lower lip.

She rushed out of the infirmary and headed for the women's campus. She had missed two classes already and was almost late for a third. The quadrangle on her way down was blank and uneasy. Tension surfaced on the brown lawns, the dust floating in the air, the sun beaming hot and heavy. She could have hid herself with a veil. But there was no point in hiding. She was not going to suffer the defeat of quitting the university.

Through open windows on the quadrangle she could see the heads of students. She could hear the faint tapping of chalk on blackboards. She could not go on. She did not know where to go or whom to tell. She sat on a line of steps near an empty classroom facing the cement wall. This wall barred the campus from the sprawling city. The administration building to her left, the men's dormitory to her right. The breeze, the echoes of full classrooms, her throbbing lips, and then the pleasure of feeling sorry for herself. The quivers of release came and went in intervals. But it did not work. She could not force a single tear.

While her face reformed and the bruises on her body shrank, she remained silent and buried her nose in books. She avoided Tazula as best she could. She wrote her mother short lines about longing for the city and her old friends. She hungered for her mother's hand upon her fine hair, gently stroking it free of all the wasted time and uneasiness of being in a place where the walls stank of hate. It was all around her: in the younger ones who giggled, in the men and their chauvinism, in the older women who clung to tradition. On the walk from the women's campus to the big mosque it hung in the air. Her opposition rose through mornings of sitting in decaying classrooms and noticing how the men were given better treatment by instructors and administrators and how the women followed a path towards enslavement.

An outcast, the women had said. A product of the Jinn, they had labeled her. She entered the administration building on a balmy afternoon. She found the president's office within a vacant corridor. She opened the door and yelled at the top of her lungs:

"My name is Rashida Husseini Pendi. The methods and policies used to denigrate women are abominable. You should all be ashamed of yourselves. All of you are cowards, hiding behind your scriptures, hiding in your isolated tombs where Allah shall keep you, to awaken at the day of judgment and cast you into the fire where the flesh is roasted. Allah will understand the torment you inflict on women at this university of hypocrites. If this is the type of Islam that you preach and practice, I want no part of it. I want no part of this university. This is not true Islam. Islam is better, and if you think that yours is the true Islam, think again. I spit on your version of it."

She shattered the door window on her way out. She did not look back. She had interrupted an important meeting. The guards caught her at the entrance. They escorted her back to the women's campus with their hands clutching her arms. Her name was immediately given to Dr. Farrukh's office.

Dr. Farrukh never received the message from his secretary that a woman had been summoned for judgement. Rashida jumped at the opportunity to stand in front of these men. She knew Khozem, the ringleader, was responsible. She wanted to make a fool of him. She wanted to hurt him in some way. The fleeting fear before she entered the chamber changed into a form of anger. Her anger put her on the offensive, but this anger was ill-defined. She hoped it would lead to a victory. There is no glory in futility unless one has won, and her darting mind searched for something to crack these impregnable seven.

She concentrated on Khozem. She knew she would be expelled, and she could have left the university before the hearing. Nevertheless, her protests, the hallmark of chronic disobedience for a better Islam, would not end with her alone. Other women would follow as the atrocity of living on a campus saturated by filth and paralysis developed like algal scum over a pond.

"Before we expel you and send you to Mecca for the high crime of apostasy, we give you this moment to hear your plea," said Khozem. "It's no secret that you are the first woman this university has ever judged..."

"So no matter what I say, I will still be expelled and sent to Mecca?"

"Yes, to put it bluntly."

"So then what's the point in saying anything?"

"Allah will hear you. That's the point."

"Doesn't Allah already know what I'm about to say?"

"Yes, Allah knows everything, but he is waiting to hear your apology to this committee and this university for betraying the faith."

"And how did I betray the faith?"

"By what you shouted in the administration building, in the president's own office. Don't play games with me."

"I never betrayed anything. Your president got what was coming."

"And we will give you what is coming. This is no game. This is not a debate. Say what you have to say and get out of my sight."

"I don't have anything to say."

"Of course you do. Didn't someone tell you how these proceedings are run?"

"Yes, but these proceedings are absurd. You sit there in ignorance, pretending to represent what Allah wants. You don't know the first thing about what Allah wants. You go against His will."

"How's that?" laughed Khozem.

"Just look at the condition of women. Our living conditions are deplorable, our food is second rate, the library has no books. You are not educating us. We are learning only how to be submissive. We are slaves down there."

"Nonsense. If that were the case we would be hearing from the lot of you. It's obvious that it is you alone who has turned against Allah and His will. The punishment for apostasy is severe, not only in this life but the one after."

"I had no other choice. You people gave me no other choice but to shout those things. And by all means I do not take it back. The people running this pit, especially you, should know that women have the same rights in relation to the man."

"I think you are grossly misinterpreting the Qu'ran. The Qu'ran clearly states that women have the same rights only in marriage and the man will always stand a step above them. It is very clear in sura two, aya 228."

"Well I don't believe in that. Something must be wrong with the Qu'ran."

"That is exactly why you have been called to this committee."

"This committee is a joke."

"Then I guess you'll be laughing all the way to Mecca."

"There are no punishments prescribed for apostasy in our scriptures. Apostasy remains the greatest of all sins, but there are no real world punishments for it. My plea is based upon 'no compulsion in religion.' Sura two, aya 256, and that our holiest of scriptures does not outline any punishment for apostasy. Our prophet never had an apostate put to death or sent to Mecca."

"You are quite right, but this committee will make an exception starting with you. We interpret apostasy in a different way. Apostasy is a fixed punishment, not a discretionary one. Because it is fixed, you will be expelled from this university and sent to Mecca for another hearing in front of the religious police."

"Then why say anything at all?"

"We are waiting for your apology."

"You will never get an apology. It is you who ought to apologize to all those women who are learning to be nothing more than slaves to these corrupt clerics. Some women may be happy being the caretakers of the family. They may be happy rearing children and depending on the husband for all the decision–making, but I warn you, Islam will die without reform, and reform begins at the women's college. Can't you see what I'm getting at? Islam cannot survive unless its women are treated with dignity. All you are doing is training housewives and baby-sitters."

"I don't think we need to hear any more of this," said Khozem. "The women must remain women, and if you take exception to this then I suppose you were never meant to be a part of this fine university."

"You will realize things when it is too late," responded Rashida. "I almost feel sorry for you. While the world changes, you will be stuck in the dark ages relying on a book that is too old to be practiced anymore."

"We follow the words of Allah, and his words transcend time. What you call slavery Islam calls the most direct route to heaven. Don't feel sorry for us. Rather it is we who should feel sorry for you."

"Oh really? Take a good look at the women of this university."

"Certainly they did not choose you as their mouthpiece."

"And who elected you? No one did. You clearly do know the condition of women, but you refuse to do anything about it. Not only are you a coward, but you are an ignorant coward. A dumb coward. A coward who doesn't even know he is a coward. You can get away with expelling those who are smarter than you are, all because you wish to build your reputation, or maybe it's because you think your power is something special..."

"I don't need to hear any more of this," said Khozem. "Get her out of here."

"No. You will hear this. You act as though you have some divine right over the minds of the students who have stood before your committee. Always remember that these ideas will remain. They do not go away through torture, expulsion, or death..."

"Get out of here, or I'll have the guards kick you out!"

"Well that's just fine," as Rashida ripped off her headdress and veil. "Take a good look, all of you. This is the only time you shall ever see a woman, so take a good look."

"Put those garments back on! Have some respect!"

"It's impossible for anyone to respect a slave, so take a good look, a hard look, at this slave."

Her exposed body lay in front of the seven members, six of whom fought the temptation to override Khozem's authority on this matter. Khozem could do nothing but stare. He sat mystified by her youth. He remotely recognized the face. It was a version of what he had seen before. From her dark eyes and skin he explored the new territory of her abundant chest, thin waist, and denim-covered legs which made up the bulk of this slave who represented the uncontrollable evolution of the woman. Khozem could not bear looking at her, but could not peel his eyes from her skin. The longer he looked, the more power he lost. He measured the energy draining from his body. His anger settled as hers expanded. He questioned where his wrath had gone. He felt in his chest the tables turning, as though this one woman had found a vulnerable point into which she plunged the knife, twisting it with the force and celerity of a drill. He tried to rid himself of her poison.

"Get out right now!"

"That's right," shouted Rashida. "Call the guards. Let other men do your dirty work. You won't get rid of me this easily. Yes, I've heard about you. Spoiled, infantile. You get these dunces to clean up your mess. We all know it. Even your cronies know it. How does it feel to have such a powerful father, while you have no potential? Don't kid yourself. You are nothing without your father. You have contributed nothing of value to our faith. You are detrimental to our religion."

The guards, stiff and mechanical, grabbed Rashida's arms.

"There is still time," she said as the guards dragged her from the room. "It doesn't have to be this way. You have the power to change things. Change does not mean apostasy, it means growth..."

And then an awkward silence with the residue of Rashida's ramblings. He could not digest such statements and could not fathom having her gone. Her strong black hair which fell to her shoulders, those full and symmetrical breasts which were never meant to be touched, her fiery elocution which captured the ovum of truth, all of these things held him in the grip of uncertainty and doubt.

Khozem could not classify this woman as psychologically unstable. He could not fit her into any category. She brushed against an elusive truth that even Khozem could not define for himself. As in the earlier hearing in which her veil slipped, he could not come to a conclusion. She had been the first student, male or female, to penetrate him with the might of her scorn. Even the professors knew it. He attempted in great difficulty to organize the chaos into some form of order. In the absence of Khozem's remarks, Dr. Farrukh rose from his seat.

"My holiness, this woman is hysterical. Instead of sending her to Mecca after the expulsion, perhaps we should send her to a sanitarium. She couldn't have meant the things she said. Evil spirits have taken her mind's capacity to be a good and dutiful woman. No one, man or woman, in their right mind would say such things. She's possessed, as most women tend to be after being put under so much pressure. May I suggest we lock her in a sanitarium for the time being until she repents for her high crime of apostasy. After she has been rid of these evil Jinn who mess up everything, then we can send her to Mecca. I'm sure I speak for all of us when I say this woman is undoubtedly deranged. She did not mean to speak those filthy comments."

Khozem sighed deeply. This Rashida may have been deranged, hysterical, or imbalanced, but simultaneously she made far too much sense. He burned for more.

"Where have the guards taken her?" asked Khozem.

"Back to the women's campus, I think." replied Farrukh.

"Good. I must order her expulsion. Give me the proper papers to sign. Have the guards watch her pack. As soon as she is ready to leave, tell the guards to bring her to my room. She is not to leave this campus without seeing me first."

"But my holiness, why would you even want to speak with such a heathen?"

"That's none of your business, Doctor. Just do it."

"Yes, my holiness. And what about future hearings in Mecca? The idea of the sanitarium?"

"No. We will not send her to Mecca. Neither will we commit her to a sanitarium. She is to be expelled. Just make sure she sees me. And by the way, this meeting is not, and I mean not to be reported in the newspapers. Not one word."

After the professors and the obedient reporter bid their salaams and left the room, Khozem did not have the motivation to move. The clash of heat and humidity pricked his skin, but like the horse swatting flies, he did not mind it so much. He had been reduced to something sickly. He wanted to be respected, not for his father's position, but for his own piety and wisdom.

He questioned how many people of the Shia Muslim faith felt like Rashida. Not many. Most of his people did not think it necessary to change the rules. The Qu'ran made things clear and unambiguous. So the question still loomed like the sunlight pestering the chamber: how did this woman come up with such ideas?

At first he blamed Cairo, the city beyond the walls. Heathens must have influenced her. But then why would Rashida insult him and at the same time embrace Islam? As he sorted through the details of what Rashida had said, Khozem recognized she did not abandon Islam itself. Rather she parted with a version of it as defined by its establishment. When closely reexamined, she technically did not commit apostasy. Her insults, her attitude, and her demeanor, however, merited expulsion.

And how could he forget that shameful act of removing her cloak and veil, such that her face and breasts and legs were shown in full view? Ah she deserved to be punished, if not for apostasy, then for undermining his power and control of the hearing. He could not brush her away like the other students he had so arbitrarily expelled. The sight and sound of her, the way she yelled, and the curves of her body astonished him.

The rest of the day went by like lava. Instead of classes Khozem waited for the guards to arrive in his room. He checked the quadrangle from his window, but no sign of the guards or Rashida. He fell into boredom. He found within his schoolwork a deeper boredom. Relief came while rehearsing what he would say to Rashida. His excitement found him pacing. He did not picture Rashida wearing the traditional uniform. She would come to him in those skin-tight jeans and loose tee-shirt, but she would not be angry or upset. His rehearsals for the event became repetitive after an hour of trying to find the right words.

All too suddenly he heard a light knock on the door. He opened it to an uncloaked Rashida flanked by two, very tall and beefy guards. Disdain and irritation hung on her face. Khozem was the last person she wanted to see, let alone talk with. With a wave of his hand Khozem dismissed the guards and shut the door. They were alone, and Khozem was scared of the silence. He feared her as he feared Allah, but not due to the overwhelming power she had over him, but from an attempt to please her regardless of what she stood for. His burning would not simmer, and the sight of her made it worse.

"What do you want from me?" asked Rashida as Khozem mixed her a cold glass of Rooh Afza.

"I just want to talk, that's all."

"I have nothing to say to you."

"Please try and relax. This is not the university chamber. This is not a hearing. Try some of this. A colleague of mine just returned from Pakistan, and he gave it to me as a gift."

Khozem cautiously handed over the glass, and she sipped the sweet raspberry liquid.

"How do you like it?" asked Khozem.

"It doesn't taste like anything. Kind of a dull drink."

"That's exactly what I thought when I tried it back in Teheran a few years ago. It's an acquired taste, but once you're hooked, you can't stop drinking the stuff."

"What is it that you want, Mr. Bengaliwala?"

"Call me Khozem."

"I don't have much time. A taxi waits for me at the entrance."

"Tell me, what is it like living at the women's campus?"

"It has been the worst experience of my life."

"Go on."

"We are not treated equally as the men are. A constant stench of urine. Strange insects, small and tiny, bury into your skin at night. A male student's vomit would be more palatable than the food at our cafeteria. Our library is stripped of the essential books. The walk to the main campus is particularly troublesome. I don't understand why there isn't some van or shuttle bus to take us to the big mosque. What few teachers we have train us only to cook and clean and how to become faithful wives and caring mothers. What scares me the most is the other female students. They don't realize what's happening. I've tried to make them aware, but all I got were cuts and bruises. Shall I go on?"

"And so you became sick of it?"

"Almost immediately. I could not carry on. I saw their complacency. When I tried to break them out of it, their response was to keep quiet and whisper bad things about me. When I pushed a bit more, they became angry.

They found that oppression suited them just fine. They beat me up real good, but I am no longer angry about it. I pity them. I pity you as well."

"Why me?"

"Because you refuse time and time again to see the big picture. You refuse progress. You look back and do not look ahead."

"I don't understand. We are doing what Allah wants. We follow what is written in the Qu'ran. We follow what the Prophet has said in the Sunnah. Muhammad has delivered Allah's message. From that message we know how to please Allah."

"But this is a very old and ancient message, a message meant for those who knew nothing about Islam. The Qu'ran is an introduction, written nearly fourteen hundred years ago. How can you expect Muslims to follow the same commands? How is it that a society such as ours remains in stasis for that long? It's impossible. A Muslim society must evolve. It must develop. We have already learned how to crawl by Muhammad's message. We are learning to stand and walk, even run. We no longer suck on Allah's bosom. Like more advanced, mature, and able sons and daughters we are given more freedom from our creator. We have the ability to make choices. These choices empower us. We grow as individuals, separate from Allah. It's no wonder that my plea was Surah two, verse 256. This is an example of Allah giving us a choice. Through our own free will we are allowed to make choices. We shape, make, and mend our own destinies."

"Are you even a Muslim? A Muslim doesn't talk this way."

"I am. I will always be. But if Islam means that I must be enslaved, oppressed, and beaten down, then obviously that version of Islam is not Islam at all. It is false."

"You are speaking of the university's version of Islam?"

"Your Islam retards development. Your punishments are cruel. You have no sense of justice. You have no concept of human rights. Your version confiscates freedom in its rawest form. Islam as you practice it is like a family inbreeding. At first it may strengthen and unite the family. It may preserve family traditions and values. It may keep future generations pure. But over time, as the same genes cannot protect the family from the demands of external factors and evolution, the family shall collapse. It does not have the inherent strength to withstand new dangers and new ideas. So I'm not angry about being expelled. Eventually Islam as we know it will have to change. Those who resist change will be determined weak and unfit. This fragile planet will be filled with lonely and vulnerable Muslims. Islam will collapse and constitute less than a footnote in history."

"Why don't you have a seat?" offered Khozem.

"I'd rather stand. I don't have time for this."

"Please. I insist. I must tell you a few things before you leave-"

"I don't want to hear it. Save it for the other students you'll expel."

"We are not sending you to Mecca. We have accepted Sura two, aya 256 as your defense, and besides you never departed from the faith, technically speaking."

"You expect me to jump and celebrate?"

"Aren't you at least relieved? You're a lucky woman. All you get is expulsion."

"Thanks to Allah for my expulsion. I can't stand another minute here."

"Then go," said Khozem angrily. "Don't say another word of your outlandish philosophy. Maybe Farrukh was right. You do belong in a sanitarium."

"He said that?"

"I declined the proposal. What gibberish sprouts from your mouth! Such nonsense was never meant to make any sense, but for some reason I can't let go of it."

"That's because it does make sense. Don't deny it."

"I'm not concerned about what you say about Islam. I do, however, need your help in reforming the women's college. Most of us up here don't know anything about what women do. Only security persons have been down there, but even they don't go down there much. Maybe once a month."

"What makes you so concerned all of a sudden?"

"This is the last time I ever want to see a woman in the university chamber."

"Why? Do I scare you? Were you frightened when I took off my clothes?"

"That outburst is the main reason why we are expelling you."

"Answer my question. Do I frighten you?"

"I'm not scared of anyone," as Khozem looked out the window.

"I think you are. You're afraid what I said makes sense. I'm not the only woman who will frighten you. I know you were afraid when I ripped off my clothes. It's no wonder you don't want to see any more women. They may tell you the truth. They may say you really are a coward, that you aren't much without your family name."

"That's not true! I'm not afraid of anyone. Now I've agreed to discuss reform at the women's college. Stop insulting me."

In the warmth of the room Rashida approached Khozem. She put her hand on his shoulder.

"My taxi is waiting," she said. "If you're serious about this, you'll call me. I'll be in Cairo."

The door closed. The ice in his glass melted leaving a red, syrupy residue. He saw her leaving with the guards who refused to assist her with the luggage. He could not extinguish the fire which immolated him. He was afraid of her, but this Rashida failed to see the reason for his fear. The insults hurt him, her philosophy on Islam confused him, her decloaked body surprised him. But the real fear rested in that condensed and bluish flame that devoured his heart with each painful moment of her absence.

Chapter Nine
KHOZEM GOES HOME
17th of Jumaada al-awal 1417
(September 30, 1996)

On the day Rashida left, Khozem received a call from his mother asking him to Mecca. She said his father desperately needed to speak with him. Khozem chose not to question his mother. She urged him with enthusiasm to make haste from Cairo as soon as he had finished judging the students.

Khozem packed his belongings, which included three pairs of white pants and kurtas, two formal skull caps, and his favorite Copy of the Qu'ran. He met with two bodyguards at the front gates of the university.

Before getting into the Mercedes, Khozem took a deep breath of the dry Cairo heat. He dreaded losing Rashida's phone number. He focused on what his father would say. He heard the Indian tour worked out successfully without the expected violence and mayhem. Yet thoughts of Rashida prevailed.

Vasilla did not meet him at the Jeddah airport as he usually did. Instead Khozem found a shorter, younger version of him standing by yet another white Mercedes. The two bodyguards who accompanied Khozem from Cairo and this replacement bodyguard made their way from Jeddah and through the busy Meccan streets. In the several months of being away from the ancient metropolis Khozem noticed not a single change. The older women in their black gowns waddled with their children, while the men in white robes and head-gear darted about; a familiar scene which did not move him. Like the pilgrims circumambulating the House of Allah, the city revolved in a singular time. In the past and in its present it never needed adjustment.

As Khozem watched the commoners moving, running, and conversing, as the car engine moaned while climbing the steep Meccan hillside, a simple truth eluded him: these mosques, these rituals, these pilgrims who came in the name of Allah, these palpable reminders of heaven and hell so unmistakably sacrosanct and untouchable were at the root of humankind's gradual demise and destruction. Yet an idea so tiny and insignificant explained his mood entirely.

The customary scenes of the city vanished. The idea of talking with his father no longer stirred him. He yearned to be back in Cairo so that he could telephone Rashida. After reminding himself of his pledge to reform that wasted section of land called the woman's college, he really did not care what happened to them. Besides, in no way could he undertake the task of reforming the women's college without his father's permission. He decided not to ask him about it.

The car pulled to the entrance of the two–story house. The intermittent sunlight forged weak shadows along the driveway. Khozem wore common dress for schooling and carried a notebook under his arm. He exchanged salaams with his father who greeted him at the door.

"It has been a long time, but I have become used to it," said Khozem, blending the right mixture of nonchalance and sentiment.

Tariq cupped his hand and gave him a firm pat on the meat of his arm. Samira gave Khozem a tremendous kiss on the cheek after meaningful salaams.

"I have been touring," began Tariq.

"And has that been the usual or something exciting?"

"The riots in India, although they did not affect us. That was on everyone's minds. But really, I was not intimidated by it. I will have to decide how to handle the affair. But really that's all. I did think of you often on the road, or up in the air most of the time. How's the training going?"

"Smooth and steady, just as it has always been. No problems."

"It's good that I broke you away from Cairo for my period of rest. You are able to understand a bit of your future, and I am hoping that school is teaching you properly as it had taught me."

"Yes, father. No problems with school," replied Khozem.

This was far from accurate. Not once had Khozem fed him a truthful line. Per chance the day would come when he would have to tell his father that things were not going as planned, that he could not shake from his mind the appearance of a young Muslim woman. But such a lack of discipline would be a severe anomaly, a strong, perfect impossibility.

He was satisfied with the relationship as it was; a direct and to the point jumble of platitudes. But Khozem detected a change in his father, as though he held him in higher esteem.

"So tell me about the latest tour," asked Khozem again.

"Same old mosques in the Indian provinces. The turnout gets bigger every year. The faith is getting stronger, the faith that you will be leading, and you are nearly ready."

"I have many more years at university, father."

He invited his son to sit in the living room. They leaned against firm pillows placed along the perimeter.

"See this picture?" asked Tariq pointing to his portrait. "That was taken nearly twenty years ago, before Allah brought you to this world. I remember praying to Allah day and night for a son to be delivered. He granted my request for a son, because he knew you would be chosen, one of two men in all of Shia Islam to lead us into the next millennium. One of the proudest days of my life."

"What's bothering you, father? You speak as though someone died."

"As a matter of fact, things are changing, and these changes are happening quite quickly."

"What changes? Things never change around here."

"You must really like it in Cairo. I cherish those years of attending Al-Karim, although back then there weren't many students to be judged. Son, I called you here because I have something important to tell you. It involves you more than it does me."

"The Indian tour?"

"No, nothing like that. The riots did not affect us. I will have to do something to stop those corrupt Hindus. The Indian tour has nothing to do with you. It has nothing to do with what I'm telling you."

"Then what can it be?"

"Someone is about to die, my son, and I must remind you that what I say cannot be shared with anyone, neither your friends nor colleagues at Al-Karim. Not even your own mother."

"I understand."

"Son," as Tariq gripped Khozem's thigh," in a period of two years you will take over my position. You will have full authority over all religious and organizational operations."

"I don't understand," said Khozem.

"I don't expect you to understand. It will take a few days, perhaps a few weeks for this to settle in. But I will give full power to you within the period of two years, maybe sooner."

"But why? There is so much more I need to learn."

"After you left Cairo I spoke directly to the dean of the university. What's his name?"

"Dr. Farrukh."

"That's right. Under my close vigilance he will put together for you an advanced, very intensive curriculum for your training. He will compress ten years of study into two years of training."

"I can't handle that."

"You can and you will. After completion you will be known as the youngest bavasaab ever in our short history. I, of course, will be guiding you once power has changed hands. I will bring you to our meetings, I am even going to select a wife for you."

"A wife? What do you mean a wife?"

"Don't be silly. You ought to know this. You will be married before you leave Al–Karim. Your mother is in charge of this. After today she will be accepting applications and photographs from prospective wives. This doesn't excite you."

"This is all happening so fast."

"I know my son. It's an equal mix of excitement and fear. Don't let it confuse you. There are two years of training, long days and short nights. From it you will be fully knowledgeable. You will be ready to lead and prepare our soldiers of Islam."

"Prepare what?"

"Don't worry about that now. Go back to Cairo ready to work hard. I have told you enough. Let it rest for some time. The next two years are extremely important. Don't disappoint me."

"I won't, I suppose."

"Good. Don't be afraid. I will be there every step of the way. I won't let you down, just so long as you understand what's ahead. To celebrate this event we will go to the Kaa'bah and perform a small pilgrimage. I'm proud of you son. Very proud."

Khozem ascended the stairs behind his slow father who seemed exhausted from relating the news. His room a few feet away from the master bedroom seemed smaller and unacceptable. The warm and bitter air engulfed him. He clicked on the ceiling fan which broke the heavy dust over his small bed, desk, and bureau. The breeze brought a window of serenity. Such information from his father's mouth would have normally made him overjoyed and impatient, but instead he slipped into a blurry delirium. The dizziness and mental confusion forced him to sit on his bed. He put his head into his hands and admitted he did not want his father's position so soon. Such a position, no matter how powerful and enviable, would control the rest of his days. His slow and steady movement towards adulthood, that cloudy, misty, grayish area between irresponsibility and sophistication had been reached by his sudden discovery that his days were now numbered.

His father knocked softly at his door. Tariq was covered with two pieces of white, seamless cloth: one for his upper body and the second for the lower. He had performed a detailed ablution, for his hair was neatly combed, and Khozem smelled a hint of cologne.

"What's the matter?" asked Tariq. "You should have been ready by now."

"Just a few more minutes, please," as Khozem returned to normalcy.

Khozem performed a quick ablution. Through his conscientious scrubbing of hands and feet he tried to come up with seven prayers to complement the seven rounds of the Kaa'bah. His father would also wonder what verses he would use for the small pilgrimage. He came from the bathroom with white cloth covering him and an expressionless face, stoic almost, as he hid his uncertainty and worry beneath a decorum of an eager Muslim supplicant.

Khozem met his father downstairs and was amused by the bodyguards, four of them, covered with identical pieces of cloth. They were clean shaven and solemn.

"Where's Vasilla, by the way?" asked Khozem.

"He's on special assignment. He'll be back any day now," said Tariq.

They walked under the hot sun. Because Tariq and his son wore only cloth without their caps, they were not recognizable to the inspired throng of Muslims. Tariq, Khozem, and the bodyguards entered at the rear of the mosque. Time afforded them a leisurely pilgrimage. With the bodyguards sandwiching them from the front and rear they opened their palms towards the corner of the black stone and cried aloud:

"Allah is the greatest."

Each time they circled it, they cried the same greeting. Khozem knew his father would use his favorite verses while walking around the great, black fixture which, quite literally, commanded the center of attention. Some of the believers closer to the center read directly from the Qu'ran in their valiant attempt to curry favor with Allah. Khozem understood, however, that there were no specific supplications for this ritual. The verses people usually recited were baseless. He remembered well the prayers he used to recite. One of them came into mind as he crossed that specific corner. He whispered to the sky:

"Oh Allah, I seek refuge in thee from
incapacity, from sloth, from cowardice, from
miserliness, decrepitude, and from the torment
of the grave.
Oh Allah grant to my soul the sense of
righteousness and purify it, for Thou art the

Best purifier thereof. Thou art a Protecting
Friend thereof, and Guardian thereof.
Oh Allah, I seek refuge in Thee from the
knowledge which does not benefit, from the
heart that does not entertain the fear
of Allah, from the soul that does not feel
contented and the supplication to which there
is no response."

He continued this march with his father who seemed to be in another
world. They took their time amidst the hypnotized believers. With each new
lap came a new prayer, and Khozem chose randomly some of the more
traditional verses. But as the end of the round grew near, he could not deny
that basic Muslim right to pray for what he truly wanted. His heart throbbed
with each request.

He asked Allah for the gift of leadership and political acumen. And
then a second request: that he be made a special bavasaab unlike the rest, for
he wanted to live on the lips of his people like the great ones: the murdered
Ali, the poisoned Hasan, the decapitated Husain.

As this brief list of martyrs came to mind, he was thereafter stunned and
ashamed while making the final round. These martyrs were Imams, precious
and dead. He almost forgot in the flaring ambition of his prayer that he could
neither be as great nor as powerful as the Imam who would ultimately be his
sovereign. He would be recognized, yes. Powerful, absolutely. The next Imam,
however, reigned a step above him. He was a servant to this invisible Imam,
this lost Imam.

He had ruthless questions to ask his father, for Tariq knew much more
than he revealed. Khozem threw these questions aside in the rush of making
one final request to Allah. Against a pall of shame and guilt he prayed Rashida
would pick up the telephone when he called.

They ran between the two hills of Safi and Marwa, but did not run too
fast at the green fluorescent lights. They took it slowly, surrounded by the
bodyguards. The green of the runway tile felt cool under their feet. As they
ascended the small incline, the tile became grooved for better traction. They
ran the track seven times and partook in zamzam water stocked in orange
coolers. Persian rugs, with the emblem of Saudi Arabia stitched in the center,
blanketed the floors. They could see their home mounted upon the rocks. The
'Umrah cleansed their souls of all things negative and instilled a renewed
cleanliness and vitality, as though reborn.

After leaving the mosque, they shaved their heads and all other body
hair. Their loins took the most time.

Even though the small pilgrimage was a success, Khozem could not stop thinking of Rashida.

Late the next morning Khozem awoke with his mother by his side. She rubbed his arm until he woke.

"What time is it?" asked Khozem while rubbing the sleep from his eyes.

"It's around noon."

Khozem's dream placed him in a mild dust storm. The memory of his father's talk settled before he could speak.

"I've overslept haven't I?"

"Yes. You must have been very tired."

"Well, I still have time for afternoon prayers."

"Better than nothing."

"The timing must be special if Allah wakes me at this point."

"How did the talk with your father go?"

"He told me my time is near."

"He also must have said not to discuss these things with me," smiled Samira.

"He always says that. Besides, you probably knew already."

"Yes, I know. Your father told me when he arrived from the Indian tour. You must be a very excited young man to be hearing the news. Your father would have loved to be so young. My first priority is to find a wife for my handsome son. She will be the most beautiful woman in Islam. I can picture your wedding day, all those powerful men, all of Mecca, all those gifts of diamonds and gold, the singing and the dancing. It had to be the most memorable part of my life."

"Mother, how did you and father come to be married?"

"Haven't I told you this before?"

"Tell me again, but tell me how you met each other first. You said your father was an important man in Teheran, a radical, a devout Muslim who predicted the Twin Revolutions."

"Your grandfather was a very great and powerful man who saw such corruption in Iran at the time. He helped make Iran what it is today. He was exiled. He advised Khomeni and supported Rafsanjani. What a time it was. The whole of Iran changed in such a short time, and your grandfather led that change, because he knew Allah had a hand in ousting that culprit who cared nothing about Allah. Strange, isn't it? Allah always has his way no matter what type of government.

"Your grandfather gave me a photograph of your father, and he told me he would be the one whom all Shia Muslims would bow down to, listen to, pray for. He gave the photograph to me, and I accepted."

"Are you happy?"

"I'm happy with your father and with my position. I have a lot of work to do, but my work is confined to Mecca. Your father goes all over. You will be doing the same."

"You married someone just on the basis of a photograph?"

"His position too. Your grandfather would never let me marry but the greatest of men. I also thought your father was quite handsome, at least from the photograph."

"So you did have a choice."

"Not really," she chuckled. "Actually my father ordered that I accept, and I did as he wished. But I wanted to marry your father. I was quite lucky."

"Times have changed, mother. We marry now for different reasons."

"Not you. Your father and I united two very powerful political families. It made your father's position much stronger. The same will happen with you. Within the next few weeks we will be getting hundreds of photographs flowing in from the Middle East. Women from Egypt, Jordan, Syria, Iran, and Iraq. These women would die to marry you."

"What if I don't want to get married?" asked Khozem.

"There is always that fear. I felt it. Your father certainly felt it. But over time you will learn to love your wife. Your wife will be your partner and will always be faithful to you, unlike the women of the Western world who keep on getting divorce after divorce. You are only human, so of course you are afraid. Who wouldn't be? Understand that your particular marriage serves a greater purpose. Because of your future position, which is now two years away, Insh'Allah, you are not marrying only for yourself but for others."

"How can I be happy if I'm marrying for others?" asked Khozem. "Shouldn't I marry for myself first?"

"You will have plenty of choices."

"Yet you will be the one narrowing those choices. I will have never known them or met them or seen them in the flesh."

"You've never met any women before anyway."

"That's not true."

"Really? When did you meet a woman before, besides your cousins?"

"At the university."

"That can't be. Don't women have their own campus?"

"Yes, but they visit the mosque on the main campus."

"Don't they wear proper clothing?"

"Yes."

"So you have talked with one of these women?"

"Maybe."

"That's impossible. Women don't talk with the men. Whom did you meet?"

"Her name is Rashida. We expelled her for apostasy before I left."

"You judged a woman? Oh Allah..."

"The first woman in Al–Karim's history. Don't tell father about this. I've tried to keep it quiet."

"Whatever you say I will never reveal. We've always had that understanding."

"I have feelings for this woman. We talked after the hearing..."

"Did she expose herself to you? Did you see her face or her body?"

"That's not the point."

"That is the point. Never be fooled by a woman's appearance. No wonder you like this woman. Her looks have taken hold. Any man would have reacted the same way. You must put her out of your mind."

"I've tried, but I can't. She's a permanent distraction. Ever since I talked with her, I can't forget her. For these few days I couldn't think of anyone but her. Reading the Qu'ran, praying, performing Umrah, walking, sleeping, eating, nothing works. Don't suggest I try to blot her from my thoughts, because I can't. And now you talk of my marriage. It's the furthest thing. I'm not sure what to do, and I know what your about to say, but don't say it. I already know I can't pursue her. Yet I can't get rid of her. She has made an impression. That's where I am."

"Let me tell you a story. It's a short one, and I don't mean to lecture, but when I was a young girl in Teheran, I couldn't have been more than sixteen or seventeen years old, I knew my wedding was near. I was to marry a mystery man, and my father never dropped a hint. He never told me of his plans. I had imagined the shape of this man, his looks, and so on. We women covered ourselves and congregated behind the men at one of the holiest mosques in Teheran. Then I saw a man who stood in the front.

"He must have been older than I. When I saw his dark, handsome face and his blouse I imagined he was the one I would marry. Every evening we gathered at that mosque. A curtain divided us. He could not see me, but I could see him.

"As the days moved on, I imagined myself married to this man, dressing in my best clothing for social gatherings or cooking his dinner after work. My thoughts became so intricate that I imagined having my family with him. I was so young, can you imagine? And for restless nights I would think of him, that he would one evening lift that divider and take me far away from Teheran. We would travel the world. I would serve him, and he would be my sovereign. After long nights of lying awake, after secretly praying to Allah for this man to come calling under my window, my father gave me a picture of your father. I'd never seen him before. He was a man I had never known.

"I knew it would happen that way, but even though I undertook the duty of a Muslim bride, I kept kidding myself. I hoped in my young, immature heart this man would somehow notice and, even one day, marry me.

"So when I say very cheerfully time and again that I immediately accepted your father, I accepted him with pain also. I endured, and after a while I got over it. I married your father. I love your father, but it was a different love. I learned of him, and he of me. We shared in the learning of each other, and therein lay love's novelty. Each day is a new discovery.

"Marriage was like embarking on some journey made more precious and solid by our searching, not necessarily for the mysteries of Allah, but the mysteries within ourselves. Of course your father soon conducted the business of the faith, but that yearning to learn more of each other never ended. It kept us young. Certainly it was not always like that. Even through the most strained difficulties, we endured. It was better for me to end my dreaming of that man at the mosque. I was lucky enough to lose the man of my dreams and gain the man of my reality.

"I could never dream of being without your father. You will feel the same way. At least this woman made you feel what it's like for Muslim women. Rarely has such insight been bestowed upon a man your age. Some say falling for a woman whose face and body you have seen is a curse. I assure you it isn't. You learn from such things. This will go away. Your wedding is not far. Time will make you forget about her. Don't underestimate your own strength. You will overcome it, because you are my son."

Samira kissed Khozem on the forehead and retreated to her bedroom. Khozem readied himself for afternoon prayers. He did not understand what his mother meant but appreciated it. Conversations with her were not usually this emotionally charged or awkward. Leading the faith in two years, however, commanded his attention. He gave thanks to Allah for his mother's confidence in this matter.

Chapter Ten
THE ORGANIZATION COMPLEX
18th of Jumaada al-awal 1417
(October 1, 1996)

After morning prayers, Tariq made plans to visit the Organization complex. He wanted to browse through membership files for potential adoptive parents for the new Imam. Before he left, he checked Khozem's room and found him sleeping. He did not wake his son as sleep would give him a rest from thinking too hard. The mind needed recuperation. Better for Khozem to sleep long hours in Mecca than in Cairo where alertness and endurance would determine his success. Tariq closed the door and went downstairs. His wife had been waiting for him.

"In the name of Allah, and upon the blessings of the Lord," said Tariq before breakfast. Tariq ate quickly.

"Praise and thanksgiving to Allah who gave us to eat and to drink and who made us Muslims," he said.

Both put a pinch of salt on their tongues. The servant removed the remnants of breakfast collected beneath the thal.

Tariq met the pistachio-chewing bodyguards in the driveway. Minutes later he arrived at the Organization's complex. A medley of short-story buildings were linked by glass walkways. Narrow footpaths stretched across beige quadrangles. Vast, empty parking lots surrounded the buildings.

Three military men stood at the front door as Tariq entered a small antechamber. The building was named after his father. The soldiers scrutinized Tariq's features, including the mole on his cheek. After a brief interrogation and salutations, they allowed Tariq to enter.

A long, bright hallway with white tiles ran ahead of him. The walls were interrupted by heavy oak doors. These doors were numbered but unnamed. As he progressed, the hallway grew narrow. The lights faded. The hallway split into three passageways.

He journeyed through the middle path. The sensors caught foreign movement and electrified the tube lights caked with dust and dead insects.

The walls grew thicker, and similar doors appeared. Lost and confused, he found one of the doors unlocked. He ventured in and discovered a room without windows, a hard metal desk with papers scattered all about, and an antiquated air conditioner fixed into the wall. The compressor rattled and shook. By the desk he found a flashlight. He sorted through a pile of folders on the desk. They contained records of former employees of the Organization. Black and white passport photographs of rough men were affixed to the top corners of each report. Their names were typed onto a thin application paper. He could not find the typewriter.

The lights in the hallway turned themselves off. He read the files by flashlight. The men were unshaven. One of them wore a black leather jacket. A stiff collar choked his neck. 'Saheed Khan' read the name followed by an address in Jordan. The report included a brief family history. This man was born and bred in the territories between the Jewish colony and Syria. He then immigrated to Jordan. The history did not mention any family moving with him.

He delved deeper into the files and found they were all clones. Different names, different photographs, but the same addresses, the same family histories.

The air grew thin. He adjusted the rattling grate in the wall. He tried the file cabinet. The first drawer kissed open. A black typewriter rested on a block of paper. A small box sat next to the typewriter filled with dozens of passport photographs. Towards the back of the drawer, a shotgun, heavy and cold. In surprise, he dropped the flashlight which broke upon hitting the floor. The bottom drawer had been locked as he tried to pull it free.

He found his way to the door and entered the pitch-black hallway. The yellowing florescent lights flickered. He refused to venture back through the main corridor, into the arms of the guards. His footsteps echoed.

He trudged into the belly of the complex. The lights guided him a few steps at a time. The spaces he had passed and the spaces ahead faded into blackness. Surrounded by these black poles, he stood frustrated in the dim light. He had come too far to turn around. The hallway narrowed just wide enough for Tariq to fit. As the lights from behind went off, he expected the lights ahead to turn on . But he was caught in darkness, feeling the walls as he went. He wiped the sweat from his face. He called aloud. The echoes bounced.

After crawling for a good hour, he heard voices. The sounds became stronger. He hoped these voices came not from his own mind. He heard telephones ringing, the manhandling of papers, the snapping of typewriters. He had two options for the persons responsible for this: exile or death. Exhilaration and anger pushed him. The voices became definite: men and women colliding into work. He sat on a cold, damp floor. His legs touched the other wall.

He yelled out. The voices paused. He yelled louder. The voices resumed. Out of the darkness ascended a slit of light. Tariq caught the silhouette of a man in the elevator car.

"What is the meaning of this?" asked the silhouette. "We are not escorts here. If you can't find your way, you shouldn't be down here at all."

Tariq moved into the light. The young man moved closer. He then collapsed to his knees and held Tariq's legs.

"Oh, my holiness, the pure, and the just, the righteous and the sublime, I beg your forgiveness. I couldn't see you in the dark. I beg for mercy. I beg..."

"Get up!" yelled Tariq. "You are young and foolish to be speaking in such a tone, and even if you were not speaking to me in such rudeness, you would still be young and foolish. And Allah has made the young foolish, so foolish that they engage in nothing but foolishness all their lives. You are nothing but a fool, and instead of hanging fools in public squares in front of other fools, the fools remain alive, because Allah, being all-knowing and merciful, forgives absolute fools for their foolishness. Even fools know when to follow instructions.

"I will say this only once. Summon Mr. Abbas, the supervisor of the complex, and Mr. Nadjir, Director of Membership. Have them meet me at this office. You will do this instantly, and if they think you are practicing your foolishness, you best tell them they are relieved of their duties, effective immediately!"

The young man broke at his feet, apologized, wept. He then took Tariq to the din of the office below.

The room was larger than Tariq expected. Plush sofas lined the walls. Cubicles stood in the middle of the room. Large, fake date trees were thrown into corners. Once guiding him to a supervisor's vacant office, the young man lowered the blinds. Although Tariq soon realized he had come before working hours, he was enraged by their negligence.

He was filthy and wanted to perform an ablution. Tariq poked between the blinds of the office. It met Western standards quite well. His picture hung on the wall. He thought of replacing the old photographs in the mosques, government facilities, and other offices with color photographs. He quickly abandoned this idea as the black and white pictures lent austerity and venerability.

Tariq reclined on a comfortable love seat and drifted in and out of sleep. He was startled when he heard a knock at the door. Mr. Abbas and Mr. Nadjir entered. Tariq gave them his hand for salaams. He remembered he was not supposed to be pleasant with them.

"Gentlemen, would you be proud of your bavasaab looking like this?"

"We are always proud of our bavasaab no matter how he looks," replied Nadjir: a tall, thin, middle-aged man with square glasses. His coal suit and silk tie impressed Tariq but also irritated him. Nadjir tried to settle Tariq with a salesperson's smile.

"In other words, Mr. Nadjir, you would have the bavasaab looking like this?" asked Tariq.

"No, your holiness. We accept our bavasaab no matter how he looks, no matter how he acts. If his clothes happen to be soiled, it is of no consequence."

"So if the bavasaab were clean, that is of no consequence?"

"It is, but if the bavasaab happens to be wearing dirty clothes, there is no consequence, for we know that our bavasaab is the most pristine no matter how dirty he is."

"Are you mocking me, Mr. Nadjir?" roared Tariq.

Nadjir hung his head in silence.

"Mr. Abbas, when I walk into my complex searching for important information, I should be able to find it without a problem. Granted this is my fourth time here in ten years, but don't you think you should have seen this coming? It's very easy to get lost in this devil's pit. Wandering through the bowels of this complex for what seemed like hours, without lights, without air? Is this the condition of my complex? And it is *my* complex, is it not? I wonder what other pitfalls we have in here. For my toil, I blame you. I want this place lighted. I want signs posted everywhere, names on the doors, maps of the place. Do I make myself clear?"

"With all due respect, your holiness, the departments were intentionally set up this way for security purposes, in case a stranger made it passed the guards."

Tariq paced. He wanted to fire both of them.

"I came here to undertake work of the utmost importance," said Tariq. "I am in my own complex, and I have wasted enough time. I want a map of the complex. Mr. Abbas, you are to return to your normal duties. You, Mr. Nadjir, will escort me to the Organization's membership files. They are vast, I am sure. The faster I get out of here, the better."

As they walked through the underground office, workers peered from their cubicles to witness the bavasaab. Tariq paid them little mind. They took the elevator to the blackness above. Mr. Nadjir gave him a fresh kurta which he donned in a washroom. The three walked to a small office where Abbas presented him a diagram of the complex. Tariq was looking at it upside down, but the two chose not to make the correction.

"Your holiness has asked me to direct you to the Organization membership files," said Nadjir after Abbas left. "You should know that we do not hold all of them here. We only have those living in Europe, North and South America, and the Far East. Files for the members of the Middle East and most of Asia are kept at the Jeddah complex. If you like, I can escort you to the Jeddah complex?"

"No. I'm interested in the files kept here," as Tariq tried to make sense of the map.

"The files on the Western nations and the Far East are vast," said Nadjir. "If I may be so bold as to ask what particular nations you wish to reference?"

"The United States and the United Kingdom."

"Any particular area in those countries?"

"Just show me those files."

Tariq followed Nadjir up four flights of stairs. They reached a hallway with a view of the immense parking area. He caught his breath. He followed the quick-paced Nadjir in irritation. He expected the visit to take an hour at the most, but the affair would take the entire day.

He kept Nadjir with him. He was awestruck by the mammoth size of the room. A twisted maze of file cabinets.

"After you use the files," continued Nadjir, "just place them in the basket on your way out. One of the file keepers will return them. There is a telephone should you require..."

"You're not going anywhere," said Tariq.

"Excuse me, your holiness?"

"You shall help me here."

"It shall be my honor. How may I help?"

"For starters, let's go back to the U.S. membership files. I'm looking for married couples who have not had children yet. Young couples who are in good standing with us. The husband must be earning a good income to support his wife. The husband must be educated. I need the best of the U.S., the best of the U.K."

"My holiness, that may take days, perhaps weeks. One would have to go through every one of these files."

"Why don't I give you the specifications. Then organize your staff. I need the files by the end of the week. There is a problem though. What I'm doing is confidential. If anyone finds out about the search, you will answer to me. Understood? You will be held accountable for any leaks."

"My staff will know only that I want the files, not you, and even then I will tell them to keep their mouths shut about it. Even I don't know why you need them."

"That's all you need to know. Not one slip."

"Naturally I am curious as to why you need these files so urgently," said Nadjir. "You can be assured my staff will not be. For them it is tedious work. Believe me, you don't have to worry. Your files shall be ready in a week."

"Sooner than that."

"Very well. Five days."

"Sooner."

"Three days?"

"Done."

"We will use workers from other departments," said Nadjir. "I will check with personnel immediately to see what workers can be spared. You may give me what files you want pulled," as he picked an appointment book from his breast pocket.

"I need a total of four files- two from the U.K. and two from the U.S.," instructed Tariq. "I need young, married couples without children who are devout and wealthy. They should come from good Shia families, strong and pure. No half-breeds of any kind. They must have Shia blood through and through. I want the couple to be Westernized, and can you get how long they've been in Britain or the U.S., that sort of thing?"

"Hmm. You know, if you tell me why you want these files, I can get them much faster. I mean, there may be hundreds of married couples in here. Someone will need to narrow the bulk to get the best four. I can be that man."

"I will never tell you why I want them. But you're right. Someone will need to narrow down the numbers, and you will be that person."

"I thank you, your holiness," bowed Nadjir. "I thank Allah for this opportunity."

"I give you the power to judge over these files. Present the best four, then I'll be the final judge. I will return soon, and this time I will wait out front by the sentries. If you sense a delay in my order, you best start searching for another career."

Tariq returned home in the late afternoon. He found a note from his wife to meet her in the grand mosque. The note mentioned that Khozem flew back to Cairo. Tariq studied the note as he could not believe his son would leave so suddenly. Tariq had heard before that saying goodbye, whether short or long, casual or formal, a handshake or a salaam, was not really a goodbye. His son's brief note, however, gave neither explanation nor alternative.

Tariq's chest sank. He likened the note to a disturbing telegram. Nevertheless, he gave thanks to Allah for his son's health and determination towards his training. Going back to Cairo had been the right thing for his son to do.

But Tariq yearned for more time with his son, just the two of them: camping, running errands, even praying. He was no longer jealous.

In the few days that followed, Tariq heard from neither Khozem nor Vasilla. He returned to the complex well rested for reviewing the files. Dark bags hung under Nadjir's eyes. His breath smelled of tobacco and tea. His hair had been hastily combed. He wore the same suit and tie. Tariq hoped he would never again visit the complex. The territory gave him bad omens.

In his den Tariq reviewed the files. The two couples in the United States resided in New York City, Manhattan and Queens. The other two from Great Britain resided in London, Bradford and South Kensington.

He hoped the Imam wouldn't identify with Western philosophies, as they unsettled Tariq's stomach. Islam would be the partner while dancing. Tariq sensed the danger of a Westernized Imam who might make a folly of the religion. But that would be Khozem's domain. His son still weighed on his mind.

Tariq opened the first folder to the wedding photograph of a slender man and a shorter, decorated woman. The groom seemed stern and disciplined, the bride motherly and forgiving. They were from Manhattan, a place of little spiritual health. The groom's family owned a lucrative import/export business in Karachi and New York. The bride's family flirted with oil drilling in the United Arab Emirates.

Their families stood well with the Organization. They contributed regularly to the Organization's fund. Their brief histories were attached to their contribution records. This was an ugly couple, but the most devout. He saw their Western education as a drawback to their faith. Jews must have filled their schools.

He had a preference for the United States over the United Kingdom, although he was intrigued by a more prosperous South Kensington couple. But they lacked contributions. Tariq chose the couple from Manhattan. He locked the files in his den.

In bed he did not discuss this with Samira, but complained about the trend of future generations becoming less devout. She played with his thinning gray hair. In her arms he found sanctuary from a wandering mind. He knew nothing could be solved right away. While being prodded by the ticks of uncertainty, he felt some knot undone. The more he projected, the harder he buried his face into the pillows. As Samira slept, he realized faith could not give him comfort at every moment. He had no choice but to endure and suffer the agony of waiting.

Chapter Eleven
THE KISS
19th of Jumaada al-awal 1417
(October 2, 1996)

Khozem knew his decisions had been made for him, but he mused how the stars could be swept away one day. He strolled beneath a busy, sparkling sky on the main campus and noticed these same stars set into their background like gems fixed to a crown. The world would spin with or without the wreckage of human kind.

While speeding with his bodyguards towards Al-Karim that afternoon, he was torn between his future position and grandiose thoughts of Rashida. The former represented rigidity, while the latter held sacred the right to enjoy the charms of a woman. Khozem's grandiosity was not perversion. All he had known about women came from the hard-nosed Qu'ran. He had little interest in the laws of marriage and divorce. He pondered instead a man and woman's erotic plunge:

O Mankind! fear
Your Guardian Lord, Who created you
From a single person,
Created, out of it,
His mate, and from them twain
Scattered (like seeds)
Countless men and women.

He arrived late as the university slept. He raided the fridge and drank Rooh-Afza. Schooling seemed far from his mind. The next few months would hold little glory. He would be forced into constant study and training. He expected Dr. Farrukh in the morning, and so he pondered the stars, and how they never changed. Later, he climbed into bed. As the minutes turned into hours, he accepted his inability to sleep. He lay curled in a ball as Rashida penetrated his thoughts. Was it her face in that moment of madness? Was it her hair hanging to her shoulders? Or the legs running the length of the Nile? So achingly he wanted to touch her. He clutched the pillow as though it were her body.

He awoke as the sun captured his bed. He showered and conducted prayers in the privacy of his room, under a spell of grogginess.

He waited for Dr. Farrukh to arrive. In his mind's eye he pictured Rashida from head to foot in the same outrageous clothing she revealed at the hearing. He asked Allah to stop tormenting him with such thoughts.

He saw his fellow students on their way to the big mosque. The strengthening sun moved above the horizon. He felt for Rashida's phone number in his pocket. Phoning her would relieve his duress.

He slipped into worn sandals and went to the common room downstairs. A pay phone hung on the wall. University stationary had been tacked to the entrance door. It read: 'Rashida Husseini Pendi, first year student of the women's college has been expelled for direct disobedience, conduct unbecoming of a Muslim, the improper questioning of the president, and apostasy. Let it be known: the Dean of Students' office will expel any student who violates any law of the Qu'ran and any rule in the university handbook endorsed by the Islamic Council and Syedna Tariq Bengaliwala. Let it be known the university considers this case closed, and under no circumstances are students to bring up this judgment with anyone. My peace be upon you.'

He forced a coin into the slot and dialed Rashida. A young woman answered. She said Rashida waited tables at the El Kabir cafe not far from the university grounds. Khozem was familiar with the cafe as some students occasionally went there.

He walked to this small coffee shop. He did not see Rashida at first. The temperature inside the café was warmer than outside. The small kitchen belched steam and sizzle from breakfast foods on the grill. Two old men in the corner hunched over a chess board while sipping tea. They must have been regulars, for they sat like statues before making their moves.

The cook must have been expecting a sizable crowd for breakfast.

He piled more food on the grill, which added more heat to the small area. A back room was equipped with foodstuffs. Khozem ordered a pot of tea and took his seat a few tables from the old men. He could not abolish the fear, but he wouldn't budge until Rashida showed. And so he sat drinking ten cups of tea. The café filled. The cook sweated and did all of the waitering. Khozem marveled at his speed. In a few hours Khozem drank twenty-two cups of tea, had used the lavatory seven times, and had watched the old men play four games. The cook did not mind Khozem's loitering as long as he purchased more tea. Khozem stopped ordering the tea as afternoon prayers came.

He had little hope he would see Rashida. He believed Allah had a hand in his disappointment. Half the day wasted, and with a heavy pound on the table he resolved to leave the cafe and abort Rashida from his mind. The only cures were time and distraction.

Despite his will to leave the El Kabir he found the smallest reason to stay. Something unidentifiable kept him sitting and drinking.

Rashida charged through the doorway, her hair tangled by the breeze and her face full of excuses. Khozem watched from the table as she argued with the cook. Khozem could not discern what was said. After the cook found defeat, Rashida disappeared to the back room, and Khozem reviewed his strategy.

He admitted this was a sickness but also a pleasure which comes from drowning in thoughts of a woman, untouchable yet visible, forcing him to be dominated by his emptiness, to dream of her, and to beg. She offered an exit from destiny's stronghold. If only she would accept his proposal to spend some time, to talk about anything she liked, to be close.

Khozem prepared a greeting. He rehearsed for so long that he crumbled when she noticed him.

"What are you doing here?" she asked loudly.

"Uh, hello Rashida. Remember me?" asked Khozem quietly.

"This isn't the best-time. I'm very busy here."

"Shall I come at another time?"

"I'm really very busy. I have no time."

"I know that. Maybe I can meet you after work."

"I'm busy after work."

"How about tomorrow?"

"I'm busy tomorrow.

"When are you free?"

"I'm never free, and besides we have nothing to talk about."

"Yes we do."

"And what's that?"

"The women's college. You said I could call you about it."

"I'm not in the mood."

"I walked all the way from the university. I've been sitting here for hours drinking tea, and now I'm missing afternoon prayers."

"Then go back and pray. No one is forcing you to stay here. The women's campus is made of women, not men. Women will do it by themselves. They have no need for men."

"In such a short time you've decided this? I thought you wanted my help? You're the only woman who wants to reform that college. You are alone on this."

"And I suppose I need you?"

"I'm the only one who can make it happen."

"Then I hope it doesn't happen. I'm busy here, and there are customers. Run along to that little university of yours. You're wasting your time."

"I will waste my time sitting here then."

Rashida fetched a tin tray and picked up an order of lamb. She wore beige overalls, loose in places. The cook served more tea. Rashida refused to serve him. Each time she passed she looked the other direction. Khozem stood firm.

He recalled how some of the students talked about women. In order to get a woman, one has to bother her. He heard women were fascinated by looks, that the first attraction was callously sexual in nature. Khozem never thought himself attractive. He knew money did not mean much to Rashida. What was Rashida looking for? Perhaps if he were taller with muscles she might be attracted to him. Or perhaps the way to her heart was through her father. Marriage was usually at the beginning, not in the middle or at the end of some long and drawn-out relationship. Marriage was the equivalent of a blind date in which the participants have no choice but to see each other exclusively for the rest of their lives. And he would worship her. He did, however, have the capacity to step back and examine his emotions. Khozem loved Allah but feared Rashida. At worst Rashida was sent by Satan to derail Khozem's ascension to the bavasaab's position.

Through thousands of prayers and fastings and beatings on the chest he never had such feelings for anyone before. As he missed his prayers, he watched her float in and out of the storage room, pouring the tea for all the customers. He chose to rationalize the circumstance, as rationality would justify the most ridiculous of absurdities. She must have passed by his table thirty times. At the next round Khozem grabbed her arm.

"Are you crazy? Let go of me!" she cried.

"Not unless you talk with me."

"Let go of me, or I'll call the police!"

"Go ahead and call them. They won't touch me."

"I bet they won't. Look around this dump. No one notices you. You are nothing without identification. Only then they'll know who you are. But look around. None of these people know who the hell you are."

"I expect you to sit down and talk. What's the sudden change? Before you left the campus, you wanted me to call as soon as I was ready to implement women's reform."

"I don't care about that place anymore. Now let go of my arm. Now!"

"What's going on here?" called the sweating cook. "Let her go."

"This is none of your concern. This is between me and her. Leave us be."

"Hey, this is my restaurant," shouted the cook. "I'll beat you with my skillet. Release her!"

"Do that, and I'll have your throat slit so wide you'll have to force your greasy food down your neck to survive!"

"Get behind the grill," advised Rashida to the cook. "You don't know who this man is. Let me handle it."

"This is my place," answered the cook. "And I want him out this instant."

"Please," said Rashida to the cook, "let us talk for a few minutes. He's obviously here to bother me, not you. Will you promise to leave after we talk?" asked Rashida of Khozem.

"Yes," replied Khozem.

"You get out of line once, and I'll come after you with my sharpest knife. Got me?" yelled the cook.

Khozem nodded, and Rashida took a seat. The cook returned to his grill.

"What do you want from me?" asked Rashida.

"I want your story, the story of your rebellion."

"You've heard it already. Why do you want to hear it again?"

"Because it interests me. And please, have some tea."

Khozem poured her a tepid cup, and she sipped it, telling him the torment of her dormitory and the defiant march to the administration building.

"It all went something like that," she concluded as her sips turned into gulps. "You were smart to get my boss's attention. He really hates people from the university. You would have been sitting here all night without a word from me."

"I never intended to get the cook all worked up," replied Khozem. "How about another cup?"

"Don't you have any other questions for me?"

"Yes, of course. How about another cup?"

Khozem snapped his fingers, and with a grimace, the cook brought another pot of tea to the table.

"Who was it that answered the phone?" asked Khozem.

"What does that have to do with anything? Shouldn't you be sticking to the story of my rebellion?"

"Of course. We will get to those matters as we drink, but for now I would like you to speak about your family life. Who was that girl on the line? Who do you live with? How did you stumble onto Al-Karim? Are you, uh, ready for marriage?"

"Don't be foolish. My parents don't have plans for a wedding yet. Maybe in a year or two. As for my reasons for coming to Al-Karim, my father is a member of the Islamic council, and I, like you, got a free ticket to Al-Karim, although I was admitted with many good recommendations. I thought I told you this already? Why are you asking such irrelevant questions?"

"You have something against the Islamic council or the organization, shall we say?"

"No," replied Rashida, "because they are far too detached. Their main goal is to see students transformed into good Muslims, to make the student devout and learned in the ways of the faith. They do not see the Deans treating us like dogs. They don't dawdle on the specifics of university life. They just care to see their objectives met. The Organization has been aloof from Islamic education for nearly two centuries. They listen to the clerics more than they listen to themselves. If only the council knew."

"Then tell your father."

"He doesn't listen to me."

"And your family?"

"My parents were born in Syria, and I was born here in Cairo. My mother resides in Cairo, but she knows nothing of my expulsion. I live with a roommate. My father has five wives, and therefore five separate families to feed, so he's usually out of Cairo, except for occasional meetings. The Organization meets regularly."

"Ah, a man of prominence. What is his name? Maybe I know him."

"Pendi. Iqbal Pendi."

"I don't recall. Why don't you tell him about it?"

"See, the Organization needs to meet their objectives. It's a matter of statistics to them. They leave such matters of student education to these confounded clerics. My father is buried in international issues. My problems are not worth a grain of dust. He even tells me this, but no matter how big a stink I make about the women's college, my father would side with the clerics. They have been meeting Council standards for centuries, and they think they have done an adequate job. The fault is not with him or the council. It is not the Organization I must challenge but these clerics and especially you who lead them.

"Before you it was your father, and before him your grandfather. Your family has given these clerics the leeway to degrade women and bury them in the worst possible place at the university. All the women may one day snap out of their complacency. But for now, these women are perfectly content playing whores. I'm not afraid to say it. I would even think some of the senior women are particularly intimate with the higher ranked administrators, just to ensure an easier ride through their final year."

"How scandalous! How do you know such things?"

"One night I noticed a student running off with an administrator. My bed is by the window, and since all the first year students live with the senior students in one cramped bunk room, it's easy to tell who's awake and who's not. Who stole out the hallway doors in the middle of the night, and who did not. I saw it all, even the administrator's face."

"Their names?"

"I better not. The senior woman was one of the nicer ones to me. I don't want to incriminate her. But some women at Al-Karim are actually whores."

"Have your parents ever talked to you about marriage?"

"What is your great concern with my private affairs? Don't you have anything else to ask, like how we can reform the women's college? That is the reason for your visit, isn't it?"

"So you don't have a boyfriend at all? Cairo is a pretty liberal place for a woman. All kinds of strange men must be falling at your feet."

"My question is why do you give a damn? I've had enough of this. You don't care about reform. You are just an ordinary liar and a pervert. Either I go or you go. To think I trusted you for a minute..."

Khozem sensed this was the end of it. Rashida ran to the back room. She returned with her small handbag and headed for the street. Over the shouting of the cook Khozem begged:

"Listen, we'll talk about anything you like. Just name the subject, and I will remember what you said."

Khozem chased her.

"I have a large notebook," he said. "Come and see for yourself how many notes I've taken on the abuses of women!"

Khozem pursued her. He dodged the men on their bycicles. A small car almost ran him over.

"Consider me a sympathizer! Yes, a sympathetic fool! You're lucky you got out of the university alive! You need men on your side. Otherwise you haven't a valid cause. You need me!"

Rashida marched to Khozem from the other side of the street. She breathed into his face.

"First of all, I will never have need of a man. Second of all, I am out of the university for the crime of apostasy, so the last thing I need is support. And third, you're nothing but a scrap of university trash guided by your hormones. You've been in that ivory tower of yours for so long you don't even know what hormones are. Yes, all the things the students whisper about you is true. You are nothing, and each time you step out to become a real man your father wipes your nose clean. Get back to that nursery of yours. You belong there."

Khozem grinned and his eyebrows loomed. In the street as she walked away, he grabbed her by the arm.

"You enjoyed that, didn't you?" he said.

"So what is it to you?" as her breath shook.

He planted a firm kiss on her lips. She returned the gesture with a solid, stinging smack. His sweat trickled. He gripped her arm and kissed her again.

A car shoved them from the street. Rashida stood with him not knowing where to run or how to speak. They stood suspended in some eternal time where things made sense all too quickly, all too ridiculously. And then it ended. The bikers, the cars, the cook at the door of the El Kabir, the heat and the sweat, the shouting and the stares from car windows, these expressions of annoyance and resentment which made them feel too young.

"So you are a pervert," said Rashida.

"And a liar," replied Khozem.

"What do we do now?"

"One step at a time, I guess."

"And you expect me to go along with this?"

"You don't have a choice. Did you like it?"

"Hitting you or kissing you?"

"You want to try it again? Kissing that is?"

They decided not to kiss anymore, Rashida more than Khozem. Part of her had been hidden or suppressed and suddenly released by the simplicity of a kiss. He had only just begun, and the kiss, he supposed, served as invitation. He did, however, fear she might want to conduct similar experiments with other men. Beyond the university's wall people were allowed to look at women and kiss them. This came to Khozem by word-of-mouth, as the city was shunned by his peers, degraded as a mythical city of sin.

Their long strides consumed the blocks of pavement. They headed towards the university. The urban sprawl turned residential. They left each other on the foot-part without making plans to meet again. One step at a time, thought Khozem. But the closer he came to the university, the more he wanted to turn back. He had little idea of what more a man and woman could do before marriage. Hold hands? Kiss on the cheek? Kiss on the mouth?

The sun hung heavy in the afternoon sky. He recalled her lips, wet and full, open and moist, twisting, squirming, and then her body going limp, closing her eyes and accepting him. He found himself on university grounds suddenly.

The quadrangle was empty. He wanted to confide in some one, but even his closest friend at the university seemed unworthy. His friends, by the way, were more acquaintances than friends. They were kindly to him because he feared him. No one dare get close to Khozem. He had enjoyed such an aloofness but now regretted it as his heart wanted to explode in confession.

He found notes tacked to his door. Dr. Farrukh had posted them. He remembered leaving the bed unmade and a bottle of Rooh Afza on the fridge.

The bed, however, was neatly made, and the sticky bottle back in the fridge. The room looked oddly clean, the rug vacuumed, the windows washed, the garbage emptied. His books were put away, and the bathroom smelled of antiseptic. Khozem blamed Dr. Farrukh. No one in their right mind would enter his room without permission.

In the afternoon, with the faint breeze pushed by the ceiling fan, Khozem fell asleep and awoke with drool against his cheek. Sharp knocks came at the door. He opened it to Dr. Farrukh whose grin Khozem wanted to smack off.

"What's the meaning of this?" yelled Khozem.

"I'm sorry to wake you, but by orders of your father we must begin your lessons."

"Did my father order you to clean my room?"

"I thought it would be of some help, that it may put you in an academic mood."

"It hasn't."

"The sooner we begin, the less uncomfortable it will be. It's hard to get back into the grind after a much needed break. It takes conditioning. It's always hard in the beginning. Where were you this afternoon?"

"None of your business."

"Yes, my holiness, you are quite right. It is none of my business, only to say your father phoned me this afternoon wondering where you were."

"It's still none of your business."

"Yes, none of my business. But now that I have found you, we must begin the lessons. One of our mullahs is waiting for you. He is eager to meet you."

Khozem noticed it was dark outside.

"What time is it?" asked Khozem.

"It's seven-thirty in the evening."

Khozem had missed the day's prayers, and he did not want Farrukh to know.

"Shall we go?" asked Farrukh.

Khozem ran his hands through his hair in an attempt to look presentable. He was already in his clothes, and on the way out he grabbed a pen, a small notebook, and his skull cap. He would have much rather lain in bed for the rest of the night, but the training had to begin. He could not elude it. He would no longer judge the students either. As he and Dr. Farrukh ambled across the quadrangle, Khozem craned his neck to the stars, hanging in their bluish light, begging for understanding and attention.

On the quadrangle Khozem ran into some friends. Word had surfaced that Khozem would be moving faster towards the bavasaab's position. These friends smiled while keeping a respectful distance. Loneliness accosted him as though he were passing time in solitary confinement, and these strangers just visitors. He had difficulty determining whether he was cursed or blessed and admitted he would never know. But better to assume blessedness as he was called to do the Imam's work, and by one degree of separation, Allah's work.

The warm night swelled. His long hours at the El Kabir reconfirmed his intense disliking for academia. With each step towards the barren building, Khozem's freedom melted from his body, as the purpose of his existence already had an answer.

Dr. Farrukh led him to a classroom. The walls, once white, were now yellow. The classroom housed many varieties of Middle Eastern insects. A tall, lean mullah sat at the head of the room. The mullah was middle-aged, as shown by his beard and smooth face, his eyes possessed. Dr. Farrukh left the two alone with the buzz of the lights and the insects reproducing and eating each other.

"Who are you?" asked Khozem.

"Who do you think I am?" replied the mullah.

"I don't know. A teacher of some sort?"

"I'm not a teacher, but I've been sent here from Mecca to speak with you."

"About what?"

"You don't know?"

"No. Tell me."

"I am here to help you, Khozem, and I have been waiting on this campus since morning. You never showed up. Can you tell me why?"

"That's none of your business."

"I'm making it my business. You see, in order to advance along this fragile road you have to get through me first. And many others."

"What do I have to do?"

"You can start by sitting down."

He sat across from the robed mullah.

"I'm not here as your babysitter," said the mullah.

"Then tell me who you are and why you're here."

"My name is Yamani. I am here to measure your psychological stability. I will do so by asking you questions."

"You mean the great psychologist, Abdullah Yamani?"

"Yes, but you will call me Dr. Yamani."

"But you're so young. Maybe ten years older than I. I thought you'd be much older."

"That's because I refuse to be photographed, and my intellectual abilities are much higher than the common man. In old age we find wisdom, but in youth we find genius. Do you find something wrong with my age?"

"Not really. Please, proceed with your questions."

"I will start by asking where you were this morning."

"I was in the city visiting a friend."

"Elaborate."

"We talked, and now I'm back."

"Who was this friend?"

"It doesn't concern you."

"We will sit here until it does. I expect honest answers to my questions. My time is valuable, and yours even more valuable. You will never advance unless you get through me. Who was this friend?"

"An old student."

"A graduate of Al-Karim?"

"Maybe."

"Don't say maybe. Tell the truth."

"It will only get me into trouble."

"No one will hear anything beyond these walls. Tell me the truth, the hard and stubborn truth."

"Fine. I went with a friend to the El Kabir. We talked, and then I slept for most of the afternoon."

"Harder," said Dr. Yamani.

"What do you mean 'harder?'"

"I mean tell me the brutal truth."

"I have no idea what you're talking about."

"You're hiding something. Look at me straight in the eyes and tell me the truth."

"I've already told you the truth."

"Then look into my eyes."

"It's hard."

"Then learn. Look into my eyes. Stop hiding things."

"Fine. I had twenty cups of tea at the El Kabir."

"Good. Why were you at the El Kabir so long?"

"I had a lot to talk about with my friend."

"Like what?"

"My future."

"Look into my eyes while telling me this."

"I can't."

"Because you are hiding something. We should not be afraid of the truth. Allah is truth and so are your experiences."

"But I don't even know you. You'll tell my father."

"No. All of this is confidential. I am here to help. Look into my eyes. Good. Now tell me everything. Stop running. Stop being that spoiled brat people know you as. Let the truth liberate you... Yes, the rock-hard truth of the matter. Look into me and speak."

"I was with a woman," mumbled Khozem.

"Louder. Be direct and unabashed."

"I was with a woman at the El Kabir," said Khozem with authority.

"Good. Who is this woman?"

"I cannot say."

"We can sit here all night."

"Fine."

Khozem's eyes roamed along Yamani's body. He did not look at him directly, only at his boney legs covered by loose, white pants and a heavy gold ring on his left finger.

"What is your concern about this woman?" asked Khozem.

"I'm not concerned about her. The important thing is that you are concerned about her, and in order to proceed, I need to hear that concern."

"I am concerned about this woman."

"Continue."

"I went to see her. I admired the way she looked. She's attractive."

"What's her personality like?"

"She's a rebel of sorts."

"You mean the one who got kicked out of the university the other day?"

"How did you know that?"

"I didn't until just now."

"Bastard."

"Call me what you will. Above all things, above all emotions like anger, frustration, infatuation, whatever, you need to tell the truth."

"I don't trust you."

"Who else do you have? Your father? Your mother? How would they react to your sinful thoughts?"

"You really are a bastard."

"You will realize down the line that I am participating towards your ultimate success, towards filling your father's position. And the more you tell me, the more you shall trust me."

"I like her. She will make a perfect companion. Her father is even on the Council. You can check for yourself. His name is Iqbal Pendi. This woman is not an average student."

"Was this the first time you saw a woman's body?"

"Besides my mother's, yes."

"Do the bodies of your mother and this rebellious woman share any similarity?"

"A little bit."

"Whose body do you think about more?"

"The rebellious woman's body."

"Tell me her name, and look me straight in the eyes."

"I'm afraid."

"The truth within your heart will set you free. I know you want to tell me."

"Why tell you something you already know?"

"Don't be smart. I'm not in the mood to handle your childishness. The name?"

"Why does it matter?"

"It matters if you refuse to admit it."

"I am ashamed of nothing."

"Even when you think of her without chador?"

"What?"

"Even when you imagine her in your bed?"

"Nonsense."

"Kissing you?"

"This has gone too far."

"Only because you are revealing the truth about this woman."

"You, Dr. Yamani, are relieved of your duty starting right now. We are going nowhere with this discussion. No one, and I mean no one, questions me this way. No one ever disrespects me, especially on my campus."

"Is that so?"

"Yes. Now get up and return to your Meccan dungeon. I don't care how famous you are. I know you are beneath me, and that's all I need to know."

"Why the sudden change? Are you threatened by me?"

"I don't answer to you."

"Just one bit of information. The only person who can relieve me of this post is your father. You, my insolent boy, have no authority over where I go, what I do, or what I say. I will not leave unless you admit the truth."

"I have nothing to say."

"Then go back to that room of yours until you are ready to confess it."

"I will never confide in you."

"Then there is no way you'll become the bavasaab."

"Oh, really? A monkey telling his master how things will run?"

"The only 'monkey' around here is you," countered Yamani.

Khozem walked briskly out the door.

Yamani yelled: "I guarantee you will dream of this woman, and your dreams will pile more grief and shame upon you."

Khozem marched back to his dormitory. He avoided the students in the hallway and locked himself in his room. Slipping into bed only led him back to Rashida and the afternoon visit at the El Kabir.

Khozem fell asleep in his clothes, and when he awoke he sensed he was sleeping too much. From his window he saw students in white dress traversing the quadrangle. In the sunlight he wondered whether Rashida would take kindly to him if he telephoned. He said his prayers, fighting back thoughts of her while kneeling and prostrating. Recollections of her tainted the holy ritual.

Chapter Twelve
CAIRO
20th of Jumaada al-awal 1417
(October 3, 1996)

Khozem sneaked into Cairo with a mission to see Rashida. He ignored the many notes written by Farrukh. He arrived at the El Kabir as the temperature blistered.

"Not you again," said the cook. "You are not permitted here. You cause nothing but problems..."

"My good man, I'm not here to see you. I have come to see your waitress."

"No you don't," as he flipped boneless chicken. "You are not allowed here. Get back to the university whoever you are. This is a place of business."

"I just need to see her."

"Out of this place. I have enough problems."

"I will not leave until I see her."

"I'll call the police," as the heavy cook held a spatula in his hand.

"Planning on using that?" asked Khozem

"Not unless I have to," threatened the cook.

The El Kabir was empty after the lunch rush. Khozem spotted the old men in their same clothes playing chess.

"Stop it!" yelled Rashida from behind him, dressed in those brown overalls.

Khozem could not speak.

"Calm down," she said to the cook.

"I want him out of here, now!" yelled the cook.

"I'll speak with him for a short time, and then I'll return to shelving the deliveries."

"I want him out now. There's too much work to be done. You come in late every day. You have a bad attitude, and now you want some young boy taking more time out of work? Forget it. Get back in there and shelve the food."

"Don't talk to me like that. I have plenty of time to shelve the food."

"Either he goes or you go."

"Your business would drop to a slow crawl. No one would come. You'd be out of business in a month."

"I can get any tramp to take your place."

"What did you call her?" asked Khozem.

"She's a tramp, nothing but a tramp."

"Take that back, or I'll climb over that grill and plant your face in it."

"Come and get me," said the cook with his spatula.

Rashida begged them to stop.

"You're fired," yelled the cook finally. "Leave the apron on your way out."

"Well that's just fine," said Rashida as she peeled the brown canvas from her body, uncovering a pair of jeans and a blue shirt. She threw the apron at the cook and grabbed Khozem's hand.

"Let's go," she said.

"And don't come back!" shouted the cook.

They were familiar with being in the street. The cars beeped, and the pedestrians stared. Khozem held on to her hand like a befuddled schoolboy. The sight of Rashida in a pair of jeans and tee-shirt blinded him. He could only gaze. He wanted to touch her skin, not only her hand, but along the arms, her lips, her waist. Khozem, however, seemed confused. Kissing was one thing, but now he touched her hand.

"You just had to come back, didn't you?" said Rashida. "First, I'm kicked out of the university, and now I'm out of a job, and all I have is the hand of this immature, impetuous fool. What more do you want from me? Haven't you interfered enough? This is my life your toying with. Yes, my life."

"What about yesterday?"

"What about it? We kissed, and then I hit you. So what? We move on. It was nothing."

"It was something to me."

"Okay, maybe it wasn't 'nothing,' but it wasn't that important either. We move on."

"I can't move on. I went back to the campus yesterday, and I locked myself in my room, and dove into bed, even put my pillow over my head. I tried to do my training with Dr. Yamani, but that didn't work..."

"You mean the famous psychologist Dr. Yamani?"

"He wanted to know too many things."

"What did he get out of you?"

"That I was with a woman."

"Great. That's just great. Don't tell me you fed him my name."

"I think he knows already."

"Oh Allah," cried Rashida.

"I can't stop thinking about you. Can't you see?"

"I can see just fine. You need to get over this."

"I know."

"Do it then. Although we have crossed paths, our lives were never meant to be together."

"How do you know? Who suddenly gave you this wisdom?"

"It's easy to see. What does the next bavasaab want with someone like me? I have no job, I've been expelled, my thoughts are too radical, the only friend I have is my roommate, and even she does not like me. I'm flattered by all of this. I appreciate how you think of me, but Khozem, we live in two very different worlds..."

"So what? We all live in different worlds. We pass one another pretending that it's too tough to be together, when the opposite is true. We have met because of Allah's doing. Our kiss was something sanctioned by Allah. The urge to touch you comes from the heavens, and I'm not about to let it go. I've had nothing else on my mind. I try hard to forget you. I even went so far as to curse the day I met you, but none of it works. I just keep thinking of you, as though I'm on some vicious carousel, spinning, never stopping."

"What would happen? Think about that. The least I would do is screw up your future. Your parents wouldn't want me. Your marriage has already been set. What would your parents say?"

"To hell with my parents. This is my life, and not theirs."

"That's where you're wrong. Your life belongs to everyone. You will be our leader. You have a responsibility for everyone's well being, definitely not your own. All these thoughts are selfish thoughts, too selfish. I would only cause you, your family, and the entire Middle East a great deal of trouble."

"I never knew you thought this through."

"All I see is my heart breaking and a huge scandal on our hands."

"What if I forsook my position?"

"Now you're really talking crazy."

"Seriously."

"You would do that?"

"I just might."

"Please, Khozem. Don't do this, especially with that famous psychologist on campus."

"I don't want to go back."

"You must."

"I can't and I won't. I want to spend my time with you."

"My looks are deceiving. You would never put up with my opinions."

"Try me."

"I've committed apostasy in the eyes of that committee of yours."

"I pardon you."

"I want nothing to do with the university."

"Either do I."

And Khozem pulled her close. As their mouths touched and fell apart, they noticed the cook, the old men, and the motorists along the street staring with wide eyes and hanging mouths.

"What are you looking at?" yelled Rashida. "Come on," she said to Khozem.

"Where are we going?"

"I'm taking you back to the campus."

"But I don't want to go back."

"You must. Think about this. This is not possible."

"How do you know?"

"Because I know. The sooner we part, the better."

"I'm not going back there."

"Think, Khozem. Think hard. No one will allow us together."

"I am the master of my fate."

"Allah is the master of our fate. This is all some type of freak accident."

"I'm not going back there."

"And where do you plan to stay?"

"At your place."

"This is nuts. This is absolutely nuts."

"It will be great."

"There can be no such thing. You hardly know me."

"I know you enough."

"Please. Is this some sort of twisted fairy tale you're pursuing? All I stand for is an escape from something determined. You're just using me."

"I can't grow without you."

"Save those lines for your bride."

"I've saved those lines for you. And I'm not going back. I'll sleep on the street."

"You can't sleep here. Too many rats. They'll eat you alive."

"Either your place or the street. Decide."

"I'm not deciding for you."

Khozem sat on the sidewalk.

"Get up," cried Rashida.

"Either I'm here or I'm with you."

"You're such a child, stubborn and immature. You don't give a damn about my feelings."

"I do give a damn, because within that mighty heart, you care about me. Oh, yes, don't deny it. All your life you've been fighting the urge to be with a man..."

"All false."

"Don't lie to yourself. A part of you wants me, and that's the part I've found. You don't want me on the street."

"Of course not, you big idiot. You're the next bavasaab."

"I don't care. Either I stay on this sidewalk, or I stay with you."

"That's not funny. This is not some game. What about my roommate?"

"Tell her I'm your long-lost brother."

"I can't believe I'm going to lie for you too."

"If there is a choice between lying and fulfilling your own heart, what would you pick?"

"That's not fair."

"You long for me more than your drive to be honest."

"I can't believe this is happening."

"Believe it. Now help me up."

"Get up yourself," as Rashida walked away.

Khozem followed her quietly and relished in the freedom of Cairo. Over the beige buildings he saw the municipal mosques and their wide domes. The side shops sold the lastest Egyptian fashions, appliances, and luggage. The pedestrians seemed half-naked, accepting the heat of the sun without the chador over the face and body. Khozem knew he was out of place, and Rashida walked quickly into the mess of a rubbernecking population.

"Wait up," asked Khozem.

"Is this what you wanted to see?" asked Rashida.

"I can't believe it. It's like I've been blind. That or something is wrong with my eyes."

"It seems that way, because the university is all you understood. Well, welcome to the real world. Cairo is a spiritual city but also a progressive city. You wouldn't last a week here. Luckily no one knows you."

"I've heard plenty about Cairo, and all of it seems true."

"Like what?"

"The women, for instance. They don't cover themselves."

"Some of them do, but Cairo is not a city stuck in the past. People here move ahead. People here have real needs. We are even friends with our Jewish neighbors."

"How do you know so much?"

"Because I grew up here with my mother."

"And you don't live with her? Wouldn't it be better to stay with her to avoid paying rent?"

"My mother doesn't know I've been expelled."

"The university will surely send her a notice."

"Not if I changed my address. But my problem is not my mother. The problem is you."

"Yes, you've already mentioned this."

"May I please appeal to your practical side? May I ask for once in your life that you use that big muscle called your brain and think about the consequences?"

"I listen to my heart. I have no use for the brain."

"This is obvious. With each step you take you're throwing away your future."

"The future will always be there. It's not going anywhere."

Rashida stopped on the sidewalk and held Khozem by the shoulders as rickety cars flew down the avenue.

"No, Khozem. Absolutely wrong. There comes a time when childhood ends and responsibility begins. By following me to my apartment you move farther away from the university. You are seeing too much. This is a place you were not meant to see. This knowledge is a form of corruption. The bavasaab must be holier than this. Turn around before it's too late. Go back and try to forget me. Over time you will. I will be a memory, and when you're training is complete, you shall be thankful for what I did."

"Did you like it when I kissed you?" asked Khozem.

"Yes, but I know it's wrong. You know it's wrong too."

"How can a kiss ever be wrong?"

"Kissing is not the point, Khozem."

"It is the point."

"Let's not start this over again..."

Khozem moved in for a kiss.

"Can we at least wait until we get to the apartment?"

They continued along the avenue. The past resided with Al-Karim and the future with Rashida in a small apartment in the middle of the confusion and chaos of the city.

Chapter Thirteen
THE CALL
20th of Jumaada al-awal 1417
(October 3, 1996)

"Hello?" answered Tariq.

"Yes, your holiness. So glad I got you at home."

"Who is this?"

"This is Dr. Yamani calling from Al-Karim."

"Ah, Dr. Yamani. How are you?"

"Fine, my blessedness."

"I hope Khozem isn't running circles around your intellect?"

"My holiness, I'm calling regarding Khozem."

"A very smart boy, isn't he?"

"Yes, indeed. He must take it from you."

"He does."

"Unfortunately, we have a problem here on campus."

"What is it?"

Dr. Yamani swallowed and said: "Sir, your son is missing."

"What? Come again."

"Your son is missing."

"Where did he go?"

"That's the problem, your holiness. We don't know where he went."

"Are you telling me Khozem just disappeared?"

"Yes."

"And you have no idea where he went?"

"No idea, sir."

"You mean I left my son under your vigilance, and suddenly he's gone?"

"Yes, sir, that is precise. Except that Dr. Farrukh is also responsible."

"All of you are responsible! You will find Khozem immediately and bring him back. To think I left my son under the supervision of such imbeciles. Find him now!"

"We do have a general idea where he went."

"Then go and get him, or I'll have your heads!"

"We believe he ran off...with a woman, your holiness..."

"Okay you fools. I'm on my way."

"You're holiness, I have a better plan."

"Like what?"

"Khozem had mentioned the woman's father was on the Council, the last name being 'Pendi.'"

"So?"

"At the next Council meeting maybe you can find this whore's father and persuade him to find Khozem."

"I don't need to persuade anyone."

"His daughter's name is 'Rashida.'"

"You don't have her phone number or address?"

"Apparently she now lives in Italy. "

"Oh great Allah, someone will pay for this. Someone will pay dearly"

"But your holiness, we have reason to believe they are still in the Middle East somewhere. At the next Council meeting you can ask her father for assistance."

"I don't remember there being a Pendi on the Council, but I will definitely find the rotten pimp."

"An excellent idea, sir. This Pendi would supply the address. You may reach Khozem and stop it before it starts."

"I'm a busy man, Yamani. I don't have time to chase my son all over creation."

"I understand, sir, but really, this is the only way. We have no idea where they went."

"Don't expect me to blame my son. Instead I blame you and that other dunce of yours."

"Please, my holiness. Show mercy."

"I am merciful, am I not?"

"Yes, my holiness, as Allah is our witness."

"Then accept your punishment for letting my dear Khozem run off."

"Have mercy on us."

"You are both relieved of duty. I want you off the grounds. I shall notify the Director of Education. If I can't find my son, you will be brought to a Meccan public square, the both of you."

"Please, your holiness..."

"Enough. You better hope I find him," and Tariq hung up the phone.

Chapter Fourteen
KHOZEM AND RASHIDA IN CAIRO
27th of Jumaada al-awal 1417
(October 10, 1996)

The blinds blocked the sunlight leaving them cool despite the crippling heat. Rashida wore a robe in the messy living room. Her roommate had left for work. Khozem lay on the living room sofa, snoring, and Rashida fought the temptation to wake him. Talking to Khozem was like talking to a wall. For him, being together was some sort of goal in itself.

She walked along the sofa and picked up his clothes. He at least showered every day, but the clothes were getting dirty and smelly. 'Just like a man,' she thought. She had somehow known about men prior Khozem's intrusion. 'Filthy,' 'lazy,' and 'Neanderthal' held some truth. She looked at him and shook her head.

She went to the kitchenette and made strong coffee. From the counter she smirked. She had resented men in general as they were corrupt and drunk over their own power. Khozem represented this power, and yet he seemed no more than an infant. He helped himself to food. He used the shampoo. He dried himself with her towel. A problem child, and she knew it. But with the fixity of his future position, Khozem had nothing to lose. He got up at noon, prayed towards the East, and listened to the radio, prayed at night, and asked for a long kiss before bed.

Rashida poured herself some coffee. She shook his arm but nothing worked. She poured cold water over his head.

"Wha? Who? Oh, man," groaned Khozem.

"That's what you get."

"I was having such a strange dream."

"Save it. Get up and brush your teeth. Take a shower. This has gone too far."

"Oh, I have been dreaming about you."

"That line doesn't work anymore. Now get up and get dressed."

Rashida ripped off the blanket that covered him. His body lay naked as he fought for the blanket.

"You dare sleep in the nude in my place?"

"Give me back the blanket...," fought Khozem.

"Where do you think you are? Some kind of brothel?"

Khozem ran to the bathroom, and Rashida laughed.

"It's not funny," yelled Khozem.

"You ought to lose some weight. Maybe go on a diet."

"You didn't see much did you?" asked Khozem from the bathroom.

"All of that manhood."

"You're not supposed to know such things."

"Take a shower quick. You've worn out your welcome."

She heard the shower. She hoped Khozem would regain his senses and return to the university.

"Can you hand me my clothes, please. Not that it matters."

Khozem's hair was combed neatly. A red towel hung around his waist. Rashida fed him his soiled kurta.

"We need to talk," said Rashida.

"About what?"

"You've been here almost a week, lying around like a lump, not doing anything."

"Should I be doing something?"

Khozem came out fully dressed.

"First of all, call the university and tell them you're safe. They must be worried."

"I don't want to talk to them."

"If they don't hear from you, they'll call your father."

"Let them call..."

"Let's try this using that tiny brain of yours. See, you won't get into trouble. I will."

"Nonsense. They have no clue where you are."

"So you mean I should be running away, always in hiding, like some sort of fugitive?" asked Rashida.

"As long as you're with me there is nothing to fear."

"My roommate is getting suspicious. She wants you out. The visiting-brother act is crumbling. All you do is lie around. You don't clean up after yourself."

"Consider it done. I will clean up my mess from now on."

"Khozem, you can't stay here. You know that."

"Then we can live together elsewhere."

"I need a job first. I've been out every day. No one wants to hire a person without a degree, especially a woman without a degree. The rent is due in a few days. Getting a job is my first priority, not housing you."

"I understand."

"This whole charade will cost us plenty. Now what I suggest is you do something. How about finding a job?"

"I have a plan in the works."

"What is it?"

"I'll tell you when you return."

"This is exactly the problem. You're not active."

"By the time you get back, I will have thought this plan through."

"At least do one thing for me."

"Anything, my sweet."

"Go and wash your clothes downstairs."

"Anything else?"

"Yeah. Don't call me 'my sweet.' Now move out of the way. I need to shower."

"Believe me," said Khozem. "I've figured things out. I know what I'm doing."

"Sure you do," called Rashida from the shower.

She left an hour later dressed professionally.

"Have a good day," said Khozem before kissing her.

"Without a job we can't stay here," she replied.

"Hurry back soon so I can discuss this. Aren't you curious?" as his hand slid down her arms.

"Not really."

"You should be."

"I'll be back in a few hours. Try getting out of the apartment."

After performing ablution and morning prayers, Khozem borrowed Rashida's bathrobe and laundered his clothes. Cairo had jolted his entire outlook. This Cairo, however, neglected its Islamic foundations as their citizens applied themselved towards hedonistic prosperity. Khozem figured Allah was not the first priority here. Living a prosperous life had long been the first, and within the Egyptian population stood a rebellious force waiting to topple the moderate government, just like the Iranian revolutionaries in 1979. A slight tension covered the solemn faces of the pedestrians.

While the news of the university depicted the routine of the men's campus, the news of Cairo seemed infinite, like the confusion of the streets. In every direction tan buildings wiped out the empty spaces. The tenements along the horizon usurped the sanctity of the sun. Now Khozem had options. He felt encouraged by it. He had control. He could go anywhere. He could change himself. He could be another person. He could put Islam on the back burners and explore. Yet he knew his ultimate fate rested with his father's position.

He wanted Rashida by his side, and no one else. Hence the construction of an unique design: Allah first, Rashida second, and his father third. The plan placed importance on piety more than predeterminism. He worked on the details as his clothes dried. He rehearsed the new proposal for Rashida. He listened to the hourly dramas on the radio. When Rashida returned he was sprawled on the sofa, staring at the ceiling.

"At least you've washed your clothes," she announced.

"How did the search go?"

"The rent is due."

"Come sit by me."

"I've been trying hard, but nobody's hiring."

"In crisis there is opportunity," said Khozem.

"I know all that. If at first you don't succeed, try and try again."

"When one door closes, another one opens."

"Slow and steady wins the race. Oh Khozem, I can't come up with the rent."

He brushed her hair aside and kissed her cheek.

"Is that supposed to make everything go away?"

"Nothing ever goes away. We might as well enjoy our time here."

"Khozem, we need shelter and food. Wouldn't it be easier for you to go back?"

"I'm not going back. Can't you understand how I feel? Do you feel the same way I do?"

"I think so. You give me no choice."

We're in this together. Let there be no more affirmations about how we feel. Such feelings are now implied wherever we go."

"I'm not sure about anything."

"Well, I'm definitely sure. You and me, we belong, no matter what anyone says."

"I wish I could believe that. Maybe I need more time."

"What is time but a measurement from one event to the next? When the event is dedicated to loving one another, time serves that love, but when the event is maimed by loneliness, time slows and becomes as deadly as a sand storm.

Khozem took Rashida's hand-and placed it on his chest.

"Can you feel it? My heart beating?"

"A little bit."

"Love means this beating heart won't stand a day without you. With every day our love grows stronger..."

"Is the radio making you talk this way?"

"I've been thinking about our future."

"Be practical. We cannot survive without work."

"Love is not rational. It has no practicality. Love makes us fools by default."

"Where did you pick up such talk?"

"Ah, my Rashida, love is a language that takes some time getting used to. I know you feel it."

He kissed her again.

"Khozem, can I be forward?"

"Nothing has stopped you yet."

"When you asked me to feel your heart, did you expect my heart to beat that way too?"

"Our hearts together?"

"While I felt your heart beating, while I held my hand to your chest, another part of my body stirred."

"Which part?" asked Khozem. "Do you feel it now?" as he touched her thigh.

"I also feel it when you kiss me. I can't put it into words."

"Kind of like kissing?"

"More than kissing. My roommate won't be home for a few hours yet."

"You want to get something to eat?"

"I can think of something else. Touch my thigh again...Khozem, do you really love me?"

Rashida led him into her bedroom.

After their second time, they held each other as their perspiration evaporated. They were shipwrecked on some far away island, far away from madness as though joined by their common secret, though every rule went against it.

"Khozem?"

"Yes?"

"How did that feel?"

"Wonderful. And for you?"

"I just want to lie here."

"Only Allah has given us a gift so great."

"You mean the gift of love?"

"We were meant to be together."

"Maybe Allah has blessed us."

"Nothing has felt so good."

"How are we to stay together? We have no money."

"I have a plan."

"It better be good. Otherwise I'll have to go home. My mother thinks I'm at the university."

"Rashida, all this time I've been running away from my responsibility."

"You mean filling your father's place?"

"Exactly. But this last week has allowed me to think of something better. I don't want the fame which comes with my father's position, and as a human being I have the right to choose who I want to become. I can have you, because I've chosen you. I can be whoever I want to be, because by nature man is free to build his life without having it built for him."

"Khozem, you are an only child. A male child. Don't cross your father."

"I will, because this is my life, not his. I choose my mate, not he. And the new path I've chosen is so pure and noble that even Allah shall support it. Everything is falling into place. And finally I understand what needs to be done.

"I want to contemplate Allah for the rest of my days, but not under the auspices of my father. I don't want his position. I want to do it alone as man was meant to do it. I don't want possessions. I don't need clerics or professors. I want to find Allah without the scriptures. I want to be a holy man who strives to understand the divine, and I want you to be my partner, you and I under a special shelter. Love for Allah and love for each other are the only things we ever really need."

"Are you saying what I think you're saying?"

"What's that?"

"You want me as your bride?"

"Eventually, yes. Ultimately, yes."

Rashida rolled on top of him.

"I see my future," whispered Khozem. "I need you by my side."

"I suddenly feel kind of lost," she said.

"I do too, but we'll make it."

"Where shall we go?"

"Let's go to Mecca. I must be near the Kaa'bah. Also there are many jobs in Mecca. It's much easier finding a job in Mecca than here in Cairo."

"How can you be an ascetic without marrying me?"

"That time will come. Consider us engaged for now. We'll marry in Mecca, the holiest place on Earth. The most important thing for the next few months is to find out what Allah wants from us. Being next to the Kaa'bah is essential."

"Are you sure you can handle it without guidance?"

"I have no need for clerics anymore. The university is a big waste of time."

"And how shall we support ourselves?"

"Jobs are plentiful in Mecca, good jobs for Muslim people. We'll make twice as much there. I'll get a job too."

"Are you sure? Won't people recognize you?"

"They only know my father. His portrait hangs all over the place. With the exception of the Islamic Council and the university, no one knows."

"I'm a little worried."

"I know you are, but as long as we're together, we have nothing to fear or worry about."

"It's not you I don't trust. It's others."

"A short flight for two. Mecca is an international city. We'll be free. We'll find a small place, get jobs, pray in the Kaa'bah, and after we feel things out, we'll get married."

"I hate to admit it, but I think I'm falling for you."

"Pack all your clothes tonight. We'll leave first thing in the morning. You won't need your passport. I have the keys to the city. And by the way," smiled Khozem, "bring your chador. A woman's body must not be seen by other men."

"Khozem, I have a past. You know exactly what I did at the university. Do I deserve to live in Mecca?"

"Love and love alone leads us towards Mecca. It's almost like a rebirth. Let's surrender our pasts to Allah. Let us be brainwashed by his love for us and others. Even our Jewish neighbors! What a miracle! I never knew something like this could exist. Once love is found there is no way we can turn back. There is no reason to turn back. To have found love means that we slowly change our youth into holy recipients of Allah's glory."

"The oppression of women still bothers me."

"And running from my father bothers me too, but we must let go. We must grow. If anyone deserves to be in Mecca, Rashida, it is you. We both deserve it, and after staying there for some time we will accept Allah's plan."

"Without those corrupt mullahs in the way?"

"Yes. For the first time we eliminate the middlemen. We pray directly in the Kaa'bah."

"I have to be certain there are jobs there."

"Plenty of jobs. Plenty of opportunities for a young Islamic couple. There is nothing in Cairo any longer. The rent is as high as the unemployment rate."

"But what about my mother?"

"Write her from Mecca. Tell her there is much more opportunity there. Be honest with her. Since love has found us, there is no reason to lie."

"You'll tell your father too?"

"After we are married."

They packed their stuff, and the next morning they purchased tickets to Jeddah. After hours of roaming in Mecca, they found an apartment. After two days, they found jobs. And within two weeks, they made love twenty-two times.

Chapter Fifteen
THE LETTER
11th of Jumaada al-THanny 1417
(October 24, 1996)

"Dear Mother," wrote Rashida.

"I'm sorry for not writing for so long, and I hope you are in the best of health and in the best of spirits. Many things I want to tell you, and I hope your reaction will be calm and collected. All of this has a very happy ending. I would never write anything to alarm or disturb you. I am perfectly safe, and I am doing well.

"I've recently left the university. I was expelled for apostasy and disobedience towards the administrators. So far I've been out for close to three weeks. The expulsion hit me hard, and I never want any part of that university again. I am much better off. I am free to live without the influence of the clerics. It's actually better for me. All the while I saw injustice after injustice towards women carried out day after day. The way we treat women is terrible, and the condition is so bad that such oppression is even institutionalized. The sexism is more subtle. Actually I am lucky. I have found another life with a man who has left the university with me.

"His name is Khozem, and we are to be married here in Mecca. Not right away, but soon. He's a wonderful man, and he cares for me. We are both in love. We met three weeks ago. I could tell almost immediately we belonged together. He's handsome, smart, and hardworking. He has found a job as a carpenter. I have found an even better paying job as a seamstress. The work pays well, and finally Khozem and I are building our lives right here in Mecca.

"Please don't worry for me, because I sense that you are worried. I should have written you earlier, but we could not stay in Cairo, because there are no jobs there. I could not pay the rent. We came to Mecca not only to be closer to Allah, but also for the work. We make just enough to support ourselves. We really do love each other. I want to be the mother of his children, after we are properly married. In all my life I have never been so happy. The love between us makes it that way. I assume I have your blessings. Your ever-loving daughter,
Rashida.
P.S. I've enclosed my address so you can write."

Chapter Sixteen
THE EMERGENCY MEETING
12th of Jumaada al-THanny 1417
(October 24, 1996)

Tariq worked in his second floor study in preparation for the emergency meeting of his twelve advisors. Mr. Pendi would be there. He saw an opportunity to be rid of two problems at once. As the meeting grew closer, Tariq muttered his prayers in the Kaa'bah and circled the House of Allah seven times. The arena had to be secured before Tariq could enter. He grew impatient. He over-planned and over-analyzed each circumstance until most uncertainties were taken into account. There was no more he could do. He sensed himself growing older. The bones felt weaker. They creaked each time he moved. But not a single snapping joint while praying.

The Custodian's residence was not far. The bodyguards avoided the Kaa'bah crowd by traveling in between prayer times. The car stopped at a security checkpoint before entering the Custodian's complex, a brown concrete mansion next to a five-story high rise. The drivers for other advisors puffed on cigarettes and rehashed old stories in the next lot. Mecca served as their resting spot, their vacation while on duty.

At the entrance, Tariq confronted two military men with rifles flung over their shoulders. He passed without being questioned. The elevator doors opened to a large room with a long table. His twelve advisors, draped in white silk, stifled themselves and stood from their chairs. The tinted windows blocked the sun and kept the spacious room dark and cool. Pitchers of zum-zum water were spread on the table. Tariq noticed the advisors' aides seated along the perimeter of the room. They sorted through thick folders and remained poised for notetaking. Tariq smiled to bid them welcome. To his advisors, however, he remained solemn, and they were sucked in by his mood. To Tariq's left sat a stenographer, a stenograph between his legs. To his right an empty chair reserved for his son who had attended a general meeting as a child, thrilling the assembly. To see the chubby future bavasaab became a rare occasion for them. They did not expect the chair to be filled at this meeting. The topic remained confidential.

Tariq stood at the head of the table. He missed not a single advisor. He saluted each of them with peace and permitted them to sit. The stenographer tapped soft keys. The meeting concerned the Hindu-Muslim riots in India, particularly Bombay. One of the advisors began his report.

"As we already know, the violence began when Hindu militants, primarily from the Shiv Sena terrorist group, marched upon the Babri mosque at Ayodha and demolished it using domestic tools and arson. Our members within Bombay, in the spirit of defending Allah's name, encouraged our fellow Muslims to retaliate knowing the Hindu government, under the authority of Prime Minister Rao, would remain indifferent if not content with the demolition. As a result of the first wave of violence, more than one-hundred dead in Bombay alone and more than one-thousand deaths all across India. Our Muslims were killed by the hands of Hindus. Thousands were injured, hundreds of women raped, hundreds of our children molested. After the deaths and casualties of our Muslim brothers were accounted for, our beloved Syedna Tariq Bengaliwala arrived in Bombay for a short visit of strategic mosques. By this time the first wave of violence had ended. He sent word to Prime Minister Rao in Delhi strongly condemning him. Our holiness labeled his regime 'a mockery of secular government.' Rao requested a meeting with the bavasaab, but our holiness refused, as dealing with hypocrites and liars is the act of Iblis.

"The second wave of violence was instigated by the Shiv Sena, the terrorist Hindu group. By this time our Syedna was en route to Mecca. They used the murder of two Hindu dockworkers to launch a wave of organized attacks on Muslims throughout Bombay. Our intelligence reports that no Muslim is safe from the Hindu militants. Brothers are being bludgeoned, their properties burned and looted, their wives raped, their children beaten with pipes, chains, and sticks. Although police have ordered the residents to stay in their homes day and night, we have numerous, detailed reports that the police themselves are encouraging the attacks on Muslim families. Where they saw riots brewing, they turned a blind eye, and when they saw our stores being looted, they participated and abetted those who stole.

"The violence, the looting, and the fear continue in Bombay. It has not stopped, and to your holiness the Advisory Council proposes the following to combat the Hindu threat and provide encouragement for our Muslim brothers.

"First, we suggest a meeting of the Foreign Advisory Committee (FAC) consisting of delegates from Palestine, Afghanistan, Pakistan, Saudi Arabia, Egypt, Iran, Syria, Jordan, Iraq, Indonesia, Algeria, Turkey, Libya, and Tunisia. We suggest the Organization extend invitations to other Islamic republics. Through the FAC your holiness shall place international pressure on Rao's aloof regime for the protection of Muslims. There is no telling when the riots will cease. We suggest you convene the FAC as soon as possible.

"Second, we suggest the assassination of Mr. Nasir Patel, political upstart and chief propagandist for the Hindu-nationalist newspaper *The Blue Wrath*. Our sources confirm that Mr. Patel is the force behind the Shiv Sena movement. Eliminating Mr. Patel would cut the escalation of Hindu attacks. If there were one man responsible for the actions of militant Hindus, it would be Nasir Patel.

"Third, we suggest the assassination of Mr. Rajiv Chandra, commissioner of the greater Bombay police force. Our sources report Mr. Chandra has removed police protection for Muslims at areas of greatest Hindu activity. Mr. Chandra has encouraged his police force to ignore Muslim pleas for help from the rioters. Eliminating Mr. Chandra would lead to a replacement who may protect our muslim brothers from further harm. Your negotiations with Rao through the FAC may ensure an acceptable replacement. Until then, the elimination of Mr. Chandra is crucial.

"Fourth, we suggest you press leaders of the Arab nations, especially the leaders of Bangladesh and Pakistan, to accommodate all Muslims who seek asylum. They have in the past. We believe this will make a strong statement to the international community that our unity is strong.

"With these four steps, your holiness, we may make a stand in this new cycle of violence. With your blessings we shall implement this plan."

The advisor took his seat.

For five hours Tariq questioned his advisors. Tariq doubted the Rao administration would bend to the FAC. The assassinations would demonstrate to Hindus that the unity of Shia Islam would never tolerate such an assault on its own people. Tariq demanded more names.

One of the assistants stood from the edge of the room and handed a notebook to his advisor. Inside was a list of names. The Advisor of Executions distributed copies of the list. Rage made Tariq see red and blue, like staring into the center of the sun, a red and blue which turned black and blue, and then black like the soot from a cancerous lung. With a swift pound of his fist Tariq ordered their elimination. Fifty-two Hindus. An execution order came attached. He signed it. The corpses were to be mutilated beyond recognition and hidden from the Hindu press. After each assassination, a letter would be sent to Rao's office identifying the Hindus and naming a fictitious Islamic group.

The advisors believed Rao would recognize the new tide of Muslim retaliation in India and use federal power to protect Muslims. He would, therefore, prevent the riots from spinning out of control. Rao would certainly keep the Hindu deaths a secret to prevent such instability. A solid plan, thought Tariq. He knew Rao would suspect him for the assassinations. If Rao wanted to extend the rioting, a final fight, then he should accuse Tariq's organization and gamble towards that end.

Tariq circled the table with his hands behind his back. He fired at his advisors, caught them in some fallacy, or shouted. After Tariq coiled the large table and was satisfied, he left all in abeyance. No whispering, no murmuring.

He thought of the Imam and his plight. He thought it unnecessary to burden his advisors with this knowledge. He stared at his Advisor of Education and ruminated on Khozem. He wanted to call emergency meetings for every one of his hang-ups. Suddenly the urge to lash out at these creatures so obsequious and familiar.

"Fine," said Tariq. "We will implement this strategy towards India and the Hindus, but without the FAC. Rao's government has thrown diplomacy to the dogs. It's time they learn never to test our patience, our faith, and our aim to keep the unity, Sunni or Shia. It is the Organization's responsibility to look out for our best interests. Let those Hindus eat the mud from where their idols were born. We should have taken India a very long time ago. A once clean India has turned to filth.

"As you know, The Imam must approve. I will take this plan to him. If he rejects it, we shall convene again at the appropriate time. But to move on, I must ask if any of you is familiar with a Mr. Iqbal Pendi. He is a member of the Organization, but I do not know in what capacity. I hear he is someone very close to me. I can't recall ever meeting the man."

Papers rustled behind him. The stenographer rose from his chair. Tariq fed him his hand for salaams and observed this dark man with thin lips, thin eyes, and thin build. A lanky animal. Pendi placed his hands at his sides and kept his eyes forward, avoiding eye contact.

"Please take your seat, Mr. Pendi," said Tariq. "We shall talk after the meeting."

After a quick prayer, the emergency meeting adjourned. The advisors lined up in front of Tariq. Each did lengthy salaams and asked for advice. The aides sat against the wall while watching their bosses whispering to the bavasaab.

Tariq advised most of them to spend time in Medina doing prayers there, performing Umrah in the Kaa'bah, or fasting. Most requested the bavasaab to pray for them. With restrained smiles and slow nods Tariq blessed them.

Mr. Pendi took his seat near the elevator, looking over the transcripts for typographical errors. Tariq spent two hours hearing the problems of his advisors.

The corpulent Education Advisor hoarded Tariq. He was having trouble with both Al-Karim in Cairo and the University in Mashad, Iran. The advisor pointed to Khozem's withdrawal from Al-Karim and promised to change the school to suit his needs. Tariq declined the offer. He did not want to interfere with the clerics. Tariq assured him that Khozem would return with a different attitude, not knowing when.

At the University in Mashad two lower ranked clerics died mysterious deaths. The autopsy had shown arsenic in their bowels. The administration suspected foul play, and they had interrogated each student. Tariq advised the advisor to continue with the investigation and to leave the Organization's independent investigator at the university.

Pendi buckled his briefcase when the advisor was finished. Pendi reeked of loyalty. He dressed in a gray suit. He gave Tariq hearty salaams.

"So, you are Mr. Pendi. Iqbal Pendi, I presume," began Tariq.

"Yes, your holiness."

"And you have been close to my side transcribing these meetings for how many years?"

"Seven years, sir, and I have found it a real privilege working under you and the Secretary of the Council," he stammered.

"Of course you have. Is not the position all that you have hoped it to be?"

"Oh yes, your holiness. I look forward to my daily duties under the Secretary."

"You are living in Mecca now?"

"Yes. I have my family here. I also have families in Cairo, Karachi, Damascus, and Jeddah."

"I see. A very prosperous man. Come, let us leave this place of business. You will stay and talk with me a while, and then I will take you to your car. Where did you leave it?"

"I left it at the Organization's complex."

"Fine. I shall drive you there."

The white Mercedes sped beyond the gates of the Custodian's mansion.

"You must not be afraid to travel with me," said Tariq. "My intentions are only to speak with you about an important matter which involves you."

"Of course not, your holiness. This must be the greatest day of my life."

The bodyguard closed the glass that divided the front and back seats. Tariq patted Pendi's knee and watched the landscape dip and ascend.

"The city of Cairo is an unusual city," said Tariq. "One of your families lives there you said?"

"Yes. I have a daughter and a wife in Cairo."

"So you are a man of the world, eh? Cairo, Jeddah, Mecca, Karachi?"

"Nothing compared to you, your holiness. From Allah's bounty I have my prosperity. I have sound families."

"When was the last time you heard from your family in Cairo?"

"Not long ago. My daughter attends Al-Karim there, and my wife is a dutiful mother and home-maker. I try to visit them as often as I can, but my duties have me to Mecca. I see them once every three or four months."

"And what is your daughter studying?" asked Tariq.

"The history of the Sunni and Shia Islam during the late nineteenth century, or so she has told me. It's interesting how my son in Karachi is studying the same."

"Your daughter, Mr. Pendi, is no longer at Al-Karim. She is missing."

"Missing? How could she be missing?" laughed Pendi.

"Do you doubt me?"

"No...No, of course not."

"Mr. Pendi, your daughter has left the university in Cairo and has moved elsewhere. You can call the university if you doubt me."

"I would never doubt you, your holiness. If you say she's missing, she must be missing, even if she's not missing. She must have left the university."

"Yes, she has left. She was expelled two weeks ago for insubordination and rebellious behavior. I'm surprised you haven't heard. Your daughter is your own business. If she has been expelled from the best university in the world, why should I care, right?"

"Right," mumbled Pendi.

"But I do care. I care very much. You see, my son, who shall fill my place in the very near future, met your daughter at Al-Karim while she was on her way out. My son has taken a liking to your daughter. They now live somewhere illegally together. My son shall never marry your daughter. His marriage is a political arrangement determined by me. Your daughter must not interfere. Am I starting to make myself clear, Mr. Pendi?"

"Yes, your eminence."

"I trust you will take care of this matter without my son's knowledge?"

"I will try my hardest, and I apologize to you and the All Mighty for letting these circumstances come to pass. I will take care of it immediately."

"And how do you plan to do that?"

"I'm not sure. You say your blessed son wants to take her as his primary wife?"

"Perhaps. We do not know."

"I will try to get her away from him. I don't know how, but it shall be done. You needn't worry."

"Mr. Pendi I am not worried. I'm sure you will do everything in your power. But if you fail, I will carry out this task for you. I'd rather not deal with your daughter, but if I have to, I will. Let's hope you succeed. I want you to succeed."

"I will succeed, your holiness," sputtered Mr. Pendi.

They sped through the swelling streets of Mecca with meandering Muslims in kurtas and duppurtas. They ate the scenes of the city in chunks: the falling darkness, the lamb rolls on spits churning in tin warmers.

"If you must know," chuckled Tariq. "Your daughter is in no way the correct breed for my son. Don't have me deal with this. We will do it your way. You know best how to handle your daughter, and I will support you. Make sure my son never finds out about our conversation. The next time I see you, this whole matter will have been taken care of."

The pock-marked terrain of the city ended. They climbed a smooth road to the hills and came upon a cluster of buildings overlooking the busy streets. The bodyguard stopped the car.

"Remember Pendi," said Tariq, "those who fail must answer to me. I don't want to hear from you until the next meeting."

The bodyguard opened the door. In the warm wind Pendi stood with his briefcase guarding his loins. The Mercedes left him there.

When Tariq returned home, he wanted to be alone. Before bed he prayed for the Imam and his offspring. He even included a small prayer for Pendi and for the Council's plan. By the time he finished, exhaustion came over him. He crawled into bed after another ablution and recited:

"Oh Allah, save me from the
pangs of the Day of Resurrection.
Oh Allah, in thy name do I die and live."

He lay awake, fiddling his fingers, reciting the Verse of the Throne until Samira came home. She put on a worn cotton gown and slid next to him.

"I thought you were sleeping," she whispered.

"I can't fall asleep."

"You weren't waiting for me, were you?"

"Yes, I was waiting," he breathed. "Your skin is so soft. It is the one thing that makes me certain that...that I'm not losing control."

"What happened in the meeting today?"

"All I do is sentence people to death. These rotten blue Hindus continue to test my power. They are testing me until the day I crack, the day I let down my guard. When that day comes, Shia Islam will become a mockery, and I will be the person to blame."

"So you've let down your guard?"

"Not yet. I know what must be done, and I want to remain calm and rational, even peaceful. It never happens. I end up thinking this is the day I will lose my grip. Many years we have suffered for the Imam. The Imam is not helping me with anything. He hasn't helped me at all. I wish I could rip off these clothes."

"Always remember you will be given a place near Allah, and the living will always remember your name."

"Will they remember Khozem's name?"

"They will remember Khozem's name, because he shall surpass you in every way..."

"...and help the next Imam?"

"Khozem will be a fine bavasaab once he thinks things through. Give him time."

Tariq nuzzled the side of her face. Events turned too fast. He saw it unfolding. They looked for a leader. Imam Shabbir had such a vision: a leader to thwart the money-hungry Jews and the lascivious Christians. Shia Islam shall dominate the New Age. The embattled minority of the Arab world shall be given rule. The narrow roads and gutted buildings shall be restored with mosques that call Allah's name in praise and in fear.

"My, Sarmira," he sighed. "I have only the best of intentions."

She did not question him. Tariq's mumbling faded into incoherence. Soon he grew tired of revolving in the same thoughts.

"I want so very much to be a good human being," he whispered.

Samira had fallen fast asleep by then.

Chapter Seventeen
RASHIDA AND HER FATHER
14th of Jumaada al-THanny 1417
(October 27, 1996)

Rashida's mother wrote her the same day and insisted she contact her father who worked at the complex. Rashida never replied.

The Meccan streets shortened into cuts and slants as she walked closer to the Kaa'bah one evening. A northerly wind chilled the city. The shops sold pots and pans, silk garments, novelties, and religious trinkets. Food stands roasted lamb and chicken logs on spits. She passed veiled women carrying shopping bags. The streets were unmarked. The main avenues, however, were labeled by old signposts under which taxi cabs inched forward in traffic.

The neighborhood children tugged on her chador. The cripples displayed their deformities for spare change. She found a café in the middle of a short block. The male patrons in the front sections fed on bread and an assortment of spicy meats. Curtains were drawn over the family section stocked with women and children. She indulged in a chicken kabob before meeting Khozem who had been saying prayers in the Kaa'bah.

At home they read books, most of which were interpretations and commentaries on the Holy Scriptures. They lived in an apartment without a telephone, without windows. An unmade mattress served as their only resting place.

A simple truth was more difficult to tell than the grandest of all lies. She had immersed herself in illegalities, with, of all people, the bavasaab's son. She hoped to avoid her family altogether.

Khozem and Rashida found each other on the road. They walked apart from each other as the city prohibited even remote displays of affection. Rashida walked in front as Khozem followed. They turned a corner and approached their apartment building. Rashida noticed someone familiar standing out front.

"Father?" asked Rashida.

"Yes...Yes indeed. I have been waiting all day for you," said Iqbal Pendi.

Rashida bent down to kiss his hands.

"This is Khozem," she said.

"I must speak to my daughter alone regarding a very urgent family matter," said Pendi respectfully.

"What's wrong, father?"

"I came to speak to you alone."

Khozem went upstairs, after Rashida nodded in consent.

"We may talk tonight, sure," replied Rashida. "I'm sorry for making you wait. How did you find me? Did you call Cairo?"

"Sure I did. Your mother is very worried about you. I had to see what was going on."

"I have to pray now."

"Prayers can wait. I'm disappointed. I guess Al-Karim is not the place for you. I heard you moved on. Your mother said something about a job?"

"Just a few blocks from the corner."

"You must have long hours to be coming home so late."

"I was with Khozem."

"What does this Khozem do for a living? You two are planning to get married?"

"I was going to tell you all about him. He works on carpentry, and when he is not doing that, he remains in the Kaa'bah."

"So you must be supporting him?"

"His pay is low. I'm supporting him until he finds something suitable."

"Do you realize what you're doing is illegal? The Qu'ran clearly outlines this. Both of you are young, very young."

"But we love each other, father. This is proof of our relationship's validity under Allah."

"It is neither a suitable time nor a suitable circumstance for you to be living with him. You cannot live with another man unless you are married to him. You know that better than I. Without consent how will you live? No job pays that much money. Don't insult me. A seamstress can't pay that much."

"It does pay that much, and we are happy with the arrangement."

"Nothing but filth. It stands for two people having no direction. What is it you are trying to prove? That you love him? At such an age you know nothing of love. Love will grow cold if the union is not properly matched. What does your Khozem's family think?"

"They have agreed."

"Lies! The Pendi family does not agree. You will return to Cairo into the arms of your hysterical mother. She has been worried sick. She has written dozens of letters. You haven't replied to one of them. It's just plain reckless. The holiest city in the world, and now this."

"I'm sorry about not writing her, but I needed time to think. I'm sorry father. My life is with Khozem now. You will accept this, whether you agree or not. We are doing fine with each other."

"You will go back to Cairo."

"I won't. Suddenly I see why you came. Now excuse me, I have to make dinner."

"And if I say you cannot live with him, you will disobey your father?"

"I disobey you for the greater good of Khozem and me."

"And what shall I tell your mother?"

"Whatever you want. It's better the truth be known. She will have to agree as well."

"Oh really? You have been supporting her as well?"

"What do you mean?"

"Do you have enough to support your own mother?"

"What are you getting at?"

"That your job isn't that high-paying to support the three of you. Get to Cairo where you belong, and I tell you this as your father. Don't disobey me, or I will stop sending money to that weeping mother of yours."

"You wouldn't dare."

"Get to Cairo, or you'll have your mother to support. Your place is with your mother. She has been trained to do nothing but mother you. So get there.

And if you're smart, you'll get to another university. I will be available at the complex when you awake from your childish dream. Think hard, Rashida."

In the apartment Khozem had started his prayers, and she picked the clothes from the floor. The cleaning absorbed her anger. She soon let out slow tears. Khozem pulled her into his chest. From there her tears flowed. She held on tightly as their fate depended on what Allah had instilled in the minds of others. A flicker of sophistication came to them. They grew older amongst the old. Their embrace marked an end to something that bloomed. Her eyes were red and still tearing. An occasional sniffle. No words. Khozem's dopey expression, however, finally made her smile.

Chapter Eighteen
TARIQ AT THE IRANIAN UNIVERSITY
12th of Jumaada al THanny 1417
(October 25, 1996)

Tariq had been in Iran, lecturing at the University of Mashad. A full investigation into the deaths of two lower ranked clerics failed to produce results. Tariq left Mecca like he wanted to: away from his anxiety, alone with his suitcase, and in the careful vigilance of his bodyguards.

Cloaked soldiers in long black robes stood at a respectful distance during a weeklong series of lectures. The lectures were well received. Tariq talked for hours about the political situation in Hindu India and the diplomatic initiatives of the Islamic council. Lies, of course. Over the years Tariq, as an international figure, had become adept at lying to large groups.

The plan for India had been successful for the most part. Violence, however, still remained. His detailed lectures praised the Islamic Republic of Iran for sticking to its revolutionary principles. He further extended thanks to the university for creating the most righteous Muslims. The cloaked clerics congratulated themselves, despite the mysterious deaths of the lower-ranked clerics.

The university marked the burial place of Tariq's great grandfather's sister. He visited the grave several times and had his bodyguards carry away some soil from the burial ground. All seemed peaceful in Mashad, as the only tumult came from the restless desert sands that swept over the pilgrims who camped there. Most of the tour, however, was spent in Teheran under close protection. He gave a brief sermon in a stadium that served as one of the many cultural centers in Iran. He led prayers for five thousand at the Teheran University mosque. Twenty thousand pilgrims prayed outside. He traveled to Kerbala. The bodyguards gathered more pail-fulls of soil, adding to Tariq's collection back home. At the most sacred tombs he presented a sermon to a small, privileged audience. He said that a new direction for Islam was taking shape, a theme he had stuck with throughout his tour of Iran. At Kerbala, however, he included a note about Western nations, a quick note which left the audience confused. He claimed in his ramblings that Islam should prepare to adopt the West as a mother does a bastard son.

Most of the believers from Mashad, Teheran, and Kerbala insisted he stay longer. But Tariq had nothing left to explain. His words were mysterious as he told a final group to look to the West for Allah's message. He did not say more. He then returned to Mecca.

He arrived in Mecca with the sands of Iraq and Iran still in his sandals. He had received dozens of messages from Pendi, several from the Advisor of Touring, and one from Sakina in Lahore.

Sakina's message came in a telegram. Her husband, Imam Shabbir Hussein, had died. It asked that Tariq travel to Lahore and perform the burial. Among the heaps of recorded messages and the one telegram, still no message from Vasilla. Too many things depended on other people. Tariq feared Vasilla lost in Pakistan, never to return. He feared that his departing orders may have been too difficult for him.

Tariq phoned Pendi at the complex. Pendi tearfully claimed that Khozem and Rashida could not be broken apart. Even though the couple suffered from Pendi's strategic move to stop sending support to his wife, Rashida would not leave Khozem. Pendi asked for more time, but Tariq could not wait. He relieved Pendi from his duties on the spot as the council's stenographer. He then summoned his Advisor for Executions and waited in his Meccan home.

Chapter Nineteen
A SPEEDING TAXI CAB
20th of Rajab 1417
(December 2, 1996)

Rashida left the garment shop for lunch and dropped by the apartment for prayers. She found Khozem lying on the mattress. She dropped her things noisily and stood above him. She compared him to an invalid with neither legs nor arms nor brains to function. Her softness with him in bed turned rough in the day time.

"Khozem, why aren't you up?"

"I am up. I'm talking to you, aren't I?"

"Don't be smart with me."

"It's nothing."

"You've been telling me that every day for the past month."

"Add one more day then."

"You need to find a job. We need to be married. Money is too tight."

"I know all that."

"Are you upset because of something I did?"

"It's beyond our control."

"Have you been visiting the Kaa'bah? What happened to that?"

"Everything falls apart. We spend most of our lives waiting for things that never come."

"What has happened to you? This is exactly what you wanted. We have the Kaa'bah around the corner, a place with me in the holiest city on Earth, and we're getting married soon. Isn't this what you've been dreaming about?"

"The Kaa'bah is so beautiful, isn't it? The angels come down and shed their light upon the minarets like a celestial waterfall. They float around without being seen, high in the air and swoosh! down onto that cool marble, checking us out, watching our every move as we circle that black thing around and around. And what's the purpose of that? Why is one holier just because one prays near the Kaa'bah? It's all some sort of twisted game. The more one borrows from the Kaa'bah, the more one needs."

"The more you lie here the more twisted you'll get," said Rashida. "You have to move around, take part in some activity, maybe make new friends. You can't close everyone out. We need some sort of social support. Why don't you ask some of your friends down in the Kaa'bah to go out to dinner one of these days?"

"What if they find out who I am?"

"Don't tell them your last name. It'll be fine."

"The time for making friends has come and gone."

"We are still young, Khozem. You can't expect to become a holy man overnight. It takes years of discipline, and right now you need other people, not only me, but other friends."

"I don't need friends."

"Well, I do. I want to have a woman friend."

"Then go out and get one. Why bother me about it?"

"What is bothering you? Get up. Get up now."

She pulled at his arms, but he just lay there numb. She let out tears.

"It's a long road," Khozem sighed, "and I've let it get beyond me. I'm not sure why, but I'm not myself anymore. I need to be mylself again. Being myself demands that I run into some sort of failure..."

"With me?"

"You will always be my first success. I mean that I run into these failures. I lost it somewhere. It just vanished. I'm not cut out for much. I'm trying to be someone I can't be. I can't concentrate, and I've been sleeping so much."

"Why not start by taking a shower?"

"And then?"

"We'll talk about it. What else can I say? You've got to take a shower sometime. You haven't said prayers for a while. So start with a shower, and then we will overcome the next obstacle, okay?"

"I don't want to move unless it's all laid out plain, and until that time comes, I'll just lie here and daydream about it."

"You won't get very far. By the time you think it out, you'll be dead."

"One starts with his dreams. When you lose that, then your faith will be next. After that, you lie in bed and ponder how to get out of bed. What am I going to do? I don't feel like getting up. I don't feel like talking. It's impossible to be anything in this place, to get married, to be a holy man. What's so glorious about becoming a wise man of Islam? Is it nobility in being totally anonymous? It's a prison. I've tried. I've done my best. I contemplate Allah all day. I picture him sitting above a blue and open sky, breathing life into the rotating planets, balancing the sun upon his finger tip, and leaving his creation spinning without an unambiguous book of instructions. Allah is so far beyond contemplation, like staring into the sun and taking away a collage of white spots."

"You're thinking too much," said Rashida.

"So what does Allah look like? Does he have eyes to see, a nose to smell, and a mouth to taste? Did he have a string of selected children? Does he have a wife to reproduce similar worlds? Is Allah guilty of neglect? Who is to blame for street children at the age of five? There are never stupid questions, only stupid answers. When an answer is not known, the answer becomes Allah, because Allah alone is the reason behind reasoning itself. Let me lie here. Leave me alone."

"If you feel that strongly, fine. Just lay there the rest of your life. Lay everything to rest. If you want to do it, you can do it. You can stay in the Kaa'bah all day. Is that what you want? Some sort of permission slip from me? Remember you have to get a job in order for us to live here. It's not what I want. It's what we want. If I am your first success, you will get out of bed, not for yourself, but for me. If you can't do it for yourself, do it for me. We need to work on your state of mind. An ascetic's life has gotten you into trouble. Your state of mind has gone. We will do it together, unless you rather not...be together that is."

"I don't know. I just don't know about anything anymore."

Rashida donned her chador. She slammed the door shut. Their apartment became a dark cave: drool on the pillows, stains on the sheets, and tangled clothes. When she returned, she found Khozem still in bed.

"What's going on?" as she approached their bed.

"I've lost my motivation," he said.

"That's obvious."

"I don't know what to do about it."

"Did you take a shower?"

"What's the use? I'm waiting until I get really dirty."

"The point is not the shower itself. It's getting you to move, to get up. Whatever is happening we can do something about it, together."

"Come by me," asked Khozem.

With a sigh Rashida undressed and crawled next to him.

"We can't go on," she said.

"I swear to you I'm working on it."

"Maybe we should move to an apartment with a window at least."

"Do we have the money?"

"Take anything that comes, Khozem. We won't have enough to pay the rent."

"Did you send your mother the money?"

"I had no choice. I can't support both of you. Khozem, we have to get serious now. We should get married."

"In due time. Ah, your skin is so soft. I've been waiting for you all day."

"Don't even try it."

"Try what?"

"You know what."

He put his arms around her.

"I would try nothing of the sort," as he kissed her lips and neck.

"And to think you couldn't take a shower," she whispered.

Khozem awoke before Rashida did. He was tangled in her body. He stopped the alarm clock from blaring. He tried to rehearse in that bed the reasons for their being together. Yet the shadows along the wall of their embrace did not seem so enchanting anymore. He thought that returning to his family might be the remedy. He went to the bathroom, and Rashida soon followed. He heard her vomiting into the toilet.

"Are you okay?" he asked.

"I'm sure it's nothing," replied Rashida.

"How long has it been happening?"

"Every now and then. Especially when I wake up."

"We better get you to a doctor."

"It's nothing, and we can't afford a doctor."

In the haze of the light he begged her to move closer. Khozem whispered that he would change himself. Rashida kissed him softly. He showered and put on clean clothes. She kissed him again and departed for the garment shop. As soon as she left, Khozem fell into bed again.

He awoke in the late afternoon. The evening crowd at the Kaa'bah was large. The spaces were jammed with believers on the carpets. The stadium lights made the minarets glitter. Other lights were placed near the House of Allah. The black covering on which Arabic and gold embroidery was stitched glowed in the pink sky. The possessed crowd circled it. Many fought to kiss the black stone.

He recited the Verse of the Throne as he went around. The adhan would be called soon. He finished the orbit of the house, getting a good spot for prayer. He promised to perform a lesser pilgrimage the next day. He promised never to return to a job. If Khozem had to live with his parents, he would do so for Rashida. They would be apart temporarily until financial circumstances changed. But while in the Kaa'bah he felt Allah reading his mind, scanning every ridge of his brain, and so he prayed for their longevity as a couple.

When he returned home, Rashida was not there. He thought it unusual. Instead of going to bed, he walked to the garment shop. The shop had been closed for several hours. He canvassed the area and poked his head in the places she might have gone. As evening came, he thought of phoning Rashida's mother in Cairo. He paced the room with his palms sweating.

An infantryman and a plain-clothed police inspector visited Khozem in the fifth floor apartment. They said Rashida had been hit by a speeding taxi cab just outside the garment shop. The infantry man handcuffed Khozem. He was arrested for living with a woman without being married to her.

Chapter Twenty
THE ADVISOR OF EXECUTIONS
21st of Rajab 1417
(December 3, 1996)

Tariq waited for Asif Mohammed, Advisor of Executions for the Islamic council. Tariq hosted a dinner for this very dear friend who returned from a successful tour of India, Malaysia, and Indonesia. When he arrived, Asif looked ill, but his wife was buoyant, radiant, and talkative. She and Samira sat close together, while Tariq and Asif stood stiffly with warm tea. Asif dressed in a cotton kurta and topee, while Tariq was arranged in a top heavy turban and gold kurta.

Asif pushed the FAC idea further, even though it was a social occasion. Tariq was also in the mood for business. He resisted convening the FAC, even though Asif insisted that all Islamic republics supported the ending of violence against Muslims in India.

"Islam shall have the last word in all of this. The FAC must wait. Timing is everything. I have been consulting with the Advisor of Tours. When I say the time is right, the time will be right," announced Tariq.

"How long will you wait, my holiness?"

"Let's give it two months or so. We must read our intelligence in the area very carefully. We obviously knew the violence wouldn't end with a few assassinations. Our actions were only catalysts for more violence. Delhi will realize that Islam would never permit itself to be dragged through the mud. They will find that our Muslim brethren have more confidence in what I say than in their own elected officials."

"Hmmm," said Asif sipping his tea, "I agree with the Advisor of Information. He says there is a lot more we can do on the inside."

"And this is your specialty," smiled Tariq.

"We got every one of those militants, and our intelligence reports that our men are hungry for more. Really you must think of the whole spectrum. All of the advisors are ready."

At these moments Tariq saw his advisor full of life. In the meetings Asif usually remained cold and calculating, highly respected by the other advisors. He was known as one of the bavasaab's closest friends. Asif usually asked for work on clandestine projects. Challenges made Asif happier.

But it was Tariq who had asked a small favor of him. Asif followed orders without questioning them. As their wives chatted, Tariq guided Asif Mohammed to his study filled with books on Islam, old copies of *The Arab News*, and an unabridged Qu'ran on his desk. The short and sickly advisor handed over an envelope of photographs: Rashida outside the garment shop heading towards the apartment.

"So this is what she looked like?" said Tariq.

"She died of some freak accident," replied Asif. "Allah had willed it."

"Good. No woman tempts my son and gets away with it. The killing should not have a single stamp on it. Keep it quiet. It was an accident. An act of Allah. A quick, quiet accident."

"Quick, easy, and routine."

"Good. Burn these photographs."

Chapter Twenty-One
PRISON
22nd of Rajab 1417
(December 4, 1996)

The iron cage had no seats or bunks, only a floor, bars, and a hole in the ground leading to the city sewers. They confiscated Khozem's belongings, closed his apartment, and stripped him of clothes. They did not threaten him. The guards remained cordial, almost pleasant. They were not permitted to bring him food. They tolerated Khozem's screaming. These screams were mostly curses. The guards reclined on swivel chairs, reading the newspapers or playing cards. These guards thought of putting the tin can over him but instead ignored his insults.

Khozem collapsed in the middle of the cell, plaintively calling Rashida's name. He refused to believe she was dead. He suspected a conspiracy to imprison both of them in separate areas of the kingdom.

He threatened the guards with his father's name for a few hours, but they continued reading. Khozem vowed revenge. Justice would come to the whole, corrupted lot, and he and Rashida would be together again.

The next morning, the guards shook Khozem awake. In his exhaustion he was escorted to another wing of the precinct. He was the only prisoner kept there. As he walked with the guards, he noticed rows and columns of steel doors installed in the walls. The chill of the hallway, powered by a large metal fan, numbed his toes.

One of the guards pulled open a drawer from the wall, which exposed Rashida's bare shoulders and mutilated head. Khozem caressed what remained of her face. When his tears fell over the corpse, the guards stepped away.

"Oh my Rashida," whispered Khozem. "My sweet, gentle Rashida. What have they done to us? We were to be married. Don't leave me like this. I have changed..."

The guards gave him handkerchiefs and led him back to his cell. The more he lamented, the drowsier he grew.

The guards awoke him for a plate of rice under a cold stew. He threw it across the room. He muttered things and laughed to himself. He thought of the punishment he would receive for the crime of zina.

The punishment was public flogging and banishment from the kingdom for one year. To say Allah sanctioned this made him think Allah could not be perfect as the scriptures demanded. But this was one thought among thousands. His thoughts became as tortuous as the red ants biting his body and feeding on the food he threw away.

The guards ignored his requests to call his family. Khozem moved to the corner of the cell, away from the red ants. He slept by the sewage dump. He awoke as he heard footsteps and greetings exchanged. He stood and paced. The footsteps came closer. The guard let out tears as he opened the gate, releasing Khozem to his father. Khozem collapsed on his father's shoulders.

"She's dead. Rashida's dead."

"I know."

"She's gone. I loved her more than myself. Why has Allah cursed me? What did I ever do wrong?"

Khozem, smelling terribly from the prison, wet his father's shoulders. Tariq led him from the Meccan precinct and into the Mercedes.

Night had fallen on the city, and within the blur of tears Khozem saw the minarets of the grand mosque, shaded with aquamarine colors. Tariq placed his hands upon his. At the touch Khozem regained some of his senses.

"Tomorrow morning, you and I shall go to the Kaa'bah, together, and pray for better times," said Tariq.

"What's going to happen to me?"

"We shall ask Allah what he thinks, and only he may fill us with ideas. Don't be afraid. Remember, Allah does things for reasons. He steers us in directions to satisfy the greater good. Don't be afraid. We will talk more when you are clean and better rested."

After a long bath and a penetrating look at the Kaa'bah through his bedroom window, Khozem slid into his cool bed. 'Things happen for a reason,' he repeated. 'Events in a life are not isolated moments that cut a person down by the brutality of chance. There must be an ordering to these events, whether they take place in the abyss or high atop a Meccan hill.'

His father wakened him around noon. Khozem was reassured by the sunlight. He had neither seen the sun nor remembered his father ever sitting by his side. He told his father he wanted to attend Rashida's funeral. Her mother in Cairo had been phoned from the precinct and was to perform the rites in a few days.

After performing an ablution, they both strolled into the Kaa'bah. They performed Tawaf and rested on the side for a bit of zum-zum water. Khozem had never been by his father's side for so long. He felt awkward and uneasy, like a kid confronting a familiar stranger.

"You know, besides camping, your grandfather and I used to visit the Kaa'bah on days like this. Truly we are blessed to be able to come here so much. I think of him. A very strict fellow skilled in the ways of the faith, and while I knew I would one day follow in his footsteps, I often questioned the level of my faith."

"I question my faith every day," added Khozem. "Obviously I'm not so faithful."

"The intent is there, my son. If your intentions are true and good, then Allah will always lead you, whether you are conscious of it or not. We have all transgressed one way or another. It is Allah's way of making us see the difference between good and evil. We pay the price and move on. Allah keeps his accounts, but He is oft-forgiving and most merciful. You must not forget that."

"And has the All Mighty filled your head with ideas of what is to become of me?"

"While you slept, I had a word with the commissioner. You are to carry out your punishment under my supervision. Who else is more qualified than I really? You must agree to my punishment and my terms."

"Of course I agree. I'd much rather be with you than those dogs."

"They were only doing their jobs, Khozem. Without my intervention your back would be burning, and you would have been kicked out of the kingdom. You must never forget the crime you committed. I will punish you in accordance with Qu'ranic law."

"You will have me flogged, is that it?"

"I have not thought about it yet."

"Oh come now. You would whip me? Your own flesh and blood?"

"I can send you back to the mutawafs."

Khozem gazed into the crowd.

"Don't think you are getting off easy on this," continued Tariq. "The All Mighty has set rules for a reason."

"So how are you going to punish me, father? You are the bavasaab, and without a doubt you must follow what has been written in the Qu'ran. Whip me, if you must, but from thenceforth don't regard me as anything. I'm not your son any longer. No one else but you tried to break us apart from the very beginning. You must have spoken to her father. How clever."

"I did nothing of the sort," claimed Tariq.

"I've lost my bride. And for some reason your hand was in on it."

"Lower your voice when you address me. There are to be no arguments in the Kaa'bah, and no, I never talked to her father. I don't even know who her father is. I don't have time for such meddling. Her father must have seen or heard of the illegality somehow. If I were him, I'd turn you in all the same."

"If only you knew how I felt about her. But you'd never understand. You come and go like our home is some hotel, and then you choose to butt into my life whenever you please."

"And you think it was not right of me to pry you away

from some woman, some revolutionary who had been expelled from our holiest university?" said Tariq. "We are lucky the Commissioner did not publicize all of this. Damn right I was concerned. I was concerned about you and my reputation. And now it is my concern to punish you as I see fit."

"Whip me then. Right here in front of all your loyal subjects."

"Khozem, sit down and lower your voice."

"Arrest me again, and throw me into that pit."

Khozem spread his arms to the sky and twirled about in the Kaa'bah. Mutawafs approached, but Tariq flashed the palm of his hand.

"Stop it this instant! This is not a loony bin, this is a place of worship!" said Tariq hotly.

"Then whip me here in the Kaa'bah with all of these people cheering you on. It is the holy thing to do, isn't it?"

"Please, Khozem. Come here. I never intended to have you flogged, okay? I knew nothing about Rashida. Now please, come here. That's better. I only want to teach you a valuable lesson. Let's go."

They made it out as the crowd prepared for prayer. Khozem wanted to stay, but Tariq pushed him into the car.

"I'm sure she was a fine, fine woman," said Tariq. "But see, Allah has a plan for you, and that is to take my place after I'm gone. You wanted the position so much, remember? The bavasaab position is open to you and to you only. My flock is wondering what will happen to me when I pass away. Don't deny Allah's grace. You can be so much. You have been selected as the leader of the Shia race, its assets, its mosques, its entire organization. You will work directly with the Imam."

"And what of my punishment?"

"That is the first step, and it shall not involve whipping. I would have myself whipped before my only son was whipped."

"So what is my punishment then, if I submit to your plan?"

"You must be banished from Saudi Arabia."

"This is my home!"

"I know that, but you have a choice. You may either be banished to Al-Karim in Cairo or to the university at Mashad, not to return unless your studies are completed."

"If I refuse?"

"I have not thought enough about that, but for sure you will no longer stay with us. You will be on your own without a title, without direction. I dread for it to come to that. I have no other children. You remain my only hope, the muslim hope."

Khozem chuckled. This chuckling gathered into deranged laughter.

"What? What is it? Is this actually amusing you?"

"No," answered Khozem catching his breath. "Just think of it. You have a son who has just committed zina. A son you might have to throw out of the house and deprive, and all of a sudden I'm your only hope? You are going to trust me with all you've worked for? Or perhaps it's because you don't have any alternative. I don't have a choice, and either do you. We're stuck."

"I guess you're right," said Tariq solemnly.

They came upon their guarded driveway.

"When will my punishment begin?"

"Let's say I give you until my return from my next trip. I won't be touring. I have some business to take care of in Pakistan."

"It's not the rioting again, is it?"

"Be concerned about your own life. You are at the beginning of a short but strenuous journey: to finish your studies in Shia theology and your training. Think of it as a second chance. After the funeral, I want you either in Cairo or Mashad. I have called the administrators of each university. They are expecting your answer to very open invitations."

"Great. They'll be fawning all over me."

"They will not. You are ready to be taught. I trust your diligence in study. We will talk further, so don't worry."

In the days before Rashida's funeral, Tariq and Khozem spent more time in the Kaa'bah. They said prayers and recited different verses from the Qu'ran while circumambulating the giant black house. Tariq sang his most favorite verses and was delighted to see his son impressed. But Khozem never recovered. He believed Rashida's spirit could hear his reciting of the verses. He continued to suspect his father of wrongdoing. Ultimately Khozem thought himself responsible. This began a long cycle of self-hatred and disgust.

Chapter Twenty-Two
THE TELEGRAM
23rd of Rajab 1417
(December 5, 1996)

Tariq arose early the next morning. The house was quiet. Samira was in the bathroom. The night guard slid an orange envelope undern the door. The telegram from Lahore read: MOST GRACIOUS SIR, I HAVE FOUND THE PROSTITUTE. CALL THE LAHORE MARRIOT ROOM 233. VASILLA.

Tariq telephoned immediately. Vasilla's slow, husky voice was refreshing over the static-ridden line. Before Vasilla finished, however, Tariq ordered him to stay put.

"Samira," yelled Tariq.

He could hear the water running. He knocked frantically. He had never doubted Allah's plan. There was so much to be done. 'Such an important child at the hands of a prostitute,' he moped. He removed two heavy suitcases from the closet. Samira came from the bathroom, wiping her face with a hand towel.

Stumbling over one of the suitcases, she threw the damp towel to the floor. She threw the kurtas and skull caps into the suitcases. It was time for Tariq to return to the rest of the world.

He strung up the blinds. The sun blared through the room. Samira kept packing, rhythmically moving from bureau to suitcase.

Tariq scouted the Kaa'bah. He gazed at the station of Abraham who built this house of stone, the meteorite from the heavens providing the last piece to this overwhelming puzzle.

Allah had empowered him to bring the faith to the West. Tariq shivered at the thought. He despised the West and its cursed lands, which bedeviled Allah's will. He remembered Imam Shabbir and his dying words. He remembered a slogan on a wall in Lahore: CRUSH ISRAEL, HATE AMERICA, LOVE ISLAM.

Tariq explained coolly to his wife he was to perform the burial rites and that she could not attend. The burial was subject to restrictions. Traveling was meant for Tariq himself. He was not about to share this with his wife. He had been accustomed to being without her. Religious business was not meant for her, only that she should pray the required times per day and fear her husband.

Samira made up her face in the mirror, gobbing on skin cream. Her face would never be shown. Tariq never objected to her imported cosmetics, but he preferred she not use them. The woman was man's tragic weakness. To see her on the street with heavy mascara might be too tempting for other men. She rubbed her thick cheeks. She applied lipstick to her full lips, a color that enhanced the shade of her skin. She kept her natural look, which pleased him.

"Tell Khozem he should leave for the university before I return."

"And if he doesn't?" asked Samira, closing her beauty jars.

"Then I'll have to deal with him when I come back, but you will press him onwards."

"And if he goes to Iran?"

"Then push him in that direction. The difference between Mashad and Al-Karim is minimal. They are both the best."

"Khozem should decide on his own what he should do. You push too much. You meddle too much in his affairs. How will he grow if he can't decide for himself?"

"I merely pushed him in the direction of the All Mighty. It was meant for him. He has been selected. He will have plenty of decisions to make. He shall develop through one path, not through many different ones. There are reasons why Allah provided us with a male child."

"And did Imam Shabbir (may peace be upon him) leave us with a male child?"

"That's none of your concern. Stay focused on Khozem."

The Qu'ranic archway marked the end of the city. The pleasure of freedom returned. The headlines of his newspaper failed to interest him, with the exception of Egypt under siege by radicals. The Organization sponsored some activity. The Iranian government had matched those funds, and citizens for a pure Islamic state gained more control. And when the Imam in the West gathers the believers, Egypt would submit to its calling and prostrate towards Mecca instead of London or Washington D.C., hung up on their lofty commands, arrogance, and false Gods. Tariq was sure Egypt was the next to be delivered by the All Mighty.

He threw the paper to the floor, and from the window he saw the city devolve. They passed Jeddah with its undeveloped land fixed between low buildings and residential compounds. A mile of white awnings, the landmark of the airport. For Allah's plan to work, self-sacrifice beyond basic obligations needed to be met.

'Beyond basic obligations,' thought Tariq. For now the move was to build a network within the West. This network would expand and undercut the roots of the unbelievers. As the Imam grows, so would his followers, hungry to punish those who interfered, while embracing those who understood the ultimate beauty of Allah, Muhammad his prophet, and in all ways, Ali, the rightful successor. Tariq sensed that Allah himself put thoughts in his mind, falling from the sky, absorbed into one clear message: to push Islam further into time. 'Glory be to the heavens, for the leader, my son, and glory be to the Imam who will break the horse and gallop through the West which shall part for him.' He pulled his subha beads and counted his worries.

On the plane his thoughts of the opposition to the new Imam grew intense.:

"But there are, among men
Those who purchase idle tales
Without knowledge (or meaning),
To mislead (men) from the path
Of Allah and throw ridicule
(On the path): for such there will be
humiliating chastisement."

He kept an eye on his bodyguards taking shifts in the dark.

Allah's plan already produced Vasilla's call and the Imam's timely death. Yet there was reason to keep up his guard. He needed to lead the believers along an infinite path as wide as the sky for the righteous and as tough as a brick wall for those whom sought comfort from excess.

'Things shall always swing towards a state more pure, and the Imam will split the West.'

Tariq gave it fifty years. A slow progression like a well-oiled machine, a network spanning the continents.

The plane ride did him some good, but left him groggy. The Lahorian breeze burned his lips. He never understood why the Imam chose Lahore. Perhaps one could understand the workings of Islam while farther away from it. Imam Shabbir had somehow found what he was looking for.

The West was too dangerous. The new Imam would be assaulted by false information. He would be confronted by a gutter morality and promiscuous women. Shabbir's grand idea was too far out of whack, his dream too fantastic, even though it proved to be attractive and carried Tariq to the jumbled city of Lahore in the heat and haste.

'Let the Imam be known, and he will live a short life, not accomplishing anything. The leader of the Shias has to be the visible catalyst for unification.'

Imam Shabbir's main request was to unite the flock, but his words loomed uncertain and vague.

Tariq, however, wanted to move quickly. He wanted to be alive to see the effect of planting this Imam in the impure land. The Imam must learn to despise Western culture as his own people have learned to despise it. The learning of Western thought is to be used for one purpose: to defeat it and to fit it within Islam, taking the Western falsities apart bit by bit. All the freedoms in the world are useless without Allah. If the Western world refuses this glorification, then the Imam must work against that same structure, tearing the whole thing down.

Tariq did not trust the adoptive parents Mr. Nadjir had selected. They would have to be under close watch. Sure they were devout, but they were Westerners all the same. They were taught to compromise their faith and use liberties recklessly dispensed. Tariq pondered situations and determined their outcomes. In the midst of such equations were monstrous complexities. The next Imam would be a product of the West without any adversarial instincts towards it.

After touching down and driving to the hotel, the bodyguards cleared the lobby first. Tariq was stuck on the same verse ever since his mind wandered.

He closed his Qu'ran. The hotel was a single floor building. They walked through an empty lobby.

The bodyguards were happy to see Vasilla. He had lost tremendous amounts of weight. His former brawn had distinguished him from the other guards. But now he had a darker, thinner face and had shaved his mustache, making him look younger, almost boyish. Tariq gave him his hand, and Vasilla performed lengthy salaams. The one bedroom unit pleased Tariq. The Organization's money was spent wisely. The room was immaculate. Vasilla's clothing had been shoved in the closet. Tariq was too afraid to hear his report, but his humble grin without his bushy mustache suggested good news.

"I think congratulations are in order," said Tariq.

"Thank you, your holiness. It took a long time, but I finally found this Fatima."

"Where is she?"

"She is in a slum area a few kilometers from here. I have seen her many times."

"Have you seen children with her?"

"I only see her in and out of the slums."

"And how did you find her?"

"By questioning every bureau in Lahore, searching through piles of birth certificates. I figured she must have been born here. And so when I found her old place of residence, I simply went to the bureau, submitted her name, and they pulled up the record. I went to see her old landlord who pointed me in the right direction. I went to the slums day after day, asking these strangers who looked at me a bit funny. Very poor, very sick, very unhealthy people, my holiness. And I saw her. I know where she lives, but I made sure not to get close. She may smell a rat."

"Miraculous, Vasilla. Just miraculous. Allah be praised."

Chapter Twenty-Three
TARIQ RETURNS TO DRAKNI DRIVE
11th of Sha'baan 1417
(December 22, 1996)

In the hotel room Tariq asked Vasilla to lead afternoon prayers. Vasilla tried to remember some of the verses. Nothing but whispers came from his mouth. But Tariq knew Vasilla was slow, and maybe being slow was a virtue. The bodyguards outside were quick in their deductions. But slowness yielded a bodyguard of great loyalty. Vasilla would stand by Tariq. He relied on Tariq for all the answers, even the answers the Prophet had already given the common man.

"Tell me the truth," asked Tariq, "did you pray while I was away?"

"Yes, my holiness."

"Don't lie to me."

"I'm not, my holiness."

"Then recite."

"Allah is most great. Allah is most great..."

"You dare recite without ablution?"

"I'm sorry, your holiness."

"Forget it. I don't know when you'll ever understand prayers. Don't worry about them for now. I will hold you responsible if you do not learn within the coming weeks. Understood?"

"Yes, my holiness. Please forgive me."

"Only Allah can forgive you. Don't worry about that now. We will pray together later. We are here on a very important task, Vasilla."

"Is it to pray better?" he asked.

"Don't worry about that now. The woman, Vasilla. This Fatima. Have you been down to the slums?"

"Yes, I've been down there almost every day."

"Did she take notice of you?"

"I think so. I find her very pretty. She's kind of fat too."

"Fat? A woman of the slums? How can she be fat...unless, yes Vasilla, she has to be fat. She's pregnant."

"What child is this, my holiness?"

"You will never understand unless you pray. Once you do it routinely, everything will be made known to you. Understand?"

"Yes, my holiness. Should I get her?"

"Not yet. We must plan this out. Does she know who you are?"

"I don't think so. I was careful. Since I am bigger than most of the slum people, they are afraid of me. My clothes are much nicer than theirs, so they stare a lot."

"Did you notice anyone living with her?"

"They all live together, my holiness. The shacks are the size of their bodies. But I know where this Fatima lives. It's not such a long walk."

"Vasilla, you have done well. Right now I want you to stay away from the slums. We must wait until she gives birth."

"And how long will that be, my holiness?"

"Soon. Giving birth takes time."

"What shall we do now?"

"You will stay in the hotel. Here you will learn how to say prayers without my help."

"Yes, my holiness. But what about you?"

"I must perform a funeral."

"Who has died, my holiness?"

"Stop asking questions. Pray first, and then you shall learn. Do you remember Drakni Drive, my boy?"

"No sir."

"Someone of great importance has died. I shall conduct a funeral. You did well, Vasilla. For once you are using your mind. Finding this slum woman is a miracle. You should be proud of what you've done."

"Oh my holiness, I thank you, I thank you. May you live long..."

"Unbind me! We are not finished!"

After blessing Vasilla, Tariq sped away with his bodyguards towards Drakni Drive. Tariq trusted Vasilla again and felt at ease. He left him a Qu'ran, a step-by-step praying book, and money to pay for the room.

The orange orb hung low in the sky. It settled on the horizon as Tariq traveled to Drakni Drive. His urge was to say his prayers out of routine, to celebrate the victory of the evening over the heat.

The breeze carried a brutal warmth he should have been used to. Imam Shabbir Hussein's home emanated the smells of a dead man. The pungency had increased ten-fold. He pinched his nose. Vultures circled overhead. A flock of ravens flew from bush to bush. Tariq carried a white sack filled with white cloth, vials of non-alcoholic perfumes, and instructions for burial.

He knocked once, then twice.

"Ah, my prayers have been answered," cried Shrika.

"How can you stand it?" asked Tariq.

"Even death is holy, my holiness."

"Death, yes, but this smell? How can you stand it?"

"It doesn't bother me. For years before my dear Imam employed me, I used to smell this smell every day. In a strange way it reminds me of my younger years."

"Oh Shrika, only you could find holiness out of something so repulsive. How long has the body been out?"

"At least a month."

"I should have made it here earlier. Did you disinfect the body? "

"I followed Imam Shabbir's instructions. He said not to touch the body. Wait for the bavasaab to come."

"Oh Shrika, how dare I question you. First, I want every window open."

"And what of the animals outside?"

"At least open one window. I'm about to faint."

"Yes, my holiness. The body is in the next room."

Tariq entered the room filled with big, fat flies and other insects on their way towards the prize: Imam Shabbir's decaying corpse. Tariq covered his nose and coughed. A shroud covered the body. The insects had eaten through the shroud.

"Have you even checked the room in the last month?" he asked.

"Imam Shabbir told me to stay out until you came."

"This is ridiculous. Go in there and kill those insects. It smells so bad."

"I've got the solution. We don't have insect spray, so I'll have to do it the old-fashioned way."

Shrika ran a towel under water. He smiled mischievously.

"And what do you plan to do?" asked Tariq.

"Just leave it to me," he smiled.

The snaps and whips could be heard. The effort was so loud that the bodyguards could hear it as well. One of them rushed in to see if the bavasaab was safe.

After fifteen minutes Shrika emerged from the room, his large towel covered with dead insects.

"There were so many, but the deed is done. Even the smell is gone."

"Good. I can always count on you."

"I'll be in the kitchen making tea. It will help you."

"First we need to wash the body," said Tariq. "Would you like to help me?"

"Oh my holiness, as Allah hears all, I am so very pleased and honored to help you with the rites."

"But where shall we wash the body?"

"How about the kitchen? There's a drain in the corner."

"You must call Sakina and tell her of the news."

"What shall I say?"

"That her husband is dead. I have decided to bury Imam Shabbir in Lahore. I can't risk anyone finding out. We would be attracting more zealots than insects."

"The nearest cemetery is five miles from here."

"Call Sakina and tell her to meet me there. Wait. Don't call her just yet. I need to finish with the preparation of the body."

The stench made him cough and water about the eyes.

"I can't look at this," said Tariq.

"Shall I do it?"

"No, I must do it. The burial must be perfect. On the count of three I will look."

"My holiness, shall I get a pail for you?"

"A pail for what?"

"A pail for vomiting."

"I'm not going to vomit."

"Or pass out?"

"I won't. I can handle this. We must not make a mistake. Ready? One...Two...and Three!"

Tariq pulled the sheet off like a magician. Shortness of breath, an erratic pumping of his heart, and a profound nausea touched him. He then dropped like a puppet. He awoke from his fainting as Shrika dripped ice water over his face.

"What happened?"

"You fainted, my holiness."

"Get the disinfectant. I want this place smelling like roses, but don't spray the body."

"But that's the part that smells."

"Just do as I say."

Shrika disinfected the room, and Tariq paced the hallway. Shrika opened the door a few minutes later.

"It is done, my holiness. The smell has been reduced. We can continue."

To Tariq's delight the smell became bearable. The body, a mere pocket of flesh, the protruding rib cage, the bluish tint of the face, and the matted hair were hastily arranged. They carried the corpse to the kitchen. They covered his privates with a hand towel. Tariq perused the instruction book.

"Okay, first we press the stomach."

A white foam leaked from the mouth.

"This may be disgusting," added Shrika.

"Silence. There is to be no talking."

Shrika filled a pot with warm water. Tariq added to the pot a non-alcoholic perfume, which smelled like pipe smoke. Tariq performed an ablution on the body, washing it thrice and reciting:

"In the name of Allah, the beneficent, the merciful."

Tariq rubbed the teeth and pressed the nose at its ends. He messaged soapy water over the flesh. He continued the wash with his eyes closed but opened them while washing the hair. Shrika dried the corpse and fetched five balls of cotton and stuffed them into each orifice. Tariq covered the body.

"It wasn't that bad," said Tariq, relieved.

"No, my holiness. A clean and dry body, and the soul will be released. What a special day this is."

"Right. I couldn't have done it without you. Call Sakina in Karachi and tell her of the news. We need to secure a plot."

"Imam Shabbir has taken care of that, my holiness."

"Good. Call Sakina and tell her to bring the baby Nisrin."

The body was kept in the kitchen, and soon the house soon smelled like a thick forest.

So many uncertainties. Even Tariq knew thinking ahead never helped. Best to take things step by step. He wished his advisors knew of his worries. He could then blame them if things went wrong. He could tour without cessation, praising a ubiquitous power rather than moving about incognito like a manipulator and Spy, searching for an unborn child. For this he resented Imam Shabbir.

Tariq counted on Vasilla to deal with the most important task. This added to his unease. What type of Twelfth Imam would this child be? Maybe this Fatima is carrying a baby girl, not a boy.

He stayed overnight in the Drakni Drive home. In bed he tried to control the future. He thought of his wife. How badly he wanted to touch her. The road grew old on this first night.

When he arose the next morning, he banged on the bathroom door. Sakina, Imam Shabbir's widow, emerged from the bathroom. At her knees was the baby.

"It is you, sister Sakina. Here so fast?"

Sakina bent to his knees.

"Not now," uttered Tariq as he rushed to the toilet.

After a thorough ablution he wore his most welcoming smile.

"When did you arrive, sister?"

"About twenty minutes ago, my holiness," said Sakina.

"How was the flight?"

"Quick. We haven't been home since Shabbir took ill."

"How does it feel to be back?"

"Better. We are all set to come back home."

"You mean move back in?"

"Yes, my holiness."

"I'm sorry, sister. You and the baby can't stay here."

"Why not?"

"This house will be sold. It will fetch a high price, and all the proceeds will go to you. We will relocate you wherever you wish. But this home will be sold, and with it the memory of your husband."

"I don't understand."

"This house is not glorious enough. As a widow you must learn to live more elegantly and perhaps get married again."

"As you wish, my holiness, but I'm not thinking of marriage."

"I must tell you frankly that Shabbir has been away from us for a month now. It is okay if you wish to marry again. I encourage it. The baby will need a new father."

"Are you sure we can't stay here, my holiness?"

"I'm sorry, but you can't. The believers will know Imam Shabbir had lived here. They will flock here. They will question your whereabouts."

"They won't find us. Drakni Drive is so discreet."

"Trust me. You will be able to live in a better home without being so cramped."

"We want to live here..."

"Well you can't," he snapped. "I'm sorry. The Organization will provide for Shrika as well. You have been a precious figure in Imam Shabbir's life. And so your return on that investment is your choice to live wherever you wish. It doesn't have to be Mecca. It can be anywhere in the Middle East. We will provide you with a home, food, and a servant. Why not take Shrika with you?"

"How about Karachi?"

"An ideal place."

"Can't we bury Shabbir in Karachi? How will we visit his grave?"

"It will always be here. But really I need to perform the burial quietly."

"If that's what you think is best."

"I know it's for the best. Lahore hangs in the balance. The slums grow every day like an incurable disease. The poverty will spill onto these hills. You don't want to live near people of the slums, do you? You must forget this place and reside in a nicer city. Lahore is not the place for you or your daughter."

"But my husband is buried here."

"You no longer have a husband. Don't dwell on it."

"It's so strange without Shabbir."

"How is it strange, sister?"

"Baby Nisrin loved him. When the baby found him praying, she would totter towards him as he prostrated. She would totter close and say prayers with him. Most of us learn the hard way. Some of us are forced to say them at an early age, and if we don't follow, we are scolded or beaten. Others never learn. They lead corrupt lives. But when I saw my daughter and husband praying together, a ritual that turned into their special routine and time together, I thanked Allah.

"My daughter does not understand what happened. She says: 'Time for prayer. Where's daddy?' I keep lying to her, and I let her cry. My mother lets her cry. My sister lets her cry. She falls asleep crying and wakes up asking the same things."

"Why not tell her the truth?"

"She won't understand. She'll forget about Shabbir."

"Over time, sister."

"I keep thinking that. Every morning I wonder where my husband is. Was he in pain? Did he need water? But he sent us away, too proud for us to see him like that."

"Believe me," consoled Tariq, "it is for the best. Don't you feel a release? He has passed on to sit with Allah and all the other Imams. You forget that Shabbir is up there watching us. He is alive. He lives eternally. You shouldn't be upset. You should rejoice. He is in a place so good that we cannot conceive of it. Dry your eyes, sister. There is to be no crying at the funeral."

Tariq looked upon the baby who played by herself.

He took her in his lap. He pinched her cheeks and tried to make her smile. But Tariq was reminded of the child unborn, and he lost the will to hold her.

Shrika rented a carriage drawn by Arabian steeds. The carriage served as the bier. The messenger of Allah said: "if a muslim expires and is then prayed for by three rows of Muslims, his entry into paradise becomes imperative." In the kitchen they could have formed one longer row, but Tariq insisted on having three rows.

"Allah is most great," began Tariq.

"Glory to thee Oh Allah, and Thine is the praise,
And Blessed is thy name, and Exalted is thy
Majesty, and there is no God besides thee.
All praise is due to Allah, the Lord of the worlds,
The compassionate, the Merciful, the Owner of
The Day of Judgment. Thee alone do we worship
And to thee alone we beseech for help.
Guide us on the Right path, the path of those
On whom you have bestowed your favors,
Neither of those upon whom your wrath was
Brought down nor of those who went astray.
-Amen.
Oh Allah! Bless Muhammad and his posterity
As you have blessed Ibrahim and his posterity.
Verily, you are the Praiseworthy and majestic.

Oh Allah! Magnify Muhammad and his posterity.
As you have magnified Ibrahim and his posterity.
Verily you are the Praise-worthy, the Majestic."
"Allah is great," he said again while referring to his instruction book.
"Oh Allah! forgive our living ones and dead ones
And those of us who are present and those who
are absent, and young ones and old ones,
And our males, and females.
Oh Allah! whosoever among us is kept alive by
You, cause him to live in submission to you
And whosoever cause to die, make him die In Faith.
Oh Allah! Do not deprive us of his reward,
(for patience on his loss) and do not make us
Subject to trial after him. Peace be upon you and the mercy of Allah."
The Mercedes followed the bier along Drakni Drive. They crawled up a hill to the cemetary. The graves were packed together, one on top of the other. Somehow Imam Shabbir reserved his plot in advance. Before the body was lowered:

"In the name of Allah and in accordance with The ritual of the Apostle of Allah," said Tariq.

He imagined what his own grave would look like. Plastering the grave was prohibited. He cupped some sods of the dry earth and threw it.

"We created you out of earth. Unto it we shall send thee back. And therefrom you shall be taken out at another time."

The grave resembled the back of a camel.

After Sakina and Nisrin left for Karachi, Tariq called Vasilla at the hotel.

"Hullo?"

"Vasilla, have you been saying your prayers? It's afternoon. Today our holy Imam has been buried."

"Yes, my holiness."

"Now I'm putting you to the test. You have been waiting in Lahore for good reason. You are about to accept the most challenging assignment of your life. You were put on this earth for one thing, and this is it. If you fail, I will never forgive you."

"Yes, my holiness."

"Don't use your real name anymore. Pick a new name, any name."

"How about Tariq?"

"No stupid. Another name."

"Abbas?"

"Excellent. Abbas it is. What made you think of that?"

"It just came to me."

"Do you know who Abbas was?"

"No, I don't think so."

"Of course. I'll tell you that at a later time. For now your name is not Vasilla. It's Abbas."

"Yes, my holiness."

"And Vasilla?"

"Yes, my holiness?"

"Damn you! Your name is Abbas now. You must answer only to Abbas."

"Sorry, my holiness."

"Okay. This is your moment, Vasilla, your moment to carry that water."

"But my name is not Vasilla anymore.

"To me your name is Vasilla. But for this special assignment you will use the name Abbas. You are Abbas Hussein, Imam Shabbir Hussein's younger brother.

"My name is Abbas Hussein."

"Right you are. You are Abbas Hussein. Your task is to bring the young Fatima to Drakni Drive, 116 Drakni Drive."

"That's Imam Shabbir Hussein's home?"

"Yes. Do you remember how to get here?"

"I think so."

"Don't think. Do you know?"

"Yes, my holiness."

"Bring the pregnant Fatima here. Remember you are Abbas Hussein. Your younger brother Shabbir has just died. You want the pregnant Fatima to stay with you until she gives birth. You must be convincing. This is your time. Now what is your name?"

"Abbas Hussein?"

"Excellent. You will live and breathe and be Abbas Hussein. You cannot crack under any circumstances. So after you shower and say your prayers, go to the slums and fetch her, and live with her at Drakni Drive. Make her stay. Don't take 'no' for an answer. Be Abbas Hussein."

"Yes, my holiness."

"If you succeed in this task, there will be a place for you in heaven. Can you handle it?"

"I think so."

"Don't think. Do you know?"

"Yes, my holiness. I am Abbas Hussein, Imam Shabbir's younger brother."

"When she gives birth, call me directly at the hotel. You are to move to Drakni Drive right away. I want you out before I get there."

Chapter Twenty-Four
FATIMA AND VASILLA
12th of Sha'baan 1417
(December 23, 1996)

While pregnancy in the slums was not rare, raising the child with the natural mother was rarer. But Fatima wanted to follow through. The maternal dream was possible as the father had a home on the hills. She was turned away from Drakni Drive, though. Shrika had seen her bloatedness, but like other servants he was no exception.

In the shade Fatima finished her daily inspection of her stomach. She sensed Shabbir Hussein would do everything in his power to support her. After dumping some rice into the pot, she heard a loud knock. She expected Shamima. The sun blinded her for a moment. She encountered this towering figure under a halo of sunshine.

"Are you Fatima?" he asked.

"Who wants to know?"

"My name is Abbas."

"I don't know any Abbas."

"Yes, well, my name is Abbas. I am here to take you to Drakni Drive."

"What about Drakni Drive? I haven't stolen anything."

"I'm sorry. 116 Drakni Drive."

"I don't know who you are."

"I'm sorry, I should have introduced myself. I am Abbas Hussein. You know my younger brother, Shabbir?"

"I do. Why hasn't Shabbir come himself."

"Shabbir is dead."

"Dead? What do you mean he's dead?"

"He died about a month ago."

"I knew he was very sick. What did he die of?"

"We're not sure."

"What will I do?" as tears welled in her eyes.

"Not to worry. That's why I am here. I'm here to take you to our home. I was given instructions by my brother to take care of you, through the pregnancy and after it. The slums is no place for a pregnant woman. Get your stuff together. I'm getting you out of here."

"Shabbir has remembered me?"

"He left not a stone unturned. The house is practically yours. I'll be staying with you."

"Is there enough room?"

"Enough for you and me."

"Can I request another person to live with us?"

"I guess so, but it may get crowded."

"I need Mama Khadija. You'll love her. She's a good friend. She will serve as mid-wife."

"What's a mid-wife?"

"To aid in my pregnancy and birth."

"I see. Sure. Why not? But please, let's hurry."

"Is there some sort of rush?"

"I don't like it down here. Everybody's so poor."

"I can't leave my bags of rice here."

"Leave them. You will have rice and plenty more."

"Seriously?"

"We will have three hearty meals a day, but we must hurry."

"Thanks to Allah above," she said. "What about these extra bags?"

"I'm not carrying those out of the slums."

"You look like you can lift a lot. There are only three bags here."

"Can't you give them to someone?" asked Vasilla.

"I suppose. I'll give them to a friend then."

"It's your rice. But hurry. People are staring."

Fatima tied her clothes in a bundle, and they walked along a trail that grew wider with the incline.

"You don't look anything like your brother," she said. "I mean there is no similarity at all, not in the face and certainly not in the body...I've never seen someone as big as you. Do you exercise? Huh? You don't talk much either. The silent type unless you want out of the slums, right? I'm glad to be leaving the slums, but kind of guilty about it... Where do you come from? Hello? Oh that's a great place. You were born 'nowhere.' If you can't talk, someone has to, right? You see this tiny area over here? In this one area four people sleep. I'm used to it. The people on the hills have it good. Nice house, nice floors, the kitchen, even enough to overfeed a fish. Yes, they have it good. Can you believe there's someone lower than I? The area we just passed is known as the poorest, most diseased place, not just in our country, but in the entire world. Think of that. What would it be like living in the poorest place of

Earth? Can you believe it's Lahore? You really don't talk much...Or am I babbling? Leaving this place is for the best, the best for my baby. I've seen what it's like on the hill. Cars, money, food. Some people never get a chance to set foot on the hills. They just live in the slums, and there they will die. Sad, isn't it? Something has to be done. They say it's growing out of control, and Akbir's men have moved in. Pretty soon there'll be a government plot to exterminate us. The hill folk probably pay the government for it, eh? Hey, wait up!"

The dirt and trash turned to clean pavement.

"Wait. I forgot Mama Khadija."

"We have to go back?" asked Vasilla

"I can pick her up and meet you at Drakni Drive. What's the number? 115?"

"I think it's 116. Hurry. If you're not up there in a half-an-hour, I'll come looking for you."

"Give us an hour. We're slow walkers."

Fatima returned to the slums, which she thought she had lost. She made a break towards the East. A small line had formed at the water pump. Men held empty pails. She praised her bulging stomach for a defense against the cat-calls. As the trail grew narrow, stirring with children, naked and dark from the sun, Fatima arrived at Mama Khadija's small shack.

"Mama Khadija! Mama Khadija!" she yelled.

"Yes, yes, I am here," she replied.

"Mama Khadija!"

"Ah my child, come to me. Why are you shouting? Is something wrong?"

"The greatest thing has happened. I've been invited to live in the hills. Can you believe it?"

"My God, look at you. Your stomach grows each time I see you."

"Can you believe it? I'll be living in the hills, and I have great news: You're coming with me."

"The hills? I've never been there before."

"Now it's time. Finally there is proof Allah exists."

"I'm happy for you. I don't know how you got this place, but for certain Allah has blessed you. You should go and live there. This is what you wanted all along."

"Yes, my baby will be free of this place."

"May Allah bless you. But my child, I cannot go with you."

"Why not?"

"You are too young to understand."

"Then explain it to me. I talk of this every time I see you"

"See, I'm old now. I've lived here all my life, ever since I could remember. My mother lived here, my grandmother lived here, even my great grandmother lived here. I have no need for the hills. I belong here with my people. You know the difference between the hills and the slums. I don't. I've been living here all my life. I know my way around. I know my neighbors, I have tea and rice..."

"But you lost a son to these damned slums, and Akbir's men have grown strong."

"Whatever happened and whatever is happening now is in the hands of Allah."

"It's not rational. You know how bad these slums are. It's a death machine. It eats people up, and the ones who survive run away from it. Eventually it catches up to them. People spend their lives running from its jaws. And in the process all their possessions or even the thought of having possessions is taken away from them. Now I have a chance of living in the hills, and I'm taking it, and I want you to come with me."

"I can't."

"Why not?"

"You wouldn't understand."

"Then make me understand. There is nothing here. Not one thing."

"This is where I belong. I take care of the children. Everything is here. I am comfortable here, and before long I will die here. The generations before me will have died here. I shall die with dignity. I will end the line. I have a great deal of pride living here."

"There is nothing dignified about it."

"Then accept that Allah has meant it to be this way."

"Allah? You can't be serious. Are we talking about the same Allah? What is it with you? Allah this, Allah that. I'm sick of hearing that word. You leave everything up to Allah, and then you're stuck here. I can't understand that kind of thinking. I may be young, but anyone with a dose of smarts knows that Allah may control all things and all people and all that you dream of becoming, but you have the freedom to determine your own outcome, even when Allah is a cruel heart himself. You can't rely on Allah. Don't you think he has better things to do? Allah, fine, once in a while when we have no where to turn, or when we are starving or being shot by one of Akbir's men. But Allah determining our entire life? This same Allah who has sentenced us to life in these wicked slums? Worship Allah, fine. Praise his name, fine. Like a parent he guides us. Not like some evil despot.

"Whether we agree or disagree is not the point. I'm asking you now, please, you must come with me and try for a better life. No where is it written that you must sacrifice all that you are. If you won't do this for me, do it for this baby. And if you miss the slums so much, you can visit here any time you like."

"How have you learned to be so convincing? Allah has been giving you words in your sleep?"

"No. Allah has given us both the opportunity to live the good life. There is nothing left here."

Their conversation was cut short by the boiling water which spilled over the sides of the pot. They sipped their tea from paper cups.

"Okay. I'll do it," said Mama Khadija finally, "but only if you promise I can return after the pregnancy."

"You'll do it? You'll really do it for my baby?"

"Not only for the baby but for you as well."

When they arrived at Drakni Drive, Fatima noticed for the first time that this Abbas was extremely handsome. His heavy arms and legs bulged with the strength of Arabian steeds. She searched for a security he could provide. Her attraction came on slowly but grew stronger. She thought about letting him know but remembered that she was a slum woman, and a man as handsome and well endowed as he may never want a woman so poor and pregnant. She kept this attraction inside and acted the part of the congenial sister who talked with him after meals.

She cooked the food after he did the grocery shopping during the hot afternoons. He purchased more than needed and made sure she was well fed.

She wanted to reveal her longing. Yet it would destroy the sweet rapport they had built. She tried hard to talk about different things and discovered how this strong man remained quiet and silent around her.

What did men look for? A beautiful face and body? Periodically during the day, Fatima would check herself in the mirror. She sucked in her stomach, even though it bulged with an infant inside. Perhaps men looked for social standing, and in this area she thought she failed as well. But underneath that attraction, she wanted security. She realized this suddenly at the dinner table one night. For a man to have her, the man needed to have the child in mind also. With a steady calculation, Fatima prepared to ask how he felt about the child, but not in the usual sense. She would ask as a soul genuinely enamored of this strong man who appeared at her hovel like the angel who catches the downtrodden soul from a free-fall.

"I don't know what's going to happen," she said at dinner one night.

Mama Khadija had gone to bed, leaving the two to their nightly discussion.

"It will be all right," said Vasilla.

"You seem so sure. I hope you're right."

"I know I'm right. You are almost ready to deliver the baby. You should feel blessed."

"Oh Abbas, you have been so good to me. What will happen when the time comes to leave?"

"I'm tired," yawned Vasilla. "I better get to bed."

"So early? How can you be so tired?"

"It's been a long day. I need some sleep."

"Tell me once more, before you go."

"Tell you what?"

"That everything will be okay, even if the baby has no father."

"Yes, Fatima. Everything will be all right."

"I'm so worried."

"There is no need to worry."

"Abbas, I have to ask you something, and I want an honest answer."

"What is it?"

"The baby. The father has passed on. For so many nights it's been tough getting to sleep. Once the baby is born, he or she, I don't care, I will have to support it somehow. Once the baby is born you will turn me out?"

"That time has not come yet."

"Just answer me. Will you turn us out? Are we to go back to the slums?"

"It's getting late, Fatima."

"Answer me first and then go. This baby is your nephew. Will you turn us out?"

"I must sleep."

She grabbed his arm.

"Answer me. Don't tell me we are to go there ever again. All this while I've been keeping a secret. I've been meaning to ask you, but you never tell me what you're thinking. It's like I'm the one doing all the talking. I need to know, Abbas. I need to know so that I may prepare. What will happen after the baby is born?"

"Let me think it over. I would never leave you without a place to go. You are almost ready to give birth. I would not leave you now, and I won't leave you afterwards. I must think now. I will sleep on it. Don't worry. We will plan a future for you and your baby."

"You're still not answering me."

"I promise, Fatima," he said in the soft light. "You and the baby will be taken care of."

"Can we live here? All of us together?"

"I'm not sure."

"Then what's possible?"

"We'll see. It's hard to tell at this point."

"I have to know. I can't go on wishing for things. I've been doing that for too long."

"Let's wait until the child is born."

"Abbas, if I ask you something, will you take it into consideration?"

"Depends on what you're asking."

"It's hard for me to tell you, but over the weeks we've been living together, I finally have, oh how do you say it?, I've finally come to terms with your brother. I've let him go. Shabbir will never come back. I know that now, and that spell has gone away largely due to you. Just talking, you and I, alone, away from others, has made me face the reality that this baby will be born without a father. Unless, of course, you agree to help me...raise the child."

"I don't have any money."

"Money is not the issue. I could have all the money in the world. It would help. I can't deny that. What this child really needs, however, will take more than a house of gold, a brand new car, and a ton of rice. What this baby needs, Abbas, is a father, someone to look up to and learn from. I never had a father..."

"Me neither."

"You never had a father?"

"I mean, I'm not sure what I mean, but I understand what you're saying."

"Are you sure? I want you to help raise the baby. I'm asking you, no, I'm begging you. We've been living here, a beautiful house away from the misery, and for a while that's all I thought was really needed. But I know better. This child needs a man. I'm asking a lot, but I want you to serve as his true uncle but raise him like your own son."

"I don't think..."

"Don't answer now. Just think it over. I want you to be part of our family. Sleep on it if you have no answer."

"I would never leave you alone."

"Then accept the offer."

"It's late, Fatima. I need some sleep."

She lay awake that night. The silence bothered her, and her fantasies moved from simple to grandiose. She dreamt of living in the house with this man and cooking his meals. She saw in the hazy distance an handsome father playing cricket with her son, or if the child were a girl, a handsome father buying a pink dress for her and strolling on the highest of hilltops. Then she doted on her daughter's wedding, the grandest in the city, with many rich and important people greeting the bride and groom on a stage covered with sweet-smelling orchids.

After a while of moving in countless positions, she determined she wanted to run away with this Abbas. She wanted him to love her. The need for love and to be loved was the essential part of a woman's purpose; a need to be fulfilled by love, not just passed over like scrap metal in a junkyard, but to move along with love.

The next morning Fatima answered the phone. The call was for Abbas, and the voice was curt and urgent. She took her time as though exacting a price for the caller's abruptness.

"Wake up, Abbas," she said.

Vasilla refused and rolled to his other side. She moved closer and ran her fingers through his thick hair.

"Wake up," she said again.

"What is it?"

"There's a phone call for you."

"Take a message."

"It might be important."

"Who is it?"

"I don't know."

She ran her hands over his muscles as a single sheet separated him from nudity.

"I don't want to answer it," he said. "I have a bad feeling about it."

"Want me to say you're not here?"

"No. I'll take the call."

She lay on his warm pillow. Her days of insecurity had been replaced by comfort. She inspected the stretch marks cutting across her like incisions from a scalpel, each ridge representing her gestation as though they were earned like credits. She put much of that behind her. In the darkness she searched for answers.

"What's the matter?" she asked when Vasilla returned.

"Nothing."

"Then why do you look so angry? Who was it?"

"A friend of mine."

"What did he say?"

"Nothing important."

"Then why so gloomy?"

"I'm tired."

Fatima made room on the bed. She lay next to him and nuzzled close.

"Don't be angry," she said. "Any day our child will come."

"Our child?"

"Yes. You agreed to it, didn't you?"

"Your baby shall have the finest food, the finest clothes, the finest place to play..."

"Tell me more, Abbas, more."

"He shall live in this house."

"Or she."

"He will eat lamb when he wakes up. He will be satisfied with the food. He will fall asleep in the crib."

"What type of crib will it be?"

"The finest crib, made of sanded wood, and up over his head will be a set of toys hanging in the air."

"A mobile?"

"Yes, and the baby will be so happy looking at red, green, yellow, and blue. Such little hands he will have."

"Or she," said Fatima.

"He will giggle when I pick him up. He shall have the best of everything. We'll put him on the high chair, and you will scoop the mush and feed him the food. You will put him in the sink and wash his soft body with warm water."

"And you?"

"I will teach him how to say his prayers, to respect the All Mighty Allah, and to work hard like a good Muslim. He will go to the school and graduate from the finest university, top of his class."

"He will have the nicest cars," said Fatima, "the nicest clothes, and most glamorous friends. He will go to the greatest parties and marry the greatest woman in the Middle East. And Mama Khadija will be his grandmother."

"He will play cricket and field hockey and excel in all sports."

"Most of all, this child will have a father."

That afternoon she felt something break within her: a sluice which refused to hold conspiratorial waters. She entered the kitchen, and to her quiet confusion a warm liquid gushed between her thighs.

"Go to the toilet if you have to urinate," yelled Vasilla. "Who's going to clean that up?"

She stood petrified, and suddenly screamed:

"Mama Khadija! Mama Khadija!"

"What's the matter?" yelled Vasilla.

"Go get Mama Khadija!"

"Let her sleep. Why wake her?"

"Get her now!"

"What for?"

"I have no time to argue! Get her now!"

"I will, just relax."

"Hurry, Abbas, hurry!"

He returned with the sleepy Mama Khadija. She inspected the liquid between Fatima's feet.

"It's time," she said.

"Time for what?" asked Vasilla.

"Abbas, I need a pile of towels and wash cloths. Wet some of them with warm water and make them into compresses. Get some plastic. Get some shoe strings and a pair of sharp scissors, and get a wide bowl.

"What are compresses?"

"Get them now! Don't be afraid," she said to Fatima. "Everything will be just fine."

"Is she sick or something?" asked Vasilla.

"No Abbas. Quite the contrary."

And Mama Khadija shut the door.

Chapter Twenty-Five
BIRTH
3rd of Shabanul Karim 1417
(December 25, 1996)

Pain. A knee in the groin. The ankle twisting on a misshapen rock. The fingers caught in a car door. The toe which bangs against a table leg. The elbow which can no longer swing the tennis racket. The whiplash from a tailgating taxicab. The stomach after spices. The heart pumping through hardening arteries. The liver diluting whiskey. Coughing from blackened lungs. The lower back straining upon a lumpy mattress. The hip which fractures while slipping on ice.

Or is it a splintered paddle against a warm rump? Needles poking a vein. A bone shooting through the thigh. The skull cracking from a lead pipe. A razor slicing the wrist. A bat shattering a knee. A whip stripping the skin. An ax falling on a tender foot. Scissors across a nervous tongue. An intruder ripping the hymen. A hanging from a leather belt. A bullet through the fleshy brain. A cold spike through the eye. Electricity burning the cytoplasm of cells.

Fire eating the skin. The cleaver dismembering the hand of a thief. Beating the chest on the holiest of holidays. Shrapnel from a bomb blast.

Or is it a woman giving birth?

"A boy," whispered Mama Khadija into her ear.

She held up the baby covered with vernix.

Later Fatima awoke in the darkness, ignorant of the time. She intended to hold her baby. She switched on the dim light, and saw beside the bed a small cushion made to hold his tiny body. But no baby. To her left Mama Khadija snored within the comforts of sleep. Fatima opened the door and found the household dark. Her shadow stretched along the dark corridor. She walked to the next room. She felt for the light, flicked it on, but no Abbas, no newborn. She could feel her heart beating, then pumping like a steam train on its inaugural run. Pumping harder as she entered the kitchen. Still no Abbas, still no baby. She checked the clock in the empty bedroom. Three in the morning. Her heart pumped faster. She checked the entire household a second time, then a third time, turning on and off familiar light switches and canvassing each area. In a wave of profound fear which comes from crossing the land of the dead, she shrieked in the hot darkness:

"Where's my baby? Oh God, where's my baby?"

Chapter Twenty-Six
TARIQ AND THE IMAM
15th of Sha'baan 1417
(December 26, 1996)

In the cool Lahorian hotel room, Tariq Bengaliwala held the precious, miniature Imam in his arms. The baby was wrapped in a soft woolen blanket. The baby did not stir but slept soundly, his eyes closed. Tariq noticed how the dead and the newborn were similar in their stillness. He was afraid of dropping the poor infant by mistake. He brought the baby to his breast as a mother does. He did not see this baby as a human being, like his son Khozem or his wife Samira. This baby Imam transcended the mere folly of mortals. He looked into his tiny face and understood that this indeed was the face of God, the face of Allah, brought to earth in human form, and within this small, breathing being, sleeping as the world kept spinning, as chaos brewed on every frontier of the Islamic world, he found an ounce of hope that things would turn his way, that things would finally work themselves out just as Imam Shabbir Hussein had planned.

He looked to Vasilla who sat on the bed and stared out the window. Vasilla did not respond to Tariq's quick show of admiration and affection.

Tariq brushed his fingers against the features of this young newborn: his tiny ears and sprouts of dark hair, his small lips as tender and soft as the warm sands of Iran. Along his face he pinched a fragile chin. Tariq's worrying flurried into the air, and as the worry escaped, he smiled again and rubbed his forefinger along the baby's cheek. How soft that skin, a skin soon to be weathered by the wind and cold of the Americas, a skin that would one day be kissed by a beautiful Arabian bride.

Tariq hoped to watch this child's full life unfold. This precious Imam, crafted by the gentle hands of Allah, sent down to earth and placed within the womb of a poor cleaning woman, represented not only the fate of Islam but also the fate of Tariq himself. Tariq saw his own life returned to youth, a time of imagination, wonder, and amazement. This Imam would experience this, and all the while he would be protected by the full powers of Tariq's office. Every cry, every scream, each success and failure would be carefully monitored.

Tariq chose first rate adoptive parents for him, but a brief thought entered his mind like the flash of Lahorian sun between the curtains. Tariq wanted to keep this Imam to himself. He wanted to hold him forever in the comforts of his arms and forget about his responsibilities, forget about murdering more Hidus and keeping strict watch over his son in Cairo. He suddenly saw these activities as failures. A quiet guilt surfaced.

Tariq had wondered in solitude why the world must be the way it is. Why must men have so many flaws and short-comings? But this small package would send messages of perfection across the globe. This child would be perfect, he thought. This child shall never stray from the appointed path. He would pray with others in duty, and he would serve Allah and deliver his message with all the might in his small body. Such a package would strike fear into the hearts of men. Such a glorious little package held the fate of all Shia Islam. This small package would preserve the traditions of all the peoples of Islam who knelt before him. Oh how could anyone not have faith? What is faith but a true extension of Allah?

In the Lahorian hotel room, Tariq wondered where his faith was leading him. He believed the All Mighty worked towards some fantastic end, and no matter how many Hindus he had killed at that terrible emergency meeting, no matter how he had killed Rashida, he knew Allah had the killings arranged. The killings helped this small bundle he held in his arms. Oh glorious day, the Imam had finally arrived, and Khozem would be his servant from afar. How could anything possibly go wrong?

Tariq treasured the silence of the baby Imam's slumber as well as the silence of Vasilla's absent mind. Tears welled in Tariq's eyes, tears of relief stemming from years of frustration and tense emotion, like the violin strings which break from playing too hard. This new Imam would lead the righteous and conquer the pagans. This Imam would be the greatest Imam, the Twelfth Imam, to suck up the West drunk with its false power. 'So very tiny,' thought Tariq.

He had much work to do. He had been asked to tour Indonesia but was reluctant. His mind would never focus on the task. He could never leave his post until his son Khozem finished his training.

He decided to send Vasilla to New York. Vasilla would watch and guard the baby Imam. As soon as Tariq arrived home in Mecca he would pack his bags and fly off, sit and kneel and pray in front of a chanting crowd, brown automatons bowing and kneeling and hanging their paltry lives on his every word. He preferred the solitude of the hotel room. In solitude a man touches the inner most part of his being, and once that entity is touched there is no longer an acceptable return. He held his faith. The plan had been successful.

He noticed Vasilla with tears in his eyes. He assumed they were tears of profound happiness. Imam Shabbir's plan was now set in motion. Every deed, every thought, every action would now be utilized for the preservation of this Imam. He would work not for himself but for this small bundle.

"Vasilla," said Tariq. "I'm sending you to New York."

"Where?" asked Vasilla through his tears.

"To New York. To the United States."

"But I know nothing of New York."

"Then you'll learn. Don't argue with me."

"Yes, your holiness."

As the blazing sun began to set, they checked out of the hotel room and flew back to Mecca. Tariq was happy to make it home. He reluctantly passed the baby Imam to his wife who immediately showered it with affection. The baby was placed in a small wooden crib in their bedroom. Tariq prayed in the living room and said the verses forcefully as though a new spirit had grown inside of him. He then retreated to the bedroom and gazed upon the baby Imam in his crib.

"What will you name him?" asked Samira softly.

"We'll name him Mustafa."

"Why Mustafa?"

The view of the grand mosque no longer fascinated him. Instead he attached himself to this small divine creature.

"He's so beautiful," said Samira.

"I've never seen anything so beautiful," said Tariq.

"How long will he stay?"

"Not long. The adoptive parents are flying in tomorrow."

"From where?"

"The United States."

Tariq met the adoptive parents in his study the next morning as Samira prayed in the Kaa'bah. The husband wore a bright silk tie. He had a narrow face with highly defined cheekbones. A stringy moustache adorned his upper lip. A blue, pinstriped business suit covered him. His wife dressed in a colorful duppurta.

Together the couple did not look pleasing to the eye. They seemed odd, as the husband was thin in places, plump in others, especially under the chin. His wife was scrawny and emaciated. Tariq knew this couple was not very pleasing to behold, but they were wealthy and appeared very devout. Tariq knew, had they been beautiful aesthetically, they would have never been so devout. Not that religion attracts the ugly, but most who cling to the messages of Allah don't exude such pleasing features. Tariq looked them over suspiciously. This couple may have been too young to be so devout. On paper they were ideal adoptive parents, but Tariq saw something quite different, as though this couple emanated a noticeable sorrow. Of course Tariq had to be extremely protective. He wasn't about to relinquish the baby immediately. They both gave Tariq salaams. They sat in two cushioned chairs opposite his desk.

"I want to make it absolutely clear that this baby is the most important child to me. Not only do I consider him my flesh and blood, but also my superior. I'm not about to lie and say that this child means nothing, or that this child represents one baby out of six billion. No. This child represents our religion, our creed, and our faith in Allah. Allah alone has protected this child even before its birth. It has taken many pains and many lives for him to be with us. So let me be perfectly clear. This is not an ordinary baby. He is your baby, yes, but I am only loaning him to you. You will be his guardian and sponsor in the United States, and quite frankly I don't think highly about your part of the world. Your part of the world has about as much morality as a rat in the gutter. This child must be protected from all of that. We will provide for his education, his clothes, his food. Never forget who guards him, because it is not you. It is I. If anything happens to this child, the responsibility will fall on your heads. I can't express to you what this child means."

The couple looked at each other in surprise, and then the husband said to Tariq:

"Your holiness, why choose us? America is a very different place. Are you sure we can handle such a task?"

"Do you pray the required times?" asked Tariq.

"Of course."

"Do you contribute immensely to our Organization's fund?"

"Yes, but…"

"In other words, and excuse me for interrupting you, are you devout Muslims through and through?"

"We consider ourselves Muslims through and through…"

"Fine. You have just answered your own question. You have been chosen over thousands of other couples. I personally decided that you would best serve this child."

"The child is special, yes, but we didn't count on him being so special," said the husband. "Just to be honest with you, my holiness, maybe we are not the right couple. We had no idea what this child means to you. Again, America is a very different place. I guess I need to know why this child is so important. He's important to us, because he is our son. But you make it sound as though this child is the king of some country," said the husband grinning.

"Are you mocking me?" asked Tariq.

"No, your holiness, but in all honesty, maybe we are not the right parents for this…"

"So you are disobeying my request then?" asked Tariq with more force.

"No, your holiness, it's just that…it's just that…"

"Just what?!"

"C'mon," said the husband to his wife quietly. "I think we should go."

The wife nodded in agreement. They stood from their seats until Tariq said:

"Wait, just wait, please," and Tariq smiled cordially. "America must be a very different place, you're right. Obviously my Saudi tactics don't work very well with foreigners. I didn't mean to build the child up so much, but please understand it from my point of view."

"We're just trying to be honest with your holiness," said the husband.

"This child," said Tariq softly, "is an Imam."

"There are many Imams here and elsewhere. So what?"

Tariq controlled the urge to smack the husband outright.

"I know that," continued Tariq, "but there's a difference between the Imams who are everyday clerics, and a twelfth Imam spawned from the blood of our Caliphate Ali."

"You mean?"

"Exactly. I wasn't sure whether or not to tell you such a secret, but now you know. This child, Allah's child, the greatest of grandsons of Ali, is indeed the twelfth Imam Al-Mustafa, returned to this earth in flesh and in blood."

A silence crept into Tariq's study. The couple neither moved nor uttered a word for some time. Tariq returned to his desk and sat in his chair.

"Can you at least see why this child means so much?" asked Tariq.

"Oh dear," muttered the husband. "Why America? Why us?"

"Because this child's father, the Eleventh Imam, Imam Shabbir Hussein, has decreed it, and I am here to carry out that order."

"What if we can't accept this child?" asked the husband.

"You have little choice in the matter, because you were picked from the best of four couples. You represent the best of the best, and I won't settle for anyone else. I have more confidence in you now that you've expressed your doubts about America, and about being his guardian. You must take this child and make a home and a family for him."

They again sat in silence. The intense Arabian sun flooded the small area. Tariq stared into the Kaa'bah again where a light crowd circumambulated the House of Allah. Scattered people lounged under the wide awnings of the grand mosque.

"There is one very important caveat, however," said Tariq finally.

"Anything, your holiness."

"I know America is morally bankrupt. I understand there is nothing of value there. I realize all those Westerners drink the blood of their mothers after butchering them. Believe me when I say that I understand America and their false Gods, so I say this to you with that truth and wisdom very clear in mind. Should you ever separate or divorce, the child returns to me."

"I love my wife dearly," said the husband as they clasped hands. "That will never happen."

"I hope not, but if you ever divorce or separate, you will give the child back to me. Understood?"

This couple looked at each other in bewilderment, and Tariq wondered why the wife looked so sullen, almost withdrawn from the entire conversation. While it was customary for the men to talk business and the women to mother children, Tariq found it strange the wife had nothing to say. She merely looked at her husband in tacit agreement.

He was unsure of them. He only knew they looked odd together, like a skull cap on a Sunni muslim or a winter's coat in the hot desert. He assumed they hid something. Within the wife's silent repose there lurked a secret or mystery, some darkness or trauma. She should be submissive to the husband, yes, yet she had not uttered a single word throughout this revelation.

"Yes, we understand," said the husband.

"Good, I knew you would. Many pains have been taken to deliver this child to you. Have him grow up as a most pious muslim. Count on me to help out whenever I can, although I'm touring Indonesia in the coming months."

Tariq was worried. He couldn't just leave the small creature with this couple and then bolt to Indonesia. At first Tariq decided to delay the trip, but now the decision became final. He would send Vasilla to guard this precious Imam. Vasilla had already proven himself by delivering the baby Imam in the first place. Despite having made mistakes, Vasilla developed into a bodyguard of skill, able to handle solitary missions. Tariq trusted him, not as a man alone, but as a component of his high faith in Allah. Yes, the plan had worked. All that stress paid off. For his divine plan to succeed, however, Tariq had to rely also on this sullen and homely couple admiring the view of the Kaa'bah below.

So many things could go wrong with this couple, but that was not the foundation for his fear. The fear rested in the pervasive culture of the West, the Americas, the epicenter of this powerful industrial culture, mass producing heathens, discarding their moral fiber and religious discipline. The culture itself may thwart all of his plans. He was afraid. His fight then was not with this poor excuse for a couple sitting in front of him. Rather he concerned himself with the American culture itself and how it may transform the young child. Tariq deemed New York City a vast wasteland of social and moral ineptitude.

The husband and wife held hands, and Tariq speculated that they held hands more in fear than in genuine affection.

"Would you like to see the child?" asked Tariq.

They both nodded.

"Wait here."

The Imam no longer slept. His eyes stared nervously into creation. Tariq scooped him into his arms and kissed him.

He carried the Imam to the study. The couple stood from their chairs.

"I present to you Imam Al-Mustafa, twelfth Imam of our Shia race."

With a reluctance surging trough his entire body, he handed the baby to the new adoptive mother.

"He's beautiful," she said.

"I can't believe it," said the husband. "We shall call him Mustafa you said?"

"Yes," replied Tariq. "I will be sending an allowance to you every month for his schooling, his food, his clothing, and health care. Make sure he gets all those immunization shots, although I'm not sure if we can immunize him from the West, now that he's a part of it. If anything goes wrong, you will contact Vasilla, my chief associate. I'll be away for some time, but my wife will be here. You may contact me at my home as well. Once again, I can't express the importance of this child. He shall be leading our faith. In a few years time, my son Khozem will be taking over my position. The transition should be a smooth one. When he grows I want him to marry well, and I will be arranging that…"

"What if he likes an American woman?" asked the father flippantly.

Tariq froze with surprise and fear. He gawked at the couple for a few moments. His surprise then settled into a form of contemplation. He was sure the husband meant a white American woman.

When Tariq had visited the Americas several years ago, he too could not hide his attraction for these white creatures. Many of them had curves, and they were very thin, almost pale. He remembered one he had seen along a city street, a young woman in her mid-twenties. He wanted passionately to hate her as he hated all persons of the West. But something within his heart shuddered while glancing at this woman from his Mercedes. He understood that white women from abroad had this peculiar supremacy about them. Even in Jeddah he had seen magazine covers lauding these white faces. Their natural elegance and beauty fueled his hatred. He hated the woman immediately. He wanted neither to speak to her nor touch her. The woman minded her own business. She walked mechanically, heading for work or out for a drink. Even Tariq was not immune to the white conception of beauty, a beauty pervasive and insidious, rotting the infrastructure of his soul. He hated their hold on his culture. He remembered her taut breasts, her hair falling over her confident shoulders, her eyes reflecting the Atlantic Ocean. Many in Arabia thought these white creatures devils. On the outside they attracted the hearts of all colors, but on the inside they had not an ounce of integrity, not an ounce of duty towards God.

"The Imam shall never marry a white American woman," said Tariq. "Besides, they know nothing but white men. They aggrandize their own beauty, and the Imam Mustafa, being of dark skin, shall never consort with these white Americans, not because he does not find them beautiful or filled with a false and meandering personality, but for the sole fact that they would never associate with him in the first place. As parents you should teach him to love his own kind. You are a devout Muslim couple, so I expect you to show him the beauty of his own skin, not the white skin which smells of garbage, which pierces like sharp nails, which bites like an asp. Imam Mustafa will have no time anyway. He'll be studying Arabic and attending religious schools. You will have him play with people strictly of his own race. America is no longer the interracial stew it used to be. Its citizens recognize that people of one skin belong in one area, and people of another skin belong in another."

"But I have white friends," said the husband. "Some of them are good friends, my holiness. Some of these white friends I work with, and some of them I spend some leisure time with…"

"How devout are you?" asked Tariq. "This child must command all of your attentions now. You must slowly break your connections with the white menace. How will this baby Mustafa learn of his own kind? Allah has created people of different skin colors for different reasons, that is to associate amongst themselves, to learn from each other, to thwart those who are not right and just, and in the many laws which govern this earth, Allah and his prophet and this baby Imam are the only elements which are right and just. Change your lifestyle. Change your shoddy business practices and friendships with the white disease…"

"But doesn't Islam incorporate all colors?"

"Yes and no. Allah's will is to perpetuate the species, not divide us and break us. Yes, the white color of skin is accepted within Islam, but no, these colors must remain separate. I don't make the rules. I just follow them."

"This would mean an entire change in lifestyle. I may have to leave work."

"That's exactly how you should be thinking, and I am available to you for that sole.purpose. The funds of the organization are open to you and your wife."

"I don't know what to say," said the husband.

"Don't say a thing. Just follow my instructions."

"What shall we tell our friends?"

"That they are no longer your friends."

"We have to tell them something. I just can't pick up and leave my business and my hard-earned money."

"Money is hardly the issue. Don't you understand? You are now living for the Imam. Let's say that he is now the center of your universe, and raising him won't be easy. No one must ever know he is the Twelfth Imam, especially Mustafa himself. My son will tell him when the time is right. If you do so, you will jeopardize the life of the boy."

"Maybe we should think this over."

Tariq left the husband and wife in his study and went into the living room. This couple was too Westernized, he thought. This couple may not be the perfect pair he had hoped for. But he recalled Imam Shabbir Hussein's dying words: this Imam Mustafa must learn of Islam on his own. But then he had two important safeguards, two important mechanisms for control over the twelfth Imam's life. First, Vasilla would be monitoring their every move, and if anything went wrong, Vasilla would protect his interests. Second, the couple had agreed that should they separate or divorce, the baby Imam would return to Mecca. This was acceptable. He no longer worried about his suspicions over the couple. Within his heart a weight lifted.

Tariq knew he had done right under the All Mighty, that his efforts would be rewarded in the heavens, but then the fear and worry jumped back in him. He no longer held the strings. This baby Imam would be guided directly by them. Tariq would have little direct say. Better to trust Allah's will, he thought, not his own strategies. And with a sigh Tariq decided to stick with this couple from the United States. As long as Imam Mustafa was raised a devout muslim, his son Khozem would have little problem implementing Imam Shabbir's visions and plans.

Tariq knew the future of Islam did not necessarily rest with the Imam's actions. After all, how much can one individual do in a land so morally uncouth? From the Middle East, Khozem would put the Imam's visions into action, making the illusion real. Tariq did not count on Imam Mustafa to change the United States. Tariq was too much of a realist to fall for that. Let there be then a thirteenth Imam and a fourteenth Imam sprung from the loins of Imam Mustafa. But what of Imam Shabbir's prophecy?

Tariq recalled Shabbir Hussein's words. What of the flags? What of the holy wars? What of the full glory to be gained under Islam? Tariq had to figure this out, but the heavens helped him little on this day. He could not envision the West with the new Imam implanted there. He had grown so accustomed to his own methods of solving problems. And now he would tour Indonesia.

Tariq contemplated in the living room. The husband and wife emerged from his study. The wife held the infant close to her breast.

"We have decided to do all that you request," said the husband solemnly. "In the next year or so we will break our ties with most of our friends and associates, so that this Imam may learn the wisdom of Islam. I'm sorry to have been so standoffish before, but we Westerners are so up-front about things. Before we undertake the task of raising this child, however, there is something we must know. Who are his real parents?"

"Imam Shabbir has died, and the mother died while giving birth to him. You have nothing to worry about. You must raise this child under the impression that you are his true parents."

"We accept this great responsibility, your holiness. Please bless us and this child."

"As I said, I have taken the liberty of sending one of my closest associates to New York. His duty will be to help you should any emergency occur. Feel free to call on him at any time. He will be living near you in the same neighborhood. You should meet with him once a month to talk to him on how things are progressing for you and the young Imam. Vasilla, my chief bodyguard. He alone will be distributing the Organization's allowances for the blessed child. Please meet with him as often as you like. He reports directly to me."

The engineered family left for Jeddah International airport with Tariq's full blessings. Tariq immediately summoned Vasilla who waited with the other bodyguards in the parking lot. Vasilla clumsily tripped over a fold in the carpet. He then stood at attention. Tariq resumed his authoritarian style.

"Are you ready for New York, Vasilla?"

"Yes, my holiness."

"This family, according to my records, lives on Second Avenue in downtown Manhattan. They have a penthouse suite atop this great multi-level building. When you get to New York, move into an apartment nearby. Set up a bank account. The Organization's accounting office will be sending you funds on a regular basis. Keep a very close watch over this couple. Something strikes me funny about them. I don't need to tell you how important your next assignment is. I will be touring Indonesia for the next few months, and while I'm away I want nothing to go wrong. Watch this couple with scrutiny. Not only am I counting on you, but Allah is counting on you as well. Say your prayers daily, and if anything goes wrong, call me through the complex at Jeddah. Are we clear?"

"Yes, your holiness."

From his study Tariq retrieved airline tickets and a passport.

"These are all the necessary documents," said Tariq. "Don't disappoint me. Watch them. Always have them on your mind. You are not only there to serve them but also to report to me should anything curious happen. Beware of America, Vasilla. It's a terrible place. People there are heathens. Don't fall into any traps. Do not touch their liquor or loose women. Stay devout and follow the appointed path."

Book Two

"Woman must not depend upon the protection of man, but must be taught to protect herself." -Susan B. Anthony

Chapter One
THE HOMECOMING
17th of SHa'baan 1417
(December 28, 1996)

When seen through a window of an airplane, high above in the misty clouds, Manhattan distinguishes itself by its twin towers, or the World Trade Center, jutting its mammoth hunk of steel and glass through the haze like a modern tower of Babel reaching towards God.

In the plane Maryam, the adoptive mother, held the baby Imam to the window so that he may see this incredible marvel of man, not only the towers themselves but the buildings surrounding them. Maryam never knew how man had built such a city. She thought man had a desperate need to produce instead of consume, create instead of devour, and these nervous fits of production and accomplishment resulted, with speed and with grace, this enormous complex called Manhattan, always expanding as exemplified by these buildings. She knew the baby Imam would never remember such a sight, but she held him to the window just in case.

"This is our home," she whispered into his ear.

The journey lasted seventeen hours. Maryam and her husband, Quraysh, were glad to be over with it, and when she gazed through the plastic windows upon those buildings of Manhattan piercing the sky, a joy seeped into her heart, and she hoped a similar joy possessed the baby Imam as well.

The plane veered from the Manhattan skyline and touched down safely at Kennedy International Airport. The passengers clapped in relief as the plane finally landed. While taxiing on the runway, Maryam saw fields of grass intersected by tarmac, placards in pilot-speak fixed to the ground, and other planes rolling to other destinations.

After crawling through customs where officials stamped their passports, after waiting on a long serpentine line, Quraysh and Maryam were finally free to collect their baggage, hail a taxi, and speed along the Van Wyck Expressway towards Manhattan. The winter had left its mark upon the terrain. A brownish snow covered the sides of the highway, and the air carried a Northerly chill. The city had been overtaken by a bitter cold. Luckily Maryam and Quraysh dressed properly in heavy wool jackets. They wrapped the baby Imam in an additional woolen blanket.

In the taxi Maryam held the baby Imam and had already fallen in love with him. She did not know what Quraysh thought of the new member of the family. He seemed quiet and distant in the plane and now in the taxi. She could sense neither a happiness nor sadness, but she at least knew this small child brought back an elusive purpose to her life, and that main purpose, which had been dreadfully missing, was to become a mother, since Maryam could not have children herself.

Her days had been a tumult of loss. She was born in Surat, India, and she had developed into the care-taker of her own family. Her mother died shortly after her birth. She loved her father dearly. He had died mysteriously of a heart attack when Maryam was sixteen. As a care-taker she gave her three brothers nothing less than her love, because this particular woman overflowed with a bountiful love. At a young age she changed the diapers. She fed them milk and made their food. She held them as they slept. She married Quraysh of Arabia at the age of seventeen, as her father had arranged. She was left her brothers behind in Surat. Quraysh prospered in the importation of fine silk garments.

She loved her husband but loved and missed her family more. Maryam tried to have children with Quraysh, but after a short pregnancy, she miscarried the child. The doctors said she could never have children, and this crushing blow to her maternal dream manifested itself by a lengthy depression. In the United States she had hoped her three younger brothers would someday join her. She worked vigorously for their immigration visas. She submitted affidavits and applications at the Federal Building just south of Houston street almost every day, but while doing so, her three brothers also perished, two from heart failures similar to her father's, the third from hepatitis. When she heard of their young and untimely deaths, she cried flowing tears. Her husband sent her to psychiatrists, but they never rescued her from the sorrow of losing her immediate family and the inability to have children. Her husband thought she mourned too much and the psychiatrists would keep her out of a long depression which captured her for months.

Depression, more than anything, is a form of mental apathy. The victim has trouble departing from a prolonged passive state. When one sees along a Manhattan sidewalk a woman holding a mangled coffee cup, showing her deformities, like an amputated leg or a bulging tumor from her forehead, or a single tooth hanging from her blackened gums as she cautiously stares into the oblivion of an abyss, the onlooker cannot help but find for her a loose dime. Depression is such a portrait but a portrait within. It is a mind broken by loss and hopelessness. There can be little difference between the woman who begs on the street and that woman who suffers from depression. Depression does not eat quickly. Rather it chews slowly, ripping apart the tender sinews of reality and forcing the victim to take drastic measures just to be rid of the vacancy, the loneliness, and the inherent sadness of the illness. Herein lies the paradox of depression: the woman under its spell can do nothing physical or mental to fight that hopelessness.

On many occasions Maryam found herself close to death. She envisioned slitting her wrists with her husband's razor blades, but she never had the nerve. Death is not necessarily the loss of life. Death may appear in a woman's walking down a tired, desolate road, her body alive but her soul dead. Death is not marked by a corpse but rather that point at which an insidious, inward hatred eclipses an overflowing love. Maryam possessed such a hatred, and she asked what was worse: death in its literal form, or death within the heart.

For weeks she confined herself to her apartment like a bird with broken wings unmindful of her nest, unmindful of her environment. She could do nothing but lie in bed and contemplate her own death. She thought she had nothing to live for until one glorious morning Quraysh approached her. He sat beside her in the bed and kissed her forehead.

"What about adopting a child?" he asked gently. "Our marriage, Maryam, is falling apart, and for the last few months…"

"You've been drinking haven't you?" she asked. "I smell the alcohol on your breath."

"I've been drinking," he said. "With my wife in a coma how can I not drink? All you do is lie in bed. You don't talk, you don't eat, you've been missing your appointments with the doctor. The miscarriage has hit you harder than I thought, but this was some time ago."

"You shouldn't be drinking," she mumbled.

"What else can I do? My wife just lies in bed and stares at the ceiling. So how about it? I just received a call from Saudi Arabia. We have been requested to adopt a newborn."

Maryam rolled onto her side and propped herself on her arms.

"Sounds good?" asked Quraysh.

"Boy or girl?"

"A boy. A beautiful baby boy."

A polite but subdued happiness found a way into her heart, and for the first time in weeks she smiled to her husband. Her husband broke down in tears, and Maryam held him as he shook and quivered in her arms. That smile of hers ended months of hypnotic incommunicado and mutual deterioration, for a smile when everything seems lost brings forth the sunlight amidst the most torrential rains. They held each other knowing their marriage would not fall apart, at least not yet, that this newborn son would repair what had been lost.

The adoption of the baby Imam filled a reckless and oozing void in her heart. Within the tender eyes of this small creature she saw her father and her three brothers brought back to life. As she held him in the taxi cab, she made a commitment never to let him go. She would always protect, feed, and immunize him from the desperation she had been through.

The taxi pulled up to a brick-faced structure thirty-five stories high on fifty-fourth and Second Avenue. The lobby was wide and vacant. A security guard sat at an elevated desk, watching the building's activities through a wall of video monitors. The taxi driver delivered the baggage, and the doorman conveyed his humble greeting to this new family. The elevator brought them to their penthouse suite. The suite had seven rooms including a spacious kitchen and two bathrooms. The foyer was laid with parquet tiles. Mirrored glass covered a large wall. Blue, plush sofa modules were clustered against another wall. Classic books, a small stereo, and pictures of their family adorned a series of bookshelves. A hallway led to the baby's room; a light blue paint on the walls and a small wooden crib. At its end the hallway opened into a master bedroom with a king-sized bed. A separate bathroom adjoined it. Maryam wanted to be close to the baby, so they made his room adjacent to where they slept.

After kissing the Imam on the forehead, she put him in his crib. A colorful mobile danced in the air.

'Mustafa,' she thought. 'His name is Mustafa. He is already such a great man.'

She then said her prayers in the same room. She said them aloud, hoping the Imam would hear the Arabic verses roll from her tongue. After saying prayers, Maryam joined Quraysh in their bedroom. Quraysh said solemnly that he had to meet some of his business associates. A hefty shipment of textiles was due at the office downtown. He kissed Maryam and strode out the door as quickly as he came in.

Chapter Two
QURAYSH
17th of Sha'baan 1417
(December 28, 1996)

Quraysh agreed with himself that consuming alcohol on a regular basis did not constitute a moral failure. He had been introduced to alcohol several years ago, as some of his closest associates in the garment industry drank at every conceivable opportunity. He liked drinking. He admitted that one or two drinks after work with his American friends did not break any moral code. He would casually sit at the bar and order a light beer. The beer relaxed him at first, but after three or four he felt more than loose, and in that period when relaxation gives way to a light inebriation, he knew he should stop, but he did not. Instead he kept going and found himself drunk at the end of the night.

Usually he drank to escape, to access that core of the brain which usually remains dormant during times of sobriety. He frequented a bar near his apartment called the Penbrooke Pub. The walls of this pub were made of shellacked oak. He relished in sitting down at the bar after a tremendously long day and ordering that first beer. A colorful jukebox stood towards the rear, and Quraysh had a penchant for old rock and roll tunes from the sixties and seventies. These tunes were popular in Jeddah, although most of the lyrics were censored.

Alcohol, when accompanied by music, can lead to a brief window of euphoria inaccessible to the sober mind. He knew he should indulge instead in simple pleasures, such as the sunshine, running his eyes over a beautiful blonde, or taking in a film, but these simple pleasures seemed so routine and mundane that he returned to the drink time and again. Within the drink he found truth, believe it or not. The truth of how America worked. The system demanded a confidence in the self, and without confidence success is impossible. At one time Quraysh possessed this confidence, but after the miscarriage, his confidence slipped completely. Although short-lived, the drink buoyed his ailing confidence. The drink permitted a departure from reality but at the same time a woeful perspective. On occasion he would go to the bar with associates, but after his associates departed, he would stay and drink by himself.

Quraysh was not a sorrowful man. He had wealth and close friends. But as his wife's mental health failed, as the recent miscarriage sat like a welt upon his brain, he found a substitute within the alcohol. In all his drinking he tried to enjoy life, and liquor made him enjoy it more. A typical evening would run like this: He would call his wife from the office at five in the evening. He would say he was stuck in a meeting. He would give his love to his wife, and once he determined all was well, he would hop in a taxi and head straight for the pub. He would sit close to the bar, on a warped wooden stool, and drink for a couple of hours before returning home. He usually had a friend accompany him, but recently he entered the bar alone. He left the same way.

The drinker shares a special bond with his drink. When that bubbling glass of cold and crisp brew is placed before the drinker, he knows intuitively that the drink provides an ultimate companionship. The glass doesn't speak in monotonous tones. The glass of beer doesn't talk back or offer criticism. Rather, as the drinker sips slowly, allowing it to drown his tongue and loosen his body, the beer itself shares the man's experience. Quite arguably, the alcohol never takes away, only gives. He begins to relax. The drink pauses the treacherous grind, and when this sublime relaxation sets in, the man finds a kernel of truth within the mountains of desperate lies. At this point precisely a special relationship is formed with that particular glass of beer. Ah, the texture of it. Cold and penetrating, so penetrating that the man glances into his own soul and discovers through the joy of inebriation the purity of it. With each sip, leading to voracious gulps, the alcohol removes the man from the hard reality. Does this mean the man is some scoundrel, some blemish needing a removal by the hypocrites who follow some established good? Certainly not. A departure from reality through that bountiful elixir only conveys, to anyone in a position to observe, the highest respect for that reality. The drinker manifests such a reality, a collection of forces interacting, an unbearable history penetrating the present, a routine of rising at dawn and sleeping at dusk. Call the drinker reckless, irresponsible, and weak. But the drinker who feels that numbness also understands that reality is a much stronger opponent, and only through his inebriation may he size it up and wish for things with intentions more pure. Notice how the drinker talks of some distant plan that would conquer reality once and for all. Notice how the drinker's fantasies interact with his imprisoning reality. With that cold brew he is grappling with reality, this same reality which can never be beaten. Deep in his brain, the solitary drinker knows reality will never be overcome. But when those dreams, those visions, those fantasies battle the accepted reality, therein lies the ultimate self-respect for the man, because his nobility within these mottled intentions transcend the accepted reality. And through the drink the man conquers it, at least for a short time.

There are some drinkers who get away with drinking like this. They permit the alcohol to reveal some divine truth through the waking dream or that movement toward purity of thought and intention. There are other drinkers, however, who react quite differently.

Quraysh fit into this latter category. It's the simple difference between moving up towards purity of thought or spiraling down towards bestiality. Quraysh drank heavily at times, but could seldom control it. The alcohol unearthed a belligerence that lay deep in his own heart. He had very little to be thankful for at the time of his wife's miscarriage. He asked himself, while gulping down a variety of mixed drinks, sometimes hard, bitter liquors, whether or not the fault of the miscarriage was somehow his own. He concluded that his genetic constitution was not virile enough to create and sustain another life. Although he had adopted Imam Mustafa from the Saudi sands, he still wandered into the Penbrooke Pub that evening as his wife and baby stayed home. He freed himself from his wife in the same manner, by telling her he had business to conduct, that he was in the slow process of cutting ties with his American associates.

He tipped the cabby well. At first he was quite pleasant. He had a beer and played the jukebox. After two more beers, he ordered a scotch and water.

"Y'know it's not good to mix beer with harder alcohols," said the bartender.

"Leave me alone, I'm celebrating!" said Quraysh loudly.

The entire bar heard him. The bartender poured him the drink. Quraysh downed the bitter liquid and ordered another and another and another. He danced to the jukebox and selected more music. On his way he spotted a woman with long brown hair drinking with a thin, whiskery gentleman. As the music blared, and the alcohol hit with quick, unmerciful jabs, he moved in close to this quiet couple and overheard their conversation.

"…Yeah, so maybe in a few weeks we'll make the move to Long Island."

"That's great," said the brunette. "A change is in the works, and Long Island would be the best thing for you."

"The best thing for you," mimicked Quraysh.

The couple ignored him, but he instantly barged into their conversation. He slurred:

"Whatz a reeel man you ask? A reeel man would take this here lonely woman and do the old in-out. That's right. Absolutely. The old in-out."

The bartender approached and said to the couple:

"Let me talk to him. He's usually not like this."

The couple at the bar nodded their heads.

"Lemme talk to you for a second," said the bar tender.

"Talk to me? You have a problem with me? The whole fucking world has a problem with me. My wife, my lovely, delicate wife has a problem with me, and now you, you puny little scum-sucker, you think you have a problem

with me. Well, I'm a man," he slurred. "I am a man, and I deserve to be treated
with reeespect. You hear that? Reeespect. I've got enough money to buy this
place and pay your stinking salary for the rest of your frucking life. Don't talk
to me that way…"

"If you don't cool it, I'm gonna have to ask you to leave. Now I know
you come here often, but please mind my other…"

"Mind your other what? Mind theez people? They'll go home and screw
all night, and what do I get for living? Whatz due me?"

"I'm sorry," said the bartender to the couple, "he rarely gets like this."

"…and then I'll go home, and my wife will be there with this small
baby…guess what, this baby is the closest living being to God. Can you
believe that fucking shit? He's closer than Jesus fucking Christ the Lord…"

"That's enough," yelled the bartender. "I'm cutting you off."

"Cut me off? Meee? Well, I'll just go to another fucking bar then, how
'bout that, and you can't stop me. My wife can't stop me, this woman and his
ugly friend can't stop me. Now pour me another drink before I terminate your
employment you no good white piece of meat…"

"That's it. Out you go. Goodnight."

"You can't kick me out, you scum-sucker…"

"Out, now!"

"…please, I'm sorry, okay? I'm sorry. I won't do it again. Just pour me
another drink before I leave, just one more to get me nice and tight. One more
for the road as they say…"

"Goodbye…"

"Just one more freakin' fuckin' drink man…"

"Get out, or I'll throw you out."

"Okay, okay, I'm going, I'm going."

Quraysh unhooked his woolen winter's coat from the row of pegs by the
front of the bar. He walked into a chilling winter's breeze. The snow below
him froze, making the sidewalks slippery. He moved along the sidewalks in
slow steps. He demanded another drink from himself, but the icy chill sobered
him. He hailed a taxi. From the windows of the taxi the city unfolded like the
perpetual wind gusts. The lights grew blurry, and at each traffic light he rested
his head against the back seat. As the taxi cruised over bumps and potholes, his
head shook and snapped. He paid the driver and stumbled into the lobby. A
fierce rage captured him and would not let go, like a wolf tearing its meat.

Chapter Three
MARYAM
18th of Sha'baan 1417
(December 29, 1996)

He stumbled to the bedroom and undressed in the darkness. Maryam had heard his keys and spare change jingling. She turned on the light next to their bed.

"What time is it?" she asked in a wave of fatigue.

"It's one in the morning. Shhh. Go to sleep. Turn off the light."

"Then how will you undress?"

"I can undress fine."

He crawled into the bed beside her. Maryam turned off the light.

"You've been drinking again. I can smell it."

"I know. I know. I shouldn't, but business is so rough these days. Everyone's out to get me."

"Would you like to talk about it?"

"Sure, why not."

She felt his arm sliding underneath her back.

"How's the baby?" he asked.

"Mustafa is such a beautiful child. When you were gone, I just held him, and he burped, can you believe it? His first burp. He cried a little, so I made him some warm milk, and then he slept in my arms. I kept thinking how great this child will be, and yet now he's so helpless. He needs me, and more than anything, he needs you too."

"I'll spend some time with him tomorrow. We have plenty of time."

"But you must cut out the drinking. What would Mustafa say about the drinking?"

"He's not old enough yet. Give me some time. I could drop it any time if I wanted to, it's just that things at work have gotten really out of hand."

"Like what? What's happening?"

"Oh Maryam it's too technical for you…Listen, I was wondering, do you need anymore money for the baby? I know we need tons of food, and it's important we get a pediatrician. Doesn't he need to have his shots and stuff? That's what the bavasaab said."

"I'm taking care of all that," she said. "Oh how I love it when you talk responsibly."

"I'm a very responsible man."

Maryam rolled into him, and the two snuggled for a bit. Quraysh then kissed her lips and messaged her back.

"Oh that feels good, Quraysh. I'm still so tired and grumpy from the flight..."

"So am I."

Quraysh knew it risky, but he slid his hands down to her breasts. Maryam removed them.

"What's the matter?" he asked.

"I'm not ready."

"Ready for what? I'm not doing anything."

"You know exactly what you're doing. You're trying to seduce me."

"Is it a crime? Seducing your own wife?"

"I'm not ready. I'm just not ready. I know we've had our troubles, and now these troubles seem to be over, but I'm not ready. It doesn't feel right."

"When will it feel right?" demanded Quraysh.

She lay in silence. Sex, after the miscarriage and loathsome depression did not appeal to her. She had escaped just barely from the torment of a personal hell, a mental journey where one travels alone, without any defense. When she emerged from that living and breathing nightmare, she freed herself of complications, even the complications of pleasure. She had been so alone in that journey. She had trouble associating with other people, even her own husband. At one point she slept for nearly fifteen hours a day. How blissful sleep becomes, not only for purposes of rest, but for purposes of avoidance. Maryam never spoke of her journey to anyone, not even her appointed psychiatrists, and yet such a journey, even after being pulled out of it, consumed her thoughts and affected her simplest behaviors.

She felt a foreign hand on her breast and immediately removed it. She could think only of protecting her small baby from the encroaching elements of that hell. It's not the case that life appears rosy after a walk through hell. Even after the walk, even after the stale coldness and the unmerciful heat which freezes and scathes the soul, hell still appears in the rains which fall, in the snow which sways plaintively, in the winds which burn and bite. The journey returns in the form of its apparitions. Elements of that hell reappear in the faces of men, in the night skyscrapers, and with a foreign hand on her breast.

"I don't know when I'll ever be ready," she said.

"I'm getting sick of this, Maryam. I'm really getting sick and tired of this coldness in you."

"But I love you, I really do."

"Then show it once in a while."

"We have Mustafa to think about."

"What possibly goes on in that head of yours?" he asked while moving away. "Is it the miscarriage? Is that it? Is it that depression of yours? I took you to the best doctors in the city. Aren't you cured of it by now? You sit there and pray all the time like Allah has taken a vacation..."

"I don't pray that much, and besides, maybe some of it will rub off on you."

"Don't you ever talk to me like that. I'm still the man of this house, Maryam. If you won't make love to me, you'll at least address me with the highest respect."

Maryam thought him still drunk. By tomorrow he would approach their relationship with a level head. She walked carefully to the baby's room. The eternal city glowed beyond the expansive windows. The baby Imam slept soundly, and she fought the urge to cradle him. She did not wonder so much about the baby Imam's future. She thought the future inevitable no matter the twists and turns destiny provided. She only envisioned feeding him in the morning with warm milk and baby's mush, and changing his diapers; She understood she would play a pivotal part in making this small, sleeping child a great man, but was unsure of the specifics. She knew only to protect him from sinister elements, and that protection meant learning his prayers in Arabic and keeping him under close watch. Let this young Imam fly but only within the acceptable limits of her watchful gaze. She hoped he would be awake so they may share the darkness of the city. She empathized in his need for sleep.

She grew fatigued and joined her husband in the bed. Quraysh had fallen asleep. Her husband needed to get to the office on the early side.

Maryam then awoke with a start. She had beaten the alarm clock and quickly prevented it from blaring. Her husband still slept. She went to check on Mustafa. She donned her bathrobe and went to the next room. He was awake, and she silently rejoiced. She picked him up and cradled him. She walked to the wide windows and glanced upon the city streets at daybreak, covered with snow and swelling with activity. A strong wind whistled against the windows. The wintry sun flooded the baby's room with light at odd angles. She kissed Mustafa on the forehead. She placed Mustafa back in the crib and prepared breakfast in the kitchen. She toasted some bread and scrambled three eggs. She poured cold orange juice into a small glass. She warmed some applesauce for the baby. She woke her husband who headed for the shower. She thought it would be pleasant to eat as a family for the first time. She set the table. She did not wait for Quraysh. She fed the baby Imam the heated apple sauce in a miniature spoon. The baby Imam accepted the apple sauce but regurgitated most of it. Maryam wiped the corners of his mouth with a blue towel.

"I'm sorry about last night," said Quraysh after his shower.

"Don't you notice anything different about today?" asked Maryam with a smile.

"It's not snowing?"

"No, guess again."

"You're actually smiling for once in a very long time?"

"Close. We have a new addition to our family."

"Yes we do. Ah he's beautiful. Hello, my little baby Mustafa, yes, eating your apple sauce in your cute little spoon, yes, my little Mustafa. You're so beautiful you're making your mommy smile."

Maryam giggled.

"It's good to see you this way," as Quraysh picked at his eggs. "How do you feel?"

"Wonderful, just wonderful. Today will be a busy day. I have to go shopping for food and clothes and a bunch of necessities. Are you taking a taxi to work or are you taking the subway?"

"What does Mustafa think?"

"He wants you to take a taxi. It's really cold out there, isn't that so my little angel?"

Chapter Four
CUTTING TIES
18th of Sha'baan 1417
December 29, 1996

Quraysh hailed a taxi on Second Avenue. He arrived along Seventh Avenue South. His office was large and spacious. A small nameplate, a green cloth blotter, and stray business papers armed his heavy wooden desk. He checked his appointment book and found he had scheduled a meeting with his good friend and business associate Alan Rothenberg. As he waited for Rothenberg, he was reminded sourly of the bavasaab's words that he must break connections with his American friends. He had little idea how he planned to sever these connections. When his good friend Rothenberg arrived, he tried to explain his intentions.

Rothenberg, a small, thin individual, dressed meticulously in a coal black suit, wore a pair of orange, polka-dotted suspenders under his jacket. He took a seat. Quraysh had always thought him quite handsome.

Rothenberg had been married twice already, and Quraysh envied his zest for living. He met Rothenberg at a small gathering and immediately took a liking to him. He had a glorious sense of humor. Rothenberg loved to tell tasteless but humorous jokes, mostly involving escapades with young women.

"The market is doing well, my man," said Rothenberg. "We're lucky to be in such a market. It's a good morning. The sun's shining, the women are getting anxious…"

"Yeah, I guess."

"Whaddaya mean you guess? Hey, smile a little will ya? I'm inviting you and Maryam to this get-together Saturday. A lot of big people will be there including, you know who, John Rimpington. Does that name ring a bell?"

"Yes."

"Whaddaya mean *yes*? Aren't you still interested in taking over that business of his? He's looking for a way out, last I heard. Shouldn't you be calling him?"

"We're all looking for a way out."

"Ah-ha, the philosopher on such an early morning, eh?"

"Cut it out, Alan. How can you be so happy at such an early hour?"

"Do I detect a small hangover by chance?"

"You figured me out."

"Well, I can only give you my best of advice: cut out the drinking."

"Thanks, I'll keep that in mind."

"Cheer up, will ya."

"Alan, we've been good friends for how long? Three, four, five years?"

"Yeah, so?"

"I'm thinking about…I'm thinking quite strongly about selling the business and retiring somewhere."

"You're a little too young to be retiring. Besides, didn't you just come back from a vacation?"

"And quite a vacation it was. I went with my wife, and we visited the Middle East."

"Ah, Israel will always have that effect on a man's heart. Where did you stay, Tel Aviv? I hope you didn't go into the war zones."

"Actually we went to Saudi Arabia for a spell."

"Back in Moslem country, eh?"

Quraysh paced the room. He stared at one of his prized impressionist paintings, a still-life, a basket of fruit next to a vase full of violets. He had purchased the painting from a young artist about whom many knew little. He admired its careless, thick brush strokes. He had worked hard to acquire it. He paid top dollar. This painting tried hard to remain within some established form and structure, yet conveyed confusion and uncertainty. He needed to tell Alan so much, but he couldn't utter a word. The stirrings of the troubled soul on the edge of change needs an ear to unload his most precious secrets. Like insects streaking and hunting through his body Quraysh possessed this self-doubt, devouring what remained of his confidence.

"I've never seen you like this," remarked Rothenberg.

"Oh yes you have. I've been hiding it, but you've seen it."

"When have I seen it?"

"Right now. You can say I'm going through changes."

"Everyone goes through changes. Change is not such a bad thing, ya know."

"I've got an idea. Let's go out, you and me, for old time's sake."

"Quraysh, it's only ten in the morning."

"Does it really matter?"

"I never heard of a bar opening this early. Listen, if you have a problem, just get it out and talk about it. I'm a drinking man myself, but don't drown your problems, especially so early in the morning."

"What if I told you I can never see you again, that I have to sell this business and move far away?"

"I would say you're crazy. Is it the law? Y'know I've got some really good lawyers I could hook you up with..."

"It's not the law, and I wish I could tell you everything, but I can't. Listen, I need you to handle things around here until I sell the business."

"Whatever's bothering you, I really don't think selling your business is the right move. I mean, you built this operation out of nothing, and now this small company of yours is emerging as a leader in textiles. You don't want to abandon all that. You're not thinking clearly."

"Maybe I should call John Rimpington."

"He's looking for a way out, not a way in."

"Well damn it Alan, I'm looking for a way out too."

"Settle down; just calm down and think things through. If you think a drink will help, let's go out then. I know this place in the Village which opens right about now."

Within moments the two were sitting at an old bar just off McDougal Street. Quraysh had always been impressed with the narrow streets of the Village. He marveled at the ancient brownstones, so inviting against the gusts of wind tunneling between the passageways and alleys. They ordered scotch and waters. The small bar was empty. Quraysh looked at Alan with a grimace.

"I thought this is where you wanted to be," said Alan.

"Yeah, I guess. It's a little too early to be drinking."

"For a man in your condition it's never too early. Besides, it puts hair on your chest. Oviously something's the matter at home."

"How can you tell?"

"It's certainly not business. You're business flourishes nowadays. Something at home. It's obvious."

Quraysh took a sip of the bitter liquid.

"I want you to take over for several days. Then I'm going to sell the sucker. What do you think about that?"

"I can take over. Finding a buyer won't be too difficult. You'll parachute out a pretty wealthy man, but you're looking so short term. Then you've gotta ask yourself: 'What will I do for the rest of my life?'"

"I'll be a father and a good husband."

"Are you and Maryam planning on another pregnancy?"

"We've adopted."

"So that's it. Why didn't you tell me? Congratulations, Quraysh. Really, my heart goes out to you. What's the child's name?"

"His name is Mustafa."

"Mustafa? Sounds like an inmate over in Riker's."

"No time for jokes."

"Hey, congratulations," and Alan kissed and hugged him. They clinked their glasses of scotch.

"Thanks man. I'm selling off the business and going rural."

"Mighty big step. Anyway, the city is no place to raise a child."

"I never thought a kid would change my life. Sure I expected an adjustment, but never a change this huge. Now all I have to do is find a buyer willing to pay top dollar."

"That shouldn't be a problem, but Quraysh, what's really bothering you?"

"Nothing. Everything's fine. I just have to sell, and I should be fine."

"Something else is bothering you. You'd never go out for a drink this early."

"It's my wife."

"What about her?"

Quraysh leaned in close, his voice no louder than a whisper.

"Ever since, well, ever since the miscarriage, even with adopting this child, she seems really, how would you say it, really cold."

"That's understandable."

"Yeah, but she should be over it by now. Life goes on, am I right?"

"If it's bothering you, do something about it."

"Like what?"

"If I may be so bold, I know a woman you can see."

"Jesus, you really get right down to the matter."

"She's quiet and discreet."

"Are you mad?"

"I'm just getting right down to the matter."

"I can't, and besides, the goal now is to raise a family, for better or for worse. There are so many things to do. I've got to get adoption papers signed..."

"Suit yourself, but I remember when my first marriage fell apart, I saw this woman, and after a short time, I felt much better."

"My marriage is not falling apart."

Rothenberg reached into his back pocket and pulled out a small business card.

"Take it, just in case."

They spent the next few hours drinking at the small, empty bar. They drank steadily and forgot the time. By the middle of the afternoon they finished their drinks and stumbled into the avenue replete with cold and wind.

Alan went farther downtown, and Quraysh headed towards his apartment. While searching desperately for a taxi, Quraysh stuck his hand in his pocket and found to his mischievious delight the small card Alan had given him. On the card was written a name and number of the woman Alan had recommended. He found Alan's overture amusing at best. He reassured himself that his marriage was not falling apart. Rather his marriage had passed a hurdle. He and Maryam now had a child to look after.

He arrived home and immediately went for the bedroom despite his wife's calling: "Who's there? Who's there?" He threw his coat and jacket to the floor. The baby Imam cried and wailed in the next room. He landed on the bed in a swell of incoherence and inebriation. Instantly he grew annoyed by the baby's high-pitched, screetching cries.

"Would you please shut that baby up, Maryam!"

Still the baby cried. He lay supinely on the expanse of the bed. From the corner of his eye he saw his wife carrying the small child.

"When I get home after a long day, I expect no noise in this house, damn it, absolutely no noise."

"It's only afternoon, and you've been drinking. Naturally you're upset."

"No noise, Maryam. All I want is some peace in my house."

"So how much did you drink this time," she called over the baby Imam's cries. "One? Two? Three or four?"

"What difference does it make? I'm out there cutting connections with all my friends, each and every one of them."

"They're not your friends. They're your drinking buddies."

An uncontrollable rage filled him. The tweaking of broken nerves invaded his forehead. Blood rushed to his cheeks. He had an urge to slap her, even though she carried their child who wailed as though the heavens could hear. He could either carry out his deep will to smack her or remain calm. After all, what is rage but the exhumation of a brutal, unforgiving truth? What is rage but a fire within that slowly melts that thick barrier of frost between two people? Rage can be called upon to act methodically, or it could react almost like a reflex, like a thread of lightning breaking apart a hover of clouds, or the cobra that sinks its fangs into flesh. He thought of his friends as more than just drinking buddies, especially Rothenberg who lent him support after the miscarriage. And before him stood this skinny, tan-faced woman. She used to be so beautiful, but now her long hairs sprouted like wires, distinguishable through her thin, melting skin. He wanted nothing to do with her, yet knew the obligation of taking care of them, a burden barring his freedom to drink booze and cavort with sexier women. Warm saliva engulfed his throat. He stared directly at her. He played repeatedly in his mind the point where the knuckle splinters the cheekbone. He sighed deeply and returned to bed, happy to have a drowsiness subdue him.

Chapter Five
VASILLA JOURNEYS TO NEW YORK
18th of Sha'baan 1417
(December 29, 1996)

The bavasaab's bodyguards drove Vasilla to the departures terminal and equipped him with a small book of conversational English. Vasilla had grown accustomed to eating airplane food. He was so hungry that the flight attendant served him two additional trays. The flight lasted ten hours, and he had little urge to sleep. Instead he stared out the small window as the pink sun hovered over scattered clouds. The drone of the plane's engines eventually put him to sleep for a few hours, and by the time he awoke he was approaching New York City. He filled out several forms, basic information, passport and visa numbers, where he would be staying, and whether he carried any perishable items. The plane soon descended upon the Manhattan skyline. He took out his English phrase book and practiced hailing a taxi and finding a hotel room. As the plane's wings sliced through the clouds he remembered how he stole the baby Imam from the Lahorian home. The act was simple. He crept out the door and carried him in a blanket. He had done it silently and quickly. He performed the service in the name of Allah and His representative. Yet the act saddened him all the same. The visage of Fatima recurred in his mind, turning and turning over like a dreary vision during the spell of a nervous sleep. His conscience bothered him. He was reminded of what he promised her. But he never questioned Tariq. And the plane plunged. It dipped and ascended at intervals. The plane touched the tarmac moments later.

At the customs counter Vasilla was asked a series of questions in English.

"In Arabic, please," said Vasilla, thumbing through his phrase book.

"Just go ahead," replied the customs clerk.

"Excuse?"

"Just go, andelle, move."

And the customs clerk waved him through.

New York would be unlike any other city. Already he had seen the diversity, many different faces: brown, black, yellow, and white, some in perpetual motion, some waiting impatiently, like a busy Meccan intersection. Indians, Japanese, Africans, and Swedes roamed in distinct packs, waiting for loved ones by a barrier of shabby metal gates. He wondered how so much plurality could exist. These strangers acknowledged their mutual existence under one liberating system whereby packs of Swedes were near to the Africans clad in orange and black garments. These packs moved with speed, darting between baggage carts and crying children. They lived in a tense equality and controlled chaos: acknowledging their equality, smiling upon each other, but underneath that thin surface, beneath the thin disguise, a palpable hatred, the law of the jungle coexisting with laws of conscience and good will.

In Mecca, the will of Allah determined the rules of a society set in place by a single message through a single man who brandished his saber and fought through ancient tribes and marble statues. As new situations arose, so the line of bavasaabs reinterpreted Quranic law, and things evolved slowly. The rule of the Qur'ran, however, remained intact, as did the rule by those few bavasaabs who took orders from Imams in hiding. Vasilla knew nothing of Tariq's plans but knew he was in New York for one purpose: to keep a vigilant eye over this baby Imam, the same infant he stole, and to watch over The Imam's parents who may stumble at any moment.

Vasilla had never seen snow before. He glanced through the tinted terminal windows and saw heaps of it on the ground. After wandering directionless and mute through the airport, feeling the cold revolver wedged against his rib cage, confident now that he would survive this dangerous liberation, he left the frenzy of the airport. He had been in New York scarcely a moment, and already he missed his home. Although Vasilla had his dense and error-prone moments, he realized, as the wind seeped through his coat that a man alone in an unknown universe bleeds not from loneliness or sorrow but from the betrayal of his own conscience. As the taxi cab headed into the maelstrom of Manhattan, his mind wandered neither to the cityscape nor to his new assignment, but to Fatima's face and the tears which must have tumbled from her eyes.

Chapter Six
RAGE
19th of Sha'baan 1417
(December 30, 1996)

Quraysh returned to the Penbrooke Pub in the afternoon just as his hangover from the previous night wore off. He ordered a beer and was lucky to have a different bartender. He planted himself on his usual wooden stool after forcing a dollar into the jukebox. A younger patron in the corner was lost in his own world. Above the bar hung a painting, and with each swallow of the cold brew Quraysh stared into it, getting lost in it. It depicted a gentle ocean, lapping against weathered rocks.

He imagined the shoreline and how it rapidly engulfs the rocks, the small birds pecking at the tiny pebbles. He would swim in this ocean one day, he thought. He would swim far away, enduring its swell and its calm luxury when the fish bite, or its maddening rush. The ocean calms him. The steady breeze captivates his hair. The warmth of the beneficent sun, the wind gusts, and the ocean's swell remain so silent. The ocean would always endure, astounding science and forcing the poets to dream. Ah! To touch the ocean and to hear its silent mystery, not clockwork, but a pervading mystery, and to watch the sandpiper searching the small pebbles of its shore, the seagull suspended in the air and fighting the wind, and the music of that silent ocean, undulating and hiding what lurks below its surface.

He dives into that steady swell of silence, that patient ocean of vast history, that unencumbered melody, and he fights the undertow, never letting this majesty take him alive. He moves his arms, keeping afloat, never time to rest, his arms pumping like the steels of industry, his breath moist and damp, his heart thudding with exuberance, his lungs panting, and his head slapping the cold of that water, and suddenly, for lack of air, he gasps for breath, his muscles give, but with every last bone, with every muscle aflame with work, he fights the ocean, departing far from land, so much that he can see nothing, do nothing, but grind his heavy arms into the current. He has little fear, and he is determined to survive, because he carries the weight of memories, a longing to be free, from our darker selves, free from cacophony, away from addictions and swimming towards these unearthed freedoms, not escape, because the arms will lag and the soul will drown, but moving into the horizon, his legs kicking, his torso twisting, his vision nothing but the back of his eyes, and moving steadily towards the pool of endless seas, alone and unafraid. He swims for greater purposes, neither to seek and destroy nor to win or to lose, only pumping and grinding his body upon the surface of this vast, naked, disciplined, yet childlike sea.

He said scotch, and the bartender filled his glass. With each slow sip his head grew weightless. He looked around the oak-paneled room. The young solitary drinker at the end of the bar disappeared. He spotted a newspaper at the end of the long bar. He read about Protestants and Catholics feuding in Northern Ireland, an epidemic in Sudan, a beautiful young Israeli woman arrested for depicting Muhammad as a pig. And how beautiful this woman looked in the paper. Dark hair, lightly frizzed and flowing to her chest. He could not deny her beauty, a woman who actually thinks amidst chaos, a woman willing to die for what she believes, and yet this preposterous beauty would never find him, for if they walked upon the same pavement on any street in the world they would find themselves staunch enemies. And he would never speak with her, never touch her or kiss her.

For what seemed like hours he stared at her photograph. His sips turned into frantic gulps just staring at her, regardless of her radical opinions or her hatred of Muslims, no matter the emblem of fist and Star of David tattooed on her breast, but oh her breathtaking beauty.

He gulped his scotch until he tongued bitter, melting ice. He was on the verge of destroying that newspaper as it represented madness; forty dead here and fifty dead there, the face of this radical Jew, her beauty, and her inexorable animosity. The cold ice melted in his mouth. Arms pumping against the endless sea, head in the water, gasping for breath, moving slowly towards a shore he would never reach.

"Bartender, another scotch!" he yelled into the air.

"Don't you think you've had enough, sir?" asked the young barkeep.

"It's only my first one, but yes I've had enough," as he brought the newspaper to the bartender's nose. "Now be a good lad and pour me another drink."

His legs slackened. His eyes became heavy and bloodshot. His breath fumed.

"A killing here and a killing there, smart people up, dumb people down, blacks on one side, whites on another, hatred and fear: heads, love and goodwill: tales. Now good man, another drink."

"Sir...Sir," said the barkeep. "Are you alright?" after pouring him another.

"You look like a decent young man," said Quraysh. "Are you in school, have you ever gone to school my young man?"

"I have my degree."

"And in all those years of schooling, my kind and gentle fellow, what has it taught you?"

"Why, I suppose it taught me to look ahead."

"And where will you be when you get ahead? And by the way, another drink."

"Sir, I can't serve you anymore."

"Why not damn you?"

"I'm just looking ahead," said the barkeep.

Quraysh rubbed his fingers along the hardness of his skull.

"Stop," he whispered to himself. "Stop this. Just stop."

"It's a question of attitude, sir. You can do it," chimed the young barkeep.

His stomach turned, and a hot, reckless flash accompanied the weightlessness. A curdling like sour milk pushed into his throat. He ran at full speed to the toilet. He flipped open the white lid. His eyes teared and closed, his face contorted, and the day's food and drink gushed from his mouth and nose.

He readied himself in front of a cracked mirror. He had not seen his reflection for some time. He had lost weight, his eyes of brown seemed tired and dull. His mustache dripped with perspiration. He splashed water on his face. The wetness dribbled down his neck and chest. In the mirror he saw a man who hardly looked like himself. The face scared him and yet appealed to him, as his days were shoelaces-tied and hair-combed-neatly. He checked the slits of his eyes. He asked himself:

'Where am I going? What am I doing here? I'm so lucky, such a lucky man, and yet I have nothing to live for. I have a beautiful home, a wonderful life, and a small baby to call my own. An important, a very important child he shall be, and all this time something's happening to me. It can't be the booze. My God, look at my face. I must sell off my business to Rothenberg or that guy Rimpington. Sell it all and go for broke. Isn't that the American dream? To push with nothing but the skin on your back? Everyone's against me. There is not a single man who will help me succeed, but succeed at what? There are so many people wanting exactly the same thing: to pursue their dreams and have those same dreams fulfilled within their lifetimes. Instead I have this child, this small puny infant. I have a job, a job anyone would envy, and yet I sit in this damn bar every night, the players always the same, even the same jukebox with this same music playing over and over, not necessarily in the bar, but in my head, over and over, playing again and again. Ah, another drink.'

He cleaned himself to the best of his ability. He ordered another scotch from the young barkeep.

"I will not be taken alive," he said.

"Sir?"

"You heard what I said. No one shall decide my fate but myself?"

The barkeep placed another scotch before him. Within a minute he finished the drink and rushed for the door. He found himself along Second Avenue, and the winter's breath clutched him. The cabs were all taken. He walked the distance, his shoes slipping on the icy pavement. The street lights and the stores blurred like streaks of raindrops on a windshield. The wind ran the length of Second Avenue. He bundled his coat. Tires splashed through slush. Images of his wife and small child swept through him, and he wished to return to the pub and recapture what he had lost.

He bid a small salute to the doorman on duty and tried not to fall completely asleep in the elevator. At the apartment door he removed his shoes and tiptoed to the bedroom. The light from the bedroom beamed at him. He found Maryam standing barefoot with her arms wrapped against her chest.

"Where have you been?" she asked.

"What's it to you?"

"I've been worrying half the night. I was about to call the police."

"And what would they do?"

"They at least would have told me you're not stuck in the morgue."

"I'm alive, aren't I? Stop worrying so much."

"I'm not worried. I'm concerned."

"Then stop with your concern. How's the baby?"

"Wait a minute. You're actually concerned about your own baby?"

"Maryam, this is no time for lecture or argument or whatever. It's been a long day, and it's high time I get some sleep."

"I could smell you the second you walked in here. What has gotten into you? You used to have one or two drinks after work, but this? Is this the way you want to live your life? I'm sick of it. Even the baby notices your absence."

"Gimme a break."

"Give you a break? Give me a break. We have a family now, and suddenly you're throwing it away. Maybe we need some help, you and I."

"What kind of help?"

"I know of this therapist…"

"Wait a second. You wait right there. I don't need a therapist. Maybe you need a therapist, Maryam, but I don't. Anyway, women need therapy more than men do."

"Quraysh, sit down and hear me out."

"I've heard you out, now leave me alone. I'm tired."

"I'm tired too. We need some help. At least admit it."

"I need nothing of the sort. Now let's go to bed."

"Oh no you don't. We're falling apart, and all you want to do is pass out. First, we must talk this out. What's bothering you? Can't you tell your own wife?"

"I'm a man of action. Now if you don't mind, it's way passed my bedtime, Maryam, and I'm a little on the cranky side."

"Who cares what side you're on. You must be on the side of your own family. Look at yourself. Nothing but a drunk."

"I'm warning you, Maryam."

"Warning me? No, on the contrary, I'm warning you."

"And what will you do, huh?" as he moved closer, so close that his liquored breath fell upon her.

"I can do whatever I please," she stammered.

"Like what, I might ask?"

"I can leave."

"Hah! You? Leave? Where on earth would you go? You have no food, no shelter, no job, all you have is a bunch of doctor's bills."

"Don't test me."

"Go ahead. Walk out. You used to be so beautiful, and now look at you. You're a basket-case, nothing but a basket-case."

"And you're a drunk, commonly known as an idiot."

He stepped closer, his upper lip trembling.

"What are you going to do?" whispered Maryam.

"I'm tired. Really tired."

"Do something then. Drunk."

"I'm warning you, Maryam."

His body flushed with rage, and he tightened his fists.

"Do it then," she said. "You're not only a drunk, but you're also a…"

"Don't say another word, or I'll…"

"Coward. There, I said it. You're a coward."

Again the rage brought his blood to a boil. He could only react to such a charge. His fist hit her straight across the cheekbone, and Maryam staggered. She fell to the floor. Quraysh stood over her.

"That's what you get!" he yelled.

"Is that all the strength you have?"

He grasped her arms and dragged her across the carpet. He threw her on the bed. He ripped his clothes from his body and then ripped hers. As the wind gusts bumped against the windowpanes, as the baby Imam crackled an awakening cry, his heart pumped diligently and methodically while plundering her.

Chapter Seven
MORNING
21st of Sha'baan 1417
(January 1, 1997)

Quraysh awoke the next morning in the darkness. The blinds had been pulled. Nausea and a headache captured him. He felt for another body but found only tangled sheets and a cold pillow. He reached down to his loins which burned with soreness. And then he remembered what had happened. He saw images: his wife below him. Was she screaming? Her arms fought like nervous tentacles. He felt a burning on his face. Scratches on his arms still bled. He ran his hand across the sheets and touched areas of perspiration. The sheets were stained with blood. He tried frantically to piece together last night's events.

"Was it all a dream?" he heard himself asking.

In an attempt to recover, he lifted his head from the pillow, but the aching and pounding defeated the simple act. He lay his head down just as quickly. The night went by like a taxi cab speeding down Second Avenue. He slept for a few hours more.

He knew nothing of the hour. He awoke later reaching across the bed. The stillness of the bedroom offered no response. He urinated in the bathroom, and yet he could not hear a sound, save for the splashing against the toilet bowl. He checked himself in the mirror and discovered clotted scratch marks about his face. He found the alarm clock flung far across the room. Three p.m. glowed in digital sanity. He turned on the light. His heart jumped. The stained sheets of his bed had not only been tangled but also ripped. He called for his wife. He searched through every room but could find neither his wife nor the baby Imam. He had missed a day's worth of work and checked his messages. Two messages from Rothenberg asked him to meet at the downtown office. These messages were not that important compared to the third faint message from someone with very broken English. It said:

"Hello, I'm reaching Quraysh and Maryam ---. I'm at the Hilton Hotel on Sixth Avenue. Please call to meet me and you."

Quraysh thought that he would call again. He wanted, however, a call from his wife who had rarely left the house. He wondered where she could have gone. She didn't have friends in the area. She didn't have a job. And suddenly a desperate premonition made his insides turn. He walked to the closet where Maryam had kept her clothes. He opened the wide door and found all of her clothes missing. He rushed to the baby Imam's room. The baby's clothing and a few of his stuffed animals were also missing. The phone rang. 'It must be Maryam,' he thought. He ran to pick it up before the answering machine played.

"Maryam? Maryam where the hell are you?" he shouted.

"Assalaamualaiykum. It is Vasilla. Good you are home."

"Vasilla? Oh yes, Vasilla. What can I help you with?"

"I want to see family: you, Maryam, and Mustafa."

"Listen, I'm really busy here, and besides, Mustafa and Maryam are all out now."

"When be back?"

"Not sure. Sooner or Later."

"Excuse?"

"They're not here. Call back tomorrow."

"No time tomorrow. Must inform bavasaab tonight. Must see baby."

"Listen, they're not home. They're on vacation, holiday. Call back tomorrow."

"No, tomorrow. Must see tonight. Must inform bavasaab."

"They're not here. Can't you understand?"

And Quraysh hung up the phone. The phone rang again, but the answering machine took the call. He checked the entire apartment. Not a sound. Not a lead as to where Maryam and the baby might have gone. The phone kept ringing.

"Listen, you idiot, I told you they are on holiday."

"Must see today."

"I have no idea where they went. Call back tomorrow."

"No tomorrow. Must see now. Must inform bavasaab."

"Go to hell with your bavasaab. They're not here, can't you understand English."

"I understand. I'm coming there."

"Coming where? You mean here?"

"There."

"There where?"

"Excuse?"

"Goodbye. No one home, okay?"

And he hung up the phone.

Chapter Eight
MARYAM AND THE IMAM
21st Sha'baan 1417
(January 1, 1997)

Never be fooled by how much a woman can take, for half of a woman's composition, half of her feminine fiber constitutes that moment when she dares to leave a man she loves and the same man who abuses her.

On the morning Quraysh lay sleeping, she knew her husband initiated a cycle of violence which could only be broken, not by fixing breakfast the next morning, not by accepting the abuse and then lamenting, not by dismembering his manhood. She responded simply and astonishingly.

She pulled the blinds so Quraysh would sleep through her quiet packing. She set all the clocks three hours behind. After her packing, she took money from her husband's wallet. She carried the baby Imam downstairs. They first stopped by the bank. She withdrew all of their funds from a joint account amounting to some five thousand dollars. She asked for cash, and the bank official presented her with a vinyl bag full of one-hundred dollar notes. The official lent her a telephone and the yellow pages. She found a room on the West Side. She arrived at the hotel tired and a bit confused. She asked for a room with an additional bed where the baby Imam could sleep.

She questioned the abruptness in which she left. She wanted no part of her husband. Her bruises still hurt where he had beaten her. She hurt between her legs. It all happened too quickly, and she searched for reasons to return humbly to the apartment and ask forgiveness. It wasn't pride which stopped her. An uncertainty kept her in the hotel room. She was near certain her husband would beat her again.

She had five thousand dollars and a small infant. She rushed downstairs and found a local bodega. She purchased baby food and milk and diapers. Not only did she need a job, she also needed an apartment. Most of all, she wanted independence from her husband. But she had no one.

Although the baby was with her, she noticed how alone she was. And within the void of loneliness and uncertainty the mind wanders, not forwards far enough, but backwards, as she asked herself: 'where did it all go wrong?'

She remembered her father and how he always sheltered her and her small brothers. Then she thought maybe she should return to Surat, as her five thousand dollars would go a long way there. With five thousand dollars she could buy a small house and have her son grow up on familiar earth. Instead she found herself in the middle of a swarming city with swarming people, and of all things she looked like a woman cast down and vulnerable. Nevertheless her will remained strong, and she decided with an obdurate determination to raise the child on her own.

She revised what she knew about her husband. She never loved him but only tried to love him. She had clung to him not for love but for shelter, food, clothing. 'Is this what becomes of all marriages,' she asked. Besides an initial attraction and an initial love, do two people woven together eventually use each other as love grows tired, lonely, and cold? She had been arranged to marry Quraysh by her father. Is this what becomes of such an arrangement: bare knuckles across the cheek, a penis plunging in and out of her like a knife, cutting and slicing and robbing her of womanhood?

Like the man, a woman also suffers from self-doubt which is more a crime of circumstance. She moved beyond self-doubt in her decision-making. She could see only so far, and instead of the maternal dream of having a home on some clear lake or cooking food for the father and her child, she was locked so suddenly into finding a decent job and an apartment. Sure she had ideas. She wanted to build a life with her son. Funny how dreams remain so simple, and yet to arrive at those dreams one has to cross streams of complexities, seas of conflict and confrontation, and oceans of uncertainty. There is no grander, more illustrious, and more farfetched dream than the simple dream, and most of us, through the course of our temporary lives, save those dreams like ships in a bottle, wasting our time, our years, not in pursuit of our simple dreams, but coping with realities.

On the short walk to the bodega, Maryam saw along the street corner a woman bundled in a torn jacket, a woolen muffler tied around her head. She held a mangled coffee cup with a few pennies at the bottom, her blue eyes, cloudy and dull, looking into the distance of lost dreams, broken and savagely severed, as though her dreams kept her alive while the wind petrified her hands and burned her face. She too had dreams, thought Maryam, and still this woman must be dreaming. Maryam had passed the woman without giving her a penny. She had hardly enough for herself and the baby. Maryam would never know her name or from where she came, only that this woman still dreamt.

She checked out of the hotel and moved into a fully furnished apartment on Riverside Drive after three days. She thought periodically of calling her husband but decided against it. She never forgave him for what he had done. She promised to protect and nurture her child. She remembered what the bavasaab had said about returning the child should she ever separate or divorce. She ignored the order. She wanted the small child all to herself.

While the child slept in the afternoons, she went searching for employment. Her five thousand dollars would soon run out. She thought she would do well cleaning apartments, washing dishes, or waiting tables. She searched until her feet ached. After a month in the small apartment she had been rejected by some fifty employers.

One night, as the baby slept, she had little choice but to call her husband. Although she economized by living without a telephone, purchasing cheap groceries and baby supplies, such as diapers and a few clothes, she was quickly going broke. The ceilings leaked. She opened one of the cabinets above the small kitchenette one night and found a brown rat munching on the sugar cubes she used for tea. In the middle of the night, a chunk of plaster from the ceiling fell over the toilet. The superintendent said he was too busy to fix the damage. Maryam considered moving to another place. In the end, however, she had no recourse but to call her husband. Out of the five thousand dollars she had only five hundred left. She walked to the corner one evening and called. She would not accept defeat. She called for the money. Her husband had a lot of it.

"Hello," answered Quraysh on the other end.

"This is Maryam," she said firmly.

"Maryam, where are you?"

"I'm not about to tell you."

"Not tell me? Not tell your own husband? Not only have I called the police, but I've also contacted that Vasilla who has been at me every single day, and this Vasilla may have contacted the bavasaab who will demand Mustafa back. You've caused many problems, Maryam. Are you mad? Just tell me, did you actually think that you could raise the baby alone? Not only do you need serious psychiatric counseling, Maryam, but you also have no money…"

"I'm calling you because I need money, for the baby."

"Our marriage may be finished, this I'll grant you, but if you dare think you'll get one penny from me, you're seriously deluding yourself. This is what I advise: that you bring the baby back here to the Second Avenue apartment."

"And then what?"

"We must send the baby back to Mecca."

"That I will never do. The baby is mine, and I am working on legally adopting him."

"It will never be yours, get it? It will never be yours. You've basically kidnapped our son, and not only is this son just any baby, my dear hysterical Maryam, he's a fucking Imam for Chrissakes! He's not ours to keep, don't you remember? This Vasilla has practically moved in. They want him back, Maryam. You can't take away the Imam."

"The baby will stay with me. He is my son, and I will care for him."

"Oh really? Ha! You? We are talking about the same person, right? You will care for him? With what money? Did you find a job yet?"

"Not yet, but I'm working on it."

"You must not have a penny left. You imbecile. You're hysterical, nothing but some bag lady wandering the streets with no money. Have you at least once thought about the child, his schooling, his medical care?"

"I don't need to put up with this…"

"Okay, wait. Settle down. How much money do you need?"

"A few thousand dollars."

"Bring the baby back, and I'll give you all the money you need."

"The baby stays with me. Now are you going to help us out or aren't you?"

"Tell me where you are, and then I'll help you out. At least give me the address so I can mail you the check."

"Never. I'll come myself so I can collect the check."

"And who will stay with the child?"

"I can find a day care place."

"Bullshit, Maryam. Bring the baby."

"I will come myself. Tomorrow, say in the morning."

"Not unless you bring the baby with you."

"Forget it. Maybe calling you was a mistake."

"Wait, wait, please. Don't hang up."

"I'm here."

"Come at nine in the morning."

Maryam hung up the phone and climbed the narrow, rickety stairwell of the apartment building. The baby Imam lay awake on his bed. He had grown in height and weight. She would never let him go, not without a fight. Each day she prayed tirelessly, and while in bed before dozing into a slumber she said a few personal prayers in English, begging dear Allah not to take away her child. She was uncertain whether or not Allah heard her. 'So many people have prayers that are never answered,' she thought, 'including that woman on the corner. Why should I be any different?'

Her apartment was falling apart. In the middle of the night long, indefatigable rats ran through the cabinets and under the beds. She had yet to take young Mustafa to a pediatrician. And yet through this calamity she believed her prayers had been heard, and that Allah guided her and the baby. She theorized that her prayers would be heard only if she believed. Yet she looked about the apartment: the cracks in the walls, the last can of formula in the fridge, the broken window next to the bed, and she believed the All Mighty tested her for the first time. She reaffirmed her decision to care for the child alone. She would never let him return to that abuse and sorrow she had known all her life.

Chapter Nine
KIDNAPPED
25th of Rama'Dhaan 1417
(February 4, 1997)

Maryam awoke at dawn. She said her prayers to the East. She fixed warm milk and the last of the baby's food. She was fasting and couldn't afford food for herself anyway. She changed his diaper. The long cold spell in the city broke. Maryam dreamt of spring, even though the break in the weather only teased her. She found a nursery on Amsterdam Avenue. The managers of the nursery reluctantly agreed to care for the baby Imam. Maryam paid them cash. She showed at her husband's apartment on the late side.

"Come in," said Quraysh with a smile.

"I don't need to come in. Just give me the check."

"Not unless you come in. We have lots to talk about."

"I don't want to come in. Just give me the check."

"Please, Maryam. Come in and stay a while."

Maryam looked him over suspiciously. She walked in, and Quraysh closed and locked the door. From the kitchen emerged a tall and bulky figure.

"Remember me?" asked Vasilla, having progressed in conversational English.

"I have no idea who you are," she replied.

"I represent Syedna Tariq Bengaliwala."

"If you want the baby, the baby isn't here. You'll never find him. The city is quite big, you know."

"I know that."

"And I'm not telling you where he is. I came to pick up my check."

"You will get nothing without the baby," said Vasilla.

"I guess this is a waste of time," replied Maryam as she made for the elevators.

"Silence! You are not to leave the premises without the information."

Quraysh pulled her inside and blocked the door.

"You can't be serious."

The two men made her sit in the kitchen for hours. They checked through her purse without finding any documents that revealed her address. They deprived her of food and water. They pulled the blinds so she could not distinguish the day from the night. She was free to leave, only if she told the whereabouts of the Imam.

In the darkness she sat in a coerced silence, her hands bound and her mouth taped shut, should she scream for help. She tried to scream, but her grunts and mumbles were no louder than faint whispers. Her arms, tied by plastic packing tape, burned and ached as she tried to break free. And in her suffering she cared neither for herself nor for her own plight. She was concerned only for her son. Who would greet him after daycare?

She struggled to break free so rigorously that at times she thought she might lose consciousness. In the weak darkness of the kitchen colored spots floated in the air and out of reach, moving along the room like gentle snails. Her eyes swam with tears. She could hear her blood pumping. Flashes of heat interchanged with puddles of frost, and a long stream of sweat moved from her temples into her eyes which stung and burned. The television chattered in the adjacent room. With all of the strength left in her emaciated body, she gave breaking free one last chance. She pulled her hands apart, but to no avail. The packing tape remained as strong as manacles. She poked her tongue at the tape to loosen the glue. The tape would not give. Just when she declared defeat and fainted into the murky darkness of her own kitchen, the light was turned on, and her husband stood over her. He tightened the tape around her hands. He tore an extra band and stuck it over her mouth. She winced and struggled. Her shoulders grew numb, and her entire body went slack.

"Maryam, dear Maryam," whispered Quraysh, "I'm not the one who's causing all these problems, you are. Look at you, tied up like a beast out of the wilderness, and for what, for whom? One small child, not even your own? Look at you, making us act like beasts. You think I want this, huh? All you have to do is tell us where Mustafa is, that's all, and all of this nonsense will be over. That Vasilla can go home with the child, and the rest of our lives can take place. Whether you know it or not, Maryam, I still love you, and if you're smart, really keen, you will end this childish dream of yours. The baby was never, ever yours to begin with. Don't you understand what the man in the big white turban told us? He was so serious that he sent this thug here to make sure we followed the rules. Now for your sake and mine, give me the damn address…Please, Maryam. End this misery."

In a wave of fatigue Maryam nodded her head. The gluey mounds of tape were removed easily, and she bellowed a pent-up and fuming exhalation. She breathed deeply and licked the mucus beneath her nose.

"See how easy it is. Soon you'll be free to leave and start your life without this bavasaab on your back."

"Come closer," whispered Maryam.

"What? I can't rightly hear you," as Quraysh put her face to hers.

"Closer, please Quraysh, closer, I want, I want to tell you…"

And she spit in his face.

A strong hand cracked across her lips. Warm blood flooded her mouth. A dizziness and shortness of breath accompanied the throbbing. She lost consciousness.

After some time, cold and uncomfortable water dripped over her forehead. She clutched the pillow behind her and shook the water from her face. She hardly had the strength to open her eyes. Dizziness remained. She preferred sleep. A stinging captured her lips. Yet her thirst for the water overpowered her inclination for sleep. Her eyes shut, her body weak, she reached for the glass. She gulped the water, her eyes tired and slowly adjusting to the light. Spikes of pain seized her wrists, and she dropped the glass.

A slight delirium faded when she opened her eyes. A hefty, muscular man sat beside her. His features were dark as though the sun followed him. He carried a pistol at the side of his chest. She never met him before but remembered how this man demanded information. She had the urge to yell, to spit, to fight once more for her child, but the dizziness, the stinging of her lip, and the sharp pain of her wrists prevented her.

"More water," she mumbled.

Vasilla brought her another glass.

"How do you feel?" he asked.

"Not so great."

"I'm sorry it had to happen this way. Perhaps it was a bad mistake."

"I'm calling the police."

"Go ahead. The worse they could do is send me back to Mecca. Sure my superior would get involved, and the police would have to retrieve this Imam from the clutches of the likes of you."

"Really? You underestimate the integrity of our police force."

"I'm afraid I don't understand. Calling the police would only make it worse. Your baby would return to Mecca."

"Diplomacy at its best."

"I guess you can say that, although I'm not sure what you mean."

"Enough chit-chat. Why don't you just tie me up again and have my husband beat me?"

"I've thought of that. If we were in Mecca, it would work. But this is America, land of the free. Besides, I could not live with myself if I destroyed another woman."

"I'm missing something."

"I want good memories. Not bad ones."

"Why? How many other women have you beaten?"

"Be thankful I'm sparing you. In fact, I want to help you."

"You? Help me? Haven't you done enough?"

"I will permit this separation. I will tell the bavasaab tomorrow that you and your husband have joined again."

"I'd rather drink from the East River."

"The what?"

"Forget it. Keep my husband far away from me."

"That's the plan. You may live with the baby Imam anywhere in the city you wish. I will provide all the funds necessary, provided we forget this night ever happened. Going to the police will make matters worse. If you agree to remain with your husband on paper, you may live with the baby Imam and have him as your own."

"Couldn't you have thought about this earlier?"

"I never encountered a woman as strong as you."

"I won't ever give you the address."

"I expected that. You may meet with me at some remote location. My main interest is to see the Imam taken care of. Meet me anywhere you wish so I may distribute the Organization's funds. You have proven worthy of the child."

"Tell me one thing. You have kept me here for days. You could have tied me up, deprived me of food and drink, slapped me around until I gave you the location of my Mustafa. Why didn't you?"

"Again, I want good memories, not bad ones."

Before bolting from the savagery of the apartment, she insisted on saying prayers. She asked Vasilla for a prayer cloth. She laid the cotton cloth on the living room floor. She sat on the cloth with her legs underneath her. As she muttered the opening verses, she stopped for a moment. She wondered why Allah must be worshipped in such a manner. If Allah is truly Allah, would He not hurt as she did? Would He not lick the cuts or squirm at the pain shooting through His wrists? She said the verses as a matter of routine, but while beginning her prayers she noticed how worn-out the verses had become. What if she broke free from the verses in Arabic and talked freely with Allah, perhaps asked him a few questions? She had never done so before, but the verses which spewed from her lips lost their meaning. Deviating from the guidelines of prayer frightened her. What right had she to be asking Allah questions, despite the soreness of her arms and wrists? Her fright forced her to pray routinely, and she finished in a matter of minutes. She scheduled a meeting with Vasilla after he handed over the first installment of the Organization's checks.

She arrived at the day care center on the edge of Harlem, walking distance from her apartment on Riverside Drive. The buildings along the avenue were boarded or gutted. The ornamentation at the entrances was worn, peeling, and chipped. Besides the buildings, the faces had changed, from white ruddy faces bundled in thickly-padded jackets to dark faces wearing wind-breakers, wandering in no particular direction. The divide between the races, both black and white, glared visually and economically: the boarded buildings, teen-agers loitering the fronts of grocery stores, graffiti on an old brick wall. She knew it a poor section, but it was her section as well, the place she had found herself when she had no place of her own. She could have easily drawn a chalk-line separating the white and black neighborhoods. With a high chin she accepted her African-American neighborhood as her own as it represented her first glorious days of independence.

She braced the oncoming wind. She smiled to the dark faces walking passed her. These sullen faces bloomed in the winter like violets in summer.

The pavement filled with the dustings of snow. She could have danced. She entered the day care center and sat in a small waiting area with lifeless magazines thrown upon a long coffee table. A few women waited with her. From behind a glass a day care worker emerged.

"I'm Mrs…"

"Yes, we've been expecting you," said the worker.

The worker took her behind the glass barrier and said matter-of-factly: "Our supervisor will be meeting with you shortly, please have a seat."

Maryam wondered why the supervisor had to meet with her. Her purpose was to collect the baby and leave. But she waited in a small office. The walls were painted beige, and a shoddy metal desk sat in front of her. Maryam knew it a conference room, not anyone's office, as there were no papers on the desk, no telephone, nothing which indicated the room as an actual office. She heard voices in the hallway. These voices seemed cheery, as though she would collect The Imam without delay and head home. The supervisor, however, approached Maryam with solemnity.

"You, I take it, are the mother of Mustafa?"

"Yes, and now I'm here to pick him up. I'm in a rush."

"Well, it's time to slow down."

"I see. Is there a problem?"

"Damn straight there's a problem. You said you'd pick him up two days ago, and you didn't show."

"I was tied up. I meant to pick him up, but I ran into trouble."

"Like that cut across your lip?"

"Yes, I suppose."

"What would have happened, let's say, if we had to turn your child out into the cold? What if we didn't have any beds left? What if your son were lost somewhere?"

"I hope that's not the case," said Maryam with a strain in her voice.

"It's not the case, but it might have been. You can't just leave a child somewhere and expect it to be cared for. It's irresponsible and plain reckless. Put yourself in my position. Wouldn't you be at least a little bit reluctant to return the child?"

"I don't know. I've never been in your position before."

"I want you to think about something. A mother, most likely on assistance, becomes pregnant. She has no idea who the father is, she only knows she has a baby in the pit of her stomach. She has little money. And she shoots that crap through her veins, and as she gets so high, she forgets about that child in the pit of her stomach. So with the husband gone, her mind deranged, she finds shelter in one of these burned-out buildings, even in the cold. She spends her money on the drugs, and she doesn't pay any attention to that life growing inside of her. She snorts, inhales, and injects most of her money away, and in the days before her pregnancy, she wonders why she's still so damned hungry. All of a sudden, the baby is due, and she delivers it in some crack den with all these no-good hoodlums watching her. She wants to keep the baby alive. This, at least, I'll grant her. She breast feeds the small child, and all of those drugs which float in her veins, suspended within her mother's milk, go directly into that child's body, and soon enough, that small baby who didn't do a damn thing, that young innocence wanting nothing but to bring a little love and happiness into our world, is put on death row for doing nothing else but living on this earth. And where does that mother go with this new child? She goes absolutely nowhere. She stays in that same crack den snorting, inhaling, and infecting and then passing it off to her child. But one day as she walks on the street, the cold chilling her bones, her head lost in drugs, she passes our steps and sees the sign hanging out front. She knows at this point she can no longer care for her child. She leaves the child on our doorstep, not figuratively mind you, but literally. She leaves him on our steps in the freezing cold, no blanket, no nothing. She knocks on the door and runs away into the night, her arms and lungs lost in those damn needles and glass pipes.

"Now contrary to what you've been thinking, this baby is neither black nor white or red or yellow or brown. He's a child of God, just like any other baby. This baby is filled with the same substances her mother had been abusing. And who do you think takes this child? The government? Those folks along Park Avenue? No. Men who give a damn? Sometimes. To be quite frank with you, the only people who take in these children are women like ourselves, women who care, women who understand what it means to be women, because in this day and age women are just plain lost, lost like that addict who abandoned the poor child. We care for that child, because he or she is our child. They say in all those movies that the military 'is our last line of defense.' Nothing can be farther from the truth. We are the last line of defense against a world unsuitable for small, precious infants. We took in the addicted baby. We gave him food and a warm place to sleep with warm milk. We invested so much in this child with our toil, our pain, and yet the good Lord took him away from us. Are we saddened? Are we discouraged? A little bit, but we are determined to continue, because we do God's work, and with each child who arrives we remain encouraged, and some of our children go on to see school, some of our children go to college. Some of our infants become doctors and lawyers and judges and principals. So you see, not only did you nonchalantly drop off some child, you dropped off one of our own, and all of a sudden you show up with that cut on your lip, and I see those bruises and burns on your wrists, and you expect me, you expect us, to hand over one of our children because you're in some goddamned rush? No. Out of conscience clear and respect for the welfare of our child and for all the children here I can't give you the infant."

Maryam sat in silence. Words failed her. After sitting in her chair, weak from her adversities, she still had little idea how to respond. She was neither angry nor sad, only stunned.

"What I suggest is that you leave the child with us for a while until you get back on your feet. Take a week and find employment, find adequate housing. I'll supply you with a number for a battered women's shelter down the block."

"I'm fine now," Maryam heard herself saying.

"Take your time is what I'm asking. Take some time to put yourself on higher ground. I'll make an appointment with the shelter."

"I'm on higher ground already. I've won some money from my ex-husband, and the money will provide for the baby and myself. The money is more than enough. I know I have failed, but really I want my baby back, and I'm ready and prepared to be a good mother..."

"We've heard that story too many times..."

"Please. I ask you, no, I beg of you. What was done was not my own fault..."

"Yes, they all say the same damn thing..."

"I'm being sincere. I will care for him, and I will love him. I've been through hell already, and I'm sorry, I'm sorry for putting you in this position, but all I want is my baby Mustafa back with me."

The supervisor held her chin and stared to some vague point on the wall behind her.

"This is what I'll do," said the supervisor finally. "Leave Mustafa here for a period of seven days. Come back with proof of income."

Maryam furnished the check Vasilla had given her.

"I see," mumbled the supervisor. "This is a lot of money, but that doesn't vindicate you. Are you sure you don't need any help? Perhaps a visit to the women's shelter may do you some good. The women there are genuine and supportive, and they have support groups where you can talk freely and vent all your frustrations. I can call them now, and they will admit you for a few days. Call it a sanctuary if you like, but something of that sort would be good for you. You will develop contacts with other women who have been in the same boat. How about I give them a call?"

"That won't be necessary. As you can see, the amount of the check is big, and it will allow me a different kind of life, the kind of life you would respect."

"Oh yeah? What kind of life?"

"My child, Mustafa, shall have the best medical care, the best food and clothes. He'll go to a fine school, and all the time I'll be watching him closely..."

"What about your husband? What if he beats you again? Will you return to him?"

"My husband, or my ex-husband, won't be a problem. I've left him."

"Raising a child on your own won't be as beautiful as you picture it. They'll be tough times when you wished the child had a father."

"He may see him once in a while, but that's it. I can raise him on my own. The money is there, and that's all that matters."

"Think again," said the supervisor. "How you raise your child is pretty much your own business. Listen, I'll give you my card, and some day if you find yourself in trouble, you'll give me a call."

Maryam took the card and read 'Mrs. Hale' inscribed in black ink.

"Should you need longer daycare for the child, you'll contact us. Over here we're in the trenches, so don't expect too much pampering for your child, but you can expect one thing we do have: love and nothing but love for every child who is carried into these halls. Since you have proof of adequate income, I'll return your child, not because I want to. I'd rather have you check into one of our affiliated shelters. Nevertheless I'll return your child, because our by-laws say I must."

When Maryam received her child, she hugged him with a maternal delight. She showered him with kisses. She smiled upon his tender face. The reunion of mother and son, no matter the age, no matter the location, brings forth the simple light of God within the vast complexities of his earth, and this rare light bathes the mother and child in a unison undisturbed by the wreckage of days or years apart.

She left the Harlem day-care center with her mind focused on rearing the baby Imam under her strict and vigilant gaze. She took him home and fed him until he regurgitated. Never again would her child be without his mother. She fed him at meals and in between meals. She thought he liked to watch the television, so she allowed it until he grew sleepy. With the help of Vasilla and his hefty checks she hired contractors to repair the leaks and dropping plaster from the ceilings. She hired exterminators for the rats. She found a nursery on Amsterdam Avenue, and sent him there once he was strong enough to enroll. She found a doctor. She bought clothes. She bought thermometers, band-aids, and cough syrup. She fed him at every available opportunity. She held him when he awoke, when he slept, and when he cried.

Soon this tender Imam crawled. He made sounds. His hair grew. He walked. He chewed his food. He saw his mother and opened his arms. When seasons changed she took him in the stroller and visited the city park across the street. The park was filled with other mothers and their children. Maryam felt a part of something substantive, like the trees and its foliage, the grass, and the birds that darted from bush to bush. She took him to playgrounds replete with jungle gyms, swings, and rocking horses.

Already the small Imam had been noticing things, pointing to things that made him giggle. Maryam never wished for her baby to grow. Growth and change, however, come inevitably, and soon the small Imam grew taller, and his incoherent palaver transformed into syllables, vowels, consonants, and strange idioms only understandable to young cherubs.

With the help of Vasilla and the funds from the Organization she found a parochial school sponsored by the same nursery on Amsterdam Avenue. She sent him in the mornings and retrieved him in the afternoons.

The Imam's teacher said he had the terrible habit of throwing blocks at his fellow schoolmates. Other than this small aberration in the progression of childhood, the Imam did quite well. He enjoyed drawing and got along well with most of his schoolmates. He liked washing his hands after playing with glue. He did not rebel at nap time like most. He readily accepted the nursery's wish for him to sleep an hour before playing. After the long day Maryam placed him in front of the television. He loved cartoons. Maryam brought him crayons and thick coloring books. He refused to color within the established curves and lines of the pictures. Instead he colored the furniture and the walls. Maryam grew upset by his need to vandalize the small apartment with his stray lines and circles. She chose not to confront him. Soon the small apartment was filled with many colors. 'Scribble-scrabble,' Maryam had called it.

One evening as the Imam made for the wall with his magic markers, Maryam stopped him. The Imam refused and colored the walls anyway. She scolded him. She thought he must finally be disciplined, otherwise respect would never follow him. She grabbed the markers from his hands and held the small plastic package above her head. The Imam jumped for them but was too short. He cried and yelled as his jumping proved fruitless. With his small arms he hit Maryam's legs. His yells transmogrified into shouts and screams. Tears gathered in his eyes. He planted his teeth into Maryam's arms. She slapped him, the first time she ever slapped anyone. The young Imam fled to his room opposite the walls he had marked.

Maryam held his markers in the aftermath. She dropped them to the floor. A wave of disgust for herself filled her chest, and her breathing turned rapid and hot. Her eyes watered. Her heart fluttered like a bird on its maiden voyage. She could not believe what she had done, and her anger and spite grew inward and deep like the shadows spreading over the colored walls.

After dropping the young Imam at school the next morning, she phoned Vasilla and arranged a meeting at the coffee shop where they met on the first of every month. The coffee shop itself was nearly empty in the late morning. Smells of fresh brewing coffees attacked her nostrils, and she gave into the temptation of having a cup with cream and sugar. Her table faced the window, and she watched the working people pass. A faint melody of classical music wafted into the place. Through the window she saw Vasilla walking towards the entrance. He wore a blue cotton blazer with a dull brown tie. She was thankful he had arrived.

"What is it?" he asked anxiously.

"Please, sit down," said Maryam.

"Okay, I'm sitting. What's the matter? This is not the first of the month."

"I know."

"Then what is it? Are funds low? Do you need any more?"

"How's Quraysh?"

"I haven't seen him for a few weeks. Last time I saw him he was fine. He's still working at his Seventh Avenue office."

"I hope he's alright."

"Really? I thought you hated him."

"I hate him, but that doesn't mean I wish him any ill-will."

"So why did you summon me? Not to talk about Quraysh. How's Mustafa doing?"

"He's growing. He's almost ready for the first grade."

"I see. It's good to know. I think we've done pretty well over the last few years, haven't we?"

"Mustafa's certainly growing up, but as he grows, I've found something out."

"Like what? Talk freely, Maryam. Don't hold back. You can trust me."

"I think, well, I've been thinking…the boy needs a father, Vasilla."

"Ah-ha! I was right. Always, always trust the wisdom of our bavasaab, for he alone understands the needs of our Imam. I knew it all along, that this child cannot live without a man to guide him. Now do you see why the bavasaab wanted the child back? You should have never left Quraysh. And now you have left him, and you thought you could handle the child alone in that cesspool of an apartment…"

"I didn't come here to be insulted."

"I'm not insulting you. I'm insulting myself. How foolish was I to think for a moment you could handle the Imam all by yourself…"

"I can handle him all by myself, now would you please stop being so judgmental. I didn't come here to be insulted…"

"Ah the wisdom of our bavasaab. A wisdom unmatched. He knew it. He knew the child must grow with a father. Instead he has you, and suddenly you say: 'My dear Allah, the boy needs a father. The poor boy needs a father…'"

"The child must learn some discipline, and so far I'm unable to discipline the boy, and he's such a wonderful child. He's smart, and he's doing well in school. The teacher says so, and so far I've done a good job. My whole life is devoted to him."

"Maybe too much of your life is devoted to him. Perhaps you need a break from each other. You've been together non-stop for a few years. Maybe it's time you had a break."

"Who would care for him?"

"I can ask Quraysh."

"Never," she snapped. "He's an animal, a monster, unfit to care for him."

"If you feel that way, you must care for him yourself like you've been doing."

"I guess that's what I'll do."

"I do, however, have one request, and this request comes directly from the bavasaab himself. I've been seeing his holiness periodically, and he makes one request. Have you been teaching the child Arabic?"

"He's learning English right now."

"Then you must teach him Arabic. He must learn it, and he must be fluent in Arabic."

"Can you teach him?" asked Maryam.

"Me?"

"Yes, you. He needs a man around the house. Maybe you could come in once in a while and teach him."

"I'm afraid that's impossible. I'm not the child's father. Another male around would confuse him. If you're not willing to settle your differences with Quraysh, then you must teach him yourself."

"What do you do all day? You don't have any time at all?"

"No, I don't. He is your child and your husband's child. I'm not prepared to teach him. He must learn from you alone, since you chose to be separate from Quraysh."

"The boy needs a man. He must learn responsibility. Surely you can keep a few afternoons free just to talk with him."

"I can't. I'm sorry, but I can't"

"Why not? Don't you care about your own Imam? Care enough to talk with him and teach him some Arabic?"

"I can't. I can't."

"But you're not telling me why. You sit there telling me about Arabic lessons, and all you can say is 'I can't?'"

"I'm the boy's servant. Not his master."

"You'll serve him by teaching him."

"No, I've already done enough, damn you."

Vasilla threw the next month's check on the table and left the coffee shop. He included with the check a booklet of introductory Arabic. Maryam had little idea why he became so upset.

Chapter Ten
SCHOOL
5th of Safar 1424
(April 7, 2003)

Maryam never expected it, but on one calm spring afternoon, she was called into the school by Mustafa's teacher, Evelyn Smith, a tall and quite attractive African-American woman who commanded her first grade students with an authority and knowing. The school itself on Amsterdam Avenue appeared at the end of a long driveway. Next to the school's gothic buildings stood a magnificent cathedral extending a full city block. Wide gray steps led to its august doors. The structure of dark stone and stained glass gave the campus a strong sense of God, but not a God for the few, but a God for the many, as any soul, rich or poor, humble or arrogant, could wander within this gigantic cathedral and kneel in front of its multiple alters and speak to God within its cool, dark interior.

Maryam had an initial impulse to enter the cathedral. She had been praying in Arabic each and every day, even at the appointed hours, but this magnificent cathedral seemed so grand that she could not avoid that impulse, as though the cathedral pulled into its grasp the devout and the holy from all walks of life, perhaps even the lonely Muslim who had forgotten "Allah" through his or her travels.

She met Evelyn Smith at lunchtime as the first graders flocked to the cafeteria. The two women met in the first grade classroom, books and papers piled on the floor. A long poster of the alphabet hung above the blackboard. Lilliputian tables and chairs were in disarray. Evelyn Smith extended her hand, and Maryam clasped it.

"I'm glad you came on such short notice," said Evelyn.

"No problem at all," said Maryam while eyeing some of the art work done by the students.

"I called you to discuss Mustafa and how he's doing with us."

"That's what I expected. Please continue."

From her desk she pulled a small folder filled with Mustafa's old homework and test scores.

"Here at our school we periodically administer diagnostic tests which tell us of a student's progress. Unfortunately Mustafa's scores fell way below average, especially in reading comprehension. He shows some promise in mathematics, but on a whole Mustafa's test scores fell way below average. Such a trend has been continuing. We test the students every four months."

"But he's only in the first grade. He will improve."

"Yes, and that's precisely the reason for our notifying you now. Besides the test scores, there have been additional behavioral problems."

"Like what?"

"Well, he seems to have a great difficulty paying attention. Whenever we set out a task for the entire class, Mustafa always starts well behind his peers, because he's looking out the window or staring at a spot on the wall or talking to his classmates. Usually he stares at another classmate, and I have to speak verbally in order to break him out of that spell. He only does things when he's told to do so, never on his own initiative, and this is my greatest concern. My concerns, however, are many. He gets along well with his peers, but with the girls in the class he doesn't get along so well. He has the strange habit of walking up to them and kissing them, either on the cheek or mostly on the mouth. As you can see in the corner we have added to our classroom a collection of water toys. When Mustafa goes there with his class partner, he ends up splashing his partner with the cold water. I've told him not to splash his peers, but he insists on doing so, whether I tell him or not. So the problems are mainly two-fold: first, his test scores need drastic improvement. He's falling way below average despite our efforts to re-test him. Second, his behavior with other students. While he's not exactly the rebellious type, he does create distractions for most of his classmates. I've told him over and over again not to kiss the girls, but he keeps on doing it. I'm concerned his problems might be caused by what's happening at home. Can you tell me anything about his home life?"

"I encourage Mustafa to do his homework, and I see to it that he completes it every night."

"Do you help him with it, because his homework grades are also quite low."

"I don't really check it. I just make sure he completes it. Besides that he watches a lot of television."

"You should break him out of that habit right away. You should encourage him to read books. There are many children's books out there. Perhaps you should go to the bookshop with him and pick out a few. That would certainly help. With these test scores, however, we cannot continue to teach him. This is not an ultimatum. I'm talking realistically. The school will no longer be able to teach him."

"I see," said Maryam before swallowing. "I'll help him. I'd like to continue with the school..."

"In order to do so, we need to see drastic improvement."

"When's the next testing period?"

"Right before school lets out for the summer. I would recommend summer school, but right now his future with us is so uncertain."

The spring breeze welcomed Maryam as she left the school building. She planned a course of action to remedy his behavior. She picked up Mustafa at the end of the day. He wore a blue blazer with a patch of the school's insignia ironed to its breast.

"Mustafa, what's going wrong with school? I had a word with your teacher. She says you're not behaving."

Mustafa only smiled.

"This is not something to laugh about, Mustafa. From now on there will be no more television. The television teaches you to do crazy things like kiss the other girls. Look at me. Look at me. No more scribbling on the walls. No more television. Only books and more books. And Arabic lessons. Yes, you must learn your prayers. Are you listening?"

Mustafa nodded.

"Good."

They walked to their apartment in the thriving sunshine, and above them the pigeons crouched upon the edge of rooftops and darted from ledge to ledge.

Mustafa and his mother walked hand-in-hand for some time, and Maryam ruminated on how she would discipline the boy. The teacher debunked all she had known in the six years of living with him. She could see only so far and knew no matter how far he traveled, no matter the texture of his fate, she would always be with him, holding him, nurturing him, sheltering him with a maternal passion.

Passion comes to us is different ways. It filters through the haze of an afternoon sun casting its light between branches. It accompanies a melody in the throes of uncertainty. It speaks to us in the soft unbrokenness of a mother's voice calling for her son in the middle of the night. Maryam had found such a passion, but a passion which haunts and never heals, a passion which thrives on a desperate paranoia for her son's well-being.

As the days continued beyond Mustafa's first grade year, Maryam grounded him to the small apartment. Mustafa had made friends at his new public school, but Maryam refused to let him be influenced and nurtured by anyone other than herself. When the boy wanted to go outside, she kept him inside. Everywhere Maryam went, the boy had to follow, regardless how banal the errand. Over the years something drastic had changed Maryam. Or was it she who changed while everything around her remained unchanged? Was it the crime in the streets which kept her in doors, her son within earshot? Or was it the wind and the snow turning the upper Manhattan streets into an icebox which captured, not her heart. but her brain? When one looks at a child and his mother walking the streets of a lonely city built upon the spirit of prolonged isolation, one would usually smile and glance above and know, through some ungodly intuition, that things were right in the world. One would never scratch the surface of that relationship. The onlooker would only smile at the image of this mother and son holding hands, but would never notice the child pulling away.

She collected checks regularly from Vasilla. She prayed five times a day. When she was not praying, she read the Qu'ran. When she grew weary of reading, she thumbed her worry beads. After walking her son to the public school, she waited in the apartment, pacing and longing for him to return. She saw nothing beyond her son. Such was her passion. A twisted passion, a passion that changed into a selfish obsession. She would never let her son die of heart failure or hepatitis. And when Mustafa failed to sit and take, like medicine, his nightly dose of Arabic, she slapped him, and Mustafa fought back, slapping her. Her nails pierced his fleshy arms. His spit flew into her face. The shouting could be heard in every room of the apartment building.

They mostly fought at the doorway. Mustafa would try to leave the apartment, most likely to visit with friends who he knew from the local school. She would stand in front of the doorway. Mustafa would pull her by the arms. He would shout and scream obscenities, and Maryam would smack him hard. Mustafa never retreated. He never hit her with closed fists, as he had seen countless times on the television screen. He did not hurt her physically. His true aim was to remove her from his path and frolick into the night.

After the yelling and wrestling at a door bolted with every conceivable lock, Mustafa shed tears. Nevertheless, Maryam remained ironclad in her will never to let Mustafa out of her sight. Her passion never abated. The fighting occurred almost every night. And while Mustafa's strength left him, Maryam in her high-pitched tones would criticize him in a continuous rant. This caused Mustafa to yell at her again, which prompted another bout, her nails gripping his flesh, her palms striking his face and head. It was always Mustafa who cried in his bed and dreamt of a way to escape.

When Maryam met with Vasilla on the first of every month, she hid the bruises and scratches on her arms by wearing long-sleeved blouses, even on the hottest days.

"I think Mustafa needs a pyschiatrist," said an older Maryam sipping her tea.

"Why on earth would he need a psychiatrist?" asked Vasilla worriedly.

"He needs one. He's having a tough time of it. He doesn't do his Arabic lessons."

"That doesn't mean he should see a psychiatrist."

"He's also writing things down in a small notebook."

"I don't get it. Why does he need to see a doctor? So what if he's writing things down. Let him write things down."

"I'm worried about what he's writing."

"Have you read it?"

"No."

"Then? Why does he need a psychiatrist?"

"He's getting violent."

"Violent? The Imam is not violent. Maybe you are making him violent."

"I am doing nothing of the sort. Every night he wants to go out some place, and each time he yells 'let me out, let me out.' You of all people should know how terrible it is out there. It's not safe to go out at night."

"So why does he need a psychiatrist?"

"Because he does! I need extra funds to send him to a doctor."

"Maryam, he's a growing boy. You probably suffocate him. Let him out if he wants to go out. You don't know the boundaries. You mother him too much. Now I'm heading to Mecca again. I want to hear nothing of psychiatrists."

"I'm sending him to the doctor."

"You can't, Maryam. I won't allow it. These Western doctors are all criminals."

"I'll tell him he's an Imam."

"You will never do that," seethed Vasilla. "The bavasaab only knows when the time is right. Not you. Remember, the bavasaab has loaned him to you. He knows nothing of your break up with your husband. You have kept him, because I let you keep him. Don't you dare tell him he's an Imam. That's not your place."

"Then let me send him to a doctor."

"I can't allow it."

"You will allow it, or I'll tell him he's an Imam."

"He'd never believe you."

"Is that a dare?"

"Maryam, I'll cut off all your funds, as well as your stubborn head."

"You'd never find him."

"Why, Maryam? Tell me why. He's a growing boy, so naturally he's a bit rebellious. Teach him prayers, he may find some interest in the holy verses."

"Don't you see, that's the problem. He doesn't find interest in anything. At home he's entirely quiet, too quiet, and then when I teach him the verses he doesn't listen. He may be getting involved in drugs and criminal activity. The urban lifestyle is affecting him. He doesn't want to learn. He doesn't bring home his report cards. I can't control him anymore. He doesn't listen to a word I say, not one word. He stares at the television, and when I tell him to do his Arabic, he refuses, and he doesn't talk to me. He only goes out with his friends, and at night I stand in front of the door so he won't leave."

"I never knew."

"Now you know. He needs some help, some therapy."

"Let me choose the therapist. If he is to see a therapist, let him be an Arab."

"Nonsense. He's in the United States. He needs a doctor who understands this culture and this environment. He would be diagnosed improperly otherwise."

"What do you mean diagnosed?"

"He has a problem. Let's send him to the best psychiatrist."

"Do you really think it'll help?"

"I know it will help. I'm his mother."

After ordering strong Arabian coffee, Vasilla acquiesced.

"Okay Maryam. If Allah wills it, we must send him to a doctor."

"What will you tell the bavasaab?"

"He doesn't have to know the particulars."

"I'll send him tomorrow," said Maryam.

Afraid to return to the Riverside Drive apartment, Maryam had a cup of coffee after Vasilla left. The trick was to get Mustafa to go. She could not pull him from the sofa and force him. She would have to coax him or lure him instead of battling and fighting with him.

She made an evening appointment with the same psychiatrist she had visited during the miscarriage and depression.

She went home and waited for Mustafa. He came in the late afternoon as usual, not saying a word. He immediately sat on the sofa and watched the television. Maryam quickly turned it off. Mustafa got up and switched the set back on. She switched it off. She stood in front of the television, blocking his attempts.

"Mustafa, we are meeting a good friend of mine this afternoon."

Mustafa ignored her.

"I said we are seeing someone."

Mustafa sat motionless.

"Now get up and get ready. I'm not in the mood to fight with you. You're such a sweet and handsome boy, and I'm worried about you. In fact I'm very worried."

Maryam kneeled next to him.

"Please, my boy, my baby, what's so wrong? What have I ever done to you? Maybe I mother you too much, but my sweet, sweet child, something's wrong. You only get up to fight with me, and then I have to hit you and scratch you. This can't go on, Mustafa. We can't live like this, and either can you. Say something, say anything, my sweet, my gulab, please speak to me…"

She never got him off that sofa. Mustafa looked away in his deep and troubled silence. She called the psychiatrist from the apartment. She persuaded him to make a house call. The psychiatrist accepted extra monies and showed in the early evening. He wore a brown suit with a black striped tie. His bald head and brief mustache lent him a plain but peaceful demeanor.

"Your mother tells me you like to write things down," said the doctor.

Mustafa did not respond.

"You seem to be very angry about something. Can you tell me what that might be? I see it in your face. Your mood shows through your facial expressions. Can you let me in on it? I'm here to help you. Are you having trouble speaking? Is something wrong with your tongue? Can you move your tongue? Can you nod, yes or no? Nod if you can't move your tongue."

Mustafa nodded to Maryam's relief.

"I see," said the psychiatrist. "I see it now. Why can't you talk? Is something barring you from talking? Is it me? Is it your mother?"

Tears sprung from Mustafa's eyes.

"I see," said the psychiatrist kneading his chin. "I understand what you must be going through. It hurts, doesn't it?"

Mustafa wiped the tears from his eyes and nodded slowly.

"Maybe you'd like to go someplace special, a place of rest and relaxation. You must be really, well, you must be very exhausted. Are you thinking strange thoughts? Perhaps violent thoughts?"

Mustafa did not respond this time, but tears still flowed hurriedly down his cheeks. The psychiatrist took Maryam aside. They conversed softly by the doorway.

"I need to run some tests," said the psychiatrist.

"What's wrong with him," asked Maryam in desperation.

"Well, his loss of speech certainly points to something, but right now I feel your son is confused more than anything, and I want to keep him under close observation at the Psychiatric Institute. Will you allow that?"

"If you think it'll help him."

"I know it will help him. I'd like to keep him under observation for a few days, because…because I feel in my professional opinion he may be very violent right now, and it's not safe for him to be in the house or roaming about anywhere…"

"Oh my baby, my sweet young child, it all went wrong. Oh dear Allah, it went wrong..."

"You must not blame yourself," he consoled. "Whatever has happened has happened. We can't change history, but we can change Mustafa's future."

"How long will he have to stay at the Institute?"

"It's very hard to say. But he needs immediate attention."

"How will we get him there?"

"We can send for an ambulance. That's the usual procedure."

"Doctor, what's wrong with him? Will he be all right? I never expected an ambulance or anything like that."

"He may go voluntarily, but my instincts tell me he won't, because he's in need of help."

"What caused it? Did I do this to him?"

"We don't know at this point," as he wiped sweat from his brow. "We must keep him under observation."

"How long?"

"We shall see, but we need to move him."

They moved from the quiet spot to the sofa where Mustafa looked into another world.

"Mustafa?" asked the psychiatrist, "how about you and I take a little trip to my workplace? Maybe there you'll talk. Have you had enough sleep lately, because sleep is essential to any young man like yourself. Have you been sleeping lately?"

Mustafa indicated that he had not slept for some time.

An ambulance arrived shortly thereafter. The paramedics strapped Mustafa to a padded gurney. They wheeled him from the apartment into the white van parked along the curbside, its lights flashing. The psychiatrist reassured him that this was only a routine. Maryam and the psychiatrist rode with him to the Institute on Fort Washington Avenue. Under the straps pinning him, Mustafa carried his notebook.

***

The best approach towards describing this Twelfth Imam, oh this glorious Imam, is to record what he had written in those many days away from his mother. Thus, we carefully depart from this narrative and submerge ourselves into the mind of this young man, at the age of sixteen, and to set down adequately his thoughts and ideas. Many of them are offensive and ought to be considered in light of his age. But with each breathtaking stroke of his simple pen, he described in minutiae every serious thought that crossed his mind. Some of these thoughts are nothing but insubstantial demagoguery. His writings, however, show how one young man, any young man for that matter, can transform his innermost hatreds, his negativity, his unearthed violence (because no one really knew why he kept so silent) into a gift, like a love of sorts or a thirst for life, and a duty never to allow the defeat his human spirit by his own mind. The narrative will eventually run its proper course, but not without a tour of the mind of this alleged Twelfth Imam, who has thus far remained dangerously silent.

Book Three

"A prince is nothing beside a principle." -Victor Hugo

THE PSYCHIATRIC INSTITUTE
1st of Jumaada al-awal 1435
(March 3, 2014)

In my mind, which is currently playing tricks on me, I did not see the future. I only saw the past. The death and disease, the violence and destruction, the dictators and the governments choosing war. And so I am a hostage of mind choosing to remain insane, I guess. And in my insanity I am trying to find peace, a struggle which rips me apart and tears me at the seams. My mind is pointed in many different directions. But I want to look up, not down. I want to look straight ahead, on the right side, on the left side, and even behind me. And how beautiful these black swans look on this Sunday Morning Program. So peaceful, so restful, floating in beauty, calmness, and serenity.

I do not want to harm anyone. I do not want to offend, but please understand that we must rationalize peace, not imagine it. Peace is possible within the human intelligence and exists within the mind. Haven't we determined that we, as human beings, are the most dangerous of all? And if human beings are indeed dangerous, then is not God dangerous as well? Instead of revolving in circular thought, let's choose to evolve and move ourselves to a higher plane..

I am now safe, away from ordinary people. I have decided to be that true bastard of life, shoved out of social circles, shoved out of the game of life every youth ought to enjoy. If you could see my perspective on life, you would truly see why I am a bastard.

I would like to write about my mother. She cares too much about me. She has successfully shoved religion down my throat, bit by precious bit, always in heavy doses. Religion becomes the medicine by which all difficulties are thrown into the breeze. My religion, for now, resides in the written word, so instrumentally powerful against the mood swings I have been having.

She has visited me in this place of insanity, she being the most insane of all. I have tried to commit her to this institution. A sad irony how I am here and she is free. She will never sacrifice her freedom for an institution, as I will sacrifice neither my brain nor my pen for one. I need to grow up. No one has allowed me to be that child who plays in the mud or walks a small, fragile puppy. I've always wanted a dog, and I have pleaded with God.

I am the master of manipulation. I can easily tap a psychiatrist's mind quick words. So let the games begin!

My mother will stumble always, and no one will be there to pick her up. So, who do I have to play with now? No mother, no father, no friends, for I have been left here to rot. Have you ever felt like a human laboratory experiment? Well, I do, and I'm wondering who's watching me.

Charlie Halko died today. He committed suicide, hung himself. Charlie had Parkinson's disease and was a patient here at the Psychiatric Institute. I cannot understand death yet. His suicide has made death out of us all. When will someone stop all the suicides? When will someone celebrate the brightness and glory of life instead of a death that comes all too often? He was so kind to me. He never avoided the young. He was always young at heart. And who's to blame? Who's to blame for Charlie's cop-out and sell-out? He was the father of children, and his children will continually ask 'why did you do it, Dad?' or 'Am I the one to blame?' He loved playing football, so I heard, so why couldn't he play anymore? Goddammit I do not understand death.

I write after a few days of relaxation. They have placed me under fifteen minute checks as a result of my outburst over Charlie's death. For a while I stopped speaking. I only wrote. I didn't do anything else. This served as my main line of communication to the staff members here. Fifteen minute checks means that they check up on me every fifteen minutes. This gets annoying after some time, so I had to stop writing, and I have for now. But I still must write about another incident here at the Institute.

I smoke cigarettes, Camels, even though I am underage. They relax me when my mood swings become too fierce. Within this hospital we are not allowed to have lighters, simply because many of the patients are depressed and my commit suicide or burn the place down altogether. Every day I check out a lighter from the dispensary, so that another patient here named Karen and I can hang out and smoke. On our way out of the unit, I held my cigarettes and lighter by hand, for I had sweat pants on without pockets. After returning to the ward, I put the cigarettes and lighter next to the coffee machine in the hall. As the day moved slowly into night, I noticed that my cigarettes were missing. Karen and I searched for these cigarettes to and from the unit and all along the grounds. We could not find the cigarettes. I chose not to tell anyone on the staff. I simply carried on with my normal routine.

Within this unit there is a new patient named Joe. He is a psychiatrist himself with mental diseases and many tumors in his head. His skin flakes and his eyes droop. The drool from his mouth wanders aimlessly to the floor every time he eats his lunch. His speech is incoherent, and he walks very slowly with the help of a cane. For the past few days he has been stealing cigarettes and lighters from the other patients. He has such mental problems but neither the doctors nor the nurses can do anything about them. But he stole my cigarettes from the coffee area. This was no problem for me, but I had to search most of the day with Karen. I was also going through nicotine withdrawals.

Lights-out here is at twelve Midnight. We all prepared for bed. A staff member named Steve asked me for the lighter back. I told him that I had lost the lighter. He became worried and immediately informed the staff members.

Steve is a young man at the age of thirty. He's tall and has a full beard, along with rectangular glasses. He plays Ping-Pong with me on his breaks and has complete knowledge of the history of this institution, which has been around since The Dark Ages. Steven said that my lighter privileges were suspended. I understood and found this to be a just punishment for my inability to find the lighter and cigarettes. I agreed with him, for I am a very agreeable person. After my nerves were calmed and my feelings relaxed, Kathy, the head nurse, came up to me. She is very dedicated to her work and, I guess, aspires to be the Florence Nightingale of the institution. But the egotism which marred her brain, like dense tumors encouraging an old person's senility, got in the way. She told me of my irresponsibility, my failure to follow completely the rules and regulations of the institution. Kathy asked me:

"What if Joe gets a hold of the cigarettes and lighter?"

I told you about Joe. Even though he has the unfortunate habit of stealing cigarettes and silently smoking them in his room, he is never punished for his violation of hospital rules. He has clout, authority, and seniority by virtue of his profession and his age.

But Kathy became angry and immediately searched his room. Viola! The missing lighter and cigarettes were found. My punishment was given to me by another nurse named Candice. She is a sweet gentle woman whom I would love to get into bed with. I get hard every time I see her, and believe me, I tell her all my fantasies. Celibacy is not easy. I have gone without sex for more than a week. Kathy the Nurse decided to ground me for Friday. On Friday the weather is supposed to be perfect for long strolls underneath knotted oak trees with Karen by my side. But as I heard this punishment my mood began to change, and my mind became uncontrollable. The anger and the rage, the frustration. I began to yell violently at Kathy the Nurse, such that my will became so resolute that I would not back down. Kathy then threatened me with seclusion, a procedure used to quiet those who do not comply with unfair rules and regulations. But I looked at her squarely in the eyes and told her to fuck off. She then walked off. I did not back down for once in my life. I stood up for what I believed in. To this I salute myself for being that person who always shoved the punishments of undue structure down the throats of its creators.

I have always found that the way to God is through Hell, the hell of living in an institution such as this. I will not stop until I reach rock-bottom, where the flesh burns and the bones break, where the ghosts chant sorrowful melodies and the living are tortured by demons with thick skins and florescent eyes. Question everything. Never take answers from another. You must find it within yourself to question authority.

I am now paying the price within this luxurious prison. A prison is a prison is a prison. No matter where I am I am always stuck in these prisons of thought. I need help finding answers to the questions I am always frightened to ask. So I sit within this unit, unable to accept visitors. The patients here think I'm crazy. They all whisper their concerns to each other. They all believe I had a mental breakdown. They do not realize that I am a sane person who chooses to be nuts.

The weather today is rainy and cloudy. A dull gray holds the sky in place. The threat of rain hangs over us. But for me I have only my window, my pen, and many sheets of paper. I need liquor, the stimulant which alters my mind such that my pen moves at a faster pace, and my mind races with the wind. My body remains mellow and limp while my mind is able to tap hidden banks of memory.

Today is cold and lifeless. I am stuck once again amongst the flawed persons of life, the ones that could not handle the pains of reality. Many here at one time or another have tried to end their lives, and the lifelessness they feel is a direct result of their inability to stay within certain limits of their own. Life is like a box. We cannot run away from it. We stay within these boxes and finally grow sick and tired of them. Within our boxes we have our religions, and look what has happened, like dominoes falling from one end to the other.

When I try to convince these cohorts of mine that life is much too simple to take their own lives, I get mysterious grins and suspicious eyebrows. We are indeed trapped within a box, the mental box where we gamble with chemical hormones and imbalances, like chips in a poker game.

There is a small toddler named Nicholas. He is here with his father who decided to ingest large doses of fentanyl. He wanted more meaning and substance from his life. His aim was not to commit suicide but simply to take away the anger and the pain of daily living. Fentanyl can only be found on surgical units. This seems most appropriate, because Larry has a job as an anesthesiologist over at the hospital. His family is quite nuclear, not dysfunctional like mine, and his wife is quite beautiful. I don't exactly know where his life is going, let alone my own. I have not broken nervously yet but will be free of guilt knowing that I have become insane first. What other choices do we have but to be insane? I hate the images we all comply with: these conceptions of beauty implanted within our brains to become what the system tells us to become. I am sick of following and leading. I need to get out of the way for a while and relapse into the world of roaches and rats crawling up my spine, into the world of my mother who now chases after me, never ending her selfish drive to hoard and smother me. You see, my mother is in her own box, and she wants to include me as her toy, always telling me what to do, how to feel, how to think, under the guise of Islam.

I have to admit that I like to drink. It soothes my anger and frustration. It calms my outbursts, or so I think.

I just met a new patient named Loni.

And so I am stuck like a stick in the mud. And I guess a stick in the mud can do nothing but observe the abusive attitudes of others. This will be my task. It will be a difficult struggle, to put my thoughts piecemeal upon the page. This will not be easy. I have to do it in a way so that everyone may understand. My thoughts wander as a result of this chemical imbalance, and I know I have learning disabilities as well. I am not able to read. My attention span is short, so talking to people does not come easily. I have to work at discussing thoughts. While everyone has called me stupid, I know deep down inside that I am merely a teenager who searches, just like any other teenager. I have no other recourse but to record these feelings.

The psychiatrists here believe that lithium may be the wonder drug. I may have already mentioned this, but I don't believe medication will solve my problems. My mind automatically shuts off when difficult situations approach it. For instance, what am I to do with the rest of my life? Where am I to live?

Karen and I have become very close, by the way. I think she has fallen for me. I have rejected her, knowing that my true will must rest in fierce isolation- the true lonely person who strives to correct things he or she cannot change. I will be labeled as sexist, racist, loser, and mistake. But as words sting like wasps do, so my thoughts will finally bite back at the structures that plague me.

In the background I hear children's voices. I sit at a desk with a tall ceramic lamp. A window to the city streets allows me to procrastinate. The wind sways the branches to and fro. I have such a hard-on at the moment that my pants are bulging. I think my walks with Karen have been productive. I kissed her today, and it made me feel good knowing that there is someone, finally, who understands my present situation. The box, that dreaded box, surrounds my temples and squeezes so tightly. The question becomes: where will this all end? I am not sure. Let us hope we can end it all.

I talked about the plight of Joe earlier. He is a patient/psychiatrist who unthinkingly stole my cigarettes. He was a pioneer of what the medical profession calls the EKG. This is some kind of medical device used to measure brain waves. Although Joe is ill, and I do empathize with the man, he is so full of himself. He is also in love with Karen, which does not make me jealous but gives me some perspective into her multiple personalities. She has the ability to care for everyone, if she so desires. Men of the older generation fall at her feet like she's some goddess, and at this I feel a bit slighted. I have come to need her without the bullshit of pleasant conversation.

Just now I was in Karen's room, and I kissed her passionately. She is in danger of losing her grounds card, so she must stay away from me for the time being. I am falling for her so quickly that my mind is unable to process the information, the precise reasons for falling for her. The dominant reaction is to self-destruct. "Step by step, rung by rung" I must climb the ladder, and it can only be done alone. Loneliness fills me, but as usual it is something I cannot run away from. It is included within my box of new and glimmering toys-these toys that have made me what I am today: a mistake, always wanting to create something elegant from the trash and the waste of my days.

Currently it is night time. All is quiet, and my thoughts begin to race. My mind is like a labyrinth, and I am frequently lost within its walls. My head begins to ache, and my body turns restless if these thoughts are not dealt with. Many things in life change, and these changes are coming on strong and powerful. Shall I listen to my heart instead of my mind? I think my heart may have a brain of its own, and I want to use the heart more often. These emotions I am having, they roam wild and nothing will allow me to sleep. I have flashbacks constantly. I hear voices of these people within these flashbacks. My ears never sleep. My brain is constantly awake.

A nurse is coming from behind. No, it is not a nurse, it is Edmund who has been here for thirty-three years. He is pacing up and down the hallway. He is a very lonely creature, even though he has all the money in the world. His father runs a large corporation, and Edmund is his only son. Their corporation makes shot guns and rifle cartridges supposedly. Edmund is now scaring me. His insomnia matches mine. He seems to know all. He has read many books, but we earlier concurred that there still is no viable explanation for anything. We are trapped within the maze of our own heads, unable to get out. It's scaring me; it is a nightmare that is real, and if my thinking continues in this manner, my mind is likely to explode. I need to calm my mind. I need to think in a more mellow way. Edmund comes closer again, his feet stomping on the thin scratchy carpet, my back towards him, my eyes staring through the window into the black pit of night and his reflection, and these shivers and bumps are forming along the length of my arms, my blood begins to boil, and here comes Edmund again and again and again. He will not stop pacing. Stop. Please stop Edmund's awkward pacing.

I want to fall asleep but these recurring nightmares haunt me. The ghost of Charlie will not allow me to sleep unless I give it an answer, a solution to the ultimate complexity of life.

To a large extent, Karen, who is a well-known actress, has tapped those feelings again. She seems to care about everyone. I want her to care about me only. The way I kissed her today! Although she is thirty-eight years old, I have found her to be a wonderful child at heart, always willing to learn from someone else.

My crushes, or the stages of my development at which these crushes for females took place, are now ending. I have had a handful of crushes, and each has driven me to points of no return. I recall my first. Her name was Linda. Her hair bleach blonde and her skin as soft as a baby's. This was the first grade here in New York City, right on Amsterdam Avenue. I bothered her every day, but she hated all boys. Similarly, all the boys hated the girls. Our gang was led by a big, ignorant grunt named Louie. He had been left back a year, so he knew the ins and outs, the do's and the don'ts, the hidden system of the classroom. I wanted Linda badly. I thought about her night and day, so much that I bade my mother to buy Valentine's Day chocolates during this loveliest of all holidays. I gave these to her in the hopes she would fall in passionate love with me. That evening at the playgroup I gave her the chocolates. She gave me a quick and stealthy peck on the cheek to show her surprise at such a gift. I sneaked away quickly knowing that I had an effect on her. I moved her to the brink of poignancy- so deep I wounded her, so infinite her memory to remember my gift. She must still remember it today. I was the first person ever to express my feelings for her. We were both six years of age.

She brought the chocolates back to school the next day, and I made sure to bother her more. We had our usual battle of the sexes using the water toys in the tub, the yelling of 'stop bothering me' next to the bookshelves, and the perpetual poking each other at nap time. We hated each other as well, not hate in the pure sense, but the hate that comes with the union of male and female. We both found that it never comes easily. She dumped me on Valentine's Day, and my heart broke. I never cried, only became frustrated with her. After this, I stopped bothering her. It's funny how the end of my first grade year culminated in my intense isolation from the rest of my peers. I was so lonely that the teacher gave up. I never saw Linda again, but I'm sure she thinks of me every now and then as this person who tried valiantly to express an affection, even though it was unfashionable to do so. I miss her. I look into this strange world and ask where have these people gone? I ask myself every day: "To fuck it or not to fuck it." This is my question. I have suffered the slings and arrows of outrageous fortune. What else can I do but feel sorry for myself? Once I get out of this prison of madness I will rejoin the world much sicker than before. There is no way out of this box. I need a woman inside with me.

Someone I can trust and forever hold on to. A woman who will never abuse me, never abuse me.

I am almost out of this hell hole, and the turnover rate flies high. I am getting to know my in-patient peers less and less. We are all drifting apart from each other, and I am not sure of the reasons for this drifting. My depression is becoming severe. Karen has changed so dramatically that I'm not exactly sure who she is anymore. I try to tell my friends about her, but they do not believe she is a well-known actress. In fact, everyone is telling me the opposite. My mind is playing games within this cramped environment. My rational mind of bitter, teeth-clenched reality is slowly passing into fantasy. I see people here and intuitively know who they are, but they remain under the guise of anonymity. They will never tell me their real names. They will never reveal their true characters to me, and for this I feel cheated. When I wrote earlier that I was hanging around Karen, I was convinced that she was a famous actress. Now I am not so sure. Many have doubted me, and I guess when so many suspect me of the subtle mixing of fantasy and reality, I have to doubt my own mind. But my isolation had been unraveling, and I was starting to become my true self. Now I am scared to return to the secrecy of the pen and paper to relieve the nervousness and depression. My eyes begin to water knowing that all human beings are actors and actresses. They form their roles and hide their true problems. I have placed all of my eggs, so to speak, in Karen's basket. She has crushed them so softly and scrupulously. Again, another woman I haven fallen in deep 'like' with, and without question I am left to rot in the dusts of her trail. Like my feelings for Linda in the first grade, I identified with Karen. Her sudden change, however, has thrown me into a depression. I cannot rely on her resonant voice anymore, so soft and soothing. I cannot rely on her bewildering looks, her appearances that change as a result of her drive to reduce her weight. She has always been beautiful to me. When I met her on the first day of admittance I immediately knew who she was. Her voice stung my ears and prompted me to compose melodies to pay tribute to an actress who had lost her way. The bitch hardly acknowledges my existence anymore. All women are like this, always turning their backs on men truly in need. These men, who are vile and bestial creatures, need these women to save them from the drowning. I do not choose water to drown in. I choose liquor: a simple, sweet substitute for the pain into which I was born. This pain has grown and nurtured a madness so terrible, so unqualified that the only route left to self-preservation is the route to self-destruction. The implosion of my mind, slowly and dismally collapsing, has fueled my hand, igniting it with the only thing I know how to undertake at this time: masturbation.

Oh there is no escape from these doldrums of loneliness. The impeccable, the innocuous, yet deadly subtlety of going mad and at the same time being alone.

I will never admit defeat, for only the seriously sane choose insanity. I will bring down the pillars of Islam so that the masses will understand the terrible manner in which they treat their young. Let us go beyond the morality of religion and see the power struggle among the different territories. The Middle East is a dictator's monopoly board. Arab and Jew fighting for territory, and at the same time dragging the world into its problems. Some of my best friends adhere to the Jewish faith, and my friendship will never wane. But both the followers of Islam and Judaism do not understand what they are doing to religions meant for peace, not the provocation of war. As someone once told me, in these games of war, no one wins. We all become divided and indeed fall with the nooses wrapped tightly around our necks. I am so tired of politics and economics. I am so tired of these two disciplines which dominate daily life. I want to exercise my exit option and finally leave this world of self-destruction. The sickness lies within the world, not within my brain. I cannot be cured unless the world is cured. Generals with their minds lost in games. Chess boards and outdated maps, borders, and troops. These thoughts will plague me until the panacea of peace reigns upon us all.

Women bring me peace of mind. Yes, they somehow bring me peace of mind. I must start writing about these women to stop the chemicals from traveling so fast within the maze. Women are the true peace-seekers, the only beings that care about the world. Let them stand in the name of peace, for they have earned that right, and they did it on their own.

It is mid-morning now, and the sunshine blares through the window at the end of this long hallway. Once again I sit at this desk next to my trusty ceramic lamp. I just quit the discussion group. I have trouble speaking in groups, and my alienation is now showing. My mentality will not allow me to participate in trivial conversations with other people. The day, however, is so glorious. Patients are walking to and from their meeting points. I'm not sure where Karen went. I hear the voice in the background now, and although I cannot see her, I can hear her presence.

As usual these psychiatrists are using me and my family to fill their research books. The human guinea pigs of these mental institutions are the patients who stay here. Sex is on my mind, and a blow job would suit me just fine.

Karen has just spoken with me. She tells me that I am setting myself up for self-destruction. The slightest remark may set me off or make me angry. She is a good person who cares so much about everyone, and I guess she takes pity on me. She doesn't understand, however, that the last thing I need is for someone to feel sorry for me. I have enough trouble feeling sorry for myself. I enjoy self-pity at any rate, for it has a cathartic effect. It allows me to cry without anyone seeing me. It allows me to understand my problems by myself without anyone helping me. I am learning how to help myself. I do not need others to advise me on my many problems. My goal in life is to make sure these problems do not harm other people.

I must reach out, as Karen has suggested. She feels scared, and I guess with all women, they do all the feeling for you. They do the feeling for mankind. Of course we should not stereotype all women that way.

I'm happy I dropped the discussion group. It wasn't helping me. The psychologist leading the group told me that I had an attitude problem. But she also said that I could leave whenever I wanted to, and no one would stop me. I spotted her feeble attempt at reverse psychology immediately and proceeded to tell her that I had already signed contracts for the discussion group, which would prevent me from quitting. She disagreed and called my psychiatrist from her office. She talked to him for a short time. I heard her say that she was not quitting on me and was sick of the power games I had been playing with the other group facilitators as well. She came from the room with an air of arrogance and told me that the Institute was not in the business of spoon-feeding its patients, and as a result I was not welcome in the discussion group. This was all the incentive I needed to walk away. I hold no anger towards the staff. They have valiantly tried to assist other people. I have followed in the footsteps of the fat man with arthritis and a spotted liver, battling addiction not with alcohol and drugs but an addiction with the mind. The problem for him and me both is depression, and it is depression which leads to his drinking binges.

I don't mean to be so melodramatic, but these things are slices of truth within the pie of life, and so I have left the discussion group flunking it. The dirty looks on the faces of demure facilitators have given me more incentive to brand these staff members as Nurse Rachetts- all of them, always loving the power struggles with the patients, because they always win. They have more power, after all. I guess I see this even within the kind creatures of life.

As my psychiatrist has duly said, I have started to blend fantasy with reality. This is a part of my illness. This blend, however, has been perpetuated by the family and the abusive education I have received from these fake schools in which children are sent, parceled, and packaged. Parents should begin to instill a sense of curiosity within all children. Always ask questions, regardless if they are stupid. There are never stupid questions, only stupid answers. No matter how many books we read, no matter how much television we watch, the questions still remain, and the enigma of life remains untouched, uninhibited even with the help of insecure teachers.

This illness is a curse, for I am not normal, and I am unable to fit in. I have never been able to fit in with the 'cool' crowd, because my skin color is different. Everything seems different and strange to me, and because of this I isolate myself from others. I have the ability to tug on other people's emotions. They become toys after a while. The dictator has no choice but to become the artist. Just like the painter who splashes the canvas with violent colors to portray different moods and different emotions, so a dictator moves troops along the board game of the world, creating his art by the changing of borders. The dictator's prize is peace of mind, not a peace from war and bloodshed. His use of control allows his world to reign free, where he destroys families and children, destroys homes and commonality among all peoples, no matter the color of their skins, the sizes of their wallets, their choppy language, and especially their gender. Lysistrata seems like a better alternative to me than the current offerings of politics. Oh women! I so eagerly await you!

But we must set one rule by which we all must live: non-violence. Violence helps no one. Be kind to each other, always say kind words, never the words which provoke anger and fear amongst all peoples of humanity. This extends to animals as well. Let us stop experimenting on others. Let us start living and thrive in life with honesty among fellow human beings. These are the things I wish could come true, but for me these dreams have been shattered. I have been abused and tormented, not necessarily by other people, but by myself. I am the victim of a depression that pounds on my brain night and day. Currently I am taking medication, but still this is not enough to soothe and relax me. Anger must be pointed within instead of out.

My life is not over, and there is happiness somewhere to be found. But right now I feel so depressed that life lacks hope. It is stuck with me like luggage, the bulk of reality hanging heavily on my hands. I feel for everyone. I cannot hold on anymore. I cannot feel happy unless everyone is happy. I want to be happy, but my mind continuously plays these games, and I keep losing myself. This feeling of loss and confusion suddenly changes into feelings of frustration. This is something I was cursed with. If there is a God, He, She, or It marked me to be damned among the downtrodden. It is not fair that this has to happen to me. Why can't I be someone else? This is truly the problem.

'Love' is a strange word, so strange that I am frightened to use it. It doesn't make rational sense. It remains a feeling, and I am so numb to feeling that people don't matter. My mind has its own dictionary; words I have memorized. Watching television becomes difficult, because I see the fakery of it, the fake people, the glamorous actors and actresses who truly do not know who they are. The best actors continually act and become their characters, a method by which the human being within the act is substituted by another fake character. Oh the insanity!

My mind can only recall visual images, nothing else. My ears can only record sounds and playback those sounds within my head. The recurrence and repetition of music, sweet music, which calms and soothes me. Depression is like this: the mental stress, the phobias, the drive within your gut that burns so hard that the fire moves through your spinal column and into your brain so that the chemicals burn for freedom. I ask for some crucifixion to take these pains away. Oh please make it stop. I cannot help but fall under these maddening pains. I never want to hurt others. I want to use wisdom for peace instead of war, kindness instead of anger. I must balance my emotions with rationality. Finding a common ground is difficult, for the battle field lodges within my head. To the world I ask of it on my hands and knees: let the wars, the poverty, and the hatred all take place within my head, so that all may rest in peace. If everyone uses their own mind for an iota of time, we may all realize the true wisdom of peace.

Technology can be used against us, and I am afraid of technology, although it brings efficiency into the world. Manipulators will always use it to achieve their own ends, never humanity's end of peace, non-violence, and mental stability. We are all turning into robots. Try to write by hand, even if your cursive is not perfect. The best word processor is the pen, a direct connection to the brain and the heart. My brain and heart are finally starting to join, and all the world must know that this can be done without the aid of machines, without the aid of medication. All I need is this to happen for one short period of time. Humanity will feel better. We must do it when times are rough, when all are downtrodden and sick. We are a sick race and to cure our world we must rely on each other, never weapons, never on war, only on peace.

I awoke this morning with the dream of peace still floating in my head. I put on my jeans and my shirt and walked casually into the common room. The television flashed the violence. I walk down these halls of disability which allow me to see the true nature of human kind. African-Americans leave me with the same tendencies of war, of bloodshed. The hypocritical race which strove so hard to free themselves from the chains of slavery are now becoming the same slaves of violence and destruction. They must help all of us see the light of peace and the hopes for peace. What are the children to think? Don't we all remember the Los Angeles riots? Do we not remember the lost battles of war and the chaos that came with it? I immediately retreated to my bed and hid under my pillow, knowing that the violence in my mind will not stop, these sanguinary images. These chemicals are playing games of violence in my head.

Justice in this country has gone to hell as a result of the cyclical process of revolution. We have approached that cyclical process by which revolution must occur. Not the revolution in which we tear down the structures of our precious Constitution or our precious ideals for a liberal democracy. By revolution I mean a time of questioning, a time of rattling the people who make all of us frustrated and depressed. We must not, however, tear them down. Instead let us rattle these people who are so old and grumpy, so idiotic and ignorant that my mind wishes to take them by hand and lead them to the streets among the rats and the sewers and show them real life, not their theoretical worlds of fake justice and politics. Not for the humble and most sublime goal of peace.

The Humility comes with the job of justice, the ability to allow the mind to speak, to allow the mind to roam free and learn from the human being rather than the books. I have problems reading and watching television screens. This does not mean we should destroy these items. Let us figure it out for ourselves instead of relying on our teachers. The individual must overcome the inner battles. Start with yourself and delve deep so that your true emotions are tapped. All of us will find that the truly rational choice is for peace, never for war. I can't tell you enough how the violence affected my mind, for it yearns for the ultimate freedom of peace.

Is this what they are teaching us? Is this what I have to learn from them? Do they want power, that warlike will to conquer and enslave? Do they want to obtain the sweetness of revenge, so incredibly powerful its grip?

My mind battles these negative thoughts, but for how long do I have to fight? Enough.

Karen is leaving the unit, and I am very upset. I need her more than I know, and it is unfortunate that all of my friends remain temporary. I guess being alone is the only way to strive for higher, more substantial goals. I don't want to be alone but my mind knows no other way. All of you have left me, and I have left you in the same breath. This is the tragedy of life, the inexcusable reality, so bitter and so cold. Somehow I have no choice but to "rely on the kindness of strangers." What else do I have but the luggage of disease so violent that my persona becomes a time bomb ready to explode at a moment's notice? The illness extends beyond my own brain. We are cannot force an individual to be healthy. Religion, for example, may be healthy, but the people within these religions are sick. Take Islam, for example. The followers are so ignorant that they blindly follow, for they know nothing else. Isn't it obvious that those who cling to Islam are being brainwashed by those same people who are depressed like me? The understanding of humanity is found in every individual leading his or her self. It is not found in following so blindly that no one, as a result, can see.

I am currently fighting the urges of my mind. These are impulses which limit its use. Today I had a conference with my two beloved doctors, and they said I am showing early signs of schizophrenia. I sat there and wallowed in self-pity for sometime, for I know what the future has in store. I see myself running blindly through the streets, shedding my clothes, and yelling aloud: "This is me. Please take care of me, because I do not know how to take care of myself." Again the country is lost, and the leadership we must seek is the leadership of peace, non-violence, and of course a firm belief in the Constitution. The United States is a liberal democracy. The Constitution allows me to run naked through the streets and give people my undivided attention so that I may help others with their common problems. But at the same time this is how I help myself.

The problem facing me is the child's problem: an inability to take care of himself. I need deadlines for instance, but what I produce at the end of those deadlines will never make any sense. Stress instead is produced and things like drugs alleviate the problem. I would love a good stiff drink right now and also a good lay. It's unbelievable how sex cannot be used for therapy here. Instead we have fantasies like the institution of marriage. Oh! What a brilliant dickhead invented this. Stop making sense out of all the irrationality, for there will always be irrationality.

Complete and utter doom I forsee, and this does not take some falsified message from God to figure out. Using basic common sense you can see what will happen unless peace among all brothers and sisters is implemented. I mean how many times do I have to write this? Do I have to get on my hands and knees and pray to an invisible God, a God who we will never see? A God created by my own frustrated mind? It will forever be, and that the purely fanatical believe in it only leads to violence and oppression. These things are all happening, and the violence must stop. It must end. We must all take a break, a vacation from the worries of a sluggish economy, of sloppy politics. A vacation just for two weeks to calm all of our souls. To live in peace. I see that no one else can see this, and so I am blinded by it all. I cannot watch the television. The ontology of my mind, the maze, the labyrinth which hides this unkempt ounce of schizophrenia. Put this violence in my head and let it bounce around like a ping-pong ball, but do not put the violence within my fists. Never let me use it against any living thing. I never wanted to hurt anyone. The wall has finally entrapped me, and I, the first human testing animal, have lost myself in the maze. Peace will let me overcome my schizophrenia, my intense desire to mix peace with common sense, and of course my intuitions. The books have taught me this. The education I have received has been based upon war, greed, envy, and hate. These things work but only at certain times. History has its cycles. We are now in the cycle of revolutionary activity that will not stop unless we decide to lay down our fists. And I do understand the anger and the frustration that comes with oppression.

My mind is slowly fading, and as the moon begins to glow, the mentality of the sun has awoken within me. But the controls of uniformity, proper manners, these abuses are the vices which grip my temples and make me think of the bloodshed, the wars, the dictators, and the idiotic and ignorant presidents of the Western world all choosing sides. It surprises me still that all of these overgrown children of war and destruction are not placed in these same mental hospitals. I am for peace, and they have committed me. Stand for war, and you are free! Can we not learn from these sexually frustrated carriers of war and destruction that segregating human being from human being does not work? The smokers from the non-smokers, the intellectuals from the laymen, the bleeding hearts from the hawks, the good from the bad, the right from the wrong? We are all part of the same team, the team of humanity. Let us all start playing together on the same side. We are playing against violence that exists so glowingly within ourselves.

Today I received a Grounds Card from the Institute. It allowed me to take long walks and think to myself. I thought of my rage and utter frustration, and I tried to quell these feelings. To become a true citizen of peace one must change the track of thinking. For example, the religious fanatic believes that life is for suffering, and death is the only answer. And so without fully thinking, the fanatic beats his mind and body in the name of some invisible God hoping to achieve some sort of heaven. Give yourself every day to someone else. Help us get through the burdens and frustrations of life. How hard can this be?

My own problems, however, remain hidden. There is nothing wrong with any drug or alcohol. Take these things if you, the individual, so desire. But if these substances make one grit his teeth in anger, then one knows there is something wrong, and the drugs and alcohol are causing the dilemma the mind has been thrust into. If these substances make you raise your fists instead of extending a handshake, then that center of your soul is not fulfilled. The insecurities and the paranoia which run rampant will not be quenched. These burn deep within the gut and cannot be extinguished.

I am a product of very limited experience and know no one. I can only remember the faces and the names of the people I have once met. I miss these people, for I do not know where they are, and I do not need instruments, such as computers, and genes, and digital video to remind me of them. They are packed within my brain. Like luggage I carry them with me.

After thinking about the role of power in our lives, and I can't help but say that power is a human invention, a human creation, I look up and all I see is blue sky. Sure there are things further up, like planets and stars. But we cannot rely on invisibility. This is all fictional thinking, and we must separate the fantasies from the realities. But peace is not a fantasy. It has happened before. Delve for yourselves into the history books and find out what peace is like. It is joyful and blissful with children playing in the streets and the adults watching in glee at their children. Peace is not an exhaustion from war. The children have the vision for the future, for as we become adults the mind closes and segregates. These are the parental problems an adult faces. They want to protect, but at what cost? They also want the freedom to play, but they cannot afford this very simple item. Adults want peace but do not know how to achieve it. Peace, however, is simple.

Politically we have many parties: the Democrats and Republicans, the conservatives and the liberals, the libertarians and the populists. But this new party need not have a power structure. No, this is the party that has vision instead. It contains peaceful ideology. How can you not choose this party? Let us all have one big party, for it is the millennium of peace. Music and laughter abound!

I just received a phone call from my mother. She makes me angry every time I hear that broken little voice whining through the telephone. All the hatred and the violence comes through me. I know that I must control these things, but sometimes I am unable to. The mind must find a way to reduce this unknown anger. She molested me, not sexually, but with her cruel and violent love. She is the selfish being who walks the planet sick and depressed as all of us truly are. She appears in my sleep, the nightmarish old hag pounding away on the books of her evil religion. This religion that she preaches does not make any sense. She has been brainwashed by the loss and pain of her past, all of her siblings lost in thought, roaming like vagabonds and laughing maniacally. She is of the same person, and for her to separate her religion from the reality takes the goal and vision of peace. Whenever she fills me with the authoritarian, I simply think of the children and their future.

The New War. Was this the answer to America's sluggish economy, to drop bombs over innocent lives? I am truly insane if I am supporting The New War. These powers have implanted within me the dictator who releases himself sporadically. These balls of war which bounce to and fro, as though another human life has no meaning. I am very frightened of these pictures, these images of war. It is torment.

Something as irrational as war may have a certain rationale to some. After all, I have learned about war from the fathers of education. But we must extend this same rationale to peace and study these things so vigorously that peace remains the only alternative. There are no prizes for peace. No money for peace, for it is usually money which we look at and not the services that we trade.

Things have turned more happy now. But I still feel awkward and still quite depressed. I am the rat-trap, and the dictator still looms in my head. The instability of the nation and the violence tells my inner dictator to explode and release the misery and pain of violence upon the world.

A lighter was missing from the unit, so I quickly made sure to give my papers over to the nursing staff. The papers will be safe with the nurses. My mind is wandering again, and I don't have much control over it. When the pen is in the hand, however, I am trained to use words responsibly and not maliciously, so that the so-called irrationality of peace can be rational, and the rationality of war can be made irrational. This shift is needed for behavioral change. Also, I wish to explain violence in an intuitive manner, so that everyone may understand the psychology of violence.

Violence is a psychological illness. I have it. It is a result of a life experience of torment. These psychological experiences are trapped in the brain and somehow triggered by external stimuli. For instance, the pictures of the New War gave the excuse for the psychologically tormented to react against the external stimulus of let's say, economic deprivation, injustice, or past oppression. A history of slavery, for example, may trigger a similar psychological reaction but in the form of a collapse. Those who are able to read books, for example, retain the history of their own people and actually trigger some sort of chemical in the brain which forces a reaction. My brain, for example, can empathize with such an oppressive past, and use this past to act out. There exists both pain and pleasure, but a point is reached when the pain takes over this sense of euphoria. External stimuli of, let's say, music may trigger such a response.

Let us say, then, that psychological torment remains a suitable explanation for violence within the mind. How then are these violent thoughts triggered through the body? Why does the body react so maliciously when violent thoughts enter the mind? Well, external stimuli cause these violent and emotional reactions. When stress pounds on the head like a mallet, when persons are unable to find jobs in a sluggish world economy, and when the powers that be enforce rather than provide intuitive explanations, violence occurs. The solution to the problem of violence is peace, and this starts within the mind. We must understand first and foremost that the mind is the controller of the body. It tells the body what to do, how to act, what to say, how to defend. When there is an inability to communicate these violent thoughts, the body uses itself as some sort of reflex action to express violence. The human mind must get in touch with the memories of pain in order to rationalize this pain. Pain is best expressed through revenge. Revenge becomes a very simple code which lingers in the mind. (By 'code' I do not refer to genetics. The super babies should be stopped immediately. We must not flirt with destruction by the creation of super beings which are ravaging the earth. We must trust in the human brain, as it is born, to sort out the pain from the pleasure.) We are made with pain, whether that be physical or psychological or both physical and psychological. But the mind must use the pain in such a constructive manner such that pain does not include the physical. Peace is needed with the physical to curtail the effects of the psychological. It is no doubt, then, that the traumatic pictures of the New War can trigger a psychological reaction, which again triggers that same physical response. The constant ontology of psychological pain to physical pain and then the external response of violence which triggers psychological pain to physical pain and then the external response of violence which triggers psychological pain to physical pain and then the external response of violence which triggers...

Round and round and round we go. The simplistic way to end this recurrence is through peace. Simple elegant peace, a commonsensical solution to the problem of violence. We must end it in the brain by externalizing full peace. The human reaction to pain must be peace. The solution to this problematic cycle of history is to bring back common ground, human understanding. To delve into someone else's thoughts and see and feel the core of peace and tranquility which forever remains. It never expires. It is as fluid as time.

I feel that I am in danger, because I am extending the hand of peace to all human beings. But this is not some divine word of God speaking. I'm not Allah over here ranting away, or am I? I do not preach anything, nothing. My main task is to make peace rational, rather than war the dominant reaction. Irrationality is found in war, so let us stop studying the irrational. Let us commit ourselves to the rational, intuitive study of peace. Whether or not you believe in God, you can see the mutual advantages of peace.

The lunatic is within me, and I'm trying to get it out of my head. This is not a joke. It remains stuck. Oh please leave me in peace.

I started Stelazine today, and I think it's working well for me. I'm trying not to think too hard about the future, but I guess we must use our heads a bit. We have completed another cycle of history, and the revolution, which mainly exists in our heads, is at the point where there is some sort of treatment necessary. We must rely on our brainpower to overcome the torments of revolution so that as human beings we may evolve, not revolve. The madness inside of me is a result of constant revolution, trying to find an answer to things that seem insolvable.

We must understand that there are cycles in thought, and the cyclical must move to a higher plane. This is what children must do for their parents: show them the way out of this mess. Even the dictators have children. Actually they are children themselves, always trying to rationalize things within their own minds without sharing the information. I mean how hard is it for the Arab and the Israeli to join hands? I believe it is time for the youth of this country (and every single other country) to look within themselves and say "I believe in myself." Finally, the youth must teach the parents what to do, for the parents are very insecure. Look to the young for the answers, not the old. We must, however, respect the elderly, for they have brought us into the world. But the thoughts and the thinking of war are so old and archaic that we can't rely on them anymore. This is what is happening all over again. Hence, it is every being's duty to break out of this mindset. This is my first breakdown, and for good reason. No one seems to understand the rationality of peace. Maybe some do, but this courageous bunch hid themselves in closets and cried to themselves, while their families were wondering what went wrong. They sent these people to psychiatrists, but still the trauma would not end. It remained a vulgar reality. But the spirit of each human being is so strong that these psychological trauma, the mind's tricks, the sudden attacks, and the brainwashing of innocence, youth, and beauty can be arrested. These thoughts will never end, but they can be stopped and used so that the old ways, the old thoughts are pushed away, far away, so that the rationality, the intuitiveness, the common sense of peace can be heralded forth.

My pen begins to spin again, as my head, and I am so bored that my feet shake in anxiousness. Outside the New War mobilizes the aircraft and the missile. My mind is at peace, so I am laughing again. Larry made me laugh so hard that tears spilled out of my eyes.

Sunday is the most difficult day. The newswoman spoke well this morning, and I am thankful that the media has again successfully mirrored society. It played its role responsibly and gracefully. Everyone in the world, and especially the world's children are looking up, trying to find peace. All will find peace if all make a commitment to non-violence. Being a hostage in one's own country has the effect of fear. I am so lucky to be held here in a hospital while the New War is away from me. Peace is the primary object and can be achieved under any structure of government. Since I am a part of a liberal democracy, I believe in that same Constitution by which we should all lead our lives. These ideas were drawn up by rational thinkers understanding what may be in store for the future. These men were not absolutely correct, but they had a vision for the future. Oh Darwin and Mendel and all of these rational thinkers were right. You are evolving, yes you. Now, the students must express this knowledge to the other students, and finally to their elders. The students must also express this knowledge to the ones who cannot comprehend such a change. No matter who you are, no matter where you come from, no matter what you are now, peace can be with you, if you allow the mind to open and think rationally of peace. Oh I am so calm while the rest of the country begins to find the answer, the solution to the world's problem. Sing aloud so that all may hear!

I have decided to leave this institution, if they will let me go, but my mind will always remain captured by the violence and the war. Sometimes we get so lost that a map is necessary to find our way back home.

There is a war among different parts of the world. The older generation must go against it or risk fighting the war for themselves. Send the old to war. Never the young.

We must draw out the violence from within us in other ways. For instance, I use this hospital to draw out the violence from within my mind. Others may use sports, reading, or watching television and movies. We, the followers, must take a break, for peace is much too stressful to achieve when all of society is working very hard and slowly disintegrating. Segregation inhibits our search for peace, for the followers are afraid to venture from the old ways of violence. But there must be some confidence within us, some seed which gives us back that self-esteem we used to have when we were children. This is what peace is all about, and the followers must call that self-esteem to the surface and communicate the message of peace.

2nd of Jamadaa al-awal 1435
(March 4, 2014)

I did not awake with peace. Instead I awoke with a nightmare. While in bed, I had the image of the child slapping the mother many times to break the mother out of an hypnotic spell. It was a devious image, a terrifying one, and I guess I cannot sleep. Peace is a state of mind, and I must make it a part of my inner core. I don't know what's happening to my mind, but slowly it begins to flash painful images when I try to sleep. I guess when we sleep, we start to imagine things, not rationalize them. And so, when sleep comes, I guess it is in our own best interests to rationalize peace.

The birds are chirping this morning along with Edmund's incessant pacing. His father has put him in this institution for thirty-three years. By the way, I am going to keep track of time from now on. I am losing all sense of time and place.

I have been here before. It is all some kind of game. People are very nice to me here, and I think they are all looking out for me. I have human development group at one pm so I cannot sleep this afternoon. That vision still haunts me from last night, and I want it to go away.

There is so much boredom. What to do about this boredom? I have to think, but I am so bored of thinking. I only remember that children can always play the game better than adults. And so I continue to play this space cadet game, although it does get annoying sometimes.

I'm in space. Holy Bat-shit! I'm some sort of media testing agent. Oh no. The laughter is coming back to me. Giggle. Giggle. Giggle. This is all I know how to do. I guess to find peace of mind, I must look to my childhood. My feet are firmly planted on planet earth. Oh the masterminds. They think I'm taking off on a shuttle bound for Mars. No way, not me. What I saw on television, the violence of the New War, was probably an act, all fake. After all, what the hell is going on here? My mind repeats itself. I'm going up, up, and away. Oh television is so childlike. I guess that's why people watch it so much. I think all the world's just peachy keen though. Boy would I like to have that acid I once tried. Or perhaps that smooth bowl of pot. Hmmm, how nice. Or perhaps a dozen beers. Nah, much too cumbersome. My belly will fill very easily. What would be the wonder drug? Probably the combination of pot and beer. We must not limit drugs, for it should be up to the individual to decide. How far do I want to take this? I want to take it all the way to the intuitive rationalization of peace. Peace of mind and peace of body. We are all addicted to many things. My mind is not playing tricks on me, people are playing tricks on me. I finally understand it. Time is fluid, so I guess I have lived before. Time travel is possible, but the machines don't make it possible. People make it possible, but we must not let the machines take over the people. Peace is always in the mind.

The technology of the future will help our children become smarter than they already are. Microcomputers and telecommunications have advanced far beyond the rationale of children. Hence, there must be peace within these systems of communications. Peace must be the primary objective. Never violence and war, for these things are irrational.

I have found peace but am still haunted by visions of anger and violence. I wish these things would go away, but they won't. I must deal with my secret sharer that nestles deep within me.

I am stuck here at the Psychiatric Institute. I can't wait to leave. I am on thirty-minute checks, because I told the doctors that I was in a time warp.

I've got to stop time traveling. Instead I have to get on with my life. I have no objectivity anymore, but I am able to watch the news from time to time. I don't even need these pills. It's hard, very hard to be yourself and live in your own time. Relating to other people is also very difficult, but you have to extend your hand somewhere along the line. Think about it. I have been through the theory of relativity in this small psychiatric ward. All it took was three painful weeks. I'm not sure what to believe. This may be some sort of gag, I'm not sure. But I know someone's pulling the strings. It's not me, that's for sure. I guess there is a God, somewhere out there. He sees all of us on some sort of screen. Time keeps flowing. But if it flows in the way of violence then I want no part of time, for time, although rational, must stop or be arrested when violence occurs, so that the country has the time to heal psychologically. I have clung with my life to the rationality of peace, such that my mind began to lose itself in thought. A very big web we weave, don't we? I am somewhat sick and tired of my mind's own deception. Duking it out mentally with people. But time is so fluid that death doesn't exist physically, only mentally. If this is the case, then why not live in peace? I do not understand this.

I think they are holding me hostage in this joint, and I am so sick of it. Time and peace have been wallowing over me, but it's tough to hang on to them when I am suffering. I don't know what the suffering is about, but it's killing me. We have a community meeting soon, and I will be sure to voice my opinions freely. First of all, I am not an invalid and deserve to be placed on escort status immediately.

Finally, I'm on escort status, and I do believe that I have suffered enough. I'm not sure where I'm going. I've been at this institution which is the cookiest, zaniest place in the galaxy. I am constantly second-guessing the identity of people. I thought my two roommates were Abe Lincoln and Winston Churchill. I still think I am the living proof of Einstein's theories, that time travel does work. I have traveled faster than the speed of light before. No one may believe me, for I have been drugged up and washed out. I know now that in the world I must rely upon myself first and foremost. That it is impossible to care for others without caring for yourself. How quacky is that?

I originally wanted to drop out of school, but now I am anxious to get back into the swing of things. The stelazine has worked, and my brain is starting to process years of blocked up information. In the background I hear the Sri Lankan kids playing with their mother who has been staying here for sometime. I have trust in me and am ready to love and trust again. The motivation to play some ping-pong is now here. Oh how wonderful life is- to be free at last, to exude happiness from within out.

I guess what I had was a psychotic break - a very heavy psychotic break. For this reason I found myself in outer-space. So where do I go from here? After such a break it's going to be hard to adjust to the real world. I have been in the clouds. The doctors have placed me on lithium in addition to the stelazine. I have stopped taking wellbutrin. These two chemicals will help keep my nose clean as the rugged and rocky future commences.

I need some sex now, for I have been locked up for three weeks so far. The people have been very nice to me and have empathized with my problems. But my will must carry on, and the olive branch of peace must be used by all. I do not want to second guess anyone's identity anymore. The last thing I need is to come rolling back here with my thumb up my ass going through the same thing all over again. The brave new world will not be so easy this time. My evolution will again take place, so I must be on guard, ready and prepared to rationalize peace again.

Manmatha from Sri Lanka probably understands my thinking. She has been a patient here for sometime. She is also hearing voices in her head. I hear music, but I do not know why. She's a very interesting character, although she does not talk much. She has her children who come and play with her every so often. She reminds me of my mother in many ways. Because I am of the same part of the world, I feel like I owe her something. Again this is something psychological, as if I have some responsibility to this woman I don't even know. We must have a melting pot again, not a salad bowl. Soup and salad are interchangeable. Sometimes we need the soup all over again. We have been segregated from one another long enough. It takes a student to realize this.

Karen is back. Amazing. I never want to relapse like Karen. She did it to herself. I'm wondering whether or not I should talk to her. I am very afraid of relapse.

I just awoke from sleep. Manmatha's children should learn how to play baseball, two cherubic children bouncing within these halls with glee. No cares, only curiosity.

Sluggish a bit. Sitting in this ward ordering my favorite medicines to take away the pain and anxiety. My best friend nicotine sits between my cheek and gum, while I pour out random words. Unfortunately, Phil, my other roommate whom I thought was Abe Lincoln, is leaving tomorrow, and I am sorry to see him go. He and I share the same boredom with this place. I have been fenced in for so long, and it's so disappointing to learn that my mind will fence itself in, even when I leave this hell. All I wanted to do was to save the world and all the living things within it. Time is so relative within these walls, but I still…

I get so horny in here I just want to jerk off and fantasize a bit. You can say that I'm back down to earth, and I feel pretty confident that our planet will be here for many a millenia. We must instill and inculcate the rationality of peace wherever we go, no matter what type of human being we are.

A man with wavy blonde hair came in today. He wants a sex change operation in the near future, and I guess they are reviewing him for psychiatric treatment. People are not being honest with themselves anymore, not even honest with their own sexuality. But this is okay. To each his or her own I guess. I just don't want to be fooled. Everyone should be honest, and I have to start with myself. I don't particularly care for my religion or for the persons who have royally screwed it up. But I must work to change the things that do not comply with the rationality of peace. I see this as a prime objective. I must talk peace and act peace. This will be difficult.

Karen sat next to me and attempted to put her hand next to mine. I shied away knowing that I had come down from cloud nine. In my room I sit, and the place smells like bad feet, so putrid and vile that it makes me want to puke. I can't stand the stench of my roommates' feet. We have been walking about all day, and that odor just wafts through the air, as if nothing can stop it. Phil is leaving tomorrow. He still cracks me up talking about how boring it gets around here. He seems to be in a much better mood knowing he can finally leave this place of the living dead and get on with his life. I can't wait to get out of here. I think my life has direction, but I'm afraid. Oh the stench in here. It smells so bad that I might have to change rooms.

Last night I fell asleep around eleven and had another nightmare. I dreamt that I returned to my neighborhood on Riverside Drive. I had a very voluptuous and sexy African-American girlfriend. This girlfriend would kiss me with her perfect lips from head to toe in my apartment. All of a sudden we were in some grand hotel. I, in a simple golf shirt, and she in a very tight sequined dress which highlighted her very tight, very smooth curves. She kissed me, and I recall the outlines of her face. She is all I want for the evening. As we arrive at our floor by taking the hotel elevator, we walk down the corridor. My dream now shifts perspective. She is now walking behind me, and I can see a tall, more muscular body, but I cannot make out the face. So we are both walking, and I am looking at them like a camera, watching their fronts. Suddenly she takes off my shirt in the hallway. I don't do anything about it, for there exists the same golf shirt underneath that golf shirt. She does it again and again, nothing but golf shirts layer after layer. Finally she takes off the last layer, and my new African-American chest is exposed. I am now Malcolm X marching down the hallway.

That night I had another nightmare. I dreamt that I lead a crew of African-Americans to take over my public school. The scenes of violence inflicted on innocent people forced me into a cold sweat. This was the most terrible of nightmares, for innocence was being slaughtered, and peace was shoved aside for a terrible violence. When I awoke at one in the morning, I quickly got out of bed and went to the medicine dispensary to get some Benadryl.

The Benadryl worked, and I was able to sleep for another few hours until seven thirty this morning. I had a third dream. My mother, a painter, and I were traveling in a car towards South Ferry on the FDR Drive. We were going through some underpass when I brought the car into the wrong lane. I took a wrong exit, and we were on the ramp heading up. The car stopped at a dead end, as I had no control over its maneuvers anymore. But we stopped and trotted from the car to look around. We were on a yellow brick road of sorts, but this road was made of white mosaic tile. The tiled road spiraled up into the sky with no end in sight. The painter, my mother, and I noticed the many different footprints that covered the walkway, so we got buckets filled with soapy water and carefully mopped the tiles clean. The tiled road was so dirty that our arms didn't have enough strength to clean everything. I awoke around seven fifty to be precise.

We had a quick community meeting at which time I was told that I had been denied a ground's card and town's pass. I guess they want to see if the lithium and stelazine are stabilizing me. The community meeting's main subject concerned the restructuring of the in-patient professional program. We were to be the last patients living in this ward. The facility will be used as a day treatment program. All patients living here will be reassigned to other units. Nursing layoffs are expected. The whole health care system is expected to be revamped by the politicians in Washington. The world as we know it is collapsing, but for good reason. Out of this pile of theoretical rubble we will achieve something far better in favor of the next generation of idealists who believe that at certain times social change is necessary. I asked the leading psychiatrist in the meeting, the same doctor who took me from the apartment, whether or not this change had taken place before. He answered affirmatively. I also asked how this change would affect the cost. He answered that the costs will be half of the current costs. From this point I understood the revolving cycle of the earth. Every thirty years a social change among human beings will result, giving birth to a new generation. The revolution on earth translates holistically into an evolution within the universe. Our eyes must be directed towards the cosmos, directed towards other answers. I'm positive that there will be a fruition of good things that will come from this social change. New writings, new movies, new ideas. I can imagine myself venturing out across the deserts of New Mexico with my babe on the back of my Harley Davidson, her hands around my waist and her big breasts rubbing against my back. I can feel those jugs, and her hands caressing the insides of my thighs as the wind blows back our hair. We ride across route 80 west, not looking back. No sense of time, only a sense of direction. And as we ride the highway slants upwards towards the sky. The tunes, the babe, the music, and the Harley, and the highway searching for something better, more real than what everyday life has to offer.

Coming here saved me, and in the process of saving myself I royally screwed up my education. I don't have many places to go. My dreams of leaving the planet have come down to a hurt-the-buzz reality. No one will support me in my endeavors. Rather the people will label me insane and toss me into a joint like this where masturbation in the shower becomes a daily ritual.

As you can tell my mind drifts back and forth from one concept to the next. I try to add consistency to this rubble from which the rationality of peace is developed. It's just so fucking boring here. There is absolutely nothing to do. No one visits me anymore. I pace all day waiting for lunch, waiting for smoke breaks, and then waiting for dinner. All I do here is wait to leave and then once I arrive at the time to leave, I have no clue where the hell I'm going. I'm constantly bored. I want to live by an amusement park, and even if I did live next to an amusement park, I would find that boring after some time. I wish I could live my life very simply without all the delusions of grandeur or the complications of mind. All I ever asked for was simple peace of mind. The boredom gets so tedious that I end up twiddling my thumbs or changing positions in my chair. Everything about the place is boring. My former roommate knew this full well. I mean am I not boring you by writing how boring this place is? Now do you see why these sexual images come to mind? It's because I am so bored with myself. I need some rip-roaring excitement once in a while. Bored, bored, bored.

3rd of Jumaada al-awal 1435
(March 5, 2014)

I really want to get out of this place. While my world crumbles all around me, I am left here to watch it crumble. I stay here and plummet through the abyss of space. Within this room I am watching the world collapse. Cars being ripped apart by harrowing winds. Children being tossed about by tornadoes, floods rising to the east and washing every structure to the west, flooding the grass and spoiling the soil. The sky rips apart and falls as the thunder and lightning crack like sharp, wet towels on our backsides. The sun, lost above the dark clouds and filtering sky. The clouds rolling over each other towards the portent of ominous doom. I want to click my two heels together and end up in a place called home.

I have been here before, I know I have. Something looks so familiar, vaguely familiar, as if I have gone through the same thing, over and over again. Pictures in my head flashing similar things from the past. Similar photographs on the wall. Similar circular thought. Yes, my mind is going around in circles with nowhere to stop. You have been here as well, and I can't explain it, but I can look into your eyes and understand who you are. You, over there, are Winston Churchill, and you in red with your long mustache are Adolph Hitler. You have come back to haunt me. Or are you here to make ammends for the evil you have spread onto the world? Are you waiting for the next Reich, or are you here to make me go insane? The madness, all of it hurting me, stinging me like wounds. I am seeing all of you. I know who you really are, for I can see you through that clothing. Your eyes give it away. A conspiracy against me, because I know too much, way too much. And if I die I will come back again to haunt you. These ghosts, these apparitions which plague my head. I want to forget the history, the everything, and start over again. And so they have transferred me to this room with very white walls, all of them padded. To get me there they put me in a straight jacket, and this I accepted voluntarily. For I have finally gone mad. I threw in the towel and acted out on one of the nurses. I must suffer in order to understand the problems that lurk within my brain. Why do I want to kill my mother, I am not sure yet. I feel as if this has been predetermined. Stuck in this room with very white walls, and nothing to do but write about total insanity. They have given me a crayon and allow my arms free every two hours. What is the cost of this freedom? My friends are four white walls. Who knows what the costs are. Why is everyone out to get me? Why is it that my mother won't leave me alone?

The hospital attendant with his thick glasses and white uniform. I do not hate him. I only understand that he has a job to do. To lead me back to the insanity I bore myself into, back into the padded room with very white walls. And the insanity within my brain pounds harder and harder. They are now trying to give me medication. The same Lithium and Stelazine. Hmmm. Tastes so good these two drugs- both of them stabilizers of anxiety and mood. They are lodged within the back of my throat, and I am tempted to cough them back into the world. No wonder these biotech mutual funds did so well. It's all a conspiracy to make me the new human laboratory rat. They have hid me away in the middle of nowhere. They have not given me a clue who I am or where I am. I see nothing but white walls. No windows are allowed. I cannot see the fresh green grass and the little children playing in the sun, in the playgrounds. I've often wanted to play in the playgrounds of life. To sit like a child on the swings.

The attendant in the white coat gives me the pills. Each day these pills get thicker and thicker. They are in an assortment of colors. One purple, another green, and the red one before bedtime. Slowly I'm beginning to lose my sense of balance. I become more tranquil as time goes on, and the attendant has seen this in me. The pathways of this asylum are interesting. Outside the padded room there is a hallway that stretches many feet. It is a very narrow hallway. On the sides are other padded rooms, and inside them I hear screaming and yelling, also pounding and scratching. No one is trying to calm them. I guess the cells are for that purpose, a sort of self-calming effect. As the attendant and I walk ever so slowly down this corridor I notice the faint slivers of light descend through the sky windows. Ah, I am now out of the corridor and into the bigger room with other patients. We have all been released at the same time, I guess. And everyone here is pacing so slowly. I do not know who these people are, but we have all been here before. I have walked these same steps and have inhaled the same odors. Better yet, I have taken these same medications, and they are making me react very slowly. I move my arms and they move in slow motion. All of my strength is being used, but somehow I move at the same pace as all the others. We are in hospital johnnys. Everything seems at peace, but these violent thoughts bounce back and forth in my head. The medication takes it away momentarily, but then these thoughts come bouncing back. Oh it does not matter. I should follow these people who have finally made it out of their padded rooms. The attendant has introduced me to the nurse. Her name is Mary. She has one of those horrific demeanors. She's my height and a little on the plump side. All of these Florence Nightingale types are alike. I just want to get laid, that's all I need. That and a good steak. Right beside the steak I'll have a cold pint of beer- the type of beer served at those London pubs. Mary will hopefully be as nice. She hands me more medication, and I decide to ingest them. Otherwise I will be sent to my room again.

I've got seven funny looking invalids with Mary placed at the center of attention. She is called the group facilitator, and she prevents our discussion from abuse. For instance, I could call that fucking idiot sitting over there in his chair a fat, no good penis licker and ball-sucking scumbag. But this would be too abusive. Being polite is of essential importance to the staff here at this unknown hospital. The group also maintains some kind of confidentiality rule. But this I find absolute bullshit. I mean, I should be able to say whatever the hell I want to say. After all, we are in a mental hospital. Although I don't believe in the principle of confidentiality, I will abide by it, because I am afraid of the padded room. Keeping out of trouble will be my first priority.

I now sleep in a cell by myself, but the room is not padded. The room is very small and has its own sink and toilet. They have provided my own little toiletry kit, packed with all the essentials: a toothbrush and toothpaste, deodorant stick, and comb. Nothing sharp, for I may decide to kill myself, maybe by a razor or a file. There is a common shower a few doors down. Unfortunately, we have to take showers at the same time. I don't enjoy staring at everyone, although some do. Sometimes I even do it. There are penises all around me. I have no choice but to stare at a few of them. There's this one guy named Chuck who has a deformed penis. It bends and twists in many different directions like a corkscrew.

At the end of our morning shower, towels are distributed to us, and we trudge back our merry way into our cells where even more medication awaits us. Not in our rooms, but from the dispensary. Mary has gone away for the time being, so we must take the medications from Ida. She's black and unbelievably beautiful. I asked her if she wanted to give me a bath later on, but she denied me flatly. I was left to go back to my room drugged up with medication and a raging hard on.

Mary has been very nice to me. She has given me my medications on time and has assisted my mental ramblings with a smile. But as she gives me the extra doses of medications I do not swallow them. I leave them in my mouth until I can reject them in the toilet. And I do so, because the world needs to be saved, and we cannot have the medicines clouding my judgment and my memory. I must be anxious again and brood over the feelings of violence that play pinball in my head. We must together make these thoughts vanish. But wait. Why is the attendant coming towards me? He is leading me back to the padded room. Why is this mother-fucker coming near me? I'll kill him. I will take a hatchet and decapitate him. He is handling me in such a rough manner. They must have found the medication in the toilet bowl. Oh how could this be? I haven't been thinking hard enough. I must think harder and harder until the violence ends. Oh how ironic- the world will implode, because I did not flush the toilet. Save me. Please do something. Just don't put me back in that horrible room...

15th of Jumaada al-Thanny 1435
(April 15, 2014)

For another month I have stayed in this special unit, and again I am out. If I behave well, then I may be out of this facility within a year. Escape is first and foremost on my mind. With each dragging day comes new thought of climbing that barbed wire fence in the courtyard. I'm back to the room with the sink and the toilet, all of it looking vaguely familiar. Unpacking my stuff, I notice that my thoughts have changed. Quite simply, my thoughts have whittled away into the dark abyss, for I have forgotten most of what I've known and must delve again into the past in order to find what I once had. They have taken all of my papers away for the time being, and my memory has been tapped by a fist-load of medications. I cannot even remember my friends or my mother. I'm sure I have friends and family somewhere. They have not forgotten me, I hope.

I have been sitting within this piece of shit group therapy for a month. Idiots ranting about their poor dysfunctional families. Well, you idiots, all of you blew it. Never have a family unless you plan to be a great man, or a great woman; you idiots, you cutthroat fools wrapped in your own self-pity. Well, stop feeling guilty and do something that the whole world can benefit from. We must together save humanity, for only the insane would take up such a feat. And when I get out of this wasteland of thought, I will use knowledge and oh so limited experiences to work for peace in the mind. I will look deeply into another person's eyes and carefully read their thoughts and determine, first, the degree of violence. Then I will use my hypnosis to fill the fragile, violent brain with peaceful thoughts, but this time using no medication. I will use magic to explain the activities of the brain, and thus there will be only the diagnosis of violence, and I will work hard to shift that diagnosis into the cure of peace or to prevent that violence of the brain from spilling onto the physical body. Instead, all of those who declare themselves insane must think about the rationality of peace and then use the newly acquired knowledge to convince their family and friends. If they reject you, then do not feel bad. Bounce back up and think of other ways. There are infinite possibilities in the universe for every individual. Never back down. Never forsake the goal of peace for the insanity of violence and war. With every individual who understands peace, the future dramatically changes. Change the future so that the whole human race may have the chance to evolve and grow. It's that simple. It starts with the individual. And it seems as though my brain is expanding beyond the skull, as though some damned spirit is putting thoughts in my brain. Who's there? Who's in my brain? Knock-knock, who's in my brain?

You see, the question of efficiency is mutually exclusive to the equilibrium and stability that peace brings. Hence, peace does not necessarily operate on a level of efficiency, but rather on a level of stability. Hence, the size can be very large, and peace may still operate at an optimal level. But the large size presupposes that each individual is able to rationalize peace intuitively. If all individuals are able to do this, then the preferences of the persons within this large group, known as the human race, remain the same. Hence, the equilibrium of peace is also a reflexive equilibrium. It's perfect, and the perfection of peace can exist within the mind. We must also assume that preferences are a part of psychology as well as rationality. So, all human beings must have rationalized peace in order to have peace exist as perfection in the mind. Let us look at the simple supply and demand chart. (See Diagram #1).

The reflexive equilibrium of peace is always shifting, for as time goes on, we as human beings are evolving. Hence, the costs of peace for every individual will get costlier as time goes on. So, the costs for peace will be high. In order to bring the reflexive equilibrium about once again, at which quantity equals cost, we must exercise a 'voice' option. In other words, the students of the world must voice their opinions concerning the high price of peace. Their voice will drive the cost down. Thus, the costs of peace will be more affordable for everyone. And the point at which the reflexive equilibrium occurs will be brought to a higher level, as a result of evolution and time. Oh glory to the rationality of peace, for it is intuitive not moral, rational not ideological, common sense not imagination.

Let us test this theory of peace. Let us take Harry, a thirty-six year old man who lives in the suburbs with his beautiful wife Belinda and their two sons Tyler and Moonbeam. Let us say that Harry has a white-collar job. Because he works, he is not that in tune with current trends but is able to watch the news at night to make up his mind where he stands on certain issues. Let us also say that Harry has been watching television prior to this New War and cannot make up his mind whether he wants peace or war. His dominant reaction is for war, because he wants to protect his children from the wrath of the Arabian dictator. Hence, he chooses war and goes with the majority. He understands the war will kill many but also rests his mind, because peace will remain with his family. His neighborhood will not be bombed. All will be happening on the television. After the war, Harry discovers that the recession still looms large, and he anticipates peace. He thus wants peace very badly but does not know how to obtain it. What shall Harry do, for he cannot do it on his own? Or can he? Taking the knowledge of the New War into account, he thinks about what would happen if rioting were to break out in his own neighborhood. He also thinks in the long term and not the short term. Violence begets more violence. Hence, he makes a psychological decision which is functionally irrational. He makes a choice to try and intuitively rationalize peace. This is the first step. Secondly, he attempts to find the equilibrium point at which the cost of peace is equivalent to the quantity of peace. Unfortunately, Harry notices that the price tag of peace is much too high. He alone can neither afford nor change the price tag. But still Harry cannot leave his job to pursue such endeavors. He must remain in his place and make money so that his children can eat. His wife is also working, and she thinks the same. So the students of life, who understand that stability is needed in times of unrest, use their voice to lower the worldwide price tag of peace, and bring the price back in line with the quantity supplied. Harry remembers that he was once a student and sees Tyler and Moonbeam as future students who will one day non-violently demonstrate or lobby government to lower the prices of peace. Hence, as Harry grows and develops new technology, Moonbeam and Tyler are both preparing for instability, and they are preparing their voices for peaceful demonstrations. Harry can rest well at night knowing that A) he has made a psychological choice to rationalize peace and B) he has been able to rationalize peace with the help of students from around the world, old and young, who were able to demonstrate their yearning for a lower price of peace. Also, he can now evolve and create new technology, for he knows that Tyler and Moonbeam will be in the same position later in time. So goes the example of Harry, a man who has found peace of mind through the help of A) the choice and B) Students.

We may also include the news as a catalyst to peace. We must also thank a liberal democracy for helping Harry to have easy access to the students as they finally speak their minds. Because I am a student, am I not? I have nothing to lose by taking out my violence on the world. I will smash and break the very foundations of the earth, for I am insecure and must control people in order to bring them to my knees and worship me, put up pictures of me. Let me out of this box, and I will be that monster. Out of this box, and I will show all of you the power of God. I have the power of God within my fingertips and will destroy all whom worship the master, because the master has told me how foolish you peevish little insects are. Let us make war and crucify the heretics.

Turn on those gas chambers and heat the ovens. Let the Jews separate the synagogue by sex, let the Muslims divide the mosques by power. Women in the back, and men in the front. The men shall perish first. I have broken down these walls of this asylum and shall use my hands to crush what innocence remains. Take their young bodies and bash their skulls on old stone walls. Let the blood and the waste of their organs roll down these rocks and form puddles of blood. Large puddles so that the old can finally play their games and splash in the puddles with their meaningless children, dead, beaten by stone. Let me out of this asylum so that I may trample upon the world and crush the students who sit in their meager social circles and sip beer at my expense. We will segregate the fit from the unfit, Jews from gentiles, Muslims from Hindus, Americans from the Europeans, the Blacks from the Whites, the Aids victims from the healthy, the cancer stricken from the pink lunged, the rich from the poor. Divide and conquer them. Kill them all. Stab them with large bayonets and twist slowly, making sure that they feel the pain of my wrath.

I am about to be released, and I want nothing but war, nothing but segregation. I want the church and the state to mix and unleash their torment upon the young and the old alike. There will be no mercy. All will die, and the insects can finally rule the earth. The animals will grow and do the same. I, on the other hand, will be sitting on my throne high in the heavens, while all of you idiots torment in hell. I will be laughing while the demons torture you. I will be farting and burping while the demons starve you. All of you confined to the pits of hell, as I look upon my creation and say "Damn, that was fun.'

Yes, I must get out of this asylum, and I am almost ready to leave. My therapy sessions have not been successful.

We must truly ask: are people truly free when people are at peace? Let us take Harry again. Because Harry has rationalized peace, he understands the new technology he creates must be used for peaceful endeavors. So Harry is not free, for he will tell himself not to create weapons, for example. But why not abrogate 'arms' and call them 'defensive arms' so that people can defend themselves against others whom have not rationalized peace before? But won't this hurt peace if Harry has the freedom to create defensive arms?

Creating arms always hurts peace, but there must be a compromise. Let us assume there exists life out in space. Then arms must be used to defend the human race against alien attackers. Remember that we still want peace, for this is Harry's ultimate goal. But Harry must not create arms which may be used by humans to attack other humans. Rather, arms must be created such that human beings may only use them upon other alien beings, if and only if, these alien beings do not understand the rationality of peace. If these alien beings do not, then we must first try to teach or communicate with these aliens the rationality of peace. We will demonstrate to them, most likely by the younger students, that peace is possible, if intuitively rationalized. Hence, Harry is not truly free but will be once peace is rationalized among every human being on the earth and every alien in the universe. Harry will have to be a student again, if the new technology he develops is meant for war. If he develops arms for self-defense, then there will be a time when the students must demonstrate and remind Harry to lower the costs of peace which will inflate the costs of making arms. Evolution will again take place, and Harry will still prepare arms for the universe and beyond. The human race must stick together. That is why there must be the freedom of peace among all human beings, for we will be dealing with aliens soon who may not understand the earth and how we, as human beings, brought peace to our planet. If aliens do not understand peace, then we must demonstrate to them as students what peace means to us and how highly we regard it. The last resort against our alien friends is defense. Hopefully before this juncture the students will demonstrate. Remember that aliens have politics and economics as well. No one can get away from these two forces. So again the students will set Harry free. But Harry will only be free if there is peace amongst all beings. Obviously there will be an intergalactic war unless the students rise and speak out. For the sake of human beings everywhere, please lower the costs of peace.

20th of Jumaada al-awal 1435
(April 20, 2014)

Tired and groggy this morning, and the time moves slowly. Last night I woke up in the middle of a routine nightmare and needed to get some help with the ativan. Doctors, nurses, custodians. The mental unit always going mental-seizures of the mind, brainwaves unable to untangle themselves. Smoke break soon, and I will be able to fill myself with nicotine. Feeling a bit like Moses Herzog. Doctor Dave always catches me sleeping on this bed. I hear a woman crying in the hallway. She lost someone dear, I presume. Her mother informed her, and now the pain, as though they sell it like candy bars at the local kiosk; a whole range of snacks: pain, hurt, fear, et cetera, all sold through the dispensary.

While another patient and I were playing the game of Life, an old game with peg dependents neatly fit into these plastic cars, their shapes like spores or straight sperm, we were asked to sign a card for a woman whose husband had just died. The gaiety of the game plummeted to soft whispers and commiseration as we both signed the cards. I was wondering what to put on it.

'My deepest condolences,' I wrote followed by my name. I don't even know the woman, but I forced myself to care.

Fourteen water towers, hanging like pimples above the buildings of Fort Washington Avenue. I'm in Room #1, and so I can see the same boredom out there as it is in here, wandering the hallways.

Late night now. Close to eleven, and I've been having thoughts in the back of this Neanderthal brain that I am being watched, that I may use telepathy to communicate. While playing monopoly I spotted a young visitor to the unit. She is Hispanic with simple reddish hair running over her. I tried to link minds with her, and I asked deep in thought 'if you can hear me now, I am thinking of you. Turn around if you can hear me.' She turned around a few moments later taking her large brown eyes away from the television screen. I tried telepathy a second time, but it didn't work, leaving me alone and confirming my suspicions that I am a crackpot. The side effect of this truth is emptiness. It has ended, and the truth of sickness has been revealed, and now I'm leaving behind the delusions that usurped reality. Truth: understanding that I am ill, which leaves me hollow inside.

Someone is still watching me, so I am performing for them whomever they may be. At tonight's Monopoly tournament, I believed my explanation of mortgages was being monitored by some cosmic force. I don't want to give up on those delusions, or else I'll feel empty, as if this whole ordeal happened for nothing. These things happen for a reason. Now I have to rebuild. I've been tricked and betrayed. It gives me no reason to believe in an ubiquitous God. Actually, he lives in room twenty-four, down in the special care unit.

He calls himself 'God,' a bald man in his sixties. They can't get a name out of him. His first name is 'Ubiquitous.' Last name, 'God.' On the patients list the old man is listed as 'God.'

So I was ill and that is the truth, or is it? Was I driven towards the sickness, or did I start it myself? So alone. Coincidences and connections, and I'm trying to work with them. The ego so violently prodded by the forces of the unknown, and my ego responded by doing the right things. I came to this unit and sat in silence in one of the rooms and thought or imagined that wings were growing on my back, and I was learning to fly. If I could, I would open this caged window and jump until the wings burst forth. I would take the world with me as my feet are buckled to the ground and my wings batted like a captured fly. Yes, I imagined I was growing wings on my back. I feared that this place was ready to give me a sex change operation as I sent telepathic messages. Damn, did I fuck up this time, but it's getting better. I still feel I am being watched, so I am forced to perform to my best abilities. The Ativan should start closing in on me now. I need to get some sleep, just to end the boredom. Was it all some dream? The forces have left my brain, and now I wallow in humiliation over myself for actually thinking that some cosmic power believed in me. Left with nothing. Left with hollow, vapid emotions.

21st of Jumaada al Thanny 1435
(April 21, 2014)

I have taken certain amounts of lithium, haldol, cogentin, and ativan. They have set me straight for a short time, but I still have memories- only good ones, for this time around I have been good, as if it were a faith of sorts, and now I have plans to visit places.

The man who calls himself 'God' stays in room twenty-four. I have met him. Hell and Heaven, immature as they are, finally make peace within my brain, war-torn and pillaged. So much destruction. I sit in this hospital room with a bed, shower, and bathroom. I hear Jonathan in the hallway ranting on aspects of politics, his speaking so seductive, and I know he is suffering. We all are. Helen, bless her, has given me cigarettes. My mind, damaged, is beginning to heal itself, and I'm sure it's because of the medication.

More along the lines of schizophrenia, as if I have a clue. Still it is difficult to relate to persons, difficult to write, since only the longest of books can recreate this harrowing experience. But I am well enough to try with a small degree of self-confidence. I am out of the special care ward where the yelling and moaning grew intense. I tried hard to communicate telepathically with Thelma who has been restrained to a bed with leather straps. Resistance is futile. I wanted to erase all of it, as if it never happened. Sheer terror as police officers wrestled me to the bed, to the needle, which I would normally refuse. The idea I was to be aborted, a feeling of intense fear of being changed into the opposite sex against my will.

My fear has been reduced since I trusted them. Trust is never easy, but ironically trusting makes it easier. Loaded words and loaded messages, as if each word needs direction, as if the alphabet is unintelligible. But I suppose I am on my way. Divisiveness- men and women, blacks and whites, et cetera. I must learn how to deal with these divisions but at the same time resist them. I trust the direction towards which I am resisting. Slowly I am on my feet, smiling again, laughing again, learning how to aid others again. Was I ill?

Much has changed since I have been here. Sign language, as if by wiping my eyes someone understood. The touch of the nose communicating something, telling me to leave this place, to go somewhere. But where am I to go? These coincidences all around me, telling me, begging me, forcing me to leave this place of misery and go where exactly? What is causing this? Why am I heading to Boston all of a sudden? Who's behind all this? Damn it, I can't think straight. Something is wrong. My mind is on fire. It pulls me to another place, but where? Get a hold of myself.

Book Four

"I know from my own experience that telepathy is a fact. I have no interest in proving telepathy or anything to anybody. I do want usable knowledge of telepathy. What I look for in any relationship is contact on the nonverbal level of intuition and feeling, that is, telepathic contact."-William Burroughs

THE FLIGHT TO BOSTON
24th of Rajab 1435
(May 24, 2014)

The Imam Al-Mustafa received his discharge papers. His mother, Maryam, met him at the entrance to the ward carrying a box of Italian chocolates. An electric buzzer, depressed by one of the staff members, opened the door. Together the Imam and his mother left the ward in the usual silence which had marred their relationship. She guided him under a brilliant sky. They walked slowly along Fort Washington Avenue, and it was Maryam who broke the silence.

"How are you my sweet?"

"I'm fine," said the Imam, not wishing to be bothered.

When they stopped at the crosswalk, Maryam ran her fingers through his hair as she noticed how long it had grown. The Imam now wore a scraggly beard.

"Are you all right?" she asked again.

They walked along a sun-drenched street to their apartment building. Maryam wondered why her son was so sullen. She hoped he had been cured. His head hung low. His eyes drooped.

At home Maryam prepared some mincemeat and flat bread. Mustafa flicked on the television. She served him the food on the sofa, and the Imam ate while he watched. She sat down beside him and wiped some strands of hair from his brow. He pulled away, letting the television mesmerize him.

"Can you say a few words? Anything at all? Are you glad to be back?"

"I have to leave," he said.

"Where are you going? You just got home."

"I'm going further north."

"Not without eating your food."

"I need an education."

Maryam played with his hair.

"And a haircut," she said.

"Now I'm traveling farther north within the next few days. Are you listening?"

"You can't go anywhere without something to eat. Besides, all your education can be completed from this house. You're okay now. The doctors have cured you."

"I need to be on my own."

"You're a little young for that."

"I'm older now."

Maryam was not prepared for another fight at the door, but if another fight were to keep her son from leaving, she would fight. Fighting at the door was a fight against the demons within her son, as the devil himself had made him sick in the first place. She blamed the devil for her son's temptation to flee. This devil would bother him until he learned Arabic.

"You will learn your prayers before you leave," she said.

"I already know them," he said, his eyes fixed to the television screen.

"So say them. Start with the opening verse."

"Dear God," he began.

"No, it's Bismillah…"

"I don't pray that way."

"Oh really?" said Maryam, standing in front of the television. "You're not going anywhere. Arabic has been your chosen language and within that language you must pray. You'll start by learning first thing tomorrow."

"I'll be too busy packing my bags."

"And where will you go? Without money? Without shelter?"

"People do it all the time."

"In you're condition you're not going anywhere."

"You'll give me the money to do it."

"Ha! A devil is following you. And that enemy is after you. He wants to kill you, yes, the same way he killed your father. You must fight that devil. Say that special verse and spit into the ground."

"And I'm the one who was sent away?"

"That's right, because the devil was in you. Even these dirty psychiatrists saw the devil within your head, and luckily, with the might of Allah, that devil has been drawn out and cast down."

"Be certain. I'm leaving within the next few days. I'm traveling to Boston."

"Why Boston? Who's in Boston? I'm not even sure where Boston is."

"There are plenty of colleges there. I want an education."

"You haven't gotten through high school yet. You just left the hospital. Why Boston?"

"I'll attend high school in Boston."

"What gave you such an idea?"

"I met someone in the hospital, and he went to college in Boston, and now I will attend school in Boston."

"I don't know what devil put ideas in your head, but Arabic lessons are the next order of business," and she turned off the television.

On the next morning, a yellow haze fell upon the city. Some of this light dribbled into Maryam's bedroom. She didn't hear the television in the next room, an indication that Imam Mustafa still slept. She performed ablution in the bathroom, and she set out elementary books of Arabic on the coffee table. She spread her prayer cloth along the floor and prostrated herself before Allah. She said the verses aloud, hoping they would wake the Imam. Her knees cracked during the routine prostrations, and the floorboards creaked. She poked her head into Mustafa's room only to find him missing. She checked the entire apartment only to find her purse emptied of its contents. She ran to the telephone and called Vasilla as tears of worry and confusion filled her eyes.

***

4th of Thwal-Hijja 1435
(September 29, 2014)
Boston, Massachusetts

And I loaned her the money, and she injected more cocaine with her friend Harry who tried to get me out of the room as fast as he could. She stole all my cigarettes, yes this same woman who asked me if I wanted some 'nookie.' But I drank her wine. These are the people of the streets, and I'm not certain why I was lead here. Very confused, my mind racing towards some fantastic end. It's getting colder every day, yet my brain is scalding hot, boiling, and buckling under the weight of its own tyranny. (See Diagram #2).

Always, I think things are contrived for my own understanding. But in fact, I am the last one to know. I am the last one to think. I'm just like the others- anyone who dared to dream and ended up short. The tragedy with a happy ending. Such is the goal.

Cheryl was the woman I was just getting to know, injecting dope in front of me, and yet I wanted her all the more. How many years has she been into that? Her language almost alien. And yet every thought was for my understanding, as though she were here by some cosmic coincidence. But these thoughts come a mile a minute. All of this stuff will be buried one day, and I will leave the rest up to God.

That's much too easy. I want to know it all, every last ridge of the key to the universe, as the present is what we are trying to push as eternal. So weird. The greater the present, the more circular we become. Anyone is welcome, and anyone who wants to enter the circle can enter the center. It's as if this is all set up by the higher power. Suddenly I'm the center of the universe, and everything is a significant event.

She was injecting dope into her arms, and the blood trickled from the poke-hole. In a way, I thought I was ruining myself over this: one woman injecting dope through her veins, hardly intelligible, smacking me over the forehead, because she thought I was a 'zipperhead.' But I watched this, and I longed for her no more. She would never refuse me, because she likes to take the money. Forget it, maybe I shouldn't ask her. It might mean that I'm consorting with a prostitute who injects dope for a living. The blood trickled down her arms. She slapped me in the face, and then I could not understand her as she spoke too quickly. And she rolled her tongue back and forth like a lizard. She said she was a lizard. I kept on thinking tonight. The present is this wonderful ship waiting to be set free. The idea is old, but the thought springs eternal. Many of these thoughts seem eternal. But one thought, and one thought only expands the eternal. This is the thought of peace. It is the light we all want. Only then can we be truly alive. It will happen, and the present will thus transform itself. We all seem to be on the same plane, and to move ourselves upwards takes a higher consciousness, unlike economics and technology. A transformation of the human spirit. I will find this spirit. All of us together, not a single one missing. And so I am confined to live in the present. The present is the only arena whereby peace and love may permeate. The present, then, is where I shall remain. Death means going directly to God. If you want to live the hard way, you find why every single one of us can't leave. There must be some kind of misunderstanding. We all go to heaven no matter who we are, no matter what you bring, we all go to heaven, and I will wait for that day. But of course, I contradict myself. I want to die. That will be the day when I give up on life altogether. I will take the gun, cock the trigger, and squeeze. And what I'm dreaming before I die will be the greatest thought ever known to humankind.

5th of Thwal-Hijja 1435
(September 30, 2014)

    You can easily blame it on the drugs, but we were on a higher plane of reality again. It was all on purpose, as though this abandoned building were watched by cameras. Different cameras- Cheryl wanted to know what hit me, what went wrong, a barrage of questions. We made sense and then we angered each other. She is usually unintelligible, which explains my frustration.

    One day I will be on another plane of reality, and this time gyrating. Another homeless fellow gave me this idea.

    Is this life one big lie? Cheryl seemed to be one big lie. Maybe this is one big game? And we ultimately find the right woman after a long time, after an eternity. Differing planes of reality. Eliminate the hatred, the war, the paranoia. Introduce love as a concept. And perhaps I'm paranoid, afraid of violence at every turn, yet that mugger who choked me in the Commons did so in a paternal way. He wanted me to be okay. Cheryl mugged me tonight. She hit me, and I got all upset and almost thought about leaving this drug den. I never thought I'd sink so low.

A party in Hell before it's all over. But how far do I want to go? All the way to hell? All or none. Or maybe a little. I can take this all. Before it didn't make sense. Now it's starting to: imaginary friends, different planes of reality, different drugs, different prescription drugs. All these drugs to carry us on up, yet Am I ready to die, now that I have bitched about life so much? Be patient. My end is near. Suddenly death scares the shit out of me. Kill me if you dare. But we continue. This is what I'm seeing.

We wish to live in peace like any goddamned human being who ever existed. Face it. We all want this peace, and we must live together in order to achieve it. But the question becomes: how will we do it together? Understanding the same thing, or trying to achieve the same goal, will help immensely. And I am arguing for peace. The goal of peace. Beyond peace we have absolute love. (See Diagram #3).

Right? Not necessarily. I have drawn the same to the left. The point is that we all go together.

Man, why do I get into this stuff? I guess I get hit by it, and we are all hit by it at one time or another. We are all hit by the touch of God. We are all touched by God. The present will be worth something someday, even though it is worth nothing now.

Cheryl sounded intelligible after she shot up, or at least I assumed she shot some, or else it was God in the room, because she sounded intelligible. It's over. It's not happening. I have changed my tune. I'm wondering about my place in all of this. Where can I contribute? Where am I most wanted, and more importantly, where do I belong in this grand knot of past, present, and future, and peace and God? Just do what I do, and the present always has problems. Soon a woman shall appear, and I shall bow my head to her.

Tired and down from my high. It's overload, and I realize that the mind has to rest. Instead I lay awake contemplating things. I'm not concerned with my own life. What is normalcy? I want to be normal, like the normal twenty-year-old. For once can't someone find the right answer to get us out of here? It shan't be me. Sometimes it's a pat on the back that you need. I'll end up on another hospital ward before I know it. I've been running from these city cops. It seems like I've been fucked up for days. A drug is a drug no matter how you slice it. Some drugs are beneficial, some drugs are harmful and pack a punch. Millions of people can't be wrong, and I would not recommend it. It makes Cheryl magically civil. Without the dope she's violent. But with the dope she's suddenly fantastic.

It's all too stupid. The further on I go, the less I know, and it's becoming difficult for me to grapple with all this information. I'm gonna rip up those twenty dollars, or thirty dollars she owes me, and I'm gonna rip it up in her face. I expect thirty dollars from her on Monday. If they don't give it to me, then I shall not visit Cheryl ever again. She lies, and her whole life is built on lies.

6th of Thwal-Hijja 1435
(October 1, 2014)

Smoke a butt before we begin. Have a shot, a few snorts, a few hits before we begin. Where it ends I have no idea.

And I'm so stuck, needing something more, like alcohol or food or nothing, just nothing to release what has been flowing through me. I take that attitude as though I have no control over what I think. Then who am I, and what am I doing here? Why do I need nicotine every five minutes and cocktails every night? Or perhaps I'm seriously deranged? Is it me, or is it you, or is it all of us on this same wavelength? There's perhaps too much to learn, but I do have a sense of purpose. I hope I'm doing my part. I'm seeing the signs, but I'm under control, except for a few times when I turn into the beast.

The day was spent walking around. I saw some elderly folks at the pizza shop. I thought of their fears of being mugged and drinking prune juice and shopping about this ethnic-heavy town. I became mad, violently mad, because it was unfair that they lived in fear. The fat man with the thick plastic frames and swollen belly. The two women with him, one of whom I could not hear. And as these violent thoughts gelled into a complete single vision, the old man got up from his chair and looked at me, as if he knew my mind. It was a look of surprise. The three of them left the pizza parlor soon after, taking their shopping bags with them, promising to meet again. Violence is triggered, it seems, by the threat of external violence. The key is to eliminate the external violence. Violence in the mind is also triggered by external violence. When will it end?

I took a short walk in the park. Overcast sky and a bit on the chilly side. I was sober. Quite pleasant walking around for no apparent reason. I'm getting a feel for my neighborhood. Maybe this is happening to all of us, and not just me? We are all headed up the same path. But of course, I've said it all before. In other words, I can't explain all of this. It just happens, and I approach these things as objectively as I can. The difficulties are too immense to have any semblance of control over them. Wait and see. Hopefully I won't have to endure more violence- domestic, national, international, universal. And by the way, how does one act normally while ill like this? And how do I muster up enough evidence to make these false delusions a reality, or at least capture them in the present? The questions of 'why' and 'how' irritate me most. Of course, I'm getting all my information from homeless addicts, so there must be more to a delusion than meets the thought. What I would like is some validating evidence of God. But again, my delusions are not delusions. There is no invalidating evidence to cancel my theories. My ideas are not false beliefs.

7th of Thwal-Hijja 1435
(October 2, 2014)

(See Diagram #4).

    I've been trying with all my might to venture back from the great escape that my mind has taken. It's difficult not knowing where you are, whether or not the forces of the universe are with you or against you. I've been feeling horrible for most of the day. Now I know that this sensitive brain must be ill. My head needs examination from someone able to look at it objectively. I awoke this morning, after puking, and thought that we all have the capacity for powers mystical. I'm talking about telepathy. I would rather avoid the issue of telepathy in my attempt to remain normal and sane. Yet these issues are attacking me. I'm just some sort of vessel, and in the meantime I'm hurting myself. My gyration theories are most likely old, but my point is that something is filling me with these thoughts. I'm not a goddamned theoretician. I'm seeing things that aren't really there. I awoke this morning and blurted out the word "telepathy." Why me? Why did I have to think about it? My thoughts are warped and in a strange way I'm enjoying it. Maybe I'm pregnant, I don't have any clues.

    Stick with telepathy. This is all flowing through me such that I am unsure of my whereabouts or my identity. It's not getting scary. It's getting painful that I am thinking this way. My head hurts. I don't want to go outside anymore. I'm worried that I might not be getting enough sleep- that I am the conduit by which this message is being delivered. I'm just a grain of dust, a sorrowful pitiful grain of dust.

    When thoughts do not flow but turn into ramblings, then I become angry at myself and at those stimulants around me.

    All of us are on the same plane, gyrating towards the heavens by a simple process of evolution. I'm the last one to go, I'm afraid. I'm stuck being the last one to evolve. Yet we all go, and I hang on for my dreadful life.

At least I'm a bit more stable now than this morning. I've been battered by thoughts all day, and will probably be battered through the night. The realm of the imaginary and the realm of reality fight each other. Do they ever coalesce? Am I ill because I think they do unite in some way, shape, or form? And if they do, could they for once unite in a peaceful manner, to do good things, friendly acts, unremembered acts of kindness and of love? I think these issues have to be settled before there can be any talk of telepathy. I have no doubt it exists. The people look at me, and they act strangely towards me. They know what I'm thinking. And so I try hard to explain this phenomenon.

The Slinky Gyration Model

Plato in his *Republic* postulated that there were 'absolutes' in the universe. For instance, there is absolute Hate, War, Violence, Peace, and the like. We must also assume that there also exists absolute Love, and if we were, let's say, to choose among a group of absolutes, say among

A) Truth
B) Peace
C) Love
D) Hate

It is absolute Love which seems to imply Peace, Love, and Truth without Hate. Absolute Love also implies 'all of us,' so let's choose Love as a more rational goal or direction. If you don't believe absolute Love to be a worthwhile choice, then let's choose it for the sake of example. Again, absolute Love implies 'all of us' as shown in the diagram below. (See Diagram A).

In Love, Peace is implied.
In Peace, Love is not implied.
Hence, Love rests on a higher level than Peace.

So now there is a goal. There is some direction, since we have chosen absolute Love towards which we ought to travel. But the question becomes: how do we get there? What course shall we chart for 'all of us' to reach absolute Love? Let's take one chart which is closer to our reality.

THE REVOLUTIONARY MODEL/BIRTH-DEATH CYCLE

Some assume that there exists a continual cycle of sorts such as explained below. (See Diagram B).

Since we have chosen absolute love, this cyclical, revolutionary model is not particularly valid. First, because it is no where as close to being absolute; only at a certain time, after the destruction of an existing government, does it seem valid. Second, the Birth/Death cycle does not take into account the evolutionary changes involved with human nature. Therefore, the key to reaching our goal of Absolute Love is to postulate that it is "Evolution not Revolution" that gets us there. These are two reasons to discard the Revolutionary, Birth/Death cycle.

Yet there are still depressions, recessions, violence, and the like. We still have bad days, good days, and average days. Yet we still evolute somehow. How can we conceptualize this phenomena?

Well, if we plot points on an arbitrary plane, we may determine what shape our good days and not-so-good days take. For instance, assume there is a person who has good days and bad days. Feelings of peace and feelings of violence.

Let $A1 =$ GOOD DAY
Let $B1,2,3 =$ BAD DAYS
Let $C1,2,3 =$ GOOD DAYS
Let $C3 < C1 > C2$
(See Diagram C).

Let's call this phenomenon the 'roller coaster effect.' Good days and bad days, or the **Roller Coaster Effect**, does not imply revolution, but it sure seems that way, does it not? Is there not harmony to these good days and bad? Nevertheless, there may always be feelings of revolution in the air. I again recall the Birth-Death cycle for the purpose of illustration. (See Diagram D).

The roller coaster effect combined with the new evolutionary cycle shows the reality of the roller coaster as well as the assumption of evolution. (See Diagram E).

Assuming that there is evolution, we may combine the good days and the bad days with the evolutionary model or the new cycle. Yet we are still on a course towards absolute love, and so there is still a direction. Hence the roller coaster gyration or what I would like to call the '**Slinky Gyration**.' (See Diagram F).

We assume that the evolutionary process brings us to higher utility planes. In other words, the further towards Absolute Love we turn, the more utility comes to this earth for 'all of us.'

In theories such as this, there is always movement from the general to the specific. For some reason there are components of physics and astrophysics which may explain our movement up the slinky gyration. A main assumption, probably the most important, is that 'all of us' are headed towards Absolute Love. And to add another dimension to this model which may explain more regarding the infamous theory-practice gap, or the imagination-reality gap, is the concept known as **Telekinetics**. Let's take the roller coaster effect. According to the ancient laws of mechanics: (See Diagram G).

A ball rolling from Point A to B will pick up velocity and actually hit point B and some of C, but find its final resting place at point B. So the question becomes, how do we get to point C? Or the good day?

It must be energy. Some energy must be moving the ball from Point B to C. That phenomena is known (or not known) as Telekinetics. It is the common, 'all of us' push to get from point B to C. Hence the concept of Telekinetics.

Now why telekinetics? Why not use technology to get us to point C? Why not use nuclear energy or electricity? Because technology is used for love and war; it does not belong to Absolute Love. And so if something is some love but not all love, should we not find something better or closer to Absolute Love? Telekinetics is closer to Absolute Love simply because it takes 'all of us' to use the telekinetic energy to push us to Point C. Technology, if you'll notice, only takes a few of us. But what about individuality?

The individual verses the collective has long been a problem for many people. In other words, how do I retain my individuality, and at the same time, how do all of us survive and live in peace, love, and understanding? A big assumption we can make is the presence of telepathic communication to bridge the gap between the individual and the collective. Of course I'm still working on the specifics of this, and it will take lots of time to sort out how Telepathy works. But probably the most important point is that Telepathy through the individual drives the collective to induce Telekinetic Energy. Telekinetic energy moves us out of the depression and into 'the good day' once again. It takes 'all of us' to accomplish this, since one iota of depression in one individual will break or reduce the Telekinetic energy needed to get us to the good day. Both the ideas of Telekinetics and Telepathy need further investigation. But let's put these thoughts aside except to further our theory.

Telekinetic energy assumes that more telepathy is greater or more beneficial than less telepathy. In other words, the greater the telekinetic energy, the easier it becomes to move to higher utility planes and to overcome the dips of the roller coaster effect. Therefore, it is most beneficial to increase our **Life Force** in order to achieve these aims. An expansion in the life force greatly helps. Therefore, the assumption of an infinitely expanding life force, or an infinitely expanding population. (See Diagram H).

There is a necessity to create more telekinetic energy from Point B to C, hence the need for the life force. Along the slinky gyration the life force is increasingly expanding not only to get from point A to C, but also to move to higher utility planes, which takes much effort.

Let us say that 'all of us' means the earth itself. There are then vast implications for the structure of our universe. For instance, night time may imply a low point, and day time may imply the high point. Or there may be a gradual pull towards absolute Love; that is the solar system may actually be pulled in tow. But this is stretching things, as our model is merely conceptual.

ASSUMPTIONS- quite a few.

1) Absolute Love exists
2) Absolute Love implies 'all of us.'
3) Evolution rather than revolution gets us to Absolute Love.
4) A person has good days and bad days.
5) The evolutionary process brings us to higher utility planes.
6) All of us are headed towards Absolute Love.
7) Telekinetics.
8) Telepathic communication.
9) An infinitely expanding life force.
10) Love is higher than peace.

Problems or Questions which still exist:

1) Is this a conceptual problem, or a problem involving astrophysics? In other words, for instance, does night really mean that we are in a depression? If this is so, should everyone conceive birth at four in the morning in order to expand the life force?
2) Too many assumptions not supported by evidence.
3) Once we reach absolute Love, does the life force still expand? Are those who are born in Love better than others?
4) Time- our individual roller coasters may not be in sync to allow Telekinetic energy to bloom at precise times. But again through telepathy the gap is bridged.

A PERSONAL NOTE:

This model is a result of much loneliness and fatigue. It is an attempt to maintain individuality while understanding the common needs of the collective whole. The most difficult challenges are Telepathy and Telekinetics mostly because there is first, no proof of these phenomena (especially Telekinetics which relies on telepathy itself), and second, because of problems with Time and its functions. For example, we are not all upset at the same time. Yet we can measure the mood of the earth by using telepathy as a form of communication? We may be able to personify the earth and its inhabitants as having mood swings. Yet still the direction remains the same and assuming that the model is feasible we are on course towards Absolute Love as a collective.

I can't prove any of this. That is why it must remain a theory. I have tried within the Slinky Gyration to reflect as much reality as possible. This reality is evidenced in the roller coaster effect. But even the roller coaster effect is an assumption. Much more investigation needs to be made. The difficulties in bringing this theory into practice are insurmountable. But it's a start, and starting points are specious. My hope is that this model will inspire someone to think of a way to reach Absolute Love. (See Diagram I).

Telekinetics and telepathy only work for the betterment of our collection of human beings. There must be some control mechanism to monitor it. Anything violent should be cut off, and the human heart, which possesses such a mystical power, will cut off all telepathic power when thoughts become violent, even when it becomes violent and damaging to the recipient. Otherwise, telepathy doesn't exist, or at least it shouldn't exist. These are the essential parameters.

Sickness is devouring me at every turn. I need the answers and certainly not the questions. But isn't it odd that when you figure it out for yourself, life and this reality suddenly have purpose and meaning? Love. Our search for God. All of us are together, even the dead, especially the dead, and of course, the living- old and young, black through white, tall and short, slim and fat. Love ⇔ God.

TELEKINETICS IN THE 'SLINKY GYRATION' SCHEME

Telepathy belongs to the individual. Telekinetics is used by "all of us." Take the slinky gyration scheme. The force that moves us up and down on the single utility plane, the force that makes us evolve to the next utility plane, the force that makes our lives eternal surrounding the eternal present is telekinetics. It is 'tele,' because through us all the 'kinetics' may work. In other words, we all must push this envelope and push hard. Not a single person is left out. The desire is there among all of us, telekinetics- a union of persons, minds, and motion. To get from here to there takes telekinetics to move us up and down, around, and finally up the curves of the slinky gyration to the next level. A collective telekinetics is more likely to push us gently to a higher utility plane. (See Diagram #5).

A NOTE ON TIME DIFFERENTIALS.

A time differential is when two wandering thoughts from one person to another do not connect at the same time.

When I think violent thoughts, it's obvious no one wants to communicate with me telepathically. Why should anyone be hurt by my violence, and why should I want to affect anyone with my violence? Such guilt of thinking violence begets more violence. It's a trap. You are then stuck in a **Time Differential**, because no one wants to communicate telepathically with you. Your thoughts are going nowhere, so there is considerable mental anguish and suffering. There are living beings who are here to help you throughout your turbulence in the time differential confinement period, but the anguish is still there, simply because you, telepathically, cannot be included in the collective mind (all of us). But there are a few key ways to restore your place among the 'all.' They must work together.

First, NON-VIOLENT THINKING. This may take time, but without a doubt, this is the closest to Absolute Love. Second, EXTERNAL COMMUNICATION (i.e., writing, speaking, the arts and sciences, caressing, sign language, et cetera.) Third, LOTS OF PATIENCE.

These three must operate together in order for one to be among the 'all.' Time Differentials act as mental prison cells, or better yet (much better) sort of mental hospitals where one is helped through the process of channeling violent thoughts into Love-bearing thoughts. Whether you leave or stay in the Time Differential depends upon your assessment of how much 'Love' you have in your mind. But I assure you, too much love is never enough. That's why it's important to have lots of patience. What is it like in a time differential? Just look what's happening to me. I'm not part of the collective, I go through anguish, I have thoughts about hitting people or breaking things or turning into a monster. These conditions subside when I'm helped by the thoughts that visit me. Eventually and certainly you will be a part of 'all of us' once again. Thoughts in the Time Differential are delivered in fragments, from where, or better yet, from whom I'm not so sure. Or instead of a mental prison or mental hospital, think of it as a mental ashram. I still don't know how I am going to get into school. Perhaps, if things go this way, I may never get there. Hopefully I will persevere, ride out this turbulence. The thoughts that visit you in a Time Differential encourage peace and love. So don't fret.

10th of Thwal-Hijja 1435
(October 5, 2014)

I'm doing some tests on myself on how to react to thoughts of violence. Music is my helper as it is the best conduit through which moods are calmed. I wanted to wreck this shelter and beat up the people walking on the street in the day time. This next selection has calmed me as the content is not violent. Music tends to sway my mood to such an extent that I am rocked to and fro, like a child in a mother's arms.

It is better to cry externally than to react. In other words it is better to cry over it than to become angry. Violence begets more violence, even in the mind, but the cathartic effect is a better alternative to a violent action. The crying washes away the anger in such a way that there is a distancing of oneself apart from violence while still protesting it. Of course this is the process one must go through in order to free oneself from the Time Differential. Be patient.

My trouble with TIME (the concept) and the Slinky Gyration model have been much too troublesome. Also I have been grappling with the issue of the circular model verses the spiral. I was on the trolley, and I had this question. Should we discard the past, or shall we keep it intact as the spiral gyrates? Implicit within this thought is the idea of 'carrying too much luggage.' Do we want our minds to be plagued by Slavery or the Holocaust or any such violent massacre? Or the second option, do we feel these pains by telepathy and move onwards, trying most desperately to develop the telekinetic energy to move along the slinky gyration? I prefer the spiral simply because the telepathic energy is there for all of us to feel the pain of the past and patiently move along the Slinky Gyration.

The circular model involves the rebirth/death cycle which involves Death, for one thing. This closes the possibility of learning from those who are already dead. In other words, if you've come so far so slowly and it took pains to get here, do you really want to end it without the fruition of the dream? Absolute Love? Therefore the spiral construal makes more sense. It takes in all of us- past, present, and future, while at the same time builds the rebirth necessary for added telekinetic energy. So I prefer the spiral to the circle. The spiral, the ever increasing spiral, will help us towards our goal of absolute Love.

Where the hell am I? I'm moving towards Absolute Love. Time, of course, is merely a measurement by which we judge spatial distance between points. This has implications for telepathy. I'm stuck in a Time Differential, so my thoughts are not connecting at the same measurement of the collective wavelength. I must look for ways to get out of the Time Differential. It involves non-violence, external communication, and lots of patience. Patience is measured in units of time. How long can this take? Digesting pain and turning it into something positive, anything to move us along the Slinky Gyration. It involves telepathic communication.

11th of Thwal-Hijja 1435
(October 6, 2014)

Right now I am pondering the issues of time, gravity, and relativity, and of course the current predicament called the Time Differential. The time differential is a severe anomaly, and it is the current situation in which I find myself. Let's review some material.

Every human being, every living being for that matter, has up and down times (an assumption). Hence, the 'roller coaster' effect. Therefore, the 'slinkiness' of the gyration. (See Diagram #6 and #7).

To get from point A => C involves TELEKINETICS.
Telekinetics is driven by the Life Force.
(See Diagram #8).

From A => C there is a differential of Telekinetic energy. I get this from the ancient laws of kinetics. A= rest or sleep, yet the life force is still expanding. From A to B is a deep dip. Velocity is increasing, therefore less Telekinetic energy, yet the life force is still expanding. C= the life force is greatly expanding at a greater rate to create more telekinetic energy to move us to the next 'slink' so to speak.

PERSONAL NOTES:

All of us towards Love. A Telekinetc activity through individual telepathy which gets us along the roller coaster effect. I have the feeling that if my preoccupation with our destination of Love continues, then I will never make it out alive. If that's what it takes, then that's what it takes. I can feel the unison of telekinetic energy which is pulling us towards love. The question becomes, can each person in the world feel it? So then why are they here? Better yet, why am I here? The present being eternal may give us some insight. This planet is eternal as it continues along the slinky gyration- the dips into night, hence the moon, and the ascension into daylight, hence the sun.

Actually, I know why I'm here. I'm trapped in a Time Differential. Why you people are here I have no idea. You are all around me, watching me, filling me with strange thoughts. I refuse to include modern medicine as a way of getting out of a time differential. I would rather use non-violent thinking and external communication. I'm afraid of becoming the dictator, so very afraid, and I'm so screwed up right now, I'm not sure what to think. I just have a strong revulsion, a distaste for dictators or tyrants of any sort. Again, don't listen to me.

13th of Thwal-Hijja 1435
(October 8, 2014)

The course to Love through Peace is tumultuous. I am so incredibly weak that at times I feel like breaking down, either in the form of crying, all out laughter, or violence. I'm trying for an education, but even this small step has not been taken. But there are reasons for this. It is somehow the cause of love, the purging of violence over time, and the readjustment of pneumonic devices. In other words, my mind is a function of a deep-seeded psychology and a will that can't seem to let go. It hurts. I'm getting headaches, and yet this time I refuse to go to a hospital. In the meantime I have personified the earth as a living, breathing planet. I have understood that light from the stars is a form of communication, and that somehow I have been given a light communique to come back to the present. An 'SOS' so to speak. How is this so? It is only an assumption, so I will try to explain it as best I can.

As you can probably tell, I am moving from very general assumptions to very specific details. The general assumption is that all of us are moving towards Love through peace and non-violence upon the slinky gyration. The details are manifold, and this is where I am finding my greatest difficulties. Insurmountable difficulties. I seem to be remembering too much. I am also steadfast and certain on the assumption that 'all of us' does not include 'me' as of yet. In other words, I am still caught in a Time Differential where my thoughts are not connecting with others at the same time.

There must be some logic to this chaos. Suddenly I'm losing my mental faculties- the ability to ride the trolleys, the ability to talk and externally communicate effectively. I am again lost in indecision, trying so very hard to find love, almost as if it is an entity, a living, breathing form. I'm beginning to wander in thought, and as a result physically wandering in the form of pacing or circumambulating. I'm also beginning to lose my memory which kept me in touch with the violence that had plagued this planet.

Suddenly, my mind is relaxed. The violent thoughts do not occur as often. The pain, mental pain, is still present, mostly because I'm not sure what has happened to me. I can explain it away, that I'm taking the same route my mother has taken, but then again I have come so far- from the general to the specific- that it is very hard to decide between the route of reality and the route of the imagination. At this juncture a crucial decision has to be made- Do I go on with our search for love, or do I admit myself into another hospital and get back down to earth? After deliberating over a cancer-stick, I have decided that Love is worth finding, even worth contemplating. There are consequences to this decision. I may end up without a penny to my name, the pains in the head will persist, and most importantly I may find myself having no control over my fate. But then again, I am who I am, no matter how meager my accommodations. The writing will chart this journey as best as it possibly can. Regardless of where I am or what I'm doing, I will always head towards absolute Love as though it validates my existence. We are together on this search for Love. This I must believe. I can never do it alone. My theories of the Slinky Gyration will expand as conditions permit. Focus and hard work shall overcome the mental obstacles which inhibit the bloom of Love. We must be fearless in our pursuit, even so fearless as to debunk the myth of death itself. Still I'm frightened. One day all of us will reach love, and when we have found it we will be certain that we have found it. The universe, instead of an obstacle, offers us much breathing room to postulate and to make logic and harmony explain the chaos, explain the unexplainable. For me it's ALL OR NONE. Either we are all in it together, or none of us are in it at all. I am almost proud to be taking this crucial step in my life. It will come so slowly that I won't even feel it coming, but keep faith that one day this earth will reach its destination.

    S.O.S. LIGHT COMMUNIQUE AS A FORM OF TELEPATHIC ENERGY

    I really mean to say that the spiral model describing Telekinetic energy is merely conceptual. That is, it doesn't function like a drawing would, but rather as a conceptual description of telepathy. For instance, I am here now, and the earth's light communicated an S.O.S. to the life force which is constantly expanding.

    Actually it is difficult to describe. And I'm saying that the S.O.S. communique may be a result of telepathy rather than my being an orbital of the Earth on a spiral. But really these things remain foggy. In other words, the future 'all of us' has sent us some S.O.S. signal.

15th of Thwal-Hijja 1435
(October 10, 2014)

    Tired but not frustrated or sleepy. I've decided to communicate this chunk of information which I have been carrying around with me for a few days. I wrote these ideas out in an eight page essay with diagrams and explanation. It feels like I've just given birth. I'm exhausted from thinking too much. Everything around me seems pre-planned, and therefore I am curious most of the time. I'm not sure of anything anymore. My moods are swinging, but instead of going to the hospital I have decided to take medication and see a psychiatrist here in Boston.

TELEPATHY, PEACE, AND THE COMMON GOOD

Being a new inductee into the realm of telepathy, I am sensitive, extremely sensitive to telepathic violence, and so I must record my findings here to deliver, let's say, a message of peace to all those who use telepathy as a major form of communication. This short essay will sound like ideology. In fact, much of it is ideology, because I am dealing with something I don't fully comprehend. Therefore, if I seem to ramble a bit, disregard the rambling and stick to keywords such as Peace, Love, and Harmony. After all, is this not our purpose? I would also admit to you plainly that my ruminations regarding telepathy are used to further the assumptions of Telekinetics and the Slinky Gyration. But most of all, with my heart, my soul, my life, I must stress that telepathy is to be used for peaceful purposes only- to bring peace to those whom have nothing but utter torment in their minds and bread crumbs to follow. It is all for the sake of peace, and of course, the final destination of love.

Telepathy involves the imagination. Since everyone has an imagination, everyone is able to use telepathy as a tool to aid in the peace process, which is long and hard. Telepathy then implies a form of truth (i.e., what are your intentions, and are those intentions true enough.) Telepathy begins with the use of the imagination, or at least I believe so. The imagination is a realm where anything may take place, so once you know you are dealing with the imagination, exercise extreme caution. It should be obvious to you that the gap between the imagination and reality has been reduced by considerable amounts, but still remains wide. Your brain becomes very sensitive, and at crucial times you will question what are the functions of the imagination and what are the functions of reality. Remember that there is a difference. Yet trudge onwards. We may postulate here that telepathy is a part of the imagination, and that is why it is so tricky to uncover it. But remember, if you believe in Peace and Love, you will find it. Only then, with the earnest desire and heartfelt intentions for Peace and Love, will Telepathy unfold itself to you.

I had a very difficult time getting to it, and I still wonder whether I am actually communicating to someone through telepathy, or is it just my imagination trying to find an escape route through the mess of reality. Regardless, at this time, we must assume that telepathy is a concept brought about for peaceful purposes, to aid and not to hinder. If violent thoughts exist, there is the concept known as the Time Differential which has already been discussed. Of course, I might be engaging in the art of self-deception, but for me this is not a game, and it is quite real.

It's not what you see but what you think that slowly drags you into the realm of Telepathy. It's as though telepathy finds you, and then the realm of it is an open page. I do, however, get the sense that telepathy may be used for dastardly purposes. Meaning, that there are some who enter with the best of intentions and then turn away attempting to find some sort of mastery. Well, the original intention of telepathy was to help and never to hinder, to perpetuate mental peace of mind and never to stir paranoias or other such fears. In my view, the goal of telepathy is to form a mental collective when times are tough. Then we may use Telekinetics to get us out of the tough times. But this is only theory. I am just beginning to contemplate Telepathy. It is crucial to the Slinky Gyration. But most importantly, it is a tool for peace and especially for Love. If it is not, assume there is a cut off point known again as the Time Differential. The Time Differential is also used for pupils in the learning stages of telepathy. The more 'good' your intentions, the more likely it is that you will find telepathy.

THE TIME DIFFERENTIAL 'CUT-OFF SWITCH'

I am caught between wondering whether or not I actually have telepathy. I'm not sure that I want it if it is used as a weapon rather than a tool. I never invented telepathy. I just thought it useful as an aid to reach absolute Love where we may all thrive. So if there is a problem with telepathic communication, there must also be problems in the concept of Absolute Love, partially out of difficulty and partially out of fear. Perhaps it is time to contemplate Absolute Love, so that we may sort out some of the problems which haunt our future. Yet, I have given birth, it seems, to the Slinky Gyration model which uses Absolute Love as its main goal or direction. How can I give up a child like this? I am very eager to get the ball rolling and for more input.

MENTAL HEALTH AND TELEPATHY

Without sound mental health and a thirst for life, without the goal of peace and a zest for love, telepathy is not possible. Therefore, Telekinetics may not work as a result of anything opposite. Mental health is a difficult terminology. I am not a psychologist or a psychiatrist, so I am not an authority. Yet, I sense that a healthy mind is needed to transmit healthy ideas to one another. Without a sturdy grounding in mental health, mental violence is possible. Mental violence will result in a Time Differential. Hence, a sturdy mind is needed. Mental health is of the utmost importance in sending out messages of Peace, Love, and Non-violence.

TELEPATHY AND THE ORWELLIAN NIGHTMARE

Telepathy, as postulated, is used as an aid or peaceful device. For instance, we all have pains from the day to day. Telepathy may be used to empathize more effectively or to direct these pains from negative to positive energy. Nevertheless, during times of indoctrination into telepathy, the mind is ultra-sensitive. You will notice the cameras, the televisions, the non-stealing devices which surround you. Pnemonically this ought to refer you to Orwell's *1984* which predicts the lack of privacy and the total obediance to a wizard known as 'Big Brother.' The main character is caught in a maze of political non-privacy and control, such that he is unable to function. I have not read this book in a long time, but I shall reread it at the first opportunity. *1984* creatively describes such a state where thoughts and actions are never private. In other words, you are always being watched by cameras, being duped by computers.

The issue brings up the question of mind control which we will get to later, but for now we will stick to the issue of technology and its purpose. If technology is not for the purpose of Absolute Love, then we may easily do without. If technology is used for purposes of war, genocide, and the like, then telepathy steps in and bonds us against the encroaching technology. In other words, if technology ever loses its purpose for preserving the human race, then it is an exact time to reevaluate technology. There will come a time when technology gets out of hand, and the computers and the cameras begin to control human beings. At this juncture Telepathy becomes a defense for survival. Although technology is crafted by human hands, technology rarely reaches the human intention. Telepathy, then, becomes vitally important. For instance, the television may be spewing propaganda, and I may not even know it. Someone who understands telepathy and the Orwellian nightmare may introduce that iota of thought to see a concept known as truth. Telepathy moves us closer to truth, it moves us closer to ourselves. Hence, the telekinetic theory may work as a result of Telepathy versus the cameras and computers, which have run amok. The purpose, of course, is Love.

I am not the last one to know. It halts the process of evolution and thus works against the Slinky Gyration. I've thus far assumed that I would see the fruition of the Slinky Gyration theory, and I have been holding my breath until that theory comes into life. But this is actually an act of dictatorship, or as I would call it: playing God with your own theory. You must rely on the evolutionary process to take place. The 'last one to know' disregards the imagination of the children. It now belongs to the children and the life force to pick apart and either expand or disregard my theory all together, pick it apart and most importantly, find something much better. In other words, Peace and Love are only achieved through evolution. Seeing the utopia through its full fruition implies God-like mastery over the hearts and minds of the life force which expands second by second.

'I am not the last one' actually supports the Slinky Gyration theory. The life force continually expands, carrying Love or its idea to higher planes. Because I will not be there to see the theory come into its fruition, there is a break, a personal break with the theory. We may call this concept DISILLUSIONMENT. I am never the last to know. Through evolution the children are much more knowlwdgeable than I am and are capable of coming up with better theories. The inability to manifest the fulfillment of your dreams implies death and especially the concept of disillusionment. In short, if the dream becomes true in your lifetime, you are then a God over your dream. God over the dream stops the evolutionary process.

THE CONCEPT OF DISILLUSIONMENT (A PERSONAL PERSPECTIVE)

I think of Germany after the First World War. The Treaty of Versailles put Germany within lock-and-key poverty and pure desperation. Disillusionment means a break from the illusion. The Germans after World War I encountered this phenomena. The Slinky Gyration was my dream and my vision, and I had to let it go, simply because its fruition in my life time makes myself the dictator or the God over my theory. This understanding caused severe depression within me, because I so badly wanted to make the theory come true. And so I sat there on the street corner, almost in tears, having no one to turn to, and having no place to go. I had some help within the Time Differential construal, such that I imagined conversing with people. And so I responded to this disillusionment, which nearly crippled me, with a derisive attitude, not caring about violence or better yet not caring about Non-Violence any longer. Slowly I regained strength by hearing music, and then after regaining my strength I felt ashamed about letting go of Non-Violence.

Disillusionment affects the psyche in such a way that violence becomes the next best alternative. In other words, I did not care anymore. Disillusionment is hard to bear. It leads to violence, and I use the Nazi regime in the late 1940's as a vague example. I will not discuss this, but I will assume that at the time of Disillusionment a 'pat on the back' is most needed. The trick is for another person to catch disillusionment at the exact time so that violence does not occur. How do we know of these exact timings? Well, there is a need for Information Gatherers to convey to the collective when that spark of disillusionment takes place. A helping hand is reached at the precise point.

We all need help. Disillusionment, if left unchecked, is another avenue towards violence, and help is most needed at this time, the exact time, of disillusionment. Otherwise, expect violence. Information Gatherers are a function of peace and love. They help out when Disillusionment occurs. They lend a helping hand, or better yet, they communicate to the collective that a helping hand is needed. The communication device is best expressed through telepathy.

17th of Thwal-Hijja 1435
(October 12, 2014)

Without a doubt I am working with breadcrumbs here. I do not have the evidence to support telepathy, but I am struggling with great pains to penetrate what the dictionary calls a "mystical force." Yet I believe thus far that all of us have the potential for telepathy. The key is in the struggle for it, and it is leading me towards a general theory of telepathy. The main difficulty, however, is whether or not the communication device is a function of delusion, or whether or not the device is actually for real. At this stage it is hard to tell. It is best, however, to make your investigation with the assumption that you do not have telepathy.

As a student of this phenomena, I get the sense that telepathy begins with the imagination. Hence the trickiness of discovering telepathy, for there is always the thought that you may be deceiving yourself. This concept is called self-deception. For example, a holy man starved in a prison cell for many days, because he believed he was guided by God to do so. A friend of his came to the prison and attempted to dissuade him from starving. His friend claimed that he was suffering from delusions. In retrospect the holy man asserted that he was still alive, and therefore was not suffering from a delusion. It's hard to tell, but also we must remember that a delusion is a belief held despite invalidating evidence. To find validating evidence for these delusions takes intense effort, and especially patience. Nevertheless my search continues to find Love and then create a theory of telepathic communication. So this is why I currently investigate Telepathy. Instead of inductive reasoning I am relying on deductive reasoning to investigate telepathy. In many ways it is tearing me apart bit by bit. Sometimes I think my mind has gotten the better of me, and the imagination has run amok. Yet still I have bread crumbs to follow, and absolute Love to guide me. Telepathy is a function of this.

TELEPATHY AND THE IMMOBILIZATION COMPLEX

Once again the question is asked: am I dreaming, am I imagining talking to people? Your search for definite answers will sometimes keep you locked in your own thoughts, such that it becomes virtually impossible to communicate externally let alone perform daily duties for survival. This I would call the IMMOBILIZATION COMPLEX. Literally you are 'immobilized' in the reality of your situation. For instance, I was standing outside the Museum of Fine Arts here in Boston, and the Orwellian nightmare struck me. I was then so engaged in thought that I could not move from my position. A bystander had to wave me out of my trance.

Such will be the result if Telepathy is taken to an extreme. For instance, envision a society in which all its members used telepathy as a pure means of communication. The thoughts inside the mind would be so many that it would literally immobilize all of us and more importantly, stall the evolutionary process. How would it stall the process? I would imagine that principles of singularity would break down, making concentration on thought extremely difficult. Besides there may actually be an addiction to thought such that the search for knowledge, the search for Love, does not take its natural everyday course. Assuming that the society in question uses telepathy for the search of Love, there is the curiosity and the intent to communicate with every single person. Hence, immobility. Again, I'm not certain about this concept. I take it as it comes.

TELEPATHY AND THE SELF-REFLECTION SYNDROME

Let's say that we are on a trolley headed towards some location not very far away. You then attempt to communicate telepathically with a beautiful woman sitting next to you. Since you are having sight and the ability to hear [1], you catch sight of her as well as her voice. At this point the imagination kicks in, and you then imagine speaking with her. You decide to ask her a serious question regarding the course of your fate. You receive an answer which is the answer you yourself have thought about within the realm of your own imagination. In other words, she really isn't answering you, it is you who are using your own knowledge to answer the question to yourself. In other words, it is actually your own reflection through her, as if you are looking into a mirror and seeing yourself. Then you ask, is this true telepathic communication, when she is giving back to me the same answers I have already thought up? Is it real telepathy when the answer you receive does not spark anything new, does not give enough indication that communication exists? Hence the Self-Reflection Syndrome. You are imposing what you know onto her and thus receiving your own answers in return. I would submit that communication here did not take place and was just another trick of the imagination. I would advise starting the process over again.

THE IMPORTANCE OF EXTERNAL COMMUNICATION

Without a doubt external communication is essential. The evolutionary process does not head towards Telepathy itself but towards Absolute Love, and

---

[1] The blind, the deaf, and the blind and the deaf also have the potential for telepathy just as much as those with sight and hearing. As a pupil, I am not sure how as of yet.

I would submit that absolute love, in order to get there, will involve all sorts of communication such as touch, sign, English, Spanish, Yiddish, et cetera. Telepathy is but one form of communication, to be used only as an agent of Peace, Non-violence, and Absolute Love. We can see external communication as keeping a check on telepathy as well. Because telepathy takes energy and concentration, an immediate jolt of external communication will bring about a noticeable change in the communicators behavior. Besides, what about music, laughter, a beautiful woman or handsome man walking down the street? Because telepathy is a function of the mind, the mind needs to be fed with sound, sight, smell, touch, and taste in order to communicate those essential experiences through the senses. External communication feeds telepathy, not vice-versa. Telepathy is not used to hide communication but to aid and enhance it in some way, to help out in our common goals and struggles, to help with our pains.

THE SEASIDE BAR EXAMPLE

I decided to venture to Quincy Market this evening. I ate some pizza and then went to the bar to have a couple of drinks. I was feeling mighty down. I caught the sight and voice of the bartender on duty and attempted to communicate telepathically with this bartender. I began with the imagination and expected the Self-Reflection Syndrome. But what I received from the bartender was something way off the mark- something that I would have never thought, something that wouldn't have even come to mind. The bar tender said to me that many people knew my name, which implied that I was somehow to become an important person one day. I would have never thought that or imagined that at the time. If anything, I deny such vain and immature thoughts to a point where I inflict self-hatred upon myself when those thoughts do occur. So within this telepathic connection the bartender told me something that I never knew- that many people knew my name. How he had that knowledge I am not sure, but the point is that he delivered through telepathy this new knowledge, although this type of knowledge I did not care to receive. Is this an example of true telepathy? Did a telepathic connection take place?

I'm not so sure, because I have reason to doubt. I would say that his conveyance of that thought might have been a function of my very repressed ego. In short, it still may be the Self-Reflection Syndrome whereby my repressed ego, battered and torn by the sheer process of living, reflected back on to me. In other words, it may have been my imagination again, since I do have a repressed ego.

As a result, I'm not sure if that Seaside incident was real telepathy or not. But I keep in mind the assumption that I do not have telepathy; not yet.

TELEPATHY AND THE INNER VOICE (A PERSONAL PERSPECTIVE)

So far through this misery, while trying to distinguish the real from the imaginary, I have developed a strong inner-voice that guides me through this ordeal. The inner-voice questions and probes. It is strong, and yet I'm often caught immobilized even though my inner voice has developed. Each thought is somehow monitored by this inner voice. I think a strong inner voice is needed for telepathic purposes. While wandering through the imagination it gives me a sense of identity.

TELEPATHY AND SELF-LOVE (A PERSONAL PERSPECTIVE)

This is most likely the most difficult topic to write about. For many years now I have been enveloped in self-hatred. Even the most joyful times are now marred by my self-hatred. As a result of my self-hatred I find myself isolated, confused, and most of all, violent. I'm not sure how it came to be this way, most likely through mental breakdowns, and my mother, and my own past which includes a series of violence acts against kids in school, against my mother. There are still many more reasons to hate myself, but they are not worth mentioning here.

I am still a student and shall always be a student, even though I never finished high school. Through my travels I have discovered that self-hatred only halts the evolutionary process, since it takes away the energy needed to arrive at Absolute Love. Within self-hatred there may be no way out. Self-hatred builds and perpetuates itself, such that the pains are deeper, and the wounds never heal. But there is a way out. Self love is a concept needed for Telepathy itself to exist. An end to self-hatred allows one to perpetuate good will among men and women. In short, telepathy begins with the self. And if self-hate persists either within the id or openly, then the communication one delivers will be covered by a blanket of hatred. No one will care to listen.

Of course self-love does not happen overnight. Pnemonic devices within the mind make it even more difficult to achieve self-love. Yet self-love is possible, and I would dare say that it is essential for every type of communication, external and telepathic. It takes time, but at least I'm heading in the right direction. It will happen. There will come a time when self-love envelops me instead of self hatred. I'm "shedding my skin," or better yet "loosening my robes."

SCHIZOPHRENIA AND THE FIGHT FOR RECOVERY

My sickness has gotten the better of me these days. I am now obese as my mother would call me. My doctor says that I am terribly ill and confused. My brain is so sensitive that it picks up anything, and yet I still avoid the hospital, as if that is the only place which may help me. I am severly depressed and my theories of telepathy have gotten me nowhere. Increasingly I am becoming suicidal, but I know how important it is to hold on and think things through. Nevertheless, I am unable to think, I am unable to read. I'm not labeling all that has happened so far a delusion. I'm really stating that it is time to look after my own health and resign from this course of investigating telepathy. I do believe it's important, and the study ought to continue indefinitely, but for my well-being at this juncture I need to get back into the race and move on until the next time telepathy and telekinetics strikes a chord.

TELEPATHY AND ACCESS TO TELEPATHY

Telepathy involves the imagination. Now we all dream different things, but what telepathy most accomplishes is that instinctive vision into someone else's own mind. Ultimately, however, it is a product of you and not anyone else. Let's say that it is a product of absolute love. But it is essential that you attempt to access this great ability to equate everyone on common ground. The implications are enormous. The question becomes whether or not you may access this great equalizer, which only comes through a fierce dedication to equality and especially absolute love. For instance, look at that person across from you. Recall in your mind how he looks, what he is wearing, what he sounds like. Once you get the sound, the look, the face, start to imagine. Talk to him through the imagination. The imagination is the conduit through which we see things of extreme importance. Without the imagination we cease to exist. But telepathy requires access. The access comes from the imagination. Without the imagination, telepathy is as dead as a doorknob. And I am a simple man, so we must ask ourselves whether or not this is self-deception. Remember that telepathic communication is just another form of communication. And so there is the issue of access. First, there must be an access of the imagination. You must imagine talking to someone. Suddenly it will choose you. You will treat one another as equals. When it happens, you will know. But access is hard work. It takes jumping into another person's shoes.

TELEPATHY AND MENTAL BLOCK

Immature telepathic communication may lead to a mental block, whereby the subject under the block leaves thoughts within him/herself. These pent up thoughts desperately need expression, and thus the person under duress, under the stress and strain of attempting to communicate with a partner will begin to express those emotions extraneously. For example, a person will start speaking to him/herself, unable to express the thoughts which he/she holds so dear. I call this immature communication strategy, simply because this person lives in an age when telekinetics and telepathy may not exist. Think of it as a computer that cannot find proper compatibility. And in this stage, in its aboriginal stage, telepathy does not exist among the masses. And so those who wish to communicate find nothing but vapid air, nothing less but simple imaginings which fade into a form of immature communication.

Assuming strongly and quite blindly that telepathy is a next or close phase in evolutionary development, we must also assume that those who find trouble communicating posess the learned function of telepathy. We must remember that every single human being on the planet possesses this function, and mental blockade (speaking to yourself, for example) is nothing but an evolutionary stage. Much like puberty is to the teenager, mental block is to those who try to approach telepathy too quickly. So mental block is nothing but a stage in itself. I would suggest to those whom experience mental telepathic block to relax and proceed slowly. Test the barriers of your own imagination. Poke and ponder the mind, and make that valiant attempt to communicate with another partner, but do it through the imagination. Therein you will find the satisfaction of successful communication, and these beginnings are always very rough. But hold on, and what is most important, keep practicing and exercising extreme patience. We suppose that telepathy and the concept of Telekinetics will reach the human spirit in accordance with the strict confines of evolution, and with this evolution we will come at least one more step towards peace of mind, and therefore a universal non-violent peace which shall cover us in security through our exploration of the stars. Without a doubt, telekinetics will get us through the worst of times, because finally there exists a life force and a push to get us over those theoretical hills of despair. Immature communication, a search for satisfactory telepathic communication, is only a search for peace which you will find through a dedicated practice of telepathy. Remember: you are not the only one.

A PERSONAL NOTE

Drunk at the bar. Started a new medication called chlozaril. I wish these psychiatrists would make a drug moulded to one's drinking habits. I have not been bothered by illness for too long, but I have been taking these drugs for some time. A woman is at the bar. I will have to leave, but I hope she doesn't.

18th of Thwal-Hijja 1435
(October 13, 2014)

TELEPATHY AND THE NON-DICTATORSHIP PRINCIPLE

There exists the parameter known as the 'Non-Dictatorship Principle' which must be in place in order for truly beneficial communication to ensue. In essence such a principle is a safety valve so that telepathic communication, let's say, between two people, is a mutual event and is mutually agreed upon.

This in turn suggests that one person, any person for that matter, may never enter another persons mind or engage in communication with another without an implicit or explicit sign or thought of permission. We can say that such a principle acts as a repellent to those who wish to tap another individual's private thoughts. Also, such a principle has been erected so that both persons communicating telepathically are equal partners in the venture. This presupposes that both persons respect each other as equals, not necessarily in materials or wealth, but as equal human beings, as equals metaphysically, as equals under the Creator, as equals intellectually. The equality between the two persons or groups of persons involved in telepathic communication must be that rigid indeed, because this shall ensure that one person or groups of persons may never have telepathic power to 'dictate' another's thoughts. More importantly, one person or groups of persons may never have the power to control another individual's mind or break into private thoughts unless given permission by that individual. In sum, the Non-dictatorship Principle protects the individual and his or her freedom of thought. Privacy is maintained. Also, such a principle prevents any one person or groups of persons from dominating the content of telepathic communication. Since the principle maintains equality among us all, all decisions shall be made in a collective fashion, while telepathic communication is free for an individual's own use. (By decisions and collective decision-making, this means that no one person or groups of persons may 'dictate' telepathic policy. A decision on such policy must be made and agreed upon as a collective unit in which we all have equal power. (How this is done is beyond me). In order for all of us to move towards higher 'love planes' on the slinky gyration, total collective decision making must exist at certain times.

20th of Thwal-Hijja 1435
(October 15, 2014)

TELEPATHY, VIOLENCE, AND REFLEX ACTION:
Once again we are stuck in the miserable quandry of defining non-violence from what it is not. Its antonym is violence. Violence does not seem to stem from economic conditions, although some violence does stem from there. Violence, in its essence, stems from self-hatred.

'Reflex Action' is a response not only of self-hatred but of hatred in general. Suppose one is on the street and sees a child with a cut under his eyes. A small child, an innocent child. Rather than the mind focusing on the innocence and true goodness of the sweet child, the self-hating mind will focus on the cut underneath the eye. That cut represents all that is foul. The self-hating man suspects automatically that the child was abused by his parents. The self-hating mind throws out all suspicion, such as: maybe the child fell down, or that the cut under the eye is a result of some accident. No. Rather the self-hating person will concentrate on the cut itself which represents hatred of the self. The hatred consumes him, and so a mental reflex action is let out towards the child, because all the self-hater sees is the hatred symbolized by the cut under the eye. The self-hater does not notice the cherubic, angelic face of the child. Rather the self-hater sees the small cut and that alone. Thus a reflex action through telepathy. The child, of course, does not feel this reaction as all violent thoughts stay within and do not project out. The child is safe from mental anxiety and anguish due to the Non-Dictatorship Principle. But this is of no solace to the self-hater. The self-hater sees this as his/her own fault, and thus feels shame, guilt, and fear which only builds the self-hatred. The more self-hatred, or the more mental violence within, the more violence without. As a postulate or assumption, human beings by nature may be non-violent. It is our vain attempt to reach perfection that builds self-hatred. The goal of perfection is a noble cause and a challenging goal, but it is human to make mistakes. It is inhuman to be perfect. And as a very important reminder, the Non-Dictatorship Principle, or some derivative thereof, blocks violent thoughts and such transmissions to other people. Linguistically speaking, the antonym of violence, or non-violence, has greater weight and a deeper meaning and a more powerful message.

PERSONAL NOTE:

Reflex action is a result of seeing or feeling hate. In this example, the cut under the child's eye was hate, not the child himself. There is a certain shame in the reflex action, because it is something that cannot be controlled. Luckily the child is not affected by the reflex. The one who is affected is the one dealing the reflex blow or the one who hates himself. Yes, I imagined striking this child.

INVOLUNTARY THOUGHTS:

Negative thoughts are involuntary. Violent thoughts are involuntary. Thoughts which hurt others are involuntary. One ought not to listen or take seriously **Involuntary Thoughts**. Such thoughts are false thoughts. For instance, when I thought the counter persons at a local pharmacy were not doing an adequate job, I thought that they were 'incompetent.' Thus, such a thought was an involuntary thought, and such thoughts remain within me, not within the young pharmacists themselves. When I woke up this morning and had a daydream about an old teacher who was angry with me, I became scared and hurt. But such thoughts again are involuntary. These are false thoughts.

It may be difficult to sort out voluntary thoughts from involuntary thoughts. Voluntary thoughts always prevail. In other words, positive thinking always prevails over the negative. The myth that there must be evil for there to be good is absolute nonsense. The positive and the good always prevail. How do I know this? Quite frankly, I don't. I have faith that such things work out this way.

And so on this rainy morning, I set up a structure for myself. The rain still falls.

Sick and tired of these thoughts. They bug the shit out of me. I'm afraid to look at people, because in my imagination I am hitting them. Involuntary thoughts stay within my brain, although no one seems to be following any of the rules. I'd rather be alone with my violent involuntary thoughts. External, peaceful expression may be the key. All I see around me. I'm scared to go downtown. The world has changed. Or have I changed? What little sanity I have left must rest with Non-Violence. Thus I ought to make a correction. First, Non-Violence in mind, body, and spirit. Second, a journey through the imagination through which telepathic contact may be realized.

Perhaps I started off on the wrong foot, claiming that imagination comes first. Now I have changed it. Non-Violence comes first, then the imagination. Because of my shortsightedness, I am stuck with involuntary thoughts.

20th Thwal-Hijja 1435
(October 15, 2014)

TELEPATHY ONLY IF NECESSARY:
Nothing is perfect. Only Allah is perfect, and the perfection is such that our own simple minds can never contemplate the goodness of him. We are imperfect. We make mistakes. And a purely telepathic society has its side effects. My speech, for the most part, has been suppressed. Perhaps I am not ready for Allah's gift of telepathy. I am too simple a being. I have learned my lesson. I am thankful for being here. Freedom is a key word. It was a word I had pushed aside. But now I crave it- the freedom to be kind and neighborly to people. To extend a hand. The right to work. Simple dreams that will probably move on to other simple dreams. A dream of a woman with whom I may share this life.

Total telepathy among persons, or Telekinetics, is too collective, and thus we lack the individual quality that gives our lives the thrill of freedom. There is nothing better than a smile, because a smile conveys the happiness which comes with freedom. I am abandoning the 'all or none' philosophy. At this physical age, I know and realize how stubborn I've been. God must be in charge. In a way, this entire fantasy, in all its mystery and befuddlement, is to surrender myself to Absolute Love- a metaphor for God. I surrender, and I am not ashamed. There is pride in my surrender. I suppose instead of getting out of the way, I am now following God. My surrender to God is not a form of cowardice. If I had relied on my old form of stubbornness, life would not be the miracle that it is. I just want things back to normal, but I fear they will never be. I want to forget. Just forget.

PARANOID   SCHIZOPHRENIA   AND   THE   FIGHT   FOR
RECOVERY:

I cannot live in fear anymore. I must have the wisdom to know what I can change, and especially what I cannot change. I am rife with paranoia. I am afraid to die. I'm in trouble when I don't trust my own brain. I need to recover. Nowadays I'm actually afraid of the night, the same night I had once romanced, the beauty of a full moon, always reminding me to keep my mind open. A shooting star reminding me to be patient. Suddenly I hope for sunlight. I used to criticize television, but now I like television. I used to look death in the face and laugh. Now I am afraid to die. Paranoia and suspicion all around me.

What is real? What is fiction? When will it end? Or does it keep going? The steady diet of chlozaril doesn't seem to be doing much. Everyone seems to know me, but I don't know them. I am afraid to speak to others. 'Afraid' is the key word. I am a simple man with simple needs. My innocence has been lost, but yet it is retained within the self. I am not Rasputin. I am not Nostradamus. I am Mustafa with simple dreams, right or wrong.

I cannot lie anymore, My condition is severe and chronic. I can't see a vision of the future, as though I am walking through fog groping for the answer, groping for a good future for our country. Violence, violence, violence in my brain! Hitting and smacking people left and right, only it is within the imagination that I am smacking people. And the people around me know exactly what I am about. There are no secrets anymore. The television is speaking to me. The news of hate-crime is pissing me off. I have nowhere to turn but to Allah. In a way I am being tested- moral, ethical dilemmas. I am barely holding up. The imaginary violence within my head. Who am I? Have I created this? Have I been used? Yes, I am all alone, although I am being protected by good people who see right through me. What have I done? I am not God or some kind of prophet. What have I done to deserve this? Non-Violence may not work in our beloved country. This is the age of terror it seems, only that I myself have the illness. I don't want to die. I want to live. I'm not a fighter, I'm a lover. So then why does it seem that I am on another world? Are people out to get me? I'm hurting all over. So much pent up rage. I'm on the verge of collapse. Again the news gets me depressed and angry, as though this is some kind of sick and twisted game.

21st of Thwal-Hijja 1435
(October 16, 2014)

INVOLUNTARY THOUGHT BREAKTHROUGH

Once again involuntary thoughts bother me. Involuntary thoughts are all thoughts negative and false. For example, walking past an African-American, and like Tourette's syndrome, the mind comes up with the involuntary thought of 'nigger.' The thought itself is involuntary, and what's more, the good self understands that such thoughts are false and negative and have no place at all within the good person's psyche. So we ask ourselves, where do these involuntary thoughts come from? The answer: the terrible parts of ourselves, the coldest parts of our nature, not the part which loves but that part which hates. And within the psyche of the person who holds involuntary or negative thoughts comes the better side, the lighter side which knows without a doubt that such thoughts ought to be eradicated somehow, purged from the psyche. So there exists within the psyche a need for the good to control the bad. Within our hearts, then, there lurks a battle. And as all battles, such fighting against the darker parts of ourselves is best fought within our own hearts. That is where all war, violence, terrorism, anything that breaks the human family apart, must be fought. Thoughts are just thoughts no matter how overwhelming they seem. But rest assured that the battle ought to be fought within ourselves, never outside, always inside as there are children at stake, and we must show them that: No! Killing ourselves is not in our natures. Being kind and gentle and truthful to each other is the common goal. Don't crack.

22nd of Thwal-Hijja 1435
(October 17, 2014)

BIGOTRY, RACISM, AND SEXISM AS MENTAL ILLNESS:

I shall start off by saying how ashamed I am of myself. For some reason I am being bothered by involuntary thoughts- thoughts that have somehow become a part of me. I don't want any part of them, but for some reason, racism in its absolute form, is taking over, slowly but surely, and since such thoughts are purely involuntary, like Tourettes Syndrome, mainly words, since such thoughts build the foundation of racism, I would say that such uncontrollable thoughts stem from mental illness. Through my short stay on this uncouth planet, I have had mostly good thoughts, positive thoughts, open thoughts about how we are really just one big human family- a rainbow coalition an historical figure used to say. But now these racist thoughts are taking over, slowly but surely, and when I know that such thoughts are false, I get even angrier inside. The good part of me scolds the bad, false, inhuman side of me.

I would postulate that bigoted, racist, and sexist thoughts serve no purpose. These are thoughts that I wish would go away. They are undesirable, wrong, and false to the core. So I must say or deduce that such thoughts belong in the category of mental illness. Why? First, I've been fighting racist thoughts all my life. Second, such thoughts, which I've been willingly trying to purge from my psyche, won't go away. Third, such thoughts are part of a much larger social disease.

The key to attacking this wave of mental illness is to be honest about the conflict that dwells inside the human heart. I saw a black person, and I involutarily thought 'nigger.' Once this involuntary thought registers, I beat myself up. I reduce the thought, or in this case, the word by calling myself a "sand nigger." That or I call white people "white trash," or "honky," but such labels do not seem to stick. But the ultimate response to such mentally ill thinking is to be angry with the self. It is a good sign that one knows that such bigotry, racism, and sexism are an involuntary false thoughts. To admit there is a problem is the first step. The key to eradicating bigotry, racism, and sexism is to confront such thoughts. There must be a will within the heart to stop the illness before it grows and takes over. I can't understand how I would bite the African-American hands which have fed me all these years. This is why such thoughts stem from illness.

PERSONAL NOTE:

I am starting to hate myself again. I've been against these thoughts all of my life- and suddenly this? I've spent so much time boosting my self-esteem, and yet involuntary thoughts knock down most of it. Quite a shitty day, because of these false thoughts. I'm thinking about seeing a chaplain or something. Somewhere deep inside there is a raging anger that just won't rest. Who the hell put these thoughts into my brain? I am spiritually and emotionally dying from them. I pray to Allah that these thoughts be removed. Every time involuntary thoughts roll around, I feel like taking a gun and finishing myself off. I used to think I had come so far. But have I come so far only to confront the bigotry within me? Is this what it means to evolute? I thought evolution would bring us together, not tear us apart. I'm so distraught over everything. I can't go on. I'll go on. I feel a bit strange. I'm crippled. I can't stand who I am. The world is tearing me apart, breaking me down, reducing me to my essential parts, and then making me fall back into the status quo of segregation, dividing and conquering us all. Tonight it does suck to be alive. I can only hope that the future is bright. I don't want to be bothered by false thoughts. Maybe it's all in my head, and if it is, that's where it shall stay. This is my life. I choose how I live, not anyone else. I choose how I think. Or is it that force from the underworld which is slowly obscuring my view of Heaven?

23rd of Thwal-Hijja 1435
(October 18, 2014)

TELEPATHY AGAIN:
There is not a doubt in my mind that telepathy exists. The nonverbal and intuitive contact of those whom possess telepathy is a result of the natural course of human evolution. Telepathy has existed for an incredibly long time, and my role in this is to observe and record this phenomenon. It would be far off for me to claim hubristically that I invented telepathy. Nonsense. I never created it. My duty is only to record the phenomenon so we may better understand it. My thoughts on telepathy I keep within these notes, and there is no real reason to speak to anyone about this brush with telepathy. Telepathy already exists, and I believe the people with whom I come into contact all possess telepathic power. Of course, some have little need to prove the existence of telepathy. I, however, feel quite the opposite. Within me there is a definite drive to prove that telepathy exists, and I should immediately qualify this by stating that telepathy belongs to all of us, and I have employed the strictest scientific methods so that even the most skeptical may agree that telepathy exists. I, however, am nowhere close to being a scientist. I am only one who writes, for some odd reason, to prove that telepathy exists. How telepathy got here I have no clue, but I need to discuss it.
TELEPATHY, NON-VIOLENCE, AND MIND CONTROL:
If non-violence is a worth-while principle, which I do think ought to be a worthwhile and absolute principle, then telepathy may contribute to bolstering and maintaining the non-violence principle. I have a terribly limited experience thus far, and I can only use myself as an example.
In my mind there are many violent thoughts, some stemming from my battles with my mother. I take from society: the violence on television, the violence in films. We are in the Dark Ages, so to speak. But aside from this, I am a staunch supporter of free speech even though speech itself is curtailed by market forces. For example, a radio station can't say 'fuck' on the air as it will

risk losing its advertisers. Anyway to get back on track, telepathy may help in calming the violent mind. Let's take an example.

I'm walking along the street and suddenly I get some violent urge to thrash someone who passes by. The mind at this point cannot think of anything but thrashing the passerby, but suddenly I hear the word 'relax,' as 'relax,' the word, was a thought not known to me, but implanted there by some telepathic means. Hence, I now have a choice that the mind could not develop on its own. I have a choice to A) thrash the passerby or B) to 'relax' and keep walking. Notice here how the individual is empowered by being given a choice, a choice perhaps sent telepathically by a person, a third person, across the street. The point here is not to focus on the origins of violence. Rather the point is that telepathy may help to alleviate the violent thoughts which we face each and every day. Sometimes we feel like we have little choice but to react violently towards our fellows. Hence, telepathy may help curb these violent thoughts by giving the individual a choice. But does such a suggestion of telepathic communication from that third person across the street mean that I am somehow COERCED into choosing relaxation instead of the thrashing? Herein lies the danger of telepathy, specifically the danger of mind control.

It is feasible that one may have a greater telepathic ability as to coerce others into acting one way or another. So the third party across the street may be seen as acting coercively, forcing me to think of 'relax' instead of my intention to thrash the passerby. Hence, a grave ethical concern: is telepathy a form of mind control? It could be, but to avoid violence upon another I would rather my mind be controlled by the goodness of the third party, because the effect of violence is much more destructive than the effects of the word 'relax' a second before my violent mind consumes me. But then a graver ethical concern: if violence exists, is it better that this third person penetrate our thoughts to block the existence of our violence in the mind? I hate to reify this, but we must ask: what is better? The existence of our violent selves, or the oppression of being coerced by a third party who gives us that choice to 'relax?' With such a limited experience I cannot answer this question, but I personally would much rather have a choice than inflict violence on another being of humanity. Many may think differently. It's important to note here that the third person who has implanted the choice within me to 'relax' has intruded my thoughts without formal permission. This assumes that that third person has a greater power than I to influence my own thinking, but the influence comes at a greater good, because A) it has given me a choice, and B) it turned me away from thrashing the passerby. So what, more importantly, does this say about the NON-DICTATORSHIP PRINCIPLE?

TELEPATHY   AND   A   DIMUNITION   OF   THE   NON-
DICTATORSHIP PRINCIPLE:

I'm sticking with the same example. I originally proposed the Non-
Dictatorship Principle to keep public thoughts public and private thoughts
private; I also set it up to try and stave off violent thoughts and to reduce the
influence of other thoughts by other people. For instance, under the Non-
Dictatorship Principle in its absolute form, I would have never had the choice
to 'relax,' and therefore I would have never received that telepathic message
from that third person across the street. I hate to say it, but the non-dictatorship
principle must be reduced in order to accept that third person's communique.
But what's good about this is that the individual can decide how much of the
non-dictatorship principle he or she really needs. But let's say on that day I
decided to put up barriers so that the mind could not receive any
communication whatsoever. No doubt I would have violently thrashed the
passerby. Hence, the Non-Dictatorship Principle has its limits, and sometimes
coercion by greater telepathic minds is needed to stop violence. So even if I
had decided that I want absolutely no telepathy coming to me, the thought or
choice to 'relax' is a coercive effect in the cause of the greater good of non-
violence. Also for this telepathic theory to be more feasible and reliable, the
Non-Dictatorship principle may be seen as limiting the acceptance of greater
thoughts, like the thought to 'relax' by the suspicious third party. I think the
non-dictatorship principle is an extremely important part of the telepathic
theory, but it must, at least on my part, be relaxed in order to learn more about
telepathy and to reduce my violent thoughts. If non-violence is to be a suitable
principle, the mind must move towards it.

TELEPATHY AS COMMUNICATION:

Just like reading, writing, voice, smell, all the senses in general,
telepathy is a form of communication, and as with the nature of
communication, telepathy is vulnerable to all types of misinterpretations and
communicative snafus. Also telepathy may not be the best form of
communication, and I must be careful not to place it on too high a pedestal. I
realize this may sound repetitive, but telepathy is just another form of
communication when other forms fail. That old song I remember: "I'm just a
boy whose intentions are good, Oh Lord please don't let me be
misunderstood." The misunderstanding the song discusses, I think, is a
breakdown or a misinterpretation that communication often brings. And to
hammer my initial point home, telepathy is available for all of us. Let us use it
for the good of us all.

24th of Thwal-Hijja 1435
(October 19, 2014)

TELEPATHY AND VIOLENT THOUGHTS:
Violence originates with violent thoughts, and in order to eliminate violence in the mind we must take steps to find suitable non-violent expression of violent, nightmarish, and negative or involuntary thoughts. Let us call it unfair to impose violent thoughts on others through the medium of telepathic communication. As the correct thought goes: violence begets violence, and to nip violent thoughts in the bud we must construct a way, albeit a very imperfect way thus far, to extinguish violent thoughts. The following theory does not put an end to violent thoughts. Rather it ends violent thoughts within the framework of telepathic communication. But by no means is the following part of this theory at all perfect. It should just shed light on the problem of telepathic violent thoughts and how we may make telepathic theory a more peaceful endeavor. Let us construct a diagram (See Diagram #9).

TELEPATHY   AND   'EXHAUST'   OR   EXTERNAL COMMUNICATION:
Notice in the diagram the importance of external communication such as speech, language, art, voice, writing, all that stuff. Notice how the Non-Dictatorship Principle varies. Let us call this change in the non-dictatorship principle a **Variable Non-Dictatorship Principle**, whereby the individual may adjust the non-dictatorship principle to his or her needs. Thus far we have been discussing how the non-dictatorship principle protects the mind from coercion and mind control. But now we have turned the tables.

What happens when the individual him/herself has violent thoughts which he/she does not wish to communicate through telepathy? If the self is having good thoughts on that particular day, then let those thoughts be freely communicated through telepathy if that's what the self wants (Scenerio One).

But let's say good thoughts are intertwined with bad thoughts. Then the non-dictatorship principle may be adjusted to block the self from imposing negative thoughts on Person A (Scenerio Two).

And now the very difficult part of dealing with all terrible thoughts. The implicit assumption is made that there must be an exhaust function or outlet for negative thoughts, because at this point the Non-Dictatorship principle also serves as a wall almost to block those negative thoughts. But we must battle with the reality that negative thoughts may not all be stored within the self. There must be some way to exhaust those terrible, demeaning thoughts without inflicting violence mentally or physically on others. The mind or the self can put up with only so many thoughts, and the negative thoughts need some sort of expression, a movement from reckless exhaustion to constructive and good and responsible exhaustion of all those negative, involuntary feelings. This exhaustion takes the form of external communication, as that is the only means, or one of the means rather, to regain goodness of viewpoint and kindly thoughts. It should also be noted that violent thoughts, as they approach telepathic communication, may be mediated by a telepathic helper of some sort, or a telepathic friend who may alleviate the violent thinking.

EXTERNAL COMMUNICATION AND FREEDOM OF SPEECH:
Freedom of speech and expression is extremely important, if not an absolute principle. Freedom of speech in its highest level must be maintained in order to avoid physical violence. Naturally freedom of speech is often curtailed through our cultural codes of conduct, so on and so forth, but notice how external communication is more of a reluctant function, meaning that we use it most when we have terrible, even violent thoughts. So freedom of speech and expression must prevail, but it becomes extremely important that the exhaust mechanism, or external communication, be as responsible and constructive as possible. This is only advice. It is not part of telepathic theory (or at least not this one), and if we are to decide on anything, external communication is really up to the individual, but freedom of speech must prevail.
The purpose of this is not to argue for a pure form of free speech, which I am definitely for. No, the purpose is to show how important external communication is to a general telepathic theory. For instance, a comedian may use an exhaust function differently from, let's say, the President. That's fine. But again the point is to realize the importance of external communication within telepathic theory, and at the same time, drive towards an understanding of freedom of speech and the need to vent or exhaust violent, troublesome, or negative thoughts in some external way. This assumes that the self cannot store all negative thoughts. Previously, I thought this storage well possible.
TELEPATHY,   INTUITION,   AND   VARIABLE   NON-DICTATORSHIP PRINCIPLE:
I refer now to the diagram on the previous pages involving violent and negative thoughts and how the Non-Dictatorship Principle safeguards such thoughts from being imposed upon another person (Person A). The power to control negative thoughts, to exhaust them as well, comes from the individual. So it may also be assumed that the Non-Dictatorship Principle may also be adjusted according to the individual's thought pattern. Hence, the adjustment of the Non-Dictatorship 'wall' is more an intuitive function. For instance, there is no real conscious need to implement the Non-Dictatorship Principle to

combat negative thoughts, such an application becomes more intuitive than conscious. I'm talking here of the third scenario whereby thoughts are totally negative or all negative. Hopefully this third scenario will never arise, because the good in all of us, even the most infinitesimal of the good, outbalances or outweighs the most terrible of heinous thoughts. Notice here how the problem turns from telepathy to the problems of the exhaust function, or better yet, problems of external communication, since the self is not able to absorb all those malicious thoughts in our worst case scenario, where all thoughts are terrible. Hence, in such a scenario a tiny sliver of a good thought must outweigh all terrible thoughts.

TELEPATHY AND THE EXHAUST FUNCTION IN SCENERIO THREE:
(See Diagram #10).
IMPLICATIONS OF GOOD THOUGHTS SUPERCEDING AND OUTWEIGHING NEGATIVE THOUGHTS FOR/WITHIN THE EXHAUST FUNCTION:
First we assume that good thoughts outweigh negative thoughts. This opens the door to 'gradations' or by what margins good thoughts supercede the bad thoughts.

Second, since good thoughts supercede bad thoughts, the nature of all exhaust from the self is coated instead with goodness, meaning that all exhaust, all external communication from a self riddled with negative thoughts, comes with a goodness first, negative thoughts second. Hence, all forms of external communication, no matter how tainted and torn the aim, are meant for the good and to support the good.

Third, now the problem returns to the 'self' which must find that sliver of good thought from all those vile, malicious, involuntary thoughts. Again, because the good supercedes within the exhaust function, all external communication through the exhaust function is for the purpose of the good. Whether we agree on what the 'good' is, is an entirely different matter. For instance, a neo-Nazis' version of the good differs from the version of good of, let's say, Martin Luther King, Jr. But the assertion ought to be made that all external communication through the exhaust function is meant for the good, and that sliver of good thought prevails over the bad, to what extent I am not sure.

TELEPATHY AS A PRIORITY AMONG COMMUNICATIVE MEDIA:
The difficulty is great, especially for those psychologists and psychiatrists who attempt to understand the many curves and trappings of the

mind. But telepathy as a medium must prevail, since there is no thought more difficult and yet so pure as telepathy. Telepathy gets right to the source, and only in dealing directly from the source may we survive over time and over those machines that suck away the mind's busy work. I'm not sure if telepathy is a new medium or whether telepathy has been around for millions of years. The point is, however, that without telepathy, in its way of uniting our human family, we will fall under the axe of placing too much power within the hands of the few and relying on machines way too much. I understand that new technology is the driving force behind any solid economic foundation, but we must also consider how to perpetuate our own human family. But only time will tell, only history will tell if telepathy works.

A PRACTICAL EXAMPLE OF HOW THE GOOD SUPERCEDES AND OUTWEIGHS THE BAD:

Here in Boston I met an older man named Charles Dipper who frequents the same bar I do. Apparently he's a copy editor for a major newpaper, and the bar we frequent serves as a fertile ground for experimenting with telepathic theories and communication of that nature. To my knowledge Charles Dipper is an exceptional copy editor and a decent human being, and I hold him in high esteem and regard. Charles Dipper is also an African-American, and I hold the African-American people in its entirety in very high esteem and personal profound respect. But to get back on track, negative thoughts are somehow cultivated when there is an unequal power basis from one person to another. I'm using Charles Dipper as an example to show the effect of negative thoughts upon the psyche and how those negative thoughts affect telepathic communication. I'm using Charles Dipper as an example, because every time Mr. Dipper, a most distinguished copy editor, flashes his monies at the bar, I am somehow filled with negative, abominable thoughts, and I try with each ounce of mental energy to fight against such negative thoughts. I would classify such thoughts as Involuntary Thoughts, and most heinous thoughts are due to ignorance as well as the power structure upon which our relationships are sometimes based, i.e., he being more rich and successful than I will ever be. I also have negative thoughts about Caucasians, but for some reason my negative thoughts towards Charles Dipper are more important and worthy of investigation. Nevertheless, I consider Charles Dipper a brother of mine, and those negative thoughts are a result of a power pressure or power hegemony upon me at the bar.

TELEPATHY AND THE CHARLES DIPPER EXAMPLE:

(See Diagram #11)

Hence a new relationship between the Non-dictatorship Principle and power pressure. As power pressure increases, like a boss telling you what to do, the sturdiness of the non-dictatorship wall must be made stronger in order to prevent bad thoughts from communicating telepathically to Charles Dipper. But also another relationship: a window of goodness through which the only good thought within the self may pass, and that good thought which reaches Charles Dipper is only that I respect him in the highest, and no matter how high the power pressure, I consider Charles Dipper to be a very respected and highly regarded individual. This is the thought that gets through to him telepathically. But again we have the problem of the exhaust function. How do we communicate all those terrible thoughts of Charles Dipper even though the good supercedes and outweighs the bad? Good question. Unfortunately I have very little knowledge of external communication, and without such important knowledge I am unable to comment. I am only able to assume things and think them.

26th of Thwal-Hijja 1435
(October 21, 2014)

TELEPATHY AND SELF-HATRED- A REWORKING OF THE CHARLES DIPPER EXAMPLE:
It's time to come clean and discuss frankly what is happening. The early version of the Charles Dipper example does not apply, because within the context of that example, within the bar, there were hardly any pressures applied to me by Mr. Charles Dipper. So then we must ask: where does my hatred stem from, if I am still thinking the same gross and negligent involuntary thoughts towards the color of Charles Dipper's skin? We must ask: why me of all people? Why am I cursed with such vile thoughts directed towards that dreadful word: yes, the word "nigger," and for what reason am I thinking such a vile derogatory word towards my friend Charles Dipper?
These thoughts are easily communicated telepathically. The mind is exposed to people in the bar, and even with them knowing my dreadful thoughts, the dreadful word itself keeps driving me towards the realms of hatred. So the issue is not Charles Dipper himself. The problem with that term is a reflection of self-hatred on my part.
Self-hatred has serious repercussions, not only on the self but for others who have to hear your thoughts. So the reasons for thinking Charles Dipper in such a negative light is due to a deep-brewing self-hatred, and whether one is conscious of it or not, this self-hatred casts a negative and derogatory pall on all those who may creep by you. Yes, these racial slurs, this pall of depression, are nothing but hatred of the self, and nothing fuels hatred of the self more than

the hatred of others. And I admit, if there is one person I hate more than anyone, it is myself.

I'm lost between loving everyone else and hating the self. Perhaps the old saying is true: one must love the self before one can love others. Hatred of the self transmits so easily, and when one hates the self, how easy it is to pick a scapegoat, even a man of great respect, and start thinking nigger this and nigger that. I myself consider myself a nigger as well, so it is no wonder how my heart is filled with nothing but hatred for myself, and thus we come to a vicious cycle of self-hatred, hating the self and thus hating everyone else, passing this hatred along to the next generation so that they may hate as I. Stop it. Stop it.

To love the self is twenty times more challenging than hating the self, and telepathy is a theory which is pushed further by love, not hate. Hatred and hatred of the self stalls telepathy. Hatred and hatred of the self does not offer one bit to any point of humanity. It is the embodiment of moving backwards instead of forwards. Yet I must admit that I hate myself. Telepathy and the good may never move forward, it may never work if the self hates the self. Love is telepathy's guiding principle, and love is the principle that shall save all of us from self-destruction.

A MORATORIUM ON TELEPATHIC THEORY:

Telepathy at this point is too advanced for the human psyche. For me personally it is too advanced, because the biological functions of the brain cannot handle full-fledged telepathy. For now, telepathy must be labeled as a delusion in order to reevaluate it, and also to understand that telepathy's foundation is love. We must return to reading books and working against, what Dr. King calls, the forces of darkness and injustice. Since telepathy among all of us has advanced too quickly, we must slow it down and reevaluate ourselves. This is more a personal note.

I cannot continue with telepathy since I am lost and confused and filled with inconsistency of the conscience, especially the soul. But this does not mean that the dear reader should give up or stop formulating telepathic theory. No, all it means is that I must stop, because reality is getting in the way, and my exhausted, tired brain certainly needs a rest. In this light I have labeled telepathy as a delusion for now, and my wish is to depart from it in order to pursue other endeavors like getting an education. I must get an education, and attempting to do so presses on the thick walls of my brain.

9th of MuHarram 1436
(November 2, 2014)

TELEPATHY AND PROXIMITY:

We are most influenced by those who are nearer in proximity to us. For instance, within the context of telepathy, the mind is influenced more by that person who is literally nearer to us. This we shall call one of telepathy's basic principles. For example, if I am in a room with a person, and there is another person out of that room a mile down the road, I am more apt to be influenced by the person in the room than influenced telepathically by the person who is a mile down the road. This is what is meant by 'proximity,' meaning that I am more likely to communicate with that person in the same room rather than another person down the road. We assume here that the individual in question has not advanced or fulfilled the full spectrum of telepathic communication, otherwise it is easily conceivable that the individual in question would be able to communicate with the person a mile down the road without a problem. But in this case and for the function of this theory, the individual is much more likely to communicate with someone in 'proximity.' I know this sounds incredibly tedious, but this is a basic principle. Believe me, there are many more complexities soon to come.

TELEPATHY AND THE SENSES:

In order for telepathy to function there must be a heightening of the senses. Let's take the visual, just as an example. Much of telepathy relies on facial gestures, intuition, what is smelled, and what is heard, what is tasted, what is felt. But what telepathy is based on the most is the imagination's ability to recall the senses and to use that base as a means of communication. For example, I see a man or woman, let's say a woman, in a crowded room. I know what she looks like, and I know how she sounds. I smell her perfume, et cetera. Then I imagine speaking to her. Yes, as I have noted before, there is a danger towards the self-reflection syndrome, but the key is to trust the imagination and communicate telepathically with her using the senses- the voice, the look, the book she reads.

Imagine speaking with her, imagine communicating with her. Again, telepathy does not discriminate, so walk into a room and assume that all of us hold telepathy and then try to recall the voice which is heard or the face which is seen or the smell of this fantastic woman. Recall using the imagination and have an imaginary chat with her through the mind. If at first the communication is unacceptable, try and try again. Eventually you will break through.

Of course telepathy is a two-way street. Two people must want to engage in communication by this sensual recall. The person engaging initially in telepathy will surely know whether telepathy is actually taking place.

TELEPATHY AND WOMEN:
One of the many shortcomings of this theory may be that I, the writer of it, am too intensely male-oriented, and some of the theory, especially the psychological aspects of it, may be too male for women to swallow. But a female perspective, aside from a mathematical perspective and evaluation, is desperately needed as well. Let it be known, however, that I am unafraid to venture into the female psyche to help this theory. Quite often we fail to understand the female psyche, or some of us dismiss it as unimportant. Let us declare here and now that a female perspective is of extreme importance. Some say that throughout the ages of time men have never understood the female mind, that men are unable to understand women. Some men even pass off women as 'psychotic,' or 'hysterical.' This type of attitude by males towards females is complete rubbish. Even though it may never be easy, the male must at least try to understand, if not promote, the female perspective, and I have prepared an example to demonstrate only one iota of how women may contribute to telepathic theory. This is a small example, but an important example.
THE HARRY DIMPLE EXAMPLE:
Harry Dimple is another man I met at the bar, and this example was inspired by him in a very indirect manner. Like the Charles Dipper example I have little idea if Harry Dimple knows that he inspired me to create this example. It ought to be known here that Harry Dimple is of the Jewish faith, just like Charles Dipper is a very respected African-American copy writer. So let it be known that I am drawing the inspiration for this example from Harry Dimple which is very similar to the Charles Dipper example, except with this example we are closing off the exhaust function which is so ultimately necessary for bridging the external world with the telepathic world. So, in brief, this example, this male example, assumes that the exhaust function is somehow cut off or not available. (See Diagram #12).

In this example, the Self is flooded with a terrible barage of hateful, shameful thoughts, but the human being is such that these thoughts may be seen by others, and I am assuming here that a woman may see this emanation of hatred within the Self. (See Diagram #13)

(1) EMANATION OF HATRED which goes beyond the non-dictatorship principle even though the emanation itself is a good thought. Such an emanation is perceptible perhaps to a woman who

seems to "see right through" that sturdy wall of non-dictatorship. The fact that a woman may see this may distinguish woman apart from man, but what the theory ought to demonstrate is that a woman is extremely important to this male-centric telepathic theory. I encourage women to improve this theory if it is possible, but notice here how women play a crucial role in male-centric telepathic theory by understanding and providing that essential ethic of care.

TELEPATHY, WOMEN, AND AGAINST THE DEUS EX MACHINA ARGUMENT:

In the Harry Dimple example we may misinterpret the role women play. Since they may see through the emanation of hatred to the senses not known to man, it may be easily misinterpreted that women are somehow the saviors of mankind. We must exercise caution here, because we must try to understand woman as she wants to be understood. The Harry Dimple example is just one of many examples, much like the Charles Dipper example. We must remember that women may not want to be seen in this light, even though saving the Self from destruction puts women in a place of extreme importance. Again the key is to understand women within the context of telepathic theory, and this very male theory may neglect to serve that very ambitious end. In short, let us not perceive women as the 'deus ex machina' for the very male problem of dealing with self-hatred or negative thoughts when the exhaust function is blocked off. Again we must understand woman as she wants to be understood.

The greater challenge is to find out when women are not in proximity. How do we again deal with the Charles Dipper example when the exhaust function is cut off or blocked? This is the real challenge, and understanding women may be an even bigger leap in some eyes, but the challenge remains: among men, within the Charles Dipper example where women are not in proximity, what does the Self do when 'exhaust' just isn't functioning? I have no idea. I guess at that point we rely on the goodness of our souls and dream of different ways to handle a situation when there is no exhaust function. But notice how women add to the reliability and feasibility of the theory. Their presence in proximity helps the man to dispel bad thoughts just by her presence. How remarkable the importance of women in any theory, especially this one.

TELEPATHY AND THE CLOSURE COMPLEX:

The earlier Harry Dimple example shows what may happen when the Non-Dictatorship Principle prevents hateful thoughts from being exposed and, at the same time, when there is no exhaust function available to the self. At this point it becomes imperative that the self searches for some expression, and within this closure of the self there does not seem to be any outlet for the expression of those shameful thoughts characterized by the darker parts of our psyche. This is what ought to be called '**The Closure Complex**,' as seen by this example. The underlying assumption here is that within the self there is a limit to how many self-hating and other hating thoughts one can hold. Let's look at the following example. (See Diagram #14).

Notice how the self adapts to a dangerous insularity, and because the self can only handle so much hatred, the self must choose: either reduce the non-dictatorship principle to allow self-hating and hatred to be expressed to Harry Dimple, or heighten that barrier so the exhaust function may release those negative thoughts from the self. So the individual has a choice which is extremely important at this juncture, since the self will resort to something physically drastic if involved with thoughts of hatred and self-hatred, or better yet, revolving in thoughts of self-hatred. There must be some outlet by which the individual may express those thoughts.

TELEPATHY, THE CLOSURE COMPLEX, AND THE CHOICE OF THE EXHAUST FUNCTION:

Remember the individual has a choice for either lowering of the non-dictatorship principle or utilizing the exhaust function. If we keep in mind that violence begets violence, it seems that one should choose the exhaust function. This is because we are assuming A) that violence begets more violence, and B) violent thoughts beget violent actions. Many may disagree with the selection of the exhaust function, because of that old saying "thoughts are only thoughts." The point, however, is to give the battered Self the empowerment to choose.

The second point is that telepathy is not a perfect theory and that having violent thoughts may inflict more havoc than utilizing the exhaust function whereby there is tremendous knowledge available on how to channel anger, frustration, hatred, et cetera, and parcel it through external means.

Remember also that through the exhaust function the good supercedes the bad, while the Non-Dictatorship Principle blocks additional thoughts from entering the self and also blocks those hateful thoughts from emanating onto others. The best thing to do here is to examine the results of both choices and induce a theoretical compromise.

We shall examine this in three distinct settings. First, what happens when the non-dictatorship principle is at its highest and the exhaust function is completely closed? This is what we mean by the Closure Complex, and a very dangerous ticking bomb the closure complex is! Second, what happens when the Non-Dictatorship Principle is at its highest, and there is no exhaust blockage? This is the Charles Dipper example all over again, whereby external communication is good, since the good supercedes those negative thoughts. Now the big question. Can't we strike a balance between the non-dictatorship principle and the exhaust function whereby the self may regulate the non-dictatorship principle and the exhaust function through his or her own mental thermostat? Now we get into the area of gradations, and here we must set down some basic relationships:

When the non-dictatorship principle is at its highest, the exhaust function operates to its highest as well. When the non-dictatorship principle is at its lowest, the exhaust function is at its lowest as well. Let us show this through a diagram. (See Diagrams #15 and #16).

Notice how these are two extreme examples. Example One is when all thoughts are good thoughts. Example Two is when all thinking is drowned with a self-hatred and hatred of others. There must be a middle path whereby there may be a certain optimization of both Non-Dictatorship Principle and Exhaust Function to provide the self with a healthy balance. But what interests us more is the Closure Complex, because the dominant reaction when confronted with extreme negative thinking is to cut off all avenues of communication telepathically and externally. So when the Closure Complex is present, I think it better to choose the Exhaust Function rather than telepathizing thoughts, these hateful thoughts, to another person. Let us work on the Closure Complex for a spell.

TELEPATHY, THE CLOSURE COMPLEX, AND EXTERNAL COMMUNICATION:

Again the Closure Complex is a dangerous situation. The self is assailed by negative thoughts, self-hatred, and the hatred of others. Let's say we choose to vent our anger through the Exhaust Function. This would mean that an exhaust function must open up, and even more importantly, push the barrage of negative thoughts into something positive. This is the most important principle behind the idea of external communication as a means, not just to vent, but to push negative thoughts into something constructive. This is important specifically within a Closure Complex situation. Otherwise external communication will be physically violent and offer nothing of substance to the self except "meaningless chaos," as Dr. King put it.

Therefore, to move towards healthy thinking the person within the dreadful closure complex must use the exhaust function whereby the good supercedes those negative thoughts. I will bring in the idea of 'iterated contact' when using external communication as a means of escaping from the closure complex.

TELEPATHY, THE CLOSURE COMPLEX, AND 'ITERATED' EXTERNAL COMMUNICATION:

Let us take the following example: (See Diagram #17).

Notice again the implications. Within the Closure Complex the individual (self) chooses to externalize that anger and self-hatred through the exhaust function to another person. Iterated contact assumes that person is able to vent all those bad thoughts in a constructive manner, thus making way for good thoughts to enter, since the exhaust function is high, which lowers the Non-Dictatorship Principle. So through iterated contact the exhaust function is utilized, and negative thoughts are vented to another person.

This is not as complex as it seems. It takes initial contact to stimulate the exhaust function. As the exhaust function is used more through iterated contact with another, the Non-Dictatorship Principle lowers and simultaneously negative thoughts are allowed to release from the mind.

I'm sure this carries many other implications, but the first question is: why can't the same be done with the Non-Dictatorship Principle? Basically because the Non-Dictatorship Principle is the guardian of private thoughts, and thoughts which are private shouldn't be messed with. Also communication needs to be productive and constructive rather than unleashing those more pure and self-hating thoughts onto someone else. External communication through iterated contact ensures that the first thought will be a good thought, whereas the Non-Dictatorship Principle ensures that thoughts of hatred won't get through and protects thoughts that are private. External communication initiates that movement from negative thought, to venting constructively, to positive communication. Perhaps one day telepathic theory will advance, and the Non-Dictatorship principle will no longer be needed. But another question looms on the horizon: what if there is no person with whom one may utilize the exhaust function? What if the Self has no one to communicate with but the Self?

This question presupposes that external communication through the exhaust necessitates another person. But external communication is not limited to voice communication with another person. Rather there are many forms of external communication, like whistling while you work, assuming that the self has a job. All forms of external communication might be utilized except that of physical harm to another as this is not external communication, just senseless violence. But what if someone has absolutely no outlet?

This would be an extreme scenario whereby an S.O.S. Communique would be delivered, we hope. This idea hasn't fully gelled, as the theory concentrates on individual telepathic situations as they arise, but to the person who seems to have nothing at all, no way to communicate or vent that hatred, we must rely on hope: that creative spark within the individual that moves self-hatred and hateful thoughts towards more creative and positive thoughts, thus positive external communication.

As of this moment telepathy is an imperfect concept, and so external communication is essential to bridge that gap between theory and practice.

On a more philosophical note, the real question is how to transmute negative thoughts into something positive. Herein lies the key, but within the context of telepathic theory, the questions become increasingly difficult: How do we transmute negative thoughts into positive thoughts without the aid of external communication?

TELEPATHY AND VIOLENCE AS WASTE PRODUCT OF THE MIND:

The mind is even trickier, and I do not intend to write like a psychologist or psychiatrist. This theory is spawned mostly from the imagination, and the attempt to make it more feasible and reliable is an attempt to bridge the theory-practice gap.

Let's label violence as a waste product of the mind with the simple logic that violence is something the mind does not want to use, and that violence is essentially an undesirable characteristic of the human mind. Within the individual and during telepathic exchange, it may be easy to pass off thoughts of violence to the next person. But passing thoughts of violence to a fellow man or woman is harmful to the individual's psyche. So the question becomes: What do we do with thoughts of violence?

We assume the mind may only absorb so much, and so there must be some release. There must be a type of mental refinery for the mind, a refinery that converts negative, violent, and shameful involuntary thoughts into positive thought, constructive thought. But until a mental refinery is constructed on a theoretical level, we are forced with the looming assumption that violent internal thoughts must be externalized, and even though this is quite a serious assumption, a mental refinery at this point doesn't seem to be readily available (unless there is some psychological or psychiatric theory I haven't heard or read about). So in the absence of a mental refinery to move negative thought into positive thought, we must label violence a waste product of the mind, and violence ought to be compared to our own city sewers, in the sense that these thoughts must be released like food waste is released through the body. Violence deserves to be a waste product, because it does not and never will do any good to any condition or spirit.

TELEPATHY AND A RATIO OF HATEFUL, VIOLENT, INVOLUNTARY THOUGHTS TO THOUGHTS OF LOVE:

An assumption, one of many, must be made that the individual can distinguish and differentiate between thoughts of internal hate and thoughts of internal 'love.' I do not wish as of this moment to venture into 'love theory,' although such theories in a comprehensive fashion should be extended and freely discussed and criticized. The main assumption here is that the individual knows what is violence and what is non-violence in a very loose sense. The individual may also be able to quantify his or her violent, hating, and negative thoughts and compare them to the external expressions of love. Thus a ratio exists (or should exist) whereby the individual is able to quantify hateful thoughts to good thoughts. (I don't mean to play semantics here. Good and Love concepts I use interchangeably).

Let us construct the ratio. For every one violent thought, there must be at least two thoughts of love or good thoughts that must be externalized. In a very simple, rudimentary form, the ratio is indeed one type of mental refinery. Let's take an example.

Let's say I pass by a person on the street, and my immediate internal thought is to hit that man. Let this count as one hateful thought. According to the ratio, this one thought must be complemented with two thoughts of love and goodwill that must be externalized. The hateful thought does not go through to that man, due to the non-dictatorship principle. Then the mental refinery process begins. I think of kissing a woman (one thought). I think of shaking hands with my friends at the bar (second thought). Then I externalize these acts by actually doing the deed.

The first act of good will is compensation for the hateful thought. The second act is to add one more of good into the universe to outweigh the original thought of hatred.

TELEPATHY AND THE RATIO OF ONE HATE TO TWO EXTERNALIZED THOUGHTS OF LOVE:

This may not be adequate enough, but for now the ratio must suffice until a better mental refinery is created. The problem is that this ratio and its practice may not be feasible. If I have two hundred hateful thoughts per day, how may I possibly externalize four hundred actions of love? Also, sometimes violent, hateful, and negative thoughts are situational. And third, the nature of this ratio is more powerful as a symbolic tool; that love will triumph over hate.

The symbolism is a greater argument for the ratio, but whether or not the ratio can be put into practice is very specious indeed. For now, however, it must suffice, but it highlights a major problem within telepathic theory: how do we take something inherently negative and turn it into something positive worthy of the stamp of love? Tough questions, but over time as the people add to the theory, there is faith that love shall 'conquer the great divide.' So this simple ratio as a mental refinery needs much work.

Yet the idea remains that in certain situations we may not be able to count, and furthermore we may not be able to externalize thoughts of good will. For instance, if I get a bunch of hateful, violent, involuntary thoughts towards these people at the bar, how am I to externalize thoughts of good will in double the number before I leave? I could buy them each a round of drinks, but the sheer multitude of thoughts of love and goodwill may not be very feasible. If I have hateful thoughts at the bar, the first thing I want to do is leave and get away from the situation that tempted those dreadful thoughts, especially towards Charles Dipper and Harry Dimple. Hence, the situation must be examined within telepathic theory. And I will resurrect the closure complex not only as a dysfunction of communication but also as a resource.

TELEPATHY AND THE CLOSURE COMPLEX AS A RESOURCE:

Let's take a situation. Today at the bar I had uncontrollable violent thoughts towards one of my fellow drinkers who is also turning into a good friend. These hateful thoughts somehow got the better of me. But within the bar these thoughts kept hitting me, and at no time could I step away and use the ratio to convert those negative thoughts into positive external communication. So what did I do to prevent those thoughts from reaching my fellow? I used the closure complex, not as a dysfunction but as a resource. Now the closure complex is a very dangerous situation and without attention it could lead to drastic, misdirected anger towards another person. But when used as a resource during high pressure situations, namely when hatred bombards the self, it will protect the psyche to whom those hateful thoughts have been misdirected. Let us draw a diagram, keeping in mind the Charles Dipper and Harry Dimple examples. (See Diagrams #18 and #19).

I'm sure there are many implications here, but notice how the closure complex can work to keep hateful and violent thoughts from externalizing. This is only a theoretical model. In no way can this realistically combat violent thoughts due to reality itself. Nevertheless within theory the **Refinery Ratio** is key for the movement towards peace of mind. But to practice this theory would take a virtual superman. In other words, don't try this at home. Many of the kinks within this theory need to be worked out. Much more input is needed.

PERSONAL NOTES:

Okay, I think I ought to give telepathy a rest now. Each time I go into the bar I am fueled with more ideas. I'm sure there are many more theories out there which need examining. Oh I'm so glad to be done with it for one night. I'm hoping tomorrow everything will go smoothly. A lot of this is due to my interactions with good people. I need to get back, but as of I'm not sure what tomorrow will bring. Must take it a day at a time, and I must relax the mind in order to be ready.

I'm in too deep. I need help, and at the same time I have nowhere to turn. I went to the psychiatrist today, and I mentioned that the reason I am thinking such violent thoughts is because I don't like interacting with people.

So from a psychiatric angle I need to feel more comfortable around people. I can't be pushed so much, or else I'm bound to snap. My mind is like two horses going different directions. Must return. Must keep reality in mind. I need to get an education instead of hanging out at the bar. Must concentrate on the 'all of us' theme, because whether we like it or not, every person is essentially good. It's all right to feel that way about people, and I must believe this if I am to survive. I don't know what causes such terrible thoughts.

Before adjourning to the bar, I sat in a small park next to the coffee shop and looked at the sky and smoked a cigarette and almost wept for humanity. Well, now I'm taking steps to live this life. Must return, but where shall I go with this theory? Because it is getting out of hand. I'm between two worlds: the imaginary world and the world that greets me when I wake up.

Book Five

"The whole world is haunted by these ghosts of a dead past…Ah! If we only had the courage to sweep them all out and let in the light." -Henrik Ibsen

Chapter One
12th of Safar 1436
(December 5, 2014)

If madness could be captured, then let it be defined and captured. Those mysterious coincidences must be followed through and investigated regardless of the toil and sweat and brain damage. See the signs and thus investigate each sign until it leads eventually to some higher knowledge, for this is exactly what the Imam did in Boston.

He did not wait to search out these special coincidences. He traced them at his own risk and peril, and although his mind grew warped while wandering the streets in search of some strange knowledge brought down from the heavens, straight into his brain, he nevertheless aimed for a knowledge he never rightly possessed. He saw special significance in the cars which passed him, in the people who smiled in the darkness, in the women who seemed to flirt without uttering a single word.

He walked down Boylston Street, and at their passing his heart pounded. His desire for a woman was widespread. Nothing is more gratifying than encountering a beautiful woman, for all women in their own right are beautiful creatures, and these women seemed to be looking at him, talking to him without words, without expression, only walking casually, head straight, so quiet, dazzling and mesmerizing. Could they have been looking at Mustafa? Mustafa thought so.

He pounded the pavement, his heart aching at the sights of these glorious creatures, and in his mind's eye he imagined dancing with them, arm around the waist, hands together, feet moving back and forth rhythmically, like rowing a boat towards the breadth of shore. How badly he wanted one, not to touch or to argue, but simply to walk down the street and gain their attention, any woman, and when he encountered one of them glossing him over with eyes of blue or brown, he filled his heart of stored desires and lost opportunities, only to move on to the next woman and then the next one, because they all had something to offer him: their divine beauty, the hair which cascades above the forehead like sun-drenched waves, the eyes which look preoccupied, the tender lips which whisper without ever opening or closing, and that seductive figure crushing him with each step. He saw significance in every woman's face.

A conspiracy, thought he. Yes, it must be some terrible conspiracy, as women have had their clandestine networks even before the beginning of time. Perhaps they were sizing him up. He so badly needed to hold one, right there in the street and break the barrier of wasted time, wasted years spent in seclusion and extreme loneliness. He believed only a woman could lead him to salvation, because his longing for a woman plunged him into deep despair.

'Oh woman, why won't you talk to me?' asked Mustafa. 'Is it the way I look? Is it my foreign name? Perhaps the color of my skin or the size of my waist? Or is it because I don't have a home? Why so coy on this wintry day?'

For Mustafa it was maddening to see so many women walking upon the snow, for he longed for each and every one of them, and yet his tongue would only yield an avoidance and shyness.

His head pounded with each thought. His mind roamed and wandered as it found significance in every example of creation, from the trees that whistled as the wind swept through the branches to the particles of snow that fell at varying angles. But with each thought his head throbbed, and quite suddenly the women were missing from the slush-heavy street corners, and the lights along the street shut off as though the time had come to face the chill.

He wandered the streets for some hours, and it seemed like the whole world had gone on holiday, a boat that left without him. Where did all the women go? Were they hiding somewhere, not necessarily under a rock but in the arms of other men? He heard his feet rubbing on the tender snow, and as the brain rotated in circular thought, he figured he needed help, because he knew not where he was.

He had been awake for two straight days occupied in thought, as though each second carried a profound weight. The women, like strangers, had left him. The cars had gone to sleep along the side of the street. The wind died and the snow stopped. He had little idea where to sleep, for he had completely lost his way, and oblivion followed him like an invisible stalker.

He crossed the Boston Commons. The blackness beyond his immediate path beckoned him to move forward, an oblivion that made little sense but submerged in significance at the same time. His breath grew short, and his legs hung from his torso like wet noodles. He cut through the heart of the Commons and found himself treading upon the red bricks of Charles Street, the colonial shop signs swaying somberly above him. He walked slowly, not a single person on the street, not even the strangers he knew. He followed signs to the nearest hospital as home would somehow be found among the robots walking on a psychiatric ward. He had been off his medication ever since he broke from his weird imaginings, and his head burned and churned with every conceivable thought as though some higher creature cracked his skull with the sharp end of a hammer, pulling it apart as though loosening nails on weathered boards. He found meaning and no meaning at all. The strangers along the street had disappeared, and if he so happened to find one holding out for loose change he would have given his last dime, not only to be conscience-clear, but to be saved from the beasts squeezing and pressing his brain, hacking away at gray flesh.

The conspiratorial women had left him at the wrong time, because everything had a purpose, and he was at the center of it. Angels moved from Allah's heaven, and they guided him, almost pushing him along to that point where nothing matters. All of the synapses connected, neuron to neuron, the brain transforming into a pinnacle of thought both happy and sad, up and then down like riding some sinister amusement park ride at the age of eighty, at the point where senility and unbridled youth intersect, free yet confined, sober but drunk, ice on his toes and heat sizzling his brain.

And what of the mind? The mind had left him, but the memories of yesterday invaded him. Over and over he slapped his mother at the bolted doorway. The sharp teeth of rats fed upon his flesh in the middle of the night.

And what of violence? The bomb blasts in Tel Aviv, bulldozers packing emaciated and sickly corpses into a mass burial hole. The New War.

"Oh Allah," he complained, "what have you done?"

The panorama of history flashed before his eyes, and his immediate urge was to vomit upon the steps of Massachusetts General Hospital. He entered a lobby with warm air blasting upon his body. He stumbled into a bright hallway and found a heavy door which he opened carefully. A receptionist behind a glass wall gathered what little information she could. The Imam knew neither his name nor his residence, his head drowned in complete oblivion.

"You don't know your name? Can you at least try to remember? No? How about your social security number? No? Are you suicidal? Do you feel the urge to harm yourself or to harm others? Just nod. All it takes is a nod. No? Yes? Maybe?"

The Imam stood in front of her speechless. Tears flooded his eyes due to his inability to understand simple language.

"Hold on. I'll get the doctor."

He waited near the reception desk, and in a short while a tall, thin man in a white laboratory jacket entered from a door near the reception area. He had long hair tied in a ponytail, and his voice was calm and soothing, almost melodious.

"Come with me," said the psychiatrist.

The psychiatrist on duty led him across the threshold beyond the reception area, and Mustafa was enveloped by white walls with white tiles and the ubiquitous scent of surgical equipment. They sat in a small office, and the psychiatrist fired questions at him. Mustafa had no answers. The psychiatrist fed him two small pills. Mustafa was then led to a smaller room with a hospital gurney in the middle of it. The lights were bright and kept him awake as the psychiatrist locked him within the small room. He knew neither the time of day nor exhaustion. He lay himself on the hospital gurney in the hope that sleep would take over.

Sleep came in intervals of five minutes, but nothing more than that. He did notice, however, that his thoughts were slowing, and he yearned for moments of absent-mindedness. The bright lights in the small room bothered him. The hard surface of the gurney hurt his back. But by the shuffling of feet and the opening and closing of doors in the hallway, he sensed morning approach. He knocked on the door a few times but no one responded. Just as sleep covered him, the psychiatrist entered the small room.

"How are you feeling? Better?"

Mustafa nodded his head.

"Can you tell me your name?"

"Mustafa," he whispered.

"What an interesting name. Can you tell me what's bothering you? I'd like to help."

"I can't explain it. It all happened. Just happened all at once."

"Tell me, do you have health insurance?"

"I don't think so."

The psychiatrist thought this over and said:

"How about an address? Do you live in Boston?"

Mustafa was discharged from the psychiatric unit after a short psychological test consisting of trivia questions and arithmetic. He answered all of these questions incorrectly, but his willingness to respond quickened his discharge. They sent him off with a week's supply of medication. They also insisted he go home to his family, wherever that may be.

Mustafa left the hospital feeling low, because in his mind he had failed. His intention of living self-sufficiently and acquiring an education in the colonial city had failed. His drive to meet people like him had failed. He understood that being alone in an endless city only posed greater problems. And in his fit of failure he grew angry, not at anyone in particular but mostly angry with himself for believing he was at the center of what seemed to be a message from Allah. And even if his meaningful coincidences were ultimately meant for him, then why him? Mustafa knew he wasn't exactly a saint. Yet these connections and coincidences, this newfound knowledge, and the strangers on the street, seemed so very real. Could it have been his imagination? That these strangers knew exactly who he was and how he felt, and they somehow understood his relationship with his mother and his unselfish drive for Absolute Love and Absolute Peace?

He walked along Commonwealth Avenue. The whole night mysteriously vanished as though he died and now was born again into a hardened realist. The theories which filled his head disappeared. The strangers who knew him through and through now walked their separate ways, some of them holding coffee cups, some descending the steps for shelter in the subways. His heart sank with every passing footstep, for Mustafa had believed that he saw the end of the world, the end of his country and did every duty to save it.

He mused that a movement towards peace and absolute Love could only help, and now while walking among the old buildings he realized how silly it was to think that the goals of love and peace could be achieved. Yet he had not given up so quickly. He figured he had been silent for most of his life, unable to speak, unable to survive without companionship, and twice he had blown a fuse. Better get home, he thought. This too shall pass.

He boarded the bus bound for New York City that afternoon, as he sold his medications to a transient he knew. While watching the gnarled and tangled buildings change into homes, and then the entire landscape transform into long fields, he understood that man can never be changed by a few nights of synchronicity. He rested his head against the hard tinted windows and fell fast asleep.

Chapter Two
KHOZEM IN COMMAND
11th of Safar 1436
(December 4, 2014)

Khozem Bengaliwala sat against the walls of his father's home in Mecca. He propped himself on the hard pillows that lined the perimeter of the spacious room. He had been through much in the last few years. His beard had grown as well as his belly. A white turban crowned his head, and he had purchased new glasses. He finished university in Cairo in accordance with his father's instructions. Even though he completed the two years of arduous study and training, he never believed school or education in general helped anyone. He remembered his training as a fierce burden. He believed that academia, especially the type that concentrates only on Allah, His Prophet, and the Prophet's writings were downright boring and insulting. He compared such training to water dripping from a faucet or hearing a clock making its slow revolutions around and around a dial. But he had acquiesced to his father's commands. Otherwise he would have been banned from the kingdom and whipped by some proud mutawaf.

He stayed among the clerics and students of Al-Karim for three years. He withdrew himself from judging students and attending regular classes. He reluctantly studied with a select group of clerics renowned throughout the Islamic world, and he disliked each of them. He thought them too stern and laconic. Their strict codes had little appeal.

Each day he awoke at sunrise and prayed in a specially appointed room with these chosen clerics. He would have much rather judged the students or taken long strolls to the women's campus in the hopes of finding Rashida there.

Most of him died when Rashida died, although strangely he would gaze from the quadrangle of the main campus onto the dusty road that led to the women's dormitories. He never set foot on the women's campus. This would have caused a great stir, and Khozem had matured enough to avoid scandal. He no longer kept in touch with the students, as his training was confined to very old men who asked him to read and interpret page after page of text. He followed what they said, and he hated every moment, because deep in his heart he longed for Rashida.

He never escaped from this singular fascination. He created the illusion that she still lived, if not through reincarnation, then through the spirits with plaintive voices. Yet he knew these voices false and misleading. To believe in these voices he would have to leap from his cold and calculating demeanor to mystical realms, and he was unwilling to take that leap. He disliked mystical things, and at the same time he could not let go of Rashida.

Bereaved as he was, he had wandered the campus alone, mostly in the middle of the night. He had looked into the stars and searched for some sign of her presence. He found the stars twinkling at him, almost laughing at the loss he suffered. He wanted to shout into the sky in the hopes Rashida would hear. But this would alert the campus police.

In the years during his rebellion he would have done so. He would have searched through every bunk of the women's dormitory just to find a scrap of her clothing or that musky scent that once defined her. Instead he stood beneath the glittering sky, a sky that had once connoted a goodness and purity, and he found within this same sky a darkness and despair. The bright stars were only a subterfuge for the remaining blanket of darkness that consumed his soul. He thrived off this darkness. It gave him strength, a strength which he now unleashed upon those who even thought of crossing him.

In front of these clerics he performed well, but he did not perform in the usual sense. He in fact 'acted' the part of bavasaab, and such a brilliant performance, disguised by his willingness to read and interpret Islamic text, allayed these intense emotions of hatred for himself and for others. Rashida remained the only light, but a light extinguished.

He envied the young men of the main campus, for their lives would go on without tragedy. He rarely saw women, and the one's he did see he despised. They would make the men happy as wives and mothers. He found only one reason to live, and she had died.

During the first few years his sadness was profound. He cried to himself if the sun did not creep into his room at the proper angle. He read the Hadith but could no longer comprehend the words. He knelt and prostrated to a God he secretly hated, because no God, if God is to be filled with an ultimate goodness, would confiscate his Rashida and mangle her in that fashion. He played the part with precision. He had learned the ways of the faith and had not absorbed a single glint of its knowledge. He knew only his Rashida had been taken from him.

He suspected his father, Tariq. But he blamed Allah. He withheld this anger, which escalated during the remaining years of his training. Many hours within the specially appointed rooms was spent drifting in and out of affairs with her, whether these fantasies took place now or later, in his room or while wandering the quadrangle in the middle of the night. His loss eclipsed the sun and pulverized a moon that appeared in preposterous crescents. The illusion of the sky's beauty fueled his hatred.

Khozem had toured with his father through certain parts of Far East Asia. There were fewer followers there than the Middle East or Africa. Touring mosques was the most essential part of his job. The tours gave Khozem experience in the matters of his flock. Tariq handled Khozem's vocational training in a more relaxed manner. Khozem never argued with his father while on these tours, although on many occasions he thought he would burst into argument with him. He played the role of the dutiful son, not the prodigal son which had characterized his behavior before Rashida. He looked to his father for a guidance he never valued. They would enter a mosque together, sometimes hours before the followers arrived, and Tariq would advise him how to perform prayers meant for large crowds: how the verses needed to be articulated to perfection, or else the believers would lose confidence in his leadership, or the timing of kneeling and prostrating himself to remain synchronized with the crowd, or walking the optimal number of steps behind the bodyguards so that all the believers could see the glorious bavasaab. And especially the important blessings the bavasaab must give to the most charasmatic believers. Out of this performance the final benediction was most important. The small gesture of blowing a quick breath upon a believer could animate even the dullest crowd. All tours had strict protocols, and Khozem found himself learning more with Tariq than with the clerics at the university.

Although Khozem was satisfied and at times overwhelmed by the tour of the Far East, he sensed that these tours and his training for the position were only a means towards the end of unleashing that bitter hatred he kept close to his heart. His father spoke of marriage, and Khozem smiled. He would never love another woman. He thought the world too evil for his offspring, although he himself contributed to such a darkness. This same darkness made him wish his father would trip on a fold in the Persian rug, breaking a hip or fracturing a collarbone. Khozem had suspected him all along, a man who he was supposed to love but could never fathom loving, not for one moment, despite the thin smile he wore.

When Khozem and Tariq returned to Mecca, they discussed the other major responsibility of the bavasaab's position. This was the vast Organization and particularly the Organization's funds. The money came in the protean forms of vast and heavy contributions from Islamic countries, private donations from organization members, spot donations from touring, and affiliate mosques from which the organization took a cut. The Organization's fund supported an intricate bureaucracy comprised of ministries of finance, education, culture, information, intelligence, religious affairs, and a ministry of executions. The bloated fund was derived mostly from the Middle Eastern countries. The funds also supported a series of complexes and cultural centers throughout the Islamic world. Khozem was shown an organization chart that displayed these many cultural centers along with a global display of the affiliate mosques that had been growing in the Western World. Khozem made the inference that the mosques gathering in the West would eventually shape and determine his touring schedule. Lending his support to fledgling mosques would increase converts and solidify a constituency within Western cities and towns. Khozem told his father he never cared for the West, an area that thrived on infidelity and corruption, but his father said to keep a close eye on these developing countries, because "the future of Islam shall be found there." Khozem had repeatedly questioned his father about this, especially at the beginning of his tenure, but he knew he delayed this talk for a reason, even though the delay filled his curiosity.

Tariq waited for a propitious time to tell his son of the Imam in the West. Tariq constantly led him on like a horse chasing a carrot, promising he would learn when the time was right. Khozem knew already that an Imam existed, and that he was to follow to the letter and spirit his rules, advice, and orders. After a few years of handling the Organization, its apparatus, and heavy touring schedule, Khozem did find out that the Imam was living in the

West. His father told him one night after saying prayers together in the Meccan home. Khozem was surprised at what his father said, because for the first time the Imam had been placed far away, which essentially gave Khozem even more power than he expected.

All the bavasaabs at one time or another fell into this same quandary: to follow the Imam or to break free from him and ignore his commands, thereby achieving their own ends. Khozem saw how easy it would be to leave the Imam in the West, leave the Imam in hiding, and do whatever he pleased with the Organization. Every bavasaab had at one time considered this. The only reason for following the Imam was the firm faith that he was somehow chosen by Allah, that he was indeed the descendant of Ali. Beyond this blind faith, which developed into a long-standing principle reinforced by the clerics, there seemed little reason for the bavasaab to follow an underground Imam. Yet for centuries the relationship between Imam and bavasaab remained intact. Khozem, however, was a different breed of bavasaab. He kept his contempt festering, despite the many long conversations with his father.

Khozem had plenty on his mind while waiting for his father in the downstairs living room. An emergency meeting had been scheduled to discuss Palestinian Statehood. Khozem disliked the idea of peace and security with Israel, because he knew such a security came at a great expense. He saw the Jews only as an enemy supported by infidels. His father, in his usual white garments, walked slowly down the stairs from his bedroom. Khozem stood and kissed his father's hand.

"How was the Kaa'bah?" asked Tariq of his son.

"Fine. Not too crowded," said Khozem.

"Good. Have you been reading the papers?"

"The time has come to act, father."

"Act upon what?" said Tariq with a smile. "Relax. All in good time. Can you at least see now how the West so formidably supports the Jewish colony?"

"It makes me sick. They even go to war because of them."

"It has made me sick for quite some time, but I still wear a smile on my face. Cheer up, my son. The meeting approaches, and you will lead the meeting," said Tariq still smiling.

"You'll be by my side?"

"Yes, I'll be there with you. But I must ask: what would you do in this situation? Peace may eventually come, and maybe we should abide by the Western attempt to bring peace."

"Peace? Ha! Peace is only for dreamers and those who lack the courage to fight, and fight we must. I've been thinking it over, father. Peace, you say?

There shall never be peace with the Jewish colony. That's all they talk about after the war, but really it's just a ploy, a lop-sided scheme to bolster the Jewish colony as the West provides them with guns and ammunition while we throw rocks and bottles, and once in a while kill ourselves with plastique stuck to our chests. I've never known such a word so laced with hypocrisy and duplicity. Every government swears by peace, and the result is always war, because everyone's out for their own interests anyway, and interests shall forever conflict. Peace shall always be an impossibility, because a peace shall always follow war, and war constantly follows peace, a terrible cycle, father, a most vile and heinous cycle, and it will never end. To think I've even prayed for it in the past, but now I know better. Peace is only a rest before conflict. I've never believed otherwise."

"It's hard to swallow, my son, but after so many years of fighting, we must somehow find faith in Allah and know that his true intention is peace for us all. Even I haven't lost sight of this lofty goal. Whatever we do, we do it to further our people and our faith, and in the end peace shall always triumph."

Khozem noticed how his father's stance on issues had changed in their time together. He was slowly slipping, always relying on Allah for answers never revealed. Khozem thought it was senility.

"Peace is nice to hope for, father, but still it's an impossibility, and once this truth is made known to all of our followers, we could at least adopt a rational approach which should take into account our survival. At heart, father, we really are men who live by needs, not by conscience."

"You really are beyond your years," laughed Tariq, "but faith is always more important than rationality. However, you haven't told me what you would do with the Jewish colony. How would you handle the affair, because soon you will have to handle our newest neighbor."

"We shall never live as neighbors. My plan will support our special groups within the region as we have been doing for decades. In other words, I'll uphold the funding to these important organizations. We must crush the Jew. This is plain and simple."

"Are you sure about that? The Jewish colony has a very big friend, a winning friend, which is why we placed the Imam there in the first place. Have you made any attempts to contact the Imam on these crucial issues? You can't do it all on your own."

"The Imam will always be there, but for now I will mandate a policy: we must fund our allies, so much that every Jew will want to move back to their Western cauldrons and leave our lands alone."

"And how will you do this without the Imam?" asked Tariq.

Khozem sat with his father in the silence, unable to answer this simple question. He cared not for the Imam, since he was now a part of the Western world, like a virgin transformed into a harlot. The Imam belonged to something too evil, too sinister and dastardly. Khozem told his father that he would consult with the Imam on all matters regarding the faith. Tariq believed him. Khozem played the part brilliantly that afternoon, feeding his father comfortable words and phrases, appeasing him of worry and toil, yet showing his confidence and poise.

"And what about you, father? What are your plans?"

"To watch over you," he smiled. "I'm not finished yet. All must go as planned."

"What plan? You keep talking of this plan, this big grand plan, and sometimes I have no idea what you're talking about. There's something you're not telling me, and if we are to engage our enemies we must be frank and honest with each other. I know I've been honest with you. Can't you at least be honest with me? What is this plan? I've accepted the position, I've toured, I understand the financial aspects of our Organization, I've worked so hard, and yet you talk of this plan."

"Look to the Imam for answers," smiled Tariq, as though he spoke in code.

"I will contact him after we have said our prayers," said Khozem, knowing his father's tenacity on the Organization was finally weakening.

The lie worked as Tariq smiled for the rest of the night. They prayed in the Kaa'bah and circumambulated the House of Allah seven times. Khozem prayed for the hand of Allah to crush the Jewish colony and its benefactors.

Chapter Three
MUSTAFA RETURNS HOME
12th of Safar 1436
(December 5, 2014)

Mustafa arrived at the Riverside Drive apartment a bit after midnight. He carried a small duffle bag with essentials for a seven-day stay with his mother. He knocked on the door softly at first so as not to disturb the neighbors. He knocked a bit louder, and still his mother did not appear. His soft knocks turned into loud thumps, and in the adjacent apartment, a dog, a small one, barked excitedly. 'She must be home,' thought the Imam.

He banged on the door again, this time with even more force. The dog barked uncontrollably. Suddenly he heard the locks unlatch, and in the doorway appeared his mother, Maryam. Her small face, grossly thin and hollow, showed dark rings under her eyes, and she wore a cotton night-suit that fell to her ankles.

She opened the door slowly. She said not a word, and by the threadbare shawl covering her head, Mustafa knew she must have been in the middle of prayers. His mother resumed her prayers as Mustafa looked on, not knowing her reaction to his return. She finished her prayers as a matter of course and approached him in the quiet, murky glow of the apartment, the lamp in the corner of the room casting strange shadows across the ceiling.

"You must ask Allah for forgiveness," she said almost inaudibly, her finger pointing. "Tomorrow we will go to the mosque."

Mustafa wished he had stayed in Boston under the care of the psychiatrist who dismissed him. Although he had been alone in the colonial city, he felt more alone in the small New York apartment. His mother represented a twisted, misshapen loneliness far beyond being alone. Quite suddenly he longed for the television to keep him company. He sat on the loveseat and turned on the television with its imposing flickers of light erasing the stretching and ominous shadows. Maryam blocked his view.

"You dare watch TV at a time like this?"

Mustafa put his heavy arms around his mother. She wiggled free of his grasp and shouted: "You dare hug me, you dare come back after months of not knowing where you are, no number, no address, money gone from my purse, Mustafa this is terrible, it's horrible, don't come here like this, nothing doing, Mustafa. See how sick you're looking, like a devil has gotten into you, that enemy is chasing after you, that devil is after you, and you must spit him out, because that devil is following you. I know him, and he's following you.

"We must go to the mosque and see the amilsaab there, and only he can cast this devil out. You don't know your prayers, you don't do your Arabic lessons, I called the police and the missing persons bureau, I had no idea where you went or who you were with, it's so terrible, and you dare try to hug me?"

Mustafa fell back on the love-seat and held his head in his hands. He saw his mother as a caricature, a big rat embracing something too old, too ancient. His disdain for everything Arabic intensified this image of her, a large rat waving the flags of the crescent moon, not necessarily fanatical, but clinging so hard to a God who never wanted to be followed and prayed to with such an abandon, as though prayer in itself was decadent and gratuitous.

There exists a greater humanity, he thought. He saw a fleeting spark of humanity buried deep within his mother, despite her fierce devotion to God, and her incredible selfish need for prayer, as though she hogged God and forced her version in His stead. Allah in moderation, thought Mustafa, as his mother blocked the television set, because within the straightjacket of excessively rigid religion humanity has little opportunity to blossom or bear fruit. The result must be an ontology of thought and a barrier to new and innovative ideas that move us closer to Allah, not farther away in ignorance.

That night Mustafa lay under the covers moving about in every conceivable position. He wasn't sure whether or not the illness kept him awake. He had grandiose visions of America being torn apart by an inevitable civil war, and his equally grandiose concepts of peace and love would somehow prevent such a war. He had little idea how to implement these concepts, as though they were opposed to anything real. He had nothing specific, only vague ideas which had no home.

He clutched his pillow while thinking of the next great civil war, as though such an idea was communicated telepathically, whether that communication stemmed from God or ordinary mortals. He envisioned the map of America with all of its states fitting cozily together like a giant jigsaw puzzle, and ultimately he saw the Western States splitting from the Eastern ones, as though there appeared a line dividing them, straight through the middle of Kansas, Nebraska, Oklahoma, and Texas, and thus a geological chasm along this line, a cluster of jutting rocks and soil as the country split into two separate entities. And this split grew wider, he saw himself stretched with his hands clutching the soil of the West and his feet embedded into the earth of the East, and his entire body, the only body, over this large split, and his valiant attempt to close the gap and make the vast country seamless.

As sweat gathered upon his forehead, he had not a clue as to what he should do. He only saw the States tossed into the ocean, nothing remaining but scorched and pock-marked earth consumed by rolling waters, and the crying and wailing of thousands of souls. He had to do something. He couldn't just lie there. The sweat trickled down the side of his face. He was compelled to do something, but what? He lacked the courage to speak. No one else spoke. Instead they roamed the streets, the subways, and the bus stations in their apparent silence, no one understanding anyone beyond themselves, only roaming, stuck within their own self-involved worlds. They wandered and roamed beneath laden clouds.

The Imam could have prayed, but he saw prayer only for those who needed it most, as though Allah had mounds of prayers to sort through, prayers never answered or heeded or fully understood. To have many thoughts and to never act upon them is the role of the child, but to put thoughts into action is the duty of the man. Such was the Imam's line of thought, although he had no control over his thoughts.

He wished he had a woman to comfort him, any woman. He never felt so much longing before. He again clutched his pillow and wished it were a woman's tender body. The only women he had seen were the ones wandering the streets, some of them attractive. He admitted he knew very little about them. A cursory knowledge was enough to keep him going. Yet he still longed for one, someone his own age, a friendship perhaps that grows into something greater. His main attraction fell upon women who did not possess the same skin color as he. 'How unfortunate,' he thought. 'I will be alone until such an attraction subsides.'

The Imam made loneliness an art form. He kept to himself and dreamed of meeting others. He wondered if women found him attractive, and asked: 'What does a woman look for in a man? Do they want muscles, a slim waist, and a fondness for adventure? Do they crave youth and arrogance?' Surely he generalized on these finer points, but his need, he discovered, was natural, not necessarily bestial, and a product of his own nature as a man so terribly alone.

Before drifting into sleep, which he welcomed, he labeled the onslaught of a civil war absurd. He blamed his mind and its sickness for placing him in the position of saving the entire country from the split. He intended to remain silent. He would not mention the coming apocalypse to anyone. How ridiculous to think of it in the first place, and no one would listen to him anyway.

His mother was by his side the next morning, urging him to get out of bed. She poked him gently in the ribs producing, not quite a tickle, but an annoyance that woke him up immediately.

"Cut it out," he cried.

"Get up," she said.

"There's no reason to get up"

"We're going to the mosque. I've laid out your clothes."

Mustafa brushed the sleep from his eyes and found that he hated the idea. First, he would never understand what was said, and second, the only people there would be overly religious men and women on the verge of death. Third, he didn't want to hang around with his mother who would force him to pray. He rolled over and shut his eyes. His mother poked him in the ribs again.

"I don't want to go," he cried.

"We must go, we must! A terrible enemy is following you…"

"What enemy? I don't see an enemy…"

"Yes, yes, an enemy, and the amilsaab at the mosque will find this enemy and stop him from haunting you."

Mustafa realized he had done little to please his mother, and perhaps by attending a function at the mosque he would repay her for the money he stole from her purse. Besides, maybe she would leave him alone with all this talk about some invisible enemy stalking him. He changed quickly into white, silk garments. He donned a skull cap which fit tightly over his head. Mustafa had rarely seen his mother smile, but a smile so wide amused him.

They caught a cross-town bus towards the mosque on Second Avenue. Mustafa was very conscious of his clothing. He removed his skullcap in the bus despite his mother's insistence that he wear it. He saw all types of people on the bus and thought he must look very peculiar, even though he wore a winter's jacket over his garments. His mother sat as he stood over her, clutching the hand straps and rocking with the motions of the bus. They arrived at a brown marble structure with a wide dome.

The structure was surrounded by a wrought iron gate and outside stood a variety of believers, mostly African-American, waiting entrance. Mustafa had an urge to smoke a cigarette, but suppressed such an urge as his mother was with him. He searched for persons his own age among the sea of African-American faces. Some of these African-Americans looked buoyant and jovial, greeting each other with familiar salaams. He still searched the gathering, trying hard not to think involuntary thoughts. 'To understand America, one must understand the African-American,' thought the Imam, and he felt a strange but distant connection with these dark faces, dark in color and simultaneously radiant, as though their color possessed a complexity or contradiction. His negative and involuntary thoughts subsided as he discovered a group of African-American women strolling to the slushy corner. He figured they were mostly his age, and they were dressed in long flowing garments, their heads covered by cloth. He edged near them as they walked through the initial gateway and under the wide dome.

"Come Mustafa, time for namaaz," said his mother.

He had forgotten about her.

He followed his mother into the mosque, and once inside, she went downstairs where the women congregated, and he stayed on the ground floor. She said to him before descending:

"Follow along, bow when they bow, and pay attention, and soon that devil will not follow you."

He left her smiling. He filled her quota of happiness for the time being. As she went downstairs, Mustafa forgot to ask about a prayer cloth. They had left in such a hurry. He stood in the small vestibule, and he tried to find his mother by peering into the basement. He saw a swarm of women and heard the din of their conversation. A woman came up the stairs dressed in white garb. There was not enough space for her to pass.

"Excuse me, brother," said the woman.

He could only see her face at first: a smooth, soft face with crushing bright eyes and a row of straight, gleaming teeth. Through her loose garments which fell from her chest he made out a pair of firm breasts, and instantaneously his brief encounter with this woman stunned him, because he thought her attractive, and he never expected a woman so attractive to be, of all places, at a mosque.

He had assumed quite falsely that young women so beautiful never frequented a place of worship, as they were out in some bar with bulky boyfriends sipping drinks and kissing and being taken home in luxurious automobiles, weekends at East Hampton beach houses, and inevitably sparkling jewels on their fingers. He envisioned them with rich and powerful men of high society, hoi-polloi and Pollyanna, the women holding in their long and elegant hands glasses of red wine in some SoHo gallery with men of prestige and fame, and all of these women hid from him. They emerged with successful men walking with clasped hands when he was most alone, like in the middle of Manhattan resting on a strict park bench, noticing beautiful women walking to and fro, always in some direction, never dawdling or idling, caressed by arms of a man dangerous, cocksure, blatantly obnoxious, never the quiet man, only men who looked good and thought themselves talented, only men who loved many women at once, playboys with oxford shirts and mountain bikes, men with direction. He had seen many women walk along the avenues in black stretch pants and high platform shoes, as though they all flipped through the same magazine in a valiant attempt to look more beautiful than they already were. Never has a singular species, these women all about the city streets, most likely employed and definitely in the arms of other men, provided such intense inspiration, as though the most gallant of poems never described or captured their innate artistry, their fluid movements, or their melodious tones. No matter how ferocious in their militancy or subdued in their vulnerability has this particular half of the human race pushed mankind to build edifices that touched the sky, launch ships, compete with their fellows, or simply look in the mirror each morning and brush strands of hair into place. Is it not odd then that men bereft of women slowly tear themselves apart, and women without men mysteriously survive? Or that mankind by itself would disintegrate amidst squabble, conflict, and strife, while womankind would evolve and sustain their beauty, no matter their jealousies, their angers, or fears?

The Imam saw her and was touched in this manner. He never expected a woman so stunning to appear, and at her passing his chest trembled and his heart sank to his stomach. He was compelled to meet her, but had little idea what to say.

He heard the adhan being called. He could not wait the entire time for this woman to return, so he reluctantly shuffled into a room full of African-Americans and tan-faced gentlemen sitting in positions on the plush carpet, and at the head of this crowd sat an amilsaab, his legs beneath the weight of his body, a microphone jutting from his mouth, his eyes closed.

The amilsaab rapidly sang the verses in Arabic. Mustafa sat at the back, under the echoing dome, and he shared a prayer cloth with a much older African-American who smiled politely and made space for him. He bowed when they bowed, not understanding the meaning of the verses, only copying what the others did, and for the time being he got away with it, despite the curious gaze of the person next to him. The grace and severity of the amilsaab's verses and the wrenching reverberations brought the believers to their knees over and over again, but he was not taken aback by it. He wasn't fooled by it. He visualized his mother downstairs sacrificing herself to God.

After the final verses were said, the amilsaab spoke. He was a thin and older African-American with sunken cheeks and a thin, wiry beard that flowed to his chest. Mustafa felt his overbearing presence. When he spoke, no one moved. This amilsaab commanded their attention, and this command merited and pried loose a respect from the believers.

"Brothers and sisters," began the amilsaab, "praise be to Allah and his divine messenger Muhammad for granting us another day of prayer. Every morning, afternoon, and evening is so glorious under the All Mighty, and his will is embedded within us through our deeds and thoughts, because He is most high and ever-present; in our hands when we labor and in our hearts where most of our ideas sprout. Dear Allah will you look after the suffering and the downtrodden. Never be deceived by charmers who promise bounty which Allah provides alone. Allah alone is worthy of all praise. It is He who sent down death and failure upon the greatest oppressors and the strongest of men and broke the necks and backs of the greatest men, the richest men, by putting an end to their lives. Even the greatest men, hoarding their wealth, objected to Allah's promise of death and were cast into a pit and were tumbled from their palaces to the bottom of the earth, only to be eaten by worms and insects instead of eating and drinking among a convivial society of friends. There exists only one Lord, and none shares his supreme might and wrath. He has no equal, and His might is everlasting.

"Reflections of death must always be present in the minds of men and women. However long this life must be, no matter how great the possessions of this earth, death must always come and those possessions must ultimately be left behind. Thus, men should opt for something everlasting, as the height of foolishness is to opt for something fleeting. This is all but a waiting room, and our period on this earth ends with the arrival of the angels Nakeer and Munkir who examine the souls of the dead.

"However prolonged this life on this earth may be, it is an earth upon which we were put as mortals. The only life which is immortal is our eternal life and Allah's blessings. May the All Mighty Allah be kind to you. Be alert and beware! The case of death is severe indeed, and very often we fail to realize its severity. The man on the brink of death is in a critical condition. No one can help the man on the edge of death. He calls doctors and medical experts, but they offer little hope of survival. He mumbles, he recognizes no one, he hardly breathes, because his lungs ache, he cries aloud, he can't speak, and then his eyes close for the very last time. His soul releases from his body, and heaven takes that soul into paradise, never to return.

"Each day we are involved in life, not death, and with the end of the New War we rarely talk of death. Half-measures do not avail us. We should remove the thoughts of our daily pursuits and think of death as though tomorrow it may arrive. Imagine the faces of the dead, and how the earth with its worms and grubs disfigure them, their muscled bodies disintegrating into dust. Everyone in this room will inevitably meet this doom. How high we raise our laughter! How deeply we partake in worldly pleasures. Yet everyone returns to dust. We must remember our Qu'ran:

'No living being knows the time of its end.
Man makes provisions for a hundred years,
Yet knows not he might die the next minute.'

"We are each tainted with sin and wholeheartedly engrossed in worldly pursuits. We must rely on Allah, and by his good graces he will provide for us a life after this short one. If we are pulled too much by our earthly pursuits, the darkness of Hell shall cover us.

"Most of us often mention Hell while talking to other Muslims and know not how to achieve salvation from it. We must abstain from sin and our lusts so that we may perform virtuous deeds. Otherwise a Hell awaits us, and if a stone is thrown into hell it would take seventy years to reach its bottom.

"The sinners will be thrown into Hell very thirsty; They would be ordered by angels to endure Hell's fires. Then they would be dragged into Hell by their hair and feet. The feet and hands of the sinner would be twisted and joined together, and they will repent for not obeying their heavenly Father. Iblis, the Lord of Hell, will say: 'It is no avail to curse me now, for Allah's promises were true. I believed those promises and misled you, because I could not do more than this, and you followed me. You should curse yourself rather than me. Neither you are my protector nor am I yours. I myself am disgusted of your doing, because you used to make me a partner of Allah. Surely there is dire punishment.

"And then, the sinners will pray to Allah, and their prayers will be futile, for they will pray, and there will be a period of one thousand years before Allah responds, and Allah will say: 'Welter in your cursed state, and don't address me.' The sinners in Hell would then pray for salvation and lament like donkeys.

"Then pious men would visit Hell, and the sinners would confront them and ask for entrance into Heaven. The pious man will say to them: 'You are telling lies. We do not recognize you,' and the gates of Hell will be shut on the sinners forever. These sinners in their material worlds have always been drinking, have disobeyed their parents, have indulged their families to do evil deeds, and consume usury. And of women, those who are seductive and wear transparent dresses, those who are clad but appear naked, those who have been especially arrogant will be gathered like tiny termites, as that will be the size of their bodies, and a fire of maximum intensity shall reign over them, and they will drink the excrement of the inhabitants of Hell.

"Hell is surrounded by four walls, and the length of each wall covers a period of forty years of continual walking from wall to wall. Hell has seven gateways, and one of these gates has been reserved for those who draw swords against Muslims.

At first the fires of Hell were red, and after one thousand years its red color became white. After another one thousand years the white flames turned black. The fire of Hell is black as the darkest night, and this particular fire is only the seventieth part of the fire of Hell. If we add sixty-nine degrees to our worldly fire, it equals the fire of this hell. Boots and shoes filled with this fire are the lightest punishments, and such a fire will cause the mind to boil. The sinner will take this punishment as the heaviest punishment, but really the punishment is the very first stage of the tortures.

"Hell has seven levels. The first level of Hell is reserved for Muslim sinners who were polytheists but simultaneously supported the Prophet Muhammad (May Peace Be Upon Him). The remaining six levels have been reserved for atheists, Jews, Christians, and other hypocrites respectively. Every level contains nothing but pain, tortures, and tormenting houses. Take the house of 'Ghayy,' where the occupants of Hell pray four hundred times a day for salvation from its tortures. Take another house called 'Zamharir,' the region of extreme cold. In the house of 'Tubb-ul-Hazan' there exists an overwhelming well which is filled with pus and poison. How about the towering mountain Sa'ud. It would take seventy years to climb this mountain, and Hell's occupants would be thrown into the fire from its peak. Or a pond with water so hot that it burns the tongue and tears apart the human lungs, stomach, and intestines. Another pond gathers the sinners' puss, blood, and sweat. Poisonous snakes and scorpions serve as the only wildlife. The bodies of the sinners would melt due to the excess of heat. They would melt, be reborn, and then melt again, and this cycle would be repeated seven-hundred times within one moment. Skin and flesh would burn repeatedly, and it is said that some sinners have skin which is forty-two yards thick. After the inhabitants are burned and re-burned, their hunger pangs would surpass all other tortures.

"The hunger pangs would never stop, and the sinners would beg for food, and they would be given a thorny plant known as 'Zaqqum,' and such a plant would get stuck in their throats. The sinner would cry for water. The water would be delivered from the well of 'Tahim.' Such water would cause their tongues to burn, their throats to break into pieces, and their intestines to be devoured and excreted through their anuses. The sinners would be so distressed that they would pray to Iblis for death so that their punishments would end. 'You will always remain in Hell,' will say the Lord of Death. And after a thousand years the Good Lord will say: 'You have been condemned forever.'

"Then they will think that endurance will someday prove fruitful, and they will pray continuously for one-thousand years. They will receive no answer, but their bodies would be transmogrified into the shapes of dogs, snakes, and donkeys, and other wild, feral beasts. On the day of Resurrections all the inhabitants of Hell will look thus, and they would be trampled repeatedly. They will hear a roaring voice as Hell will be bursting with nothing but fury. The moment the sinners are cast eternally into Hell, they will yell and scream and ultimately yearn for a death they will never find.

"Although Hell is so large and wide, the sinners would be kept in narrow cells like nails hammered into wood. In Hell there are many snakes, and one snake bite will cause a pain for forty years. Same with the bite of a scorpion whose stinger will be as large as the sinners' teeth. The sinners shall eat nothing but dry weeds and boiling water which will neither satisfy nor satiate them. They will eat from the thorny plant, which tastes like liquid metal and which boils in the stomach like fuming waters. The Prophet (May Peace be Upon Him) has said if only one drop of the thorny plant were to spill upon the earth, it would poison all the vegetation and meat in the entire world. We must imagine the diet of those who can't eat anything but this terrible thorny plant.

"And what of the water? One drop of Hell's water would foul the smell of the earth as it contains the sinners' pus and filth, and this substance would be frozen, a cold and rotten pus, and it will be so cold that the sinners would be unable to drink it. And when they cry aloud, they will be given the dregs of oil, which will burn their faces. No liquid in Hell would ever wash away their sins. The hunger and the thirst will exceed all the torments of Hell. They will be served burning water in iron goblets. The burning pus will rip apart their internal organs, and the skin of their heads will slowly peel off.

"In addition to the wretched food and drink, there are also many other tortures and torments of the inhabitants of Hell. First, hot water will be poured over their heads repeatedly, and the intense heat will dissolve their skin and all their internal organs, and the residue will be excreted through their anuses. Such water would melt them. Second, the inhabitants of Hell will be beaten by an iron mace just when they try to emerge from Hell's suffocation. This mace is so heavy that the sum of human beings on this earth could never lift it. Such a mace would crumble the thickest mountain. Third, once their skin is burnt by boiling water and the black fires of Hell, a fresh layer of skin will grow so that the sinners would relive their horror. They will be burnt seventy thousand times, and the process would be repeated eternally. Fourth, the inhabitants of Hell will be chained to 'Sa'ud,' the mountain of fire, and this mountain would take seventy years to reach and seventy years to fall from its peak, and the cycle would continue for an eternity. The length of the chain only Allah knows, but the chain itself, if dropped from the sky to this earth, would take five hundred years to drop. The chain would be pierced into the body through the anus and out of their mouths.

"Then the body would be roasted on a fire like meat upon skewers. In addition to long chains, Hell also has its yokes which burden necks as they drag the occupants to the boiling water and fire. A dark cloud will appear in Hell, and the sinners will ask the cloud to rain, and the cloud would rain yokes, chains, and burning flames. The sinners are taken by their hair and submerged in boiling water. The water will melt their flesh and nothing will remain but two eyes and a skeleton. Their clothes will be filled with sulfur, and hot water and fire would cling to their faces, such that their clothes would be made of fire. The torture will be not only physical but psychological as the sinners will hear the same phrase: 'Endure now the torment of fire which you denied in the world.'

"Everyone in Hell would look as ugly and would be punished in accordance with their deeds. Their upper lips would touch their foreheads, and their lower lips would touch their navels, and from their eyes heavy tears would roll, and when the tears finish, blood would flow and make marks on their faces, so much blood that boats could sail upon them.

"All of this, the description which I have given you, comes directly from the verses of the Qu'ran and the blessed Hadith of the Apostle of Allah (May Peace be Upon Him). They are true, and the verses I have used are authentic. The sinner now has an opportunity to change the course of his life through constant prayer, fasting during the appointed month, partaking in Hajj, giving to charity, and the number of other duties imposed by the will of Allah. Never waste your time seeking the pleasures of the world in constant pursuit of riches, privilege, and glory. The Prophet of Allah (May Peace be Upon Him) has said that Hell has been concealed in the pleasures of the world, and Paradise lies hidden in life's hardships: 'If the believer will keep in mind the tortures and torments of Hell, how could one ever commit great sins?' This is something to think about, and remember the words of Ali (May Peace be Upon Him) who said:

> 'If Paradise and Hell are placed before me,
> My faith will be no firmer than it already is,
> For my faith in the unseen is so strong
> That to believe on seeing and to believe without
> Seeing is all one to me.
> Those who are aware of the conditions of Hell,
> They would not only shun all sins but also Renounce all laughter
> and happiness of the
> Mortal World.'"

With this verse the amilsaab ended his sermon. Mustafa had been paying attention to most of it, and what he heard sounded false and untrue, although the sermon was delivered passionately. The Imam did not believe in evil or a Hell where all the sinners were said to be sent. He believed that people react to circumstances differently. What's good to one person does not mean goodness to another. Individuals are products of circumstance, and an individual is essentially good. Survival turns people into maniacs, and the only wrong decision stems from our inability to exercise our conscience when the situation or circumstance arises. He could not probe any deeper than that, and besides disagreeing with the amilsaab's words, at least they kept him warm as cold drafts permeated the walls of the mosque. He was scared a little by the description of Hell, but to gaze into the unknown is like staring forever into emptiness. We may speculate and develop ideas as the prophets had ideas, but contemplating an end to things diminishes the importance and mystery of this world. Mustafa believed in Allah and Allah only. The rest was insignificant. These people had wild imaginations. He thought this odd, because he himself had used his imagination to develop his telepathic theory. He had been grossly ill, and he wondered earnestly whether or not the Prophet had at one time thought the way he did. If the Prophet were around today, surely he would be thrown into the psych ward. Psychiatric wards are filled with these left-over prophets who deem this world a conspiracy, or else they believe themselves God, or they see the end of the world and are suddenly compelled to take action.

Mustafa fit these descriptions, and his courage came from inventing a philosophy beyond the scriptures. He believed in the inherent goodness of human beings, a concept that went beyond the simplistic and archaic divisions of Heaven and Hell, good and evil, no matter how wild or gruesome their descriptions. He brushed off the amilsaab's sermon as there existed a greater good to which we are blinded. He did not believe in evil, only right and wrong, sanity and illness, disturbance and serenity. He refused to define goodness by what it was not.

While thinking these things, Mustafa felt a light tap on his shoulder. His mother stood behind him, and her face beamed with an extraordinary radiance. She stuck a ten-dollar bill in his palm and told him to greet the amilsaab with this money so that he may pray for him.

"To make that devil go away," she said.

Mustafa looked at her incredulously, but she pushed him towards the amilsaab. A line had formed in front of him, and instead of making a scene by his refusal, he acquiesced. Before approaching the amilsaab, however, he looked beyond his mother and saw the same woman he had met in the vestibule. Their eyes met. Normally Imam Mustafa would have darted his eyes elsewhere, but he kept his gaze fixed upon this African-American beauty, her precious skin as dark as espresso, and her eyes of chocolate so cunning that they spoke to him. Her eyes seemed to say: 'Come closer.' Was her interest in him just a part of his overactive imagination? Mustafa couldn't tell. He kept staring as his mother said:

"Move along, Mustafa. Go!"

He wouldn't move. The woman smiled, and Mustafa returned a child-like grin, fascinated beyond the sermon, beyond a set rationality, beyond any philosophical musing. Although a dress covered her charms, Mustafa already knew her curves like a winding Vermont road. He could not hide his attraction, and he stepped out of the lenghthy line leading to the amilsaab and moved closer, not heeding his mother's high-pitched squeals. He was embarrassed by her, and his face flushed. His heart raced, for he no longer denied his longing for this woman, as though she would save him from the amilsaab's Hell. He would have passed through its gateways just for a sign from her, and it appeared she sent signals with her dark, careless eyes. A smile crept upon her face.

"I don't talk to strange men," she said.

"Either do I," said Mustafa.

Her name was Nasiba.

Nasiba. The name rolled from his tongue like running waters over smooth stones, as though the name itself healed him from years of prolonged isolation and a selfish, self-seeking existence. She passed through the vestibule mentioning her name. She wore her shawl and smiled knowingly. Mustafa thought himself a stranger after her passing, for any woman with such elegance reduces the identity of the man to ashes, picked up by winds of hormonal imbalance and irregular heart beats; a change so drastic that the man ceases to know himself.

From the vestibule the Imam followed her into the street, the cold winds unable to snuff the heat that captured his insides. He was gripped by fear in pursuing her. He knew not what to say or how to act; he only felt a tremendous impulse, as though his legs walked on their own, and his mouth and tongue mumbled foreign speech.

"What a place the mosque is," he found himself saying to her on the street corner.

The believers defiled from the mosque, and soon the two of them were enveloped by dark faces.

"I've never seen you here before," she said.

"I guess there's a good reason for coming," he said with a grin.

"You must really like prayer, brother."

"More than you know. Perhaps we can discuss prayer sometime over coffee or tea or whatever you like to drink…"

"Mustafa! Mustafa, where are you? Come here. Come here now!" cried his mother from the entrance.

"You think you'll be able to stay up that late?" giggled Nasiba.

He could have strangled his mother right then and there. His face flushed as Nasiba was carried off by her friends. He followed her with his eyes as she moved farther away, like a boat drifting to sea.

His mother called him repeatedly. She shouted at him while very near. Mustafa went to her in abject humiliation.

"Would you shut up!" he whispered hotly.

"Then go to the amilsaab," cried Maryam.

"I will. Go back inside."

"No, right now, do it right now. Where's the ten dollars I gave you?"

Mustafa held the wrinkled bill in his hand.

"Good. Now go in there and bid salaams to the amilsaab. Ask him to pray for you."

Mustafa removed his shoes in the vestibule which was crowded with believers on their way out. He approached the amilsaab under the wide dome, unsure of the correct procedure. The whiskery amilsaab gave him his hand, and Mustafa kissed its smooth knuckles. He placed the ten- dollar bill in the cup of the amilsaab's palm, and the amilsaab put the bill to the side. A large amount had been collected by his knees.

"First time here, brother?" asked the amilsaab mildly.

Mustafa nodded.

"How did you like the sermon?"

"Very informative," said Mustafa. " I never knew Hell was so…so…, well, so hot."

"The angel Mik'hail has not laughed since the creation of Hell."

"What's the use of Heaven if there weren't an escape from Hell, right?"

"You're too old to be cute," said the amilsaab sternly.

"I did not mean to be cute, your highness. I'm just trying to add a little levity, since Hell is so dreadfully hot, and certainly a place worth visiting, especially nowadays with the weather like it is."

"A smart aleck too? Believe me young man, I see them come and go, and those who take Allah's verses so lightly end up in a Hell of their own, jails, institutions, and finally a slow, unmerciful death. And once their miserable lives are complete, they find themselves in burning fires as black as night. You may smile now, but believe me, you'll regret it later. It's important to read the scriptures and follow its teachings. Otherwise you're doomed. Can you get the picture?"

"Oh I get the picture alright. You talk about Hell so freely that people put money in your pocket."

"All of the money I receive goes towards the housing of the poor and the maintenance of this mosque. And besides, who are you to question me? This is your first time here, and already you have an attitude."

"Maybe I don't believe in the same things you believe. I don't believe in Hell and damnation, and already with your bombast you have scared half the mosque. Islam is not about that."

"Tell me then, what is Islam about? I've been an amilsaab for twenty-seven years. If you're so smart, why don't you tell me a thing or two."

"For one thing," began Mustafa, "there is no such thing as Hell, only Heaven and Earth, and Islam isn't the last word on religion. There are many more to follow as we are slowly and steadily moving towards a love of ourselves and of others. In Islam we must aim towards accepting every human being as an equal, black, brown, red and yellow, we are all equal under Allah's eyes."

"Those are all nice, general ideas," interrupted the amilsaab. "A lot of Islam is about equality."

"Each human being deserves an equal respect," continued Mustafa, "and since no one seems to understand or implement these concepts, I suppose Islam has failed…"

"What? Failed?" roared the amilsaab.

"Islam has failed, your lofty highness. It has failed to bring about a brotherhood among peoples. If Islam really worked there would be no war. I mean how many times do I have to hear about bomb blasts in some crowded square or guerrillas on the outskirts of Israel, or launching missiles on Israeli troops? How long do we have to put up with this? The true test of Islam is whether or not men and women can transcend their differences and create a special unity, a simple harmony with those outside these korny system of beliefs. Islam has failed precisely because we are unable to accept Jews as extraordinary brothers, and until the day comes when we may embrace Jews in the streets of Jerusalem, Islam will continue to fail and fail miserably…"

By this time a small gathering had surrounded Mustafa and the amilsaab. A tension rose in Mustafa's voice. His voice grew louder with each passing word.

"…and in many ways I'm ashamed of my own religion, because we are unable to bridge our differences with those who happen to be Jewish. But I am a man who plays with the uniform he's dealt, and I am Islamic through and through, and I can easily say that I am ashamed of my own religion…"

"I see they've Chritianized you."

"So what if I've been Christianized or have read Hebrew and Yiddish, or have donned orange robes and prayed to the sacred Buddah, who really cares? Look at yourself in the mirror sometime, and you will see a Buddhist, a Muslim, a Christian, and a Jew. Allah has been beneficent enough to let us choose amidst all the well-known religions. Ultimately my faith rests with Allah, and I seriously question where your faith lies, brother."

"You're nothing but a dreamer," replied the amilsaab angrily.

"Yes, a dreamer," shouted another man behind the Imam.

"You have been fooled, because you are young and know nothing of reality," said the amilsaab. "We do not fight because we are simply a bellicose and belligerent people. It's a fight for water and land and all the properties that the Jews confiscated in their quest for supremacy in the region. And now the Jews want security, while our Palestinian brothers are being taken truckload by truckload to the prisons just because they are upstanding Muslims unwilling to submit to the Jewish reign of terror. And you come in here with your arrogance and condescension and tell me and these others that you're a true Muslim? You're no Muslim, and you're lucky enough to be in a land which doesn't hang blasphemers."

"If I am blasphemous, then let me be, as Allah has put within me these dreams of a better world, while you sit and rot in your cold rationality, living in the history of good and evil, revenge and retaliations. I know reality enough. We all have our inner hatreds and biases. If Islam feeds such hatreds instead of evoking our love for humanity and respect for our Jewish brethren then Islam ceases to be Islam. And to think you can sit here among those who desperately want to be closer to their Creator and collect money like a holy man when in reality you are lost, all of you lost in ancient thinking, and you are fooling yourselves by calling yourselves Islamic and being so extreme."

"Have you even read the scriptures, brother? Recite for me the opening lines of prayer."

"What difference does it make? I look up at the sky and pray to my Creator. It has taken a long time for me. He knows I pray for guidance. He knows my psychology is riddled with love and hate and twisted sickness, and by keeping in dialogue with him my feelings of hatred disappeared, and the residue of that hatred is love, as love conquers the hatred. I haven't lost sight of my inner hatreds. I am a human being, and I have my shortcomings, but essentially I am good, and even though you and your followers are lost, you too are inherently good, albeit lost like sheep without a shepherd.

"Once we manifest our own darkness to ourselves, then all the battles worth fighting remain inside ourselves- the only place where any battle ought to be fought. Islam has failed, because we tend, more often than not, to externalize our inner battles and cheapen ourselves to paranoid animals afraid of the Jew, afraid of our vulnerabilities, afraid that the Jew serves a disruptive purpose than a complementing one. After all, aren't we similar creatures anyway?"

"You have a lot to learn," said the amilsaab. "I will pray for you. I can do nothing else. You are arrogant and stupid. You seem so set on your confused views. You have been set astray by demons, and with your line of thinking you will never survive. It is not we who are lost. It is you, as being lost implies that you have no one to follow. At this mosque we follow the verses of the Qu'ran. Obviously you have not read a page of it. I'm not angry with you, although your perspectives bother me. However I do feel very sorry for you. I pity you."

Mustafa glanced over his shoulder at the gathering behind him. Many of these believers wore looks of consternation, some of them looks of anger. He didn't mean to talk so freely about a subject so sensitive, but now that he did, a slight relief overcame him.

His legs were still numb from sitting on the floor. He staggered through the small crowd. Some of them said: "Dreamer." One of them called him: "Crackpot," and another "Heathen." The Imam sensed that he was alone in his intellect. He couldn't find anything in common with people of his faith, and the initial relief turned into a quiet distress. He made his way through the incensed gathering and by mistake bumped into a tall, husky man with tan skin and a bushy mustache. The large man could have squashed him, and suddenly the Imam feared for his wellbeing.

He raced for the doorway where his mother stood bracing the cruel wind, her arms hugging her body. She asked briefly whether he gave salaams to the amilsaab. She seemed calm and less persistent. He answered affirmatively, and they walked to the bus stop on the next corner.

He loved his mother at these times, how quiet and peaceful, almost serene she could be, lost in her own thoughts and breathing a spiritual sigh of relief. She of course didn't know what he said to the amilsaab. Mustafa had meant every word of it, down to the last and minutest detail, and he would never take any of it back. For the first time he relished in the privilege of speaking his own mind, no matter how offending to the listener, no matter how muddled the philosophy, no matter how fantastic. He believed every word of it and mused how wonderful it would be to put such thoughts into action, for there exists nothing more potent than an idea whose time has come, and in the bus, traveling slowly cross-town, he had faith that one day all Muslims would come to see Jews as brothers. Of course there are Muslims who consider Jews as friends and brothers already, but these voices are stifled.

'Slow change,' thought the Imam. 'The world isn't ready yet, a fruit which isn't ripe.'

And then his mind ran along the gentle body of Nasiba, up her spine and along her supple shoulders to her dazzling eyes. Would she accept him with his wild ideas? Probably not, but he believed he could seduce her with words if given the opportunity. What he would say to her he was not sure, but this woman baffled him for the duration of the ride, as all women baffled him. At first he resisted venturing back to the mosque, but he confronted his powerlessness without a woman by his side. Something natural pushed him. His intellect kept him apart. His hormones forced him near.

"Mom, what if I went to the mosque tomorrow night?"

Maryam rarely smiled in the presence of her son, but she smiled with satisfaction. She believed her trial at motherhood was finally paying off.

"You can go to the mosque any time you like," she said, "and I'll come with you."

The bus could have exploded.

"I think I need to go alone. I'm at an age when I must worship Allah alone."

"You should learn your prayers before going, and after you learn that devil will no longer follow you."

At least she acquiesced to his wishes. This was rare indeed, and to his sincere delight his mother remained quiet for the rest of the ride. He had no intention of learning his prayers.

He arrived at the Riverside Drive apartment sleepy and inert. He crawled into bed and ran through the events of the day. Perhaps he had been foolish for opening his mouth so wide. With each turn of his body upon the springy mattress Nasiba came to him; her dark African skin soft and her thick hair relaxed and flowing down her shoulders. He saw this particular woman apart from the history of her people. Several involuntary thoughts entered his mind, but such negative thoughts he attributed to his sickness. He at least realized that his involuntary thoughts were falsehoods. The darkness comes, and eventually the darkness goes. Some have said that such darkness needs to be embraced, like a broken spine or an amputated limb. Mustafa hated the hatred, yet his hatreds were merely words, not hatreds, but words which were born from a terrible time in history. Just words, and their indestructibility. He tortured himself in the meantime. He vowed never to give in. He would die before letting these words, no matter how malicious and ubiquitous, overcome him.

Chapter Four
HAUNTED
13th of Safar 1436
(December 6, 2014)

Khozem continued to live with his father and mother in the Meccan home. On this particular evening he met with Vasilla who had flown in from New York. Khozem had never met Vasilla on his own. He never had business to discuss with him, and Khozem remembered seeing him only a few times while growing up. He saw him with his father after tours.

He remembered this gargantuan figure smiling down at him, looming so large that he blocked the sun and cast a long shadow over him. Vasilla always smiled and rarely uttered a word. Khozem knew him only as his father's bodyguard, and they were away quite often. Oddly enough, Vasilla seemed even larger to him. He remained the same in weight and bulk, as Khozem remained short and pudgy.

Khozem had a child-like fascination with this towering bodyguard. It seemed that his father spent more time with Vasilla than himself, and Khozem resented their relationship. But now that he was older and experienced in the ways of the faith, Khozem quietly understood his father's obligations and the reasons for their close relationship.

On the tour of the Far East, Tariq had always mentioned Vasilla as his favorite, and Khozem mused that Vasilla must have consistently reaffirmed his father's own beliefs and values, hence lacking a mind and individuality of his own, almost like remaining invisible. Likeable characters are usually invisible, he thought. His father told him that Vasilla would always remain loyal no matter how preposterous the request or instruction, and that such a loyalty could not be found in anyone else. Khozem appreciated Vasilla in this way, because he knew his mind simple. His actions were the result of orders, not inference.

Vasilla kissed Khozem's hand upon entrance and bid him gentle salaams. He was dressed in a blue Italian suit, while Khozem wore a tan, cotton robe with matching turban.

"I see you're living like a Westerner," smiled Khozem, trying hard to appear the man in control, not the child with a dumbfounded fascination.

"I hope not to appear too Westernized, your holiness, but I just got off the plane," said Vasilla sniffling with a cold.

"And how was your flight? It must have taken a long time."

"Your holiness, the flight was good, and I am glad to be away from the unholy territory."

"Tell me, then. How is it unholy?"

"People there drink and smoke, and the women don't cover themselves. They listen to strange music with these electric guitars. No one says their prayers. There are no mosques, only a few."

"You've been attending a mosque?"

"Yes, and there I see mostly Africans as they are the only men in the city who remain pure to the faith. Certainly I see men from Arabia, but those I see are driving taxis or working at kiosks, and some of them I meet in the mosques. I'm growing sick and tired of New York. Each time I fall asleep I dream of Mecca, its warmth and companionship."

"Tell me, what have you been doing over there?"

"I see the Imam's parents every month, and I give them the monies set up by your father. I go to the mosque every night, and the other night, before I left, I saw the Imam for the first time."

"The Imam? I see. What does he look like? Did you meet him?"

"No. I only saw him in the crowd. It's the first time I've ever seen him," said Vasilla, wiping his nose.

"I'd thought you'd be much closer to them."

"I keep a good distance from them, because your father wanted him to learn the faith on his own."

"I see, yes, you've done a good job. Obviously he's found Allah now that you see him in the mosque."

"However, there is one thing I'm worried about. When I saw him at the mosque in New York I overheard him talking to the amilsaab, and what I heard made me very upset, your holiness."

"You heard him speak, did you? What did you say?" asked Khozem excitedly.

"Well, it's not easy to express, because what he said went against the grain so to speak..."

"Nevermind. Out with it."

"He said basically that we should embrace the Jews in the streets..."

"He said what?!"

"He said that Islam is not the real Islam, I only heard some of it, not all of it, but most of what he said was very hard to follow. He mentioned he was bothered by inner demons. He said we were not practicing Islam, because we fought with the Jews..."

"Vasilla, are you absolutely sure about this?"

"Yes, your holiness. He made all of us at the mosque very upset. Some were about to beat him up."

Khozem paced the living room, and for a brief moment looked at his father's portrait hanging crookedly on the wall. He straightened it with care.

"Your father would have certainly been vexed," said Vasilla.

"I'm not my father," said Khozem suddenly.

"I did not mean to say..."

"I know what you meant. Let's make it clear, shall we? I'm not my father, and I'll never be my father. It's time for a new leadership in the Organization, and I have been appointed its leader. Never compare me with my father again."

"I apologize, your holiness."

"Good, Vasilla. Anyway you won't be staying there for much longer."

"But why? The Imam and his family are there."

"I want you to stay in Mecca from now on. You will guard me here."

"Oh thank you, your holiness," as he smothered Khozem's hand with kisses.

"Enough!"

"I'm sorry, your holiness, but I can't hide my joy. New York is so terrible. I think I've caught influenza."

"I understand, Vasilla."

"Then who will guard the Imam and look after his interests?"

"Leave that to me. You no longer have to worry about the Imam."

"I must return to collect my things."

"Go, if you must, but I want you back here in a week. I shall begin touring again pretty soon, and I need you by my side."

After Vasilla left, Khozem adjourned to his room on the second floor. His parents attended a gathering in town. He had the entire household to himself, and being alone fueled a variety of ideas. His plan involved cutting off all funds to the Imam and leaving him in the Western lands, abandoning him like a junked car. He planned deep cuts in the Organization's budget. Even though Khozem had everything a man could ever want materially, he would appropriate the funds for his own use, and the funds left over would be spent fighting Israel, as he would irritate the region like salt upon a sore. He would keep his plans a secret from his father who had grown old, distant, tired, and senile. He wished him dead so that he could run the Organization as he liked.

He lay in bed that night devising the details of this plan. He gave his father ten more years, and his death would bring Khozem a horde of wealth and control. The believers would praise him like a monarch, and those who questioned his ultimate authority and divine right would be dealt with accordingly. Without the Imam and his father he could do anything, and as he lay awake he thought of wealth, luxury, and property, and how he would attend the emergency meetings to encourage strife with the Jewish enemy. Between these details, however, the visage of Rashida appeared in his mind's eye, and he fought hard to erase the image.

'I never loved her,' he thought. 'She's gone, and Allah took her away for a reason. I must live alone. I must be alone, because all rulers are essentially alone, and my destiny is to rule. I will fight those who question me. Never let a woman get in the way of my destiny. Forget, I must forget, please Allah, damn you, damn her, you put her on this earth only to take her away, you bastard. You stole her from me, and now I'm stuck with her, forever in my mind, and I'm stuck with her face, imprinted like a portrait on my brain, damn, let me sleep. I never loved her, and from now on I shall never be fooled by a woman. Away, away, they shall love me, but I shall hate them. Dear Allah let me sleep and let my father die, because I am not a fool. I never loved her, not for one second..."

He lay awake for some time, and at every angle Rashida haunted him, for the visage of her long hair and delicate skin was replaced by a crushed and bleeding skull, the same features he found in the morgue of the police precinct years ago.

Chapter Five
NASIBA
14th of Safar 1436
(December 7, 2014)

The Imam Mustafa woke up the next morning and spotted his journal book across the room. He believed writing would ease his painful memory of the sudden outburst at the mosque. 'No one will ever read this,' he thought. 'No one in their right mind will know what I'm going through,' and before his mother called him for breakfast, he wrote in his notebook and directed his puzzling and confusing thoughts towards Allah himself.

'Why am I damned?' he began. 'Why am I filled with such falsehoods? I'm placed on this earth for no reason at all. I have no money. I don't have an education. The only stuff I see is the stuff in my mind. The floating image of this slinky gyration, sometimes in motion, and for some reason all that I perceive must be false. I hardly know how to read, and writing this becomes difficult, because I lack the brain power to do anything for the common good, and here I sit at this cramped table, my mother most likely sleeping, and the morning light blares through my window like some forgotten tune. Why, dear Allah, must the light always be followed by darkness, and then light again? Why must I love so completely every single man and woman, and then suddenly I am forced into darkness, the darkness of petty hatreds and intolerance? The hatred within my soul hates completely, and yet I love completely, as though half of me loves, and the other half hates. Why am I confronted with such terrible extremities? Why am I confronted with this one involuntary word?

'Someone once said to me that that specific word sums up all the bitter years of insult and struggle in America: "the slave-beatings of yesterday, the lynchings of yesterday, the Jim Crow cars, the only movie theaters in town with its signs saying FOR WHITES ONLY, the restaurants where a man, just because of skin color, could not eat, or the jobs he could not have, the unions he could not join. That damn word in my mind like the word 'Jew' in Hitler's Germany!" And yet I walk down the street and pass a man of darker skin, and suddenly that word jumps into my head. When it comes into my head it seizes me like a hand chopping at my throat, and so badly I want it to go away like a bad dream. Don't you see that I only want to put good in this world, not hatreds or falsehoods? Everything seems to be divided, one group goes this way, the other group goes another, never meeting, only thinking about one another and creating false impressions of each other, never learning, only seeing and smelling and judging, because it's impossible to know completely, and yet I love completely and hate completely, and there is no escape from this cycle of pleasure and pain. If I cannot love completely I shall perish and die, if not by your hand, then by mine. You dare make me think those terrible thoughts, and if those thoughts continue I will die by my own hand. Because of it, the darkness blots out the sun, and the cold murders the warmth. The trick is to stick with love and its principles, but I never knew it would be this difficult. You have taken an idea, a simple word, which I loathe, and turned it against me, such that the word I loathe becomes a part of me like the love I once had. You call it the devil, while I call it a component of this terrible human nature. Well, my dear Allah, I'd rather be a plant or a flower that grows in accordance with the sun's rules, not yours. Yet even a flower must yield to the cold and darkness. Or why couldn't you have made me a fly who sees the swatting hand or the tail of a horse? By putting that dreadful word within my mind you have made me the idiot of all life's beings, the lowest creature on the face of this God-forsaken earth. Did you do this just to humiliate me? I never expected to be perfect, and I'm far from it, but surely you could have made an exception, knowing how I am unable to live when I encounter these involuntary thoughts. Damn this. I am unsure whether You are the demon or the demon is You, because most of the time I really can't tell the difference. You fill me with love, and you take away that love with petty hatreds, so offensive that love ceases to exist. And you call yourself a God? If you created Man in your image, how dare you insult our intelligence by calling yourself beneficent and all-knowing and perfect? Please, don't strike me down for asking questions, because I am human, and being human means that I have questions of the important sort. Please don't strike me down, for already you have damned me. Now that I search my mind, however, there is one small exception to this terrible and oppressive hatred: A woman.

'A woman of darker skin, no, I will never use that word with her. She rises above all of my foul hatreds, and you shall not touch her with my hatred. She belongs to that small part of me who loves and loves completely, and maybe I'm asking for something beyond my control, but this particular woman is immune from this singular insulting word. If the word comes up, I will call myself similar words, because I am no better than the words I call others. And if these disturbances threaten my mind, then put me back in the institution with its calming white walls, padded of course; lock me up and lose the key, because already I'm nearing the breaking point, because I know no one but strangers, and strangely enough I feel more comfortable around strangers than people I know. Why is that? Please, do not make Nasiba a mere stranger. When seeing her, I am touched by your calming hand, and if You really believe in Yourself, You will turn Nasiba my way, because a man without a woman is a car without a road, and on this early morning I can think of no one else. This is what happens when you place a man on this earth without a woman. The man becomes too self-involved in his attempt to defeat his own hatreds. But please, I am not fooled. A woman may never cure the man from his own mind, but the woman may at least calm the mind, so that he may think pleasant thoughts instead of words, and I don't want to hate anymore. Rather blind me with love, the love of this one woman, and I will never ask for more. You can at least grant me this as I have been through Hell already. Stuffed like a pig with involuntary thoughts. You have made sausage from my intestines and a delicacy from my knuckles, and I can't handle it, this supposed gift, but a gift it will be if you make her love me, so that I may love myself again, because along this endless road my engine has fallen apart. Heal me with your light. Fill me with crafty words, because tonight I'm visiting the mosque, and I will go there everyday just to see her and not think of the insulting word, because this Nasiba defies this word, and if the river of this world swallows me, let it be with her.

'Funny I hardly even know her, but she looks at me and smiles somehow; she smiles more with me than other men, I can tell, and if You grant her good graces I will forever be mindful of You. Have I ever asked of anything (besides world peace, an end to poverty, and the like)? In other words have I ever asked something for myself? Never. Not once. Whatever I had asked was for the greater good. Never had I asked selfishly or impolitely. I don't understand the ways in which you work. Allah, grant me Nasiba.

'Oh let me touch a woman, perhaps kiss her, smile with her, as the woman is the greatest cure-all. She is music and laughter, my fruit and my vision, for I cannot see passed her. I must have dreamt of her all night, because I woke up this morning with thoughts of her. Can you see me? Look upon me, I'm begging you. Without a woman I'm doomed, and I'll include my moderation as payment. I will listen to this idiot amilsaab. Maybe I shouldn't have said those things. Perhaps I unearthed within him words he had once believed. Are we living in a world of extremes, never that middle ground? I meant every word I said. And people called me vicious names because of it, but I am not insulted by them. The amilsaab had it coming to him. I will digest your crude verses. I will kneel before you. I will stop going to extremes and think more clearly, perhaps pragmatically. I will jump headlong into your reality. My imagination will be thrown to the dogs. I will stay with Muslims and fight for their causes, and if the Jew becomes the enemy in the Middle East, then I will treat them as enemies, because obviously that's your will, and even though your will often sucks, I will swallow it like chlozaril. Is this what you want? I will give it to you, just let me have this tender Nasiba.'

He placed his pen down and closed the notebook thankful to be finished. He lay back in bed, his hands behind his head. He welcomed the augmenting light. His mind was clear and his purpose pure and directed. He knew now what he must do.

The day went by slowly, and the Imam spent most of his time within his small room, the notebook glaring at him. At times he regretted what he wrote. Being truthful to oneself often has that awkward effect, but he chose to let the words remain. His spirit was buoyed by the prospects of seeing Nasiba. His mother had told him continuously how excited she was that he was attending the mosque. She asked him repeatedly if she could accompany him, but Mustafa flatly refused and hoped she would not follow him, as that was her nature.

His mother irritated him throughout the long day. She served him four meals within five hours and talked of demons and enemies chasing him. Mustafa played it calmly without erupting into a fit of rage. When she flew into an unrestrained rant, he simply went to his small room and shut the door tightly. He even covered his ears. He kept away from the television, and its absence contributed to a general wave of dismay and loneliness, as though he were undergoing some panicky withdrawal. Yet after the boredom and agony of patience, the night soon came, and Mustafa prepared for the mosque.

He donned his white garb and skullcap after an hour-long shower in which he prepared his greeting for the gentle Nasiba. He shaved closely. He checked himself in the mirror several times. When all was ready, he kissed his mother gently and took the cross-town bus for the mosque.

He arrived without trouble. The cold annoyed him, but otherwise all was ready. He promised to confront her immediately. He crossed the icy intersection, the winds blowing through his winter's jacket. He saw a gathering of African-Americans huddling near the vestibule. He could not make her out at first, because the crowd was quite large, even more so than the night before. He noticed a few familiar faces, but no one said a word to him. When they saw him, they turned away without their expected gentleness.

He filed behind the gathering of dark faces. He craned his neck to see ahead of himself. The men and women entered at the same time, and the crowd was densely packed, making it impossible for him. He manouvered between shoulders and was tempted to call her name, but he refrained and approached her with stealth. He followed the believers through the vestibule and at this juncture the women went downstairs into the basement while the men stayed on the ground floor, like two separate rivers flowing towards the same sea. Mustafa quietly followed the women down the narrow set of stairs.

"Hey brother," said an angry voice, "you're going the wrong way."

Mustafa feigned deafness. He followed the women a few steps more until one of them tapped him on the shoulder.

"I said, brother, you're going the wrong way. You belong upstairs."

"I'm trying to find the bathroom," said the Imam, "I heard it's down here."

"The men's room is upstairs, brother."

Mustafa had been caught, and suddenly he felt the compulsion to confess his preposterous strategy of finding Nasiba. But he kept quiet and limited his confidence to this angry woman.

"Actually, I'm looking for Nasiba. Do you know Nasiba?"

"What do you want with her," she asked suspiciously.

"I'm a close friend, and I want to say hello before the meeting, or the convocation, or whatever you call it."

"There's plenty of time after the prayer. Go upstairs, the adhan will be called soon. Prayer may help you."

He wondered what she meant by that, but insisted on seeing Nasiba.

"Listen, I have to talk to her now, I can't wait, this is a matter of importance."

"You can't see her now. Prayers are about to start."

"To hell with prayers!" the Imam heard himself saying, and when he said this the entire congregation of women seemed to turn round and listen. "I must see her, please," he said more quietly.

He followed the wave of shawl-wearing women pushing to the bottom of the stairs. There he stood looking frantically for her. The Imam remembered his journal and had faith the prayer would be delivered. He devised a plan of action, for he could not simply walk up to her and confess his deepest desires. And yet he could do no less, because plans and schemes failed him. Only women have this particular effect. The heart pumps so loudly that every believer can hear, and simple logic and rationality transmutes into a fire unquenched, and a longing that burns.

The Imam found a nook near the stairs and watched as these descending women gave him angry looks. They had heard about his defiance of prayer, but he meant every word of it. He searched for her, and the search became easier once they fell to the floor, one by one, as the adhan was called over the small speakers. The Imam did not fear the terrible faces any longer. He weaved between the believers and made it to the front of the room. He could see everyone's face, although many peered in anger, even mockery.

"You can't stand there!" yelled an older, chunky woman.

"Move away, we're praying here," said another.

And the Imam swept through their faces and discovered Nasiba sitting at the edge of the room staring directly into him. 'Ah woman!' he thought. 'How lost man would be without thee. Whether you know it or not, you bring the sun on the cloudiest of days. You exude warmth in the most bitter cold. My blood boils, and my brain looks to the heart for answers. What has come over me? Where has my mind gone? I can think of no one else. I can't speak. I can't move. She's staring at me, oh Allah, you exist within her. Oh my heart, think man, think. Just don't stand here. Say something, say the first thing which comes to mind.'

> "Allah is most great
> I bear witness that there is none
> Worthy of being worshipped except
> Allah," came softly over the speaker system.

'Prayer has started,' he thought, 'and I can't move a muscle. How do I look? Is my hair combed, are my teeth white? Have I lost weight? Anything for her. I'd walk the earth searching for her, and yet she's right there. This is crazy. Maybe I do belong in the nut-house. I can't take it.'

> "I bear witness that Muhammad is
> The Apostle of Allah
> Come to prayer.
> Come to success," as the women turned to the right and left in

unison.

He moved cautiously along the edge of the room, disturbing everyone in his path.

'This is crazy, this is crazy, this is crazy,' he thought as he approached her.

"I need to have a word with you," he said.

"Can't it wait, brother," whispered Nasiba. "I'm in the middle of something…"

"No, it can't wait. I have to tell you now."

"Please, wait until after prayers."

"I can't. Please, I'm begging you. I'm down on my hands and knees, before God, I'm pleading."

"Brother, you need help. Go upstairs. I don't even know you."

"I know you don't," he said with stern eyes. "I desperately wish to remedy that."

"Go upstairs!" she whispered hotly.

"Please, I must have a word with you."

"Leave her alone," cried the woman next to her.

"This doesn't concern you," countered the Imam.

"You're bothering her. We are saying prayers. I'll call one of the men down here."

"Go ahead!" he shouted. And then to Nasiba: "Listen, I'm not a smart man, I'll grant you that, and I'm an idiot, I'll grant you yet another, but for some reason I never knew love to be so immediate. Most people don't believe in love at first glance, but let it be known in front of all these women that I have utterly fallen for you, and ultimately I know nothing about you, because quite frankly I don't know who you are or from where you came. I care little about your history, because I'm cursed enough to live in the present, and I'm so sorry for embarrassing myself and for humiliating you in front of all these people, but I believe that you and I fit like a flower to a warm sunny day."

Two men came rushing downstairs.

"...I'm sorry, but I couldn't keep it inside any longer, and it didn't even take that long. I'm drunk over you. I'm completely powerless without you, and you should see me as a man who has the balls to tell you, when I have little idea who you are. Believe me, this is all very normal..."

The two men rushed forward and grabbed him by the arms.

"All right, let's go," mumbled one of the men, struggling.

"Wait. Hold on. Just hold on a minute!" shouted the Imam. "Don't let it be this way," he said to Nasiba, "but if you want me to go, I'll leave and never return, but I need to know, do you really want me to go?"

"Brother, I have no idea who you are. I just saw you yesterday, and I'm flattered, very flattered, but you obviously need some help, help I can't provide. You're a very sick man. Leave him alone," she said to the men.

"You heard what she said, brothers!"

"Both of you, get out!" said one of the men finally.

Nasiba folded her prayer cloth, and the Imam followed her up the stairs. The men shut the door on them as they stood alone under a dark, chilly sky.

The Imam found quick relief in her dark face which shone underneath the lamppost. Her long hair was covered with the rest of her body, and yet the Imam knew her incredibly comely and hard to resist.

"I'm sorry," said the Imam finally.

"No need to be sorry," she said quietly. "You are not the first man to react that way. I've seen it many other times. It does happen."

"I was being honest. I've thought all day about you. I have to be honest..."

"I realize that, brother, and oddly enough, in this day and age, being honest never attracted many women..."

"I'm foolish, I know, but I can't help it."

"I'm going back in," she said after a moment's reflection.

"Can I see you again? Maybe we can meet under less formal circumstances?"

"That's not possible."

"Why? Haven't I professed my desire for you?"

"Yes, brother, you have, but I'm not looking for anyone. I'm trying to avoid complications," she said demurely.

"So am I. Maybe we can get some coffee and discuss how complicated life is?"

"I'm sorry, brother, I can't."

"Please, only once, I won't ask you again."

"I'm sorry, but I'd only be seeing you because I felt guilty, not because I really wanted to. You need help. You don't even know me. And you're so intense, my God. Just calm down. Slow down."

"Don't do this. I don't believe that. Love conquers and overrides guilt and awkward feelings."

"It's good to think that way, but really, I'm flattered, really, but I could never see someone like you."

"Is it the way I look?" asked the Imam, hugging his pouchy waistline.

"You look fine, and you are very handsome..."

"Then come with me. If you think I'm good-looking, then let's not waste another minute here. We can start to build instead of leaving everything in ruins."

"I can't. I'm sorry. I belong to Allah, and obviously you need work. I'm sorry, and I'm grateful you find me attractive, but I think you need Allah more than you need me."

She left him in the dark, oppressive street without elaboration and returned to the mosque.

And she shut the door behind her.

Mustafa stood in the darkness, the only available light coming from the lamppost a few paces away. He had never wanted a woman so much.

He fought the urge to reenter the mosque. Persistence on his part would lead to another resounding rejection. He believed the power of a man and woman together somehow served a higher purpose than the revered dome or its towering minaret. That to have a woman served Allah more than these edifices built by strong backs. They were all ridiculous in his eyes. He not only wanted her, but needed her. Her beauty had surpassed his simple expectations. And he imagined kissing her slowly and simply. Gradually warm tears filled his eyes. He tried to stop them, but they flowed freely without any sense, only an overwhelming tug of his heart amidst the cruel laughter of the night, not only for Nasiba's rejection, but for his own damaged mind. He had never been so ashamed.

He walked most of the way home, thoroughly absorbed by her. He desperately took measures to purge himself, but his mind returned to her face, her body, those dark eyes which arrested and sentenced him without a fair trial. Angry and alone, he was pulled to the all-night bars which seemed welcome and promising. He removed his skullcap and drank heavily while listening to soothing melodies, but when the last call sounded, he found himself terribly alone. The drink did not conquer his suffering. Yet he drank more at another bar a few blocks over. His speech slurred, and his body slackened as the penetrating booze freed him of his anger and impatience. He even found himself in deep prayer and meditation after shooting back shots of a bitter liquor, tasting like black liquorice.

Old men with gray hair and broken words surrounded him. He intimated how he could have easily won Nasiba's affection by attending the mosque and keeping quiet. He could have cozily become her friend, and after working on her in a friendly fashion, could have taken her as his lover. He did not blame himself, though. He had released the conniption that inflamed his heart, and although he was rejected by her, he felt for certain that he grew stronger from it.

He stumbled home in the darkness, his solitary world thrown into confusion. He thumped on the door to the Riverside Drive apartment, his hands and toes nearly frost-bitten. The shriveled figure of his mother met him, the lights on behind her.

"Where were you?" she asked.

"At the mosque," said the Imam.

She moved closer to him and smelled his breath.

"Drinking? Did you drink?" she cried.

"No. Now I'm tired, and I'd like to get some sleep."

"Drinking? Yes? Drinking, Mustafa, this is no good. You mustn't drink, no, it's terrible!"

"Will you quiet down. The neighbors are trying to sleep…"

"No, I won't be quiet. Drinking, drugs, and hanging around like a vagabond. Where did you go? You were supposed to go to the mosque."

"I went, okay?"

He walked down the hallway towards his room.

"Wait, Mustafa! How dare you drink and go to the mosque! A devil is following you, I can smell the alcohol on your breath, how disgusting the alcohol smells, yes, disgusting. The enemy is at your back, and we must take this enemy out of you..."

"Would you please be quiet," said the Imam in a wave of inebriation.

"...No, Mustafa, no, how dare you go to the mosque and drink. Were you at the mosque and drunk? No, Mustafa, we must find that enemy that's following you..."

"Goodnight, mom, I'm sleeping now."

"You dare sleep?" she said in a high-pitched shrill. "No, you must pray right now, otherwise the enemy will follow you. Kneel before Allah and pray..."

He was followed into his room.

"No time for sleep," she continued. "Come, I'm putting down the musulla. You must pray all night, you must pray until the dawn, yes, Mustafa, how terrible, drinking, smoking, jazz, all of this, and the enemy keeps following you. You must say prayers and spit into the ground. All your life the enemy has been following you as it followed your uncles and your daddy and now you too..."

"We never had one. Now get out, please!" yelled the Imam.

"Say your prayers. How terrible, Mustafa. You are nothing, you don't say your prayers, you're drinking at the mosque, you come back at all hours of the night, and then you nicely go to sleep. You dare sleep at a time like this? You're going absolutely nowhere and nowhere absolutely. You will pray first and spit out that devil, because the enemy is following you..."

"Out with you," as a blind rage nabbed him.

He pushed her out of the room and slammed the door, but she forced it open and continued her long, nonsensical ranting. He ran to the living room, asking her in bursts of shouting to shut her mouth, but she kept on her steady stream, so annoying and troublesome, that the festering rage brought him to the kitchen. He could not control the rage. He fought against it. But each word brought him closer and closer. From the small plastic rack on which were stored drying plates and teacups he pulled a dull steak knife.

"Shut up, you bitch, shut up!" he cried.

"Look at his, Mustafa, oh how terrible, so sick you're looking..."

"I'm warning you. Now shut your mouth."

She kept speaking her choppy but stern and critical words, and in the middle of her rant the frightful situation dawned upon them.

"And now you'll kill me?" she asked.

"Keep your mouth shut!" shouted the Imam.

"Kill me then, you rogue. Kill me, because that won't stop the devil from following you."

"Don't push me," said the Imam trembling.

"Kill me."

Suddenly, a window of silence. Mustafa brought the point of the steak knife to her throat.

"Kill me," she whispered, "because as a mother I have failed."

Her whispering turned into tear-turgid cries.

"You are an Imam," she said, "and I have failed to raise you rightly. An Imam, I say, an Imam, and kill me if you must, but the truth must be known before I die, and let it also be known that I love you like a son. But you were not born to me, you were given to me, you hear, you were given to me by the bavasaab Tariq Bengaliwala, and I've kept this from you, my darling sweet son, but I'd rather die by your hand than die the slow, cruel death I would have died. Take me, my Imam. Kill me here and now if you must. But the truth you must hear, for you are the twelfth Imam, father and spirit to an entire people…"

"What? What are you saying? Lies, woman, nothing but fantastic lies coming out of that filthy mouth. Just because you failed as a mother, doesn't mean that your fantasy world can absolve you," as he gripped the knife tighter.

"I'm so sorry, my son. I've always considered you my son. But you are an Imam, the descendant of Ali, and please let me die tonight, because I have failed. For Allah's sake you must learn how to pray…"

"Liar!" he cried.

"I can't hide it anymore, my son. Why do you think you must take Arabic lessons? An enemy is following you, my dear Imam…"

"Stop saying that!"

"I'm speaking the truth. I love you more than you can ever know, my Imam."

"Stop it, you bitch! You're lying, I know you're lying to me! Where's my father? What happened to him?"

"Yes, my glorious Imam, leader of the Shias," she smiled through her tears.

"You're crazy. Absolutely crazy, a nut-case…"

"Oh my dear Imam…"

"Stop calling me that, or I'll kill you, here and now. Don't you care about your own life, damn you?"

"Take me, please, take me away, because now you're older and more aware. Allah has brought you here for me to tell you the truth, and now I must die, because you are the All Mighty, you and no one else, not your Daddy, not this Vasilla who has provided us with money all these years…"

"Liar! Stop lying to me, please."

He dropped the knife and embraced his mother.

She whispered into his ear: "I'm not lying, my gulab, my rose, I am telling you the truth of the matter. You belong to us Shia Muslims. You were loaned to me. Don't deny yourself the truth. An enemy has been chasing you. I've reared you wrong, and it's my fault. The Imam musn't drink or hear jazz or consort with women. The Imam must pray and give himself to Allah so that he may save others, not abandon them. Ah, my sweet, sweet son. Everything will be alright. Allah will make things alright…because tomorrow is another glorious day, and we must return to the mosque and pray, because that devil is still following you."

Chapter Six
THE EMERGENCY MEETING
15th of Safar 1436
(December 8, 2014)

Alone in his room, Khozem prepared for the emergency meeting of his twelve advisors. He asked his father not to join him at this meeting. He felt his father too weary to handle with authority and vigor the pressing problem of the Jewish colony. Khozem made brief preparations by scribbling notes on a small pad, and as the hour approached he grew excited and anxious.

Khozem would be alone to do whatever he pleased with the Organization. He relished the thought of putting ideas into action, taking initiatives, and implementing a high-octane approach towards a problem that would not go away. He spent most of his preparation pacing to and fro like a leader on the verge of a great battle, like Napoleon at Austerlitz, or gaining full support and control, like Stalin over the Bolsheviks. Although Khozem tried in vain to brush personal glory aside, he could not deny what hid within him. He believed his plans would finally succeed and avoid the malaise his father had brought to an Organization rife with bureaucracy, inefficiency, and complacency.

He sipped slowly his glass of Rooh Afza, the liquid syrupy-red and cold on his tongue. With each sip new opportunities unfolded with the ultimate aim of agitating the ridiculous peace process ushered in by the land of heathens, drug addicts, and derelics. He knew his father usually prayed before meetings, but Khozem did away with the ritual. He merely paced back and forth hundreds of times waiting in agony for the start of the meeting.

The custodian's residence was nearby. He jumped into a white, curtained Mercedes, his bodyguards in the front and himself in the rear, slapping the notepad against his thigh, the red liquid still fresh in his mouth.

At the entrance of the residence he confronted two military men, rifles at their sides. They checked his features and determined after a tireless review of documents and identifications that he indeed was the bavasaab for whom they had waited. The elevator doors opened to a long room with a heavy oak table in the middle.

The twelve advisors stood from their chairs. They were covered in white, silk garments. The room was dark and cool, blocking the intense desert sun, and Khozem glanced at each of their faces, smiling as though possessed by some divine hand. Pitchers of holy water were spread on the table. Advisor's aides were seated at the perimeter, and their eyes were instantly afire and enamored by the presence of the new bavasaab. They held thick folders at their laps, and Khozem smiled to them, knowing they came to his first meeting prepared and poised. Khozem grinned knowingly at his twelve advisors after determining all were accounted for. A new stenographer tapped soft keys on his machine. The advisor nearest to him began his report, and Khozem listened attentively.

"Since its inception," began the advisor, "the Jewish colony has been a constant source of pain and struggle for our Muslim people in the Palestinian territories. Since then, with the aid of the United States, and the United States alone, the Jewish colony has survived and even prospered to some extent despite our fledgling groups who resist their expansion into Arab-held territories. The expansion grows each day and with it comes new and sporadic waves of violence against our people, mostly retaliations against our token bombings in populous Jewish areas such as Tel Aviv and Hebron. Our will, however, has been ironclad. We have pushed for an independent Palestinian state consisting of the West Bank and Gaza, with a connecting corridor, but this simple attempt at aiding four million dispossessed Palestinians has resulted in complete failure. Currently, the United States and its Secretary of State plan to broker a new peace settlement in the region, despite numerous United Nations' resolutions condemning the Jewish settlement expansion and the United States' lop-sided, biased approach towards negotiations, even after the New War. Your holiness, we could continue for hours, recounting six decades of war between the Jewish state and the Palestinian people. We could continue tapping our resources of intelligence in the region and funding missions of violence, but your holiness, our failure at overtaking the Jewish colony is glaring and somewhat embarrassing. This is exemplified by the Palestinian people who have offered peace settlements twenty times in the last two decades. At every angle the Jewish colony has rejected the offers. The Jewish enemy has a staunch and very powerful ally. The end of the New War has shifted the balance of power inexorably towards the Western world. Our soldiers of peace are tired as we have not missed a single opportunity in derailing the American brokerage of peace. We have reviewed the most recent treaty between the two sides, and this Council endorses the current treaty in accordance with its timetable of peace and stability in the region. Overall, we would like to see an independent Palestinian state, not merely a handed-down autonomy. Second, we would also like more land in exchange for an end to more bloodshed. Thirdly, we believe ten years towards Palestinian independence is much too lengthy. More than any single impediment to peace, however, remains the thirteen thousand Palestinian political prisoners rotting in Jewish jails.

"Your holiness, if may I speak frankly, we are all very tired with the ongoing struggle, and now that we see the light, a definite talk of peace overflowing in the embattled region, we strongly believe it's high time we endorse the current proposals. Your holiness, you are our new leader, and it's a refreshing change as there is now a new leadership, a new vision, a new hope for peace with our Jewish neighbors. We've exhausted completely our funds for increased activity, and our activities have been thoroughly negative. We are all asking for a fresh start and a clean slate. We suggest normalizing our relations with the state of Israel. We urge that you convene the Muslims countries, or the FAC, and work within the framework of the accords towards security and normalization in the region. Six decades of war and bloodshed has been too much for a seventh. We suggest you convene the FAC and deliberate for a period of five months before involving the Organization in any future activity.

"This certainly does not come easily for our esteemed Organization as we have supported our collection of allies for decades of war and bloodshed. We suggest the cut with our allies be made quickly and cleanly with funds appropriated immediately to those dispossessed Palestinians who need it most, namely the women, children, the poor, and the sick scathed and scoured by the violence. We suggest the difference of these funds be placed within our Ministries of Culture and Education for the enhancement and propogation of our faith.

"You see, your holiness, we on the Council believe we may begin a new era of relative peace and security with Israel, and our further cooperation in the peace effort would stabilize the region and grant us access to many lucrative opportunities. Nevertheless the process will be painstaking and gradual, but in the end we will gain immeasurably through our cooperation. It is even conceivable that some of our funds may finance the political parties in the West, so that our faith receives due attention and due process within these governments and their courts. We urge you to accept this plan as our Organization will surely prosper from it."

And then a long silence. Khozem stood from his chair and reached for a pitcher of zum-zum water. He stood silently for a few moments.

"Nice, isn't it?" he began. "Cool, clean, and refreshing water in the middle of this vast desert? And nice, is it not, that we have our land today with this wonderful, plentiful water smack in the middle of it, the place where Abraham and his son Isaac laid the foundations of our glorious Kaa'bah? Yes?"

The advisors sat in such a silence that only the flush of air conditioning could be heard.

"Yes, my advisors, my loyal and trusting advisors. It's a gift, all of what you see, the Kaa'bah just a stone's throw away, the sands of the desert running through our fingers, our homeland, this changeling called Arabia. Our home is here, and our lives are here. Imagine, Mr. Asif Mohammad, if your home were someday taken away? Gone! Poof! Into the air like some Jinn had stolen it from you, your home and your family, and surely you'd miss this cold and clear zum-zum water, wouldn't you? You see, there's much more at stake besides our common hatred of the Jew, don't you think? They occupy our holy shrines at Jerusalem. They take our land and our water, bit by bit, lest anyone on this Council notice. And soon with the water they steal our homes and our blood, good and wholesome Muslim blood, because many of our brothers now pace within barbed wire and the watchful gaze of muscular Jewish troops, standing erect with their American rifles, and once in a while shoving the butts of these powerful machine guns into the guts of our brothers who want nothing but to return to homes mysteriously vanished, as this water will have vanished, if we submit to this idea of cooperation.

"Cooperation does not mean sharing with the foe. Cooperation with the West must mean our constant submission to the West. Have we not seen this before? Arabia makes one false move, and suddenly we hear the bombs whistling upon the mosques of Bagdhad, and Poof! The Jinn somehow take it away, our bountiful Tigris and Euphrates contaminated by the foul destruction of thousands of innocent souls. And you have the nerve to call this 'cooperation?' I call it submission! Yes, most of you have heard this word before. Submission to Allah only, my brothers. Submission to the poetic verses of the Qu'ran, yes, but you dare think me so naïve and ignorant that I would ask my friends, our brothers in the occupied territories to submit, not only to a power greater than ourselves, but a power so tiny compared to Allah? Yes, their method is to divide us, and then conquer us.

"And then there's the question of the Jew. I admit freely and openly that I have no respect whatsoever for the Jew as he has tainted our land, raped our women, and bludgeoned our brothers. And some of you sit there and ask yourselves: aren't the bavasaab's objections so petty and childish. Are they really? Look into your hearts. Can you remotely picture sitting next to the Jew at our table, after countless entreaties, after their frozen, sharp bullets have pierced the skulls of the smallest Muslim children? These same children dying of thirst, their rooftops the desert winds, and their floors the knees of wailing mothers? With the Jew it is not merely a question of fairness. We have tried fairness with the Jew, and in return for our leniency we receive bombs from their American fighter jets and grunts from their American-trained troops, raiding homes, confiscating property which isn't rightly theirs. In your hearts, my brothers, you will see that the Jew morally and socially is the lowest animal, and Allah knows their treachery and deceit and cunning. At first we tried to discuss with the Jew, and when discussion failed, we rationalized that we must tolerate them, and after they turned their backs on our suffering and wounded our children and destroyed our homes, we still tolerated their claim to divine supremacy. And you all sit here, comfortably nonetheless, and ask me in right mind to cooperate with the Jew? To sit down and pick from his plate? You ask me to accept the Jewish colony, as a Jewish nation?

"And then there's the question of America, the sole supporter of this Jew, these dim-witted cowboys drunk on their own powers, walking hand-in-hand with the Jew, while they sell their arms just to satisfy their profit margins, only to exploit our better natures with their drink and their drugs and their moral ineptitude. If the Jew is the lowest animal, then the American must be lower. He has funded and supported the Jew, and within their borders, the Jewish lobby yields so much power, that every wish, every idiosyncrasy of the Jew is catered to with a resounding affection. If we pick at the Jew's plate, then the Jew picks at America's plate, and the American feeds the Jew with automatic rifles, ammunition, and suddenly nuclear technology? Imagine that? We toss rocks and bottles, and they develop a weapon so deadly that it would erase the entity of Arabia at a single detonation? If the Jew is the enemy, then what is America but a greater enemy? And you dare ask me to cooperate? You ask me for normalization and stability? Only to have those promises of peace, those maggot-ridden lies, a fantasy, a delusion, shoved down our throats for nearly six gruesome decades?

The struggle is not over. Our objectives must be clear as this zum-zum water which we, in Arabia, take for granted. My plan will be followed strictly, and this plan is in accordance with the will of the Imam himself.

"First, the FAC will not be utilized on this occasion. They have enough trouble dealing amongst themselves. Rather our decision-making must derive from a more, shall we say, centralized body. The problem as I see it is mainly financial, and from now on I will be the one setting policy. We must lay the foundations now in order to prosper later.

"I decree with full knowledge of the blessed Imam that we cut funding across the board. Each of our ministries will take a thirty percent cut with the exception of the ministries of culture and education which will take a thirty-five percent cut. As a result we must lay-off workers at our complexes in Jeddah and Mecca. Second, out of the revenues amassed from these cuts, seventy-five percent shall aid our allies in the occupied territories. They will continue their defiance against the Jewish enemy. The residual twenty-five percent will go into a special fund over which I will have total control. This fund shall be used wisely, investing solely within FAC countries. Call it an emerging market's fund, if you like. And by devoting funds to these markets the FAC will be pacified by our will and determination. In other words, we will compete with the bribes they are already taking from America.

"You see, my dear brothers, the time has come to make our mark and take back what is rightfully ours. No longer will this Organization sit and watch as the Jewish enemy confiscates our lands and torments our people. We must fight them tooth and nail. This will be our policy until I am satisfied. And you dare propose cooperation? You dare mention that word? I say, get ready! Get ready to thwart the Jewish foe. I want my plan implemented by next week. That will be all."

The advisors sat in their chairs stunned by Khozem's response. Each of them wore faces of consternation and dismay, but they kept silent as Khozem left the room without bidding salaams or listening to their personal concerns as his father had done.

Chapter Seven
MUSTAFA REBELS
16th of Safar 1436
(December 9, 2014)

On the next evening, a dull and cloudy evening, Mustafa found himself in his bed, his body stripped to his underwear. His head pounded from the alcohol he drank the previous night. A nausea gripped him, and although chilly in his room, he wiped beads of sweat from his brow and stumbled to the bathroom where he vomited. He had been sleeping for hours, right through the day. He remembered the previous night clearly. He wished he could forget it. He didn't know whether his mother was telling the truth or telling lies symptomatic of her general maladies. After vomiting and brushing his yellowing teeth, he met his mother in the hallway; She was dressed in religious garb.

"C'mon, Mustafa, get ready."

"Quiet, please, quiet," he said, scratching his buttocks.

"No, we must go. Hurry up and change!"

"I can't. I need a few more hours of rest."

"No time for rest, Mustafa. Let's go, get ready."

"I really can't. I'm sick."

"That's the devil inside of you..."

"Oh, not this again..."

"...yes, the devil. We must go to the mosque. Don't you remember, you're an Imam! You must learn how to pray, and the mosque is the best place."

"Even the Imam must have an off-day," he said.

"No time, Mustafa, no time."

"Besides, they probably won't let me back in."

"Why won't they let you in?"

"Can we go to another mosque? There must be another mosque in this city."

"This is the closest, and it's the finest mosque."

"I just don't want to go."

"Doesn't last night mean anything?"

"You're lying. I know you are. Maybe you need a doctor. I'm sorry about last night. Really very sorry."

"No time for apologies. Come now, get ready."

"I told you. I don't want to go."

"If you consider me as anything you'll come. You are an Imam, the descendant of Ali. I wasn't lying to you. I'm telling you the truth, may Allah strike me down if I'm lying."

Thinking his mother a crackpot, the Imam donned the same garments he wore the night before. His motive was to see Nasiba again. Upon arrival at the mosque he avoided running into Nasiba, as though ignoring her would build some attraction. He avoided also the same men who threw him out. He kept a low profile and stood on the opposite side of the street while his mother entered immediately.

He considered finding a hospital for his mother. She had gone too far, and although he felt a profound sense of guilt by pulling the knife on her, he couldn't stand living with her any longer. But where would he live? He had no money. Where on earth could he go except back to the Riverside Drive apartment with his mother's lies and ill-health? He justified leaving his mother by reviewing in his mind how he could have easily killed her, and departing from her home would keep her alive should the incident ever repeat itself.

There were so many places he longed to visit, such as California, especially California where the sun continually shines and the grassy hillsides roll for eternities, and the atmosphere overflowed with new ideas. He had to make the move away from his mother. California seemed like the best place. He planned on stealing money from his mother's purse for the prized bus ticket. As a gust of wind tunneled down Ninety Sixth Street he made a firm decision to leave his mother. He imagined what he would find in California besides the bountiful sun. Perhaps the women would smile. Yes, wasn't that the real reason for leaving? To see a woman and to be embraced by one? Isn't that the ultimate reason for any man's journey through the darkness, only to be found, or at least discovered, by the tender eyes of a woman?

'A woman must provide peace of mind,' he thought. 'And in California the women are so beautiful. Maybe I'll meet a woman who looks like Nasiba, yes, exactly like Nasiba, only that she won't be so religious, and she will love me as I love her. Yes, I must leave.'

Mustafa heard the adhan being called, and through the muddled haze of his hangover, he entered the mosque inconspicuously. He went straight up the stairs making sure to avoid each and every believer. He sat on the floor towards the back of the crowded room. He followed the believers by bowing and prostrating himself at the appropriate times. He believed such actions would absolve him of his prior behaviors.

The prayers ended after a time. He fought the urge to leave the mosque before the amilsaab's sermon. He could hardly see ahead of him but smelled incense drifting above the gathering, fuming under the high dome.

The amilsaab then began his sermon:

"Most of you must be wondering about the doom which shall pass through this planet once the time elapses, once this world is overrun by infidelity and sin. If things continue on their normal course, the doomsday will be here quicker than we expect. How will we when know the doomsday approaches? Well, let me mention the ways.

"The Prophet of God had affirmed that two groups of men destined for Hell will appear in the future. One group will carry whips like the tail of oxen, and they will beat people with them. They will be openly cursed by the All

Mighty morning and night. The second group will consist of women wearing clothes that reveal their naked bodies. They will tempt us, and we will be tempted by them. Their nudity will not arise from poverty. They will go around naked just to show off their bodies to men in order to seduce them. Their heads will not be covered. They shall wear their hair in a seductive fashion. These women will not enter paradise. They will not even smell it. Instead they will wear perfumes to trick the men they seduce.

"Infidelity shall be widespread. Men shall be believers by morning and turn to infidelity by evening. Knowledge will disappear and ignorance shall prevail. Adultery, drunkeness, and debauchery will increase, and as a result the population of men will decrease, decrease so much that a single man will account for fifty women. The number of children born out of wedlock will also increase, and when this comes to pass, the entire ummah will face the danger of the doomsday. As the tradition says: the Doomsday will not come until a scantily clad woman passes through a crowd of men, and one of those men will rise and lift her short skirt and engage in copulation with her. This man engaged in such a sinful act will appear afterwards as righteous as a Caliph.

"The Prophet of God (May peace be upon him) has observed that the end will come when killers will not know why they killed, and the victim will not know why he was deprived of life. Thousands of lives will be lost due to petty divisions in dogma, such that the divisions in dogma will unleash weapons of war, and people will never know why they fight or whom they are fighting. People will be killed senselessly just for their own misdirected causes. We will cease calling the cruel man cruel, and people will follow different paths to Allah except the one appointed by his Prophet. Men will worship false deities, and these same men will manufacture lies and lead virtuous men into wrong beliefs. Of course everything flows from the past. Each succeeding period will be worse than the former. But it is useless to complain about this apparent trend. We should be content under Allah for the period in which we live. We should give thanks that we live now and have the opportunity to change our sinful ways, for the odds are against us.

"The Prophet had said that only a few God-fearing men shall adhere to the cause of Allah until the end. Their opposition or non-cooperation shall do them no harm, for they shall not care about the attitudes of the times, and these special people have a place reserved for them in Allah's heaven.

"There will come a time when Islam shall exist in name only, and the Qu'ran will be regarded as any other book. The mosques will flourish, and they will be decorated and ornamented, but the light of faith will be nowhere. Although these mosques will be filled with eye-catching colors and plush carpets, the only people who visit these mosques will engage in worldly talk and conversation, nothing at all concerning the verses of Allah, and as a result, Allah will have no use of such people.

"Let us recall an observation of our prophet:
'When the spoils of war will be regarded as personal property instead of collective estate, and things kept in trust shall be expropriated,
When zakat shall be regarded as an indemnity, and religious knowledge shall be gained merely to serve
Worldly interests,
When the husbands shall follow the counsels of their wives and shall subject their mothers to harassment,
When men shall be thicker with their friends and estranged from their fathers
When mosques shall resound with the talk of the world
When leaders of the tribe shall become unbelievers
When base people shall be appointed as leaders of nations,
When the mischievous shall be respected on account of fear,
When the number of dancing and singing women shall proliferate and musical instruments gain popularity…'

"And those in the mosques," continued the amilsaab, "the guides and scholars, will be the worst of the believers as they will spread mischief and become evil minded. These people, these leaders, will renounce the path of piety and true belief. They will hanker after worldly goods as they will gradually lose their dignity. They will be preoccupied with the business of becoming worldly leaders, hoarding their riches. And when the world is seized by conflicts and wars, these scholars and guides will perish in the warfare initiated by them.

"The followers of these men shall imitate Jews. They will follow in their footsteps, inch by inch, and advance towards the same things at the same speed. Some of these people will commit the same sins of the children of Israel, like adultery with their mothers, and they will be divided into many different unholy sects. Only one sect will be consigned to heaven, and I ask you now, will you be part of that sect?"

Now the Imam sat through this part of the sermon, but despite his intense hangover and malady he had frequent urges to shout. He controlled these urges in the beginning. He found something so very wrong with the amilsaab, nothing personally, but with the words he spoke, striking fear into his followers. He couldn't place his finger on it, but the amilsaab's sermon irked him so much that he could not simply sit there as these strong, psychologically fierce words were gobbled up by the congregation.

At first he rehearsed in his mind what he ought to say, and because the rehearsal was only that, he kept most of these words between his own ears. As the sermon continued, however, a compulsion struck him like boiling water at the center of his chest. He found himself whispering words to himself. The whispering turned into mumbling, and finally this mumbling, along with the burning at his chest, forced him to stand up midway through the amilsaab's sermon.

"Wait a second, wait there just one moment," he said. "The Doomsday? What Doomsday? Why do you insist on filling these people with fear like you did the last time? One should never live in fear that Allah won't love him or her..."

"Sit down, brother!" shouted someone in the front.

"No, no, let the brother speak!" yelled another.

And soon a chaos and calamity ruptured the mosque. Heated words were exchanged on all sides, some of the believers agreeing with him, and the majority of them telling him to keep quiet. Mustafa saw from his position the same two men who expelled him from the mosque the previous night, but they did not confront him until the restlessness of the crowd rallied into confusion and idle shouting. Apparently, the Imam raised a controversy that was already present. He saw the two men rushing towards him.

"Now everyone calm down, calm down," said the amilsaab through the microphone.

The Imam could have run into the street, but he stood there ranting almost: "...you're using fear as some way to stay holy, well, I say we should want to stay holy, because in our hearts there is love no matter what direction we travel, no matter how we evolve and progress..."

"Let the man speak," shouted a chorus of voices from the side.

Suddenly Mustafa felt a tug at his shoulder. It was his mother, Maryam, who emerged from the basement, and she used her incredibly annoying, high-pitched shrill to protect her son from damage.

"He is the Imam. My son, he is the Imam, we must listen to him," she screeched. "Vasilla, where are you? Vasilla, protect my son from these thugs."

The two men grabbed the Imam by the arms and forced him to the carpet, ready to eject him from the mosque. But suddenly the huge bulk of Vasilla caught them from behind and threw them to the side like a pair of old shoes.

"Tell them, Vasilla! They will believe you, they must believe..." cried Maryam.

"Everyone calm down. Sit down everyone, please for your own protection, sit down!" called the amilsaab over the speaker system.

Most of the congregation did as the amilsaab said. Finally the crowd settled, their backs turned, watching to their dismay the towering bulk of Vasilla who stood before the Imam.

Vasilla had a choice. He could either rebuke this rebellious creature before him, because he was vehemently against what he believed. Or he could accept him and declare openly that this indeed was the Twelfth Imam returned to earth after generations of dormancy.

All eyes were upon them. The two men Vasilla threw aside also watched in confusion. Vasilla did not act capriciously. He deliberated for a few moments as he knew himself an important member of the mosque. He had told the amilsaab and his key people that he was the bodyguard of Tariq Bengaliwala and now Khozem, the new bavasaab. He had built a strong reputation and was regarded highly by the people most close to the amilsaab.

Vasilla glanced up at the high white dome. He sighed deeply, because he had little idea what he should do.

"Tell them, Vasilla," said Maryam more calmly. "Please, for Allah's sake, tell them the truth."

Vasilla's eyes watered as he knelt on one knee, took the Imam's hand, and smothered it with his tears and kisses. The Imam Mustafa felt his moist lips and tears canvass his hands, not a knuckle left untouched, and at that moment, with the entire mosque gawking at them, the Imam kept silent. Never before did he experience such fear.

Chapter Eight
VASILLA MEETS KHOZEM
17th of Safar 1436
(December 10, 2014)

In the home high in the Meccan hills Khozem received a call from Vasilla in the middle of the night.

"Your holiness, I'm so sorry to wake you," said Vasilla.

"What is it? Why are you disturbing me?" replied Khozem drowsily.

"Your holiness, he knows. The whole mosque knows. Word is spreading."

"What are you talking about, Vasilla? Can't this wait until morning?"

"I thought I'd call you right away, your holiness."

"Who knows? And who is 'he?'"

"The Imam, your holiness."

"What?!" yelled Khozem, more awake.

"The Imam, your holiness. He knows. Everyone knows."

"How the hell does he know?"

"His mother told him."

"His mother? Well then how did the rest of the mosque find out?"

After a moment of silence, Vasilla told him about the outburst.

"Oh dear, Vasilla. Oh dear."

"The whole mosque follows him. The amilsaab, especially. He let him speak to the entire mosque."

"What did he say?"

"He used words like 'Peace' and 'Absolute love,' and how we should, well, love the Jew as much as we love ourselves."

"Oh dear, Vasilla..."

"People are talking, your holiness. People will follow him..."

"But why will they follow him? He might be some crackpot. Why did people listen to him?"

"I...I don't know," lied Vasilla, "but people believe in him. He gave an entire speech to a mosque already divided. At first half the mosque liked the amilsaab, and half did not, but now that the Imam has spoken, they are all following him."

"Vasilla, how many are following him?"

"The entire mosque."

"How many, Vasilla?! Be specific!"

"I would estimate one hundred, maybe one hundred and fifty people, your holiness."

"Okay, it's time for containment. This is what I want, and we have to act quickly. You must prepare him for a trip to Mecca. I want you and the Imam on the next flight out."

"What if he doesn't want to go?"

"Persuade him, Vasilla. Say to him that he must if he's a true Imam. He'll accompany you to Mecca."

"He's too stubborn. He won't journey to Mecca just for the sake of journeying."

"We must bring him here. This must be done. Tell him that he must involve himself in his own culture."

"Or even meet his real parents."

"Perfect! Vasilla, that's perfect, you genius! Tell him that he'll meet his real parents. He will definitely come. Yes, that's what my father was saying: 'To adopt the West like a bastard son.' Okay, Vasilla, bring him to me on the first flight. Bring him directly to me."

"Yes, your holiness."

Immediately after hanging up the phone, Khozem called Asif Mohammed, his Advisor of Executions.

Chapter Nine
MUSTAFA CONFRONTS THE TRUTH
17th of Safar 1436
(December 10, 2014)

The truth hit the Imam in waves. He returned home with his mother after the dreadful commotion at the mosque, his eyes filled with angry tears. He saw his mother as another person entirely, as though his days with her had been some terrible hallucination. He considered his trips to the psychiatric wards in a similar light. He had questions, large ones, but knew not who would provide the answers. For hours he stayed in his room with the door closed, away from his mother. He had left the mosque after giving a strong speech, like the actor, who after a stunning performance, leaves during the fanatical applause.

The snow beyond his window fell rapidly, filling the sidewalks and dusting Riverside Drive. He looked through the window, not moving a muscle, only staring vaguely at the absent-minded snow. He thought he should pray, but had little idea what he could possibly say to his Creator.

The fear. People now knew him. He had been exposed to the entire mosque, and certainly he would be followed, because people actually believed in the unfortunate spectacle. His paranoia grew with each unique snowflake.

He knew he had enemies by default who would want him dead. He did not know who to trust anymore. He could not even trust his own mother who had lied to him his entire life. A torrent of yesterdays flashed in his mind, especially the yesterdays in Boston. He dismissed such thinking a while ago, blaming mental illness. Was it all true? Still no answer save a slight wind rattling the window, and the snow falling imperceptibly as though it shared his fear and utter desolation. The snow seemed to whisper that California was a dream indeed, that loneliness, a state of being he easily grasped, would unfold in added dimensions, that responsibility towards Allah would somehow govern and direct his days from now on, this same Allah against whom he had resoundingly rebelled. At the heart of it all, however, he missed the life he once had, although the pains great and the pleasures few. It was over, and the end must also signify a new beginning, but a beginning where? A beginning for whom? A beginning with a people about whom he knew absolutely nothing, the same people he had abandoned? Islam?

He knew very little, and what he did know angered him. In a land full of options, every escape route sealed shut like the light that escapes from being buried alive. For hours the snowflakes took him into a deep trance, and a sharp knock at the door brought him out just as quickly. He opened the door and found the big, husky Vasilla, his head covered with snow.

"May I speak with you a moment?" he said.

"Come in," whispered the Imam, holding the door wide.

Vasilla ducked beneath the threshold.

"Quite a time at the mosque."

"Why didn't anyone tell me?"

"It was all arranged. Sooner or later you would have found out. I'm sorry it had to happen this way, but now you know."

"What do I do now?"

"Well, this too has been arranged with the blessings of Allah and his holiness Khozem Bengaliwala."

"Who is Kho- Kho-, who's that?"

"He is your servant, as you are his master."

"Wait right there! I'm not anyone's master. I wish to break whatever arrangements you people have set."

"I'm afraid that's impossible," said Vasilla quietly.

"I don't think you understand. I want no part of this."

"You must be feeling much right now, but soon the feelings you have will fade. Besides, tonight we'll be traveling, the both of us to Mecca. There we will meet your bavasaab."

"Mecca?" laughed the Imam. "I don't even know where Mecca is."

"Saudi Arabia, your eminence. The Land of Allah, built by the Prophet Abraham and his son, Isaac."

"And I suppose we'll leave tonight?" he laughed. "If you for one second think I'm leaving this room, you're out of your skull, my friend. I hardly even know you. One minute you're up front praying, and the next minute you're kissing my hand..."

"Don't you wish to meet your real parents?"

This simple question struck a sensitive nerve.

"How long will we be staying," he asked eventually.

"No more than two days. You'll be back on American soil before you can say 'God is great.'"

After careful deliberations, the Imam agreed. His mother enthusiastically supported his decision. He and Vasilla left on an early morning flight. He carried a knapsack. He did not even change his clothes. He was silent for the entire flight, lost in thoughts of his real parents and who they might be. He was not excited, only confused, for his real loyalty rested with Maryam, and he confirmed this repeatedly, as though his mind may change at any moment. He was sucked in by the even simpler promise of a speedy return to America.

Chapter Ten
THE IMAM AND KHOZEM
18th of Safar 1436
(December 11, 2014)

Mustafa could sense the heat of Arabia even before disembarking. The heat not only covered the landscape of scattered rocks and tan dust but also consumed the airplane as it sat idly at its gate. The sun shone intensely, and the dark faces imprinted on his recent memory were uprooted and replaced by tan faces in head gear and flowing garments.

The men of Arabia seemed to float while walking, their legs unseen, their feet snug within open-toed sandals. Mustafa held this impression at the airport as he saw passengers in these long garments gather at a long customs line.

Vasilla flashed an identification card and passed without a word. Mustafa followed in awe. They walked briskly through the tidy terminal.

Mustafa was fascinated by the simplest things, such as the customs workers emptying suitcases, the doorways marked with flowing Arabic symbols, the praying areas where believers bowed and prostrated themselves. The heat had new meaning as they left the terminal, and they piled quickly within a white-curtained Mercedes. He was surrounded by people he did not know: two silent bodyguards in the front listening to a plain, twangy music, their silence lending an unfathomable strangeness to a young man already estranged.

They went from Jeddah to Mecca along a short highway. The choppy hills ascended and dipped with regularity. Along the fields the Imam spotted a series of white canvas tents with sport utility vehicles parked beside them. These short bursts of desert prairie soon ended as they approached Mecca.

Already Mustafa could make out the Metropolis. He could smell it, almost taste its foods and meet its people.

'Only two days,' he thought, 'two days of oddity, and I'll be back home laughing about all of this.'

And yet each crumbled rock fascinated him. He was a child again, and after a short while, he forgot his reasons for traveling to Mecca in the first place.

The car stopped in front of an iron-wrought gate. The gate swung open at the touch of a remote, and soon they were parked outside of the Bengaliwala home. Mustafa was thankful to be out of the car. Khozem greeted him at the front door by taking his hand and kissing it.

"Listen, really, there's no need to kiss my hand," said Mustafa with a smile.

"Come, your eminence," as Khozem led him inside.

The sat together in the living room. For a while they simply eyed one another. Khozem then asked:

"Are you hungry? Would you like something to eat? Maybe some kitchra or biryani or meat kabobs?"

"No thanks, I ate on the flight," replied the Imam.

"How was the flight? Pleasant, I hope."

"Very nice indeed. Great service. They fed me very well, although I'm not sure what I ate," he laughed.

"You'll soon get used to your native foods. How do you like Mecca so far?"

"I'm anxious to see more of it. Maybe you could show me around."

Mustafa felt uncomfortable in the silence that followed every painful exchange. He realized this bavasaab was not much older than he, and he tried to relate on a generation level.

"Are you married?" asked Mustafa. "This house is so big. The view is incredible. The mosque down there is the biggest I've ever seen."

"No, I'm not married yet. I live with my parents. And the mosque you see is known as the Kaa'bah, the holiest shrine known to man."

"Where are you parents now?"

"They've been vacationing in Riyadh for some time."

"I see. Maybe you can take me down to that big mosque."

"Only the righteous are allowed in there," said Khozem, "but let's start with the basics. Do you know how to pray in Arabic?"

"Uh, no, I pray in English."

"Yes, of course, English. Well, here in Mecca we say our prayers strictly in Arabic as that is the appointed language ordained by our Prophet (May Peace be Upon Him)."

"I don't see anything wrong with praying in English. God would be able to translate it, don't you think?"

"Much would be lost in the translation. Nearly all of the Qu'ran's poetry would be trampled by the foreign tongue."

"Oh I don't think so."

"There is a lot you have to learn before making foolish judgements. This is typical of every Imam I've studied thus far, and I've been reading about past Imams for nearly ten years. I have noticed a commonality in the Imams I have studied. They have lofty visions without any sense of responsibility. Tell me, did you attend any schools where you live?"

"For a short time. I traveled quite a bit, and I watch the television to keep abreast of daily developments."

"So what does the television say of, let's say, the Middle East?" asked Khozem.

"There's a war going on. Maybe we can bring about a peaceful resolution to these conflicts, you and I. By the way, your friend in the car told me I'll see my real parents. Do you know anything about them?"

"All in good time, your eminence. How long do you plan to stay in Arabia?"

"Two days. No more," smiled the Imam. "At least that's what I've been told. Everyone's so secretive around here."

"Well, two days is not a long time. Perhaps you may learn a little about yourself while you're here. Perhaps our ancient ways will rub off on you."

"I don't see a chance of that happening," smiled the Imam.

"Really? Tell me, are there any Jews where you live?"

"Quite a few, quite a few."

"Yes, I hear the Americas is overrun by these Jews."

"That's only a stereotype, a myth. In America we try not to see people in terms of religion or color or creed. The human personality is more complex and demands that we treat all people as individuals. We are more similar in America than we are different. From what I've learned, Jewish people are good people. We should treat them like brothers. Only then will there be an end to this crisis in the Middle East. You know, if you and I can work together on this problem, maybe we can find a good, honest solution to this mess. After all, shouldn't we let love take its course? This same love and its powers demand that we become friends with our Jewish brothers, don't you think?"

Khozem smiled tightly and nodded along.

"Think of it," continued the Imam, "you and me, none of this master and servant stuff, but you and me, you in Saudi Arabia, myself in the United States, working together to bring an everlasting peace in the area. Can you see it? I can. Just think, Jews walking hand-in-hand with Arabs, Arabs attending bat-mizvahs, and Jews attending mishaks, and Arabs saying 'mozaltov!' and Jews saying 'mubarrak!' So much we can accomplish, you and me. In fact in the U.S. already much has been accomplished. For instance I heard in the news that a mosque opened in a small town, and at the opening ceremonies a

Christian priest and a Jewish rabbi were present, giving their blessings to the brand new mosque. See, that's just one example, and I'm sure there are many more. Why don't we do it this way? You can be in the Middle East pushing for peace, and I'll be in America doing the same thing. Of course in the Middle East there are many issues to sort out. I'm not that naïve. I know there exists hatred and strife and division. I know these bitter feelings run deep, I understand. But over time, these hatreds will all disappear, such that the Arab will learn to embrace the Jew, hug him right in the street, and say to him: 'you are my brother, and you will always be my brother no matter how far apart life has brought us.' It's so clear. Together, Arab and Jew, Muslim and Jew, enjoying life for once, loving peace and good will towards one another.

"This will take time. Nothing comes overnight. I'm sure we will have to argue and debate a lot, but I can see it, really I can. I believe in Allah's vision for peace in the Middle East, I see it as clear as the day, and once all of this history between Arab and Jew has passed, we can move on and forge new relationships, new friendships, and then we can learn from each other instead of fighting all the time. I'm so sick and tired of the fighting. It must stop, otherwise we can never grow, we can never change into the good beings Allah meant us to be. Just think of it. You and me, we would make a great team. See, it begins with the idea, the idea of peace, and then that idea we rationalize and find a path to it, no matter the history, no matter the struggle. No more, I say. We must forge a path to peace, not as separate entities, but together, Muslim and Jew, hand in hand, laughing together over a cup of coffee or having dinner, loving each other, anything. Peace is logical and rational. It is also achievable in our lifetimes. So let's do something about it. Lord knows I'm ready, and I get the feeling Allah is ready for it too. But most importantly, my friend, can you see it? Can you see this beautiful peace unfolding? It's not magic or anything. It takes an internal struggle, and when we overcome it, we all win, all of us win. And by working together, me and you, we can accomplish anything, anything at all."

Khozem grinned and said:

"You really think so?"

"I don't think so, I know so. I feel it in my heart we can work things out for the benefit of all. Can you see this vision that Allah has sent down to me?"

"Why don't you go back to your hotel and rest. We'll meet again in the morning."

"By the way, when will I meet my real parents? I really would like to see them."

"All in good time," smiled Khozem.

Chapter Eleven
DEATH
19th of Safar 1436
(December 13, 2014)

It's hard to say whether the Imam spotted the speeding taxicab as it approached. He could have moved out of the way. He could have returned to New York. He could have led his small following at the mosque and perhaps could have been a great spiritual leader for his people. Death, however, no matter the age, must come as a course of life, and death inevitably must be accepted. Arguably things may work in cycles: death as a movement towards a greater life far removed from us. And if death overcame him, Mustafa might have been content to leave this world, because life is such that dreams rarely manifest themselves to people who yearn for them most.

There must be a reason for this disturbing trend. Reality has a way of whittling our true dreams down to size, like a lump of clay shaped or the piece of wood carved by skilled hands. And if we're lucky, we hold our dreams sacred despite the cuts and scars, the flaws in character, the plans which count for nought. The Imam, assuming he had died that day, would have held his wild dreams to heart and would have never let go.

There must be a place in the darkest fires of Hell where these dreamers stay. The flesh must singe, and the brain must boil. The darkness must be complete, and the depressions maddening. And within this dark place, the Imam must have heard the cries of millions, withstood the heat, or found another dream to follow. And because of his terrible location, he must have prayed until his mind smoldered. Perhaps he fell to his knees and offered Allah verbosity, idiom, and dangling participles, all of it rushed and too convenient. Or maybe he fell to his knees and simply wept. Regardless, he must have dreamt of something greater than himself, as all dreamers do the same. He must have endured the fires, the blood, the slings and arrows, never ducking or running, but enduring. But just like a good rain extinguishes the longest fire, so he must have escaped Hell with the help of visiting angels who heard his dream and delivered it to the All Mighty. And when the cards come up empty, the chin falls upon a cold pavement, a mere nickel lines the pocket, the cell padded, the straight-jacket tight, the fires fuming, the women disappearing, and the tender heart folds, there must always be a reason, and the Imam must have found Allah instead of the world he imagined.

Within the fires he must have seen an awkward light, a dazzling light. Then a hand which gripped his own. Suddenly an effortless tug to higher ground. Finally, a warm embrace by an entity that soothed him with kind words and understood him absolutely and infinitely. Yet if there exists a duty to one's dreams, and if those dreams are good, just, and pure, then the person must act upon them. The Imam, in his deliverance from the fires, must have questioned his Creator and believed instead in those dreams given to him, regardless of Hell's consequences.

And his were only dreams, just dreams, preposterous and absurd, grandiose and misunderstood, never overt but always kept in the vault of a young person's heart. Just simple, childish dreams.

It's hard to say whether or not he moved out of the way of that speeding taxicab. In all likelihood, though, he survived.

THE END.

<u>Diagrams for Books Three and Four</u>

Diagram #1

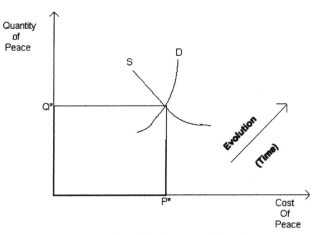

Q* · P* · reflexive equilibrium of peace

Diagram #2

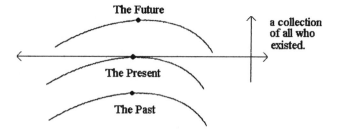

Diagram #3

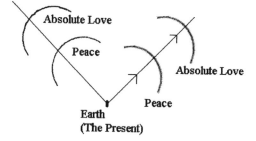

Diagram #4

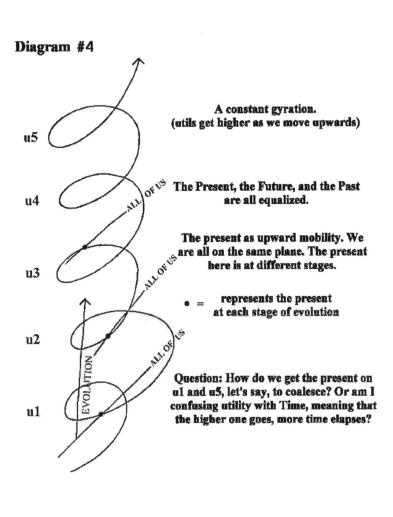

A constant gyration.
(utils get higher as we move upwards)

The Present, the Future, and the Past
are all equalized.

The present as upward mobility. We
are all on the same plane. The present
here is at different stages.

● = represents the present
at each stage of evolution

Question: How do we get the present on
u1 and u5, let's say, to coalesce? Or am I
confusing utility with Time, meaning that
the higher one goes, more time elapses?

u5

u4

u3

u2

u1

ALL OF US

ALL OF US

ALL OF US

EVOLUTION

Diagram A)

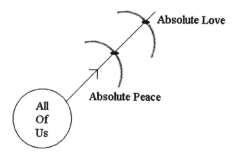

Diagram B)

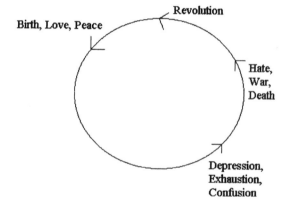

Diagram C)

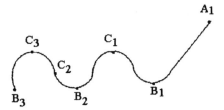

Diagram D)

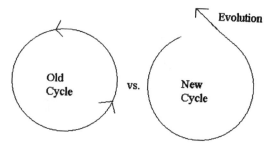

Old
Cycle   vs.   New
Cycle

Evolution

Diagram E)

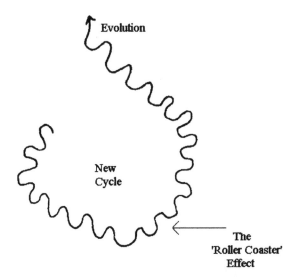

Diagram F)

Towards
Absolute
Love

$u_1 \longrightarrow u_5$

increasingly greater
good for the
greatest number

u_5

Note:
These planes may also,
be called 'Love Planes'
(i.e., $L, L_1, L_2, L_3 \rightarrow L$,
but to make it sound
more professional, I
chose 'utility.'
It does not necassarily
mean that I am "utilitarian."

u_4

u_3

u_2

u_1

Diagram G)

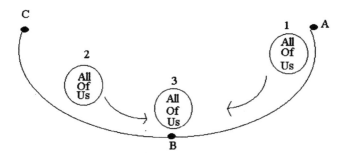

Diagram H

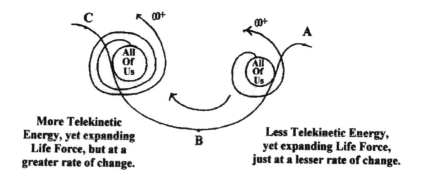

C   ↖ 00+

All Of Us

00+ ↖   A

All Of Us

B

More Telekinetic Energy, yet expanding Life Force, but at a greater rate of change.

Less Telekinetic Energy, yet expanding Life Force, just at a lesser rate of change.

Diagram I

The Slinky Gyration Model In Full Scope:

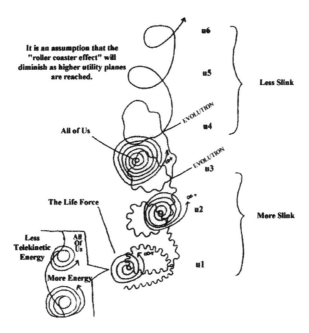

It is an assumption that the "roller coaster effect" will diminish as higher utility planes are reached.

u6

u5

Less Slink

EVOLUTION

u4

All of Us

EVOLUTION

u3

The Life Force

u2

More Slink

Less Telekinetic Energy

All Of Us

More Energy

u1

Diagram #5   A STRAND OF THE SLINKY GYRATION
                      WITH BIRTH / DEATH CYCLE

"WE ARE ALL IN THIS TOGETHER - ALL OF US."

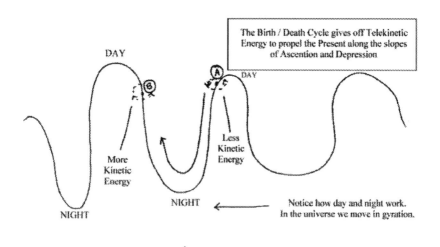

The Birth / Death Cycle gives off Telekinetic
Energy to propel the Present along the slopes
of Ascention and Depression

DAY

DAY

More
Kinetic
Energy

Less
Kinetic
Energy

NIGHT

NIGHT

Notice how day and night work.
In the universe we move in gyration.

The point is to show how the
present is propelled to higher
utility planes via Telekinetic
Energy of the Birth / Death cycle.

I disagree with the cycle concept of
Birth / Death Kinetic Energy. A spiral
would do, but this adds more
complicaion that I can bear.

Diagram **#6**

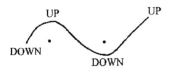

Diagram **#7**

An Arbitrary Point on the
Slinky Gyration

All of us (Earth)

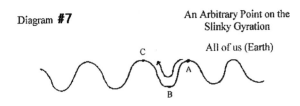

Diagram **#8**

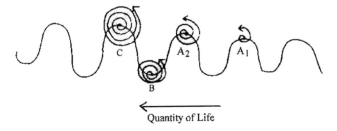

Quantity of Life

Diagram #9

Scenerio One:
Good Thoughts

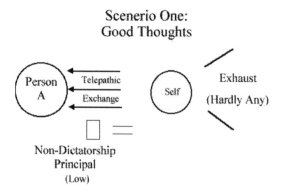

Person A ← Telepathic Exchange ← Self

Exhaust (Hardly Any)

□ ═

Non-Dictatorship Principal (Low)

Scenerio Two:
Good and Bad Thoughts

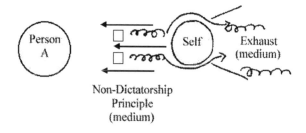

Person A

Self

Exhaust (medium)

Non-Dictatorship Principle (medium)

Scenerio Three:

Key:

□ = Non-Dictatorship Principle
— = Good Thoughts
ᒍᒍᒍ = Violent Negative Thoughts
╱ ╲ = Exhaust for Violent Negative Thoughts

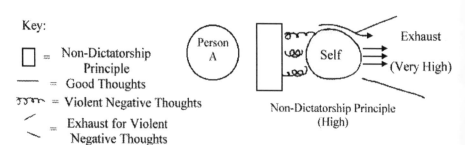

Person A

Self

Exhaust (Very High)

Non-Dictatorship Principle (High)

Diagram #10

Telepathy and The Exhaust Function
In Scenario Three:

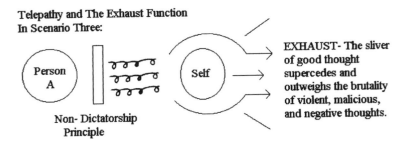

Person
A

Non- Dictatorship
Principle

Self

EXHAUST- The sliver
of good thought
supercedes and
outweighs the brutality
of violent, malicious,
and negative thoughts.

Diagram #11

The Charles Dipper Example

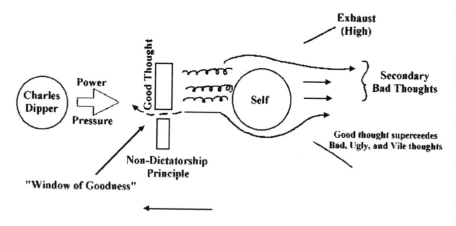

As Power Pressure increases, the "thickness" of the Non-Dictatorship Principle increases as well

Diagram #12 The Harry Dimple Example

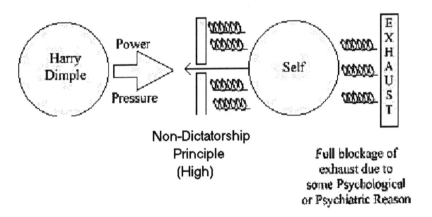

Harry Dimple

Power

Pressure

Self

E
X
H
A
U
S
T

Non-Dictatorship
Principle
(High)

Full blockage of
exhaust due to
some Psychological
or Psychiatric Reason

Diagram #13

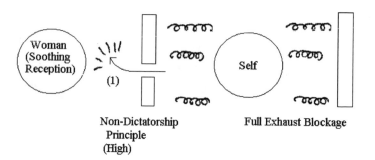

Woman
(Soothing
Reception)

(1)

Self

Non-Dictatorship
Principle
(High)

Full Exhaust Blockage

Diagram # 14

The Closure Complex

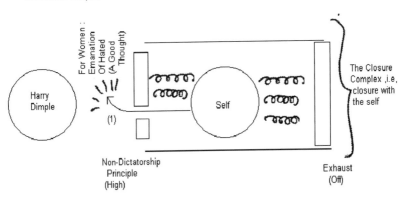

Note: Men cannot see the emanation of hatred
better than women can.

Diagram #15

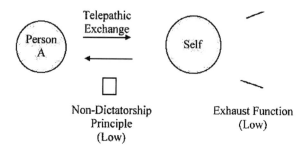

Telepathic
Exchange

Person
A

Self

Non-Dictatorship
Principle
(Low)

Exhaust Function
(Low)

Diagram **#16**

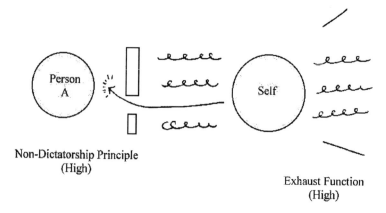

Person
A

Self

Non-Dictatorship Principle
(High)

Exhaust Function
(High)

ᒪᒪᒪᒪ = Hate

◄────► = Good Thoughts

ᐟᐟᐟᐟ = Emanation of Hatred

Diagram #17

The Closure Complex and "Iterated" External Communication
1st Communication:

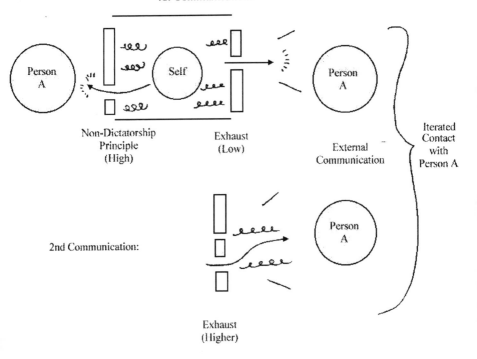

Non-Dictatorship
Principle
(High)

Exhaust
(Low)

External
Communication

Iterated
Contact
with
Person A

2nd Communication:

Exhaust
(Higher)

Diagram #18

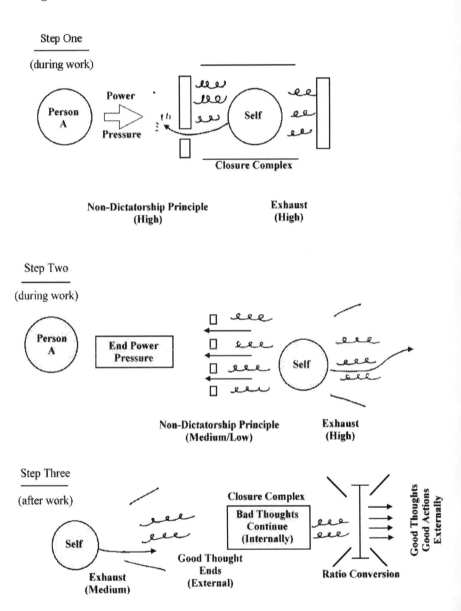

Step One

(during work)

Person A

Power

Pressure

Self

Closure Complex

Non-Dictatorship Principle
(High)

Exhaust
(High)

Step Two

(during work)

Person A

End Power Pressure

Self

Non-Dictatorship Principle
(Medium/Low)

Exhaust
(High)

Step Three

(after work)

Self

Exhaust
(Medium)

Good Thought Ends
(External)

Closure Complex

Bad Thoughts Continue
(Internally)

Ratio Conversion

Good Thoughts
Good Actions
Externally

Diagram #19   Refinery Ratio in Scope

(during work)

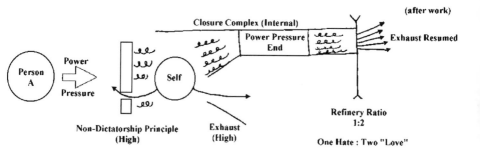

Closure Complex (Internal)

(after work)

Power Pressure
End

Exhaust Resumed

Person
A

Power

Pressure

Self

Non-Dictatorship Principle
(High)

Exhaust
(High)

Refinery Ratio
1:2

One Hate : Two "Love"

A Glossary of Historical Names, Places, and Terms

Note: This glossary does not list all of the Islamic names, places, and terms found in this novel, but it does list the most essential terms which may be not be familiar to the reader. For example, some of the names in the novel, which are not listed here, were most likely created by the author or are variants of other Islamic names.

Abbas- (al-'Abbas) A warrior who fought the Prophet Muhammad at the Battle of Badr. He was captured and thereafter converted to Islam. He joined the Prophet in the final battle of Mecca in 630 A.D.

Adhan- The opening call to prayer, which may differ from region to region.

Ali- The Fourth Caliphate of Islam. The first Imam of ***Shia*** Islam. The cousin, and later, son-in-law to the Prophet Muhammad. He married the Prophet's daughter, ***Fatima***

Amilsaab- A local cleric, usually the head of a municipal mosque.

Arafat- An area of desert about thirteen miles from the city of Mecca. During an Islamic Pilgrimage (***Hajj***), pilgrims will visit Arafat to hear sermons and take significant oaths. This is also the place where Adam and Eve found themselves after their expulsion from Paradise.

Aya- A verse of the ***Qu'ran***.

Bavasaab- In this novel, the open and visible leader of Shia Islam. Variant of the word "Bhaisaab" in the Gujarati language.

Biryani- A traditional Pakistani dish consisting of moist rice and meat.

Bismillah- "In the name of Allah."

Black Stone- (al-Hajar al-Aswad) A meteorite which fell to Earth and was used by Abraham and Isaac as the final stone in the building of the **Kaa'bah**. Pilgrims, circumambulating this corner of the House of God, will recite prayers and try to touch it.

Cairo- The present day capital of Egypt.

Chador- A cloak and veil covering Islamic women to deter a man's temptation. This type of dress is most prevalent in Iran and other Shia countries.

Custodian of the Holy Mosques- Or the King of Present Day Saudi Arabia. It is said that the King chose this title under pressure from Shia groups, mostly in Iran, who wanted to make the holy sites of Mecca and Medina internationally independent cities, much like Vatican City in Italy.

Duppurta- A traditional Pakistani dress, worn by women.

Fatima- Daughter of the Prophet Muhammad and wife to **Ali**.

Ghazal(s)- Traditional Islamic songs.

Gosh- Traditional Pakistani dish of meat and gravy.

Gulab- This means "Rose," in Gujarati language.

Hadith- A record of Islamic thought created by the Prophet Muhammad. This record is considered a close second to that of the Qu'ran, Islam's holiest book. These records are considered the traditions of Islam.

Hajj- A mandatory pilgrimage, once in a Muslim's lifetime, to the *Kaa'bah* in the city of Mecca. This is one of the five Pillars of Islam.

Hassan- In Arabic, this means "good or just." Various holy men of Islam have been named this.

Houris- Virgin women who are female companions in the Islamic Paradise, or Afterlife.

Hussein- (al-'Husayn) The Third Imam in Shia tradition, a grandson of Prophet Muhammad, and the son of the First Imam, Ali. He was beheaded in *Kerbala,* Iraq in 680 A.D.

Iblis- The Devil.

Imam- In Arabic, this means "religious or spiritual leader." It has a variety of connotations, but the term refers to the Twelve Leaders of the Ithna 'Asharis, or those Twelve essential Imams who followed the Prophet Muhammad. According to Shia legend, the Twelfth Imam, Muhammad al-Mahdi, disappeared in 874 A.D., and his return is expected at the Day of Judgement. This Twelfth Imam is portrayed in this novel by the central character, Mustafa.

Insh'Allah- "If God Wills It."

Israfil- The Islamic angel who sounds the trumpet on the Day of Resurrection.

Jinn- Protean and invisible beings made from fire. They are associated with *Iblis.*

Kaa'bah- In Arabic, this means "cube." It is a building in the center of the Great Mosque in Mecca towards which all Muslim's offer prayer. It is said that the demolished idols from Prophet

Muhammad's sacking of Mecca were at one time stored within its walls.

Kerbala- (Karbala) A site in Iraq, which is one of the holiest shrines in Islam and the burial ground for the Shia Martyr **Hussein** (Husayn).

Khadija- First wife of the Prophet Muhammad. The Prophet married her when he was 25 and she was 40 years of age.

Khalid- Historically, a renowned general in the Prophet's army, who had converted to Islam after originally fighting against the Prophet. In this novel, he is the father of the Eleventh Imam, Shabbir Hussein

Kitchra- A traditional Islamic dish, served usually on the 10th of MaHarram, the date Imam Husayn was assassinated in Kerbala.

Kurta- Traditional Pakistani dress for men, usually made of loose cotton clothing.

Lahore- A major city in Pakistan, fictionalized in this novel.

Marwa- (al-Marwa) This is a small hill enclosed within the Grand Mosque of Mecca. Pilgrims run between this hill and another, known as **al-Safi**, to imitate the back and forth running of Hajar, the wife of Ismail, who was the son of the Prophet Ibrahim. Hajar ran between these two hills to fetch water and to quench the thirst of their dying son.

Maryam- In Arabic, this means "Mary." It is the heading of the 19th surah of the Qu'ran.

Mashad- A city in Iran which is home to one of Islam's most revered universities.

Mecca- The holiest city in Islam and the site of the *Kaa'bah*, surrounded by the Grand Mosque.

Medina- The second holiest city in Islam, the third being Jerusalem. The Prophet Muhammad is buried in Medina, and his tomb rests in another magnificent mosque, comparable to the Grand Mosque of Mecca.

Mik'ail- A great Islamic angel who watches over places of worship.

Mishak(s)- The rite of passage obligatory for all young Muslim adolescents into adulthood. From this point Islam's customs take full effect. This is comparable to the Jewish bat-mitzvah.

Mubarrak- "Congratulations."

Muezzin- The person who calls the *adhan*, traditionally from a mosque's minaret.

Muhammad- The Prophet of Islam. His revelations are recorded in the *Qu'ran*.

Mujlis- A community prayer, usually in a masjid, or mosque.

Mullah(s)- A term used for respected Islamic religious figures in Asia, Iran, and elsewhere.

Munkir- An angel most often associated with Death and Burial.

Mutawafs- The Religious Police.

Nakeer- An angel most often associated with Death and Burial. Nakeer is said to be the angel *Munkir's* partner.

Namaz- "Prayer."

Namira- A hill in Mecca where sermons are given during the Islamic pilgrimage of Hajj.

Ninth of D'hul Hijja- A crucial date during Hajj, when pilgrims visit both *Namira* and *Arafat* for essential rites.

Piaster(s)- Present-day Egyptian currency.

Qu'ran- The holiest book in Islam. This is said to be that record of the Prophet Muhammad's revelations from Allah through the angel Jibril. It is roughly 115 chapters long, and each chapter contains *ayat(s)*, or verses. It is well-known that the Qu'ran, in contrast to the narrative structure of the Bible, is a poetic testament to these divine revelations.

Quraysh- In Arabic, this means "shark." This was one of the major tribes in Mecca to which the Prophet Muhammad belonged.

Rashida- In Arabic, this means "rightly guided," or "guided by the just."

Rial(s)- The currency of present day Saudi Arabia.

Riyadh- A city in Saudi Arabia.

Rooh Afza- A Pakistani fruit drink, bottled as a thick, red syrup, to be mixed with water. It is marketed as a drink that imitates the flavor of roses.

Rupee(s)- The currency of present day India.

Safi- (al 'Safi) See *Marwa*

Sajjada- Prayer rug. A supplicant will usually pray at the foot of it, and then, while prostrating, touch his/her head at its top.

Salaam(s)- Traditional Islamic greetings. In this novel, the characters kiss the backs of each other's hands when greeting one another.

Shia- A major branch of Islam, known as the "embattled minority" to some scholars. This branch of Islam holds that Ali, the Fourth Caliphate of Islam, is the rightful successor of the Prophet Muhammad, whereas Sunni Islam holds that Abu Bakr, the first elected Muslim Caliph, is his rightful successor. There are many ritualistic differences between both branches of faith, such as the reverence of the Martyr *Husayn* and the use of a carpet while praying. Also, it would be wise to note that most citizens of Iran are Shia Muslims.

Subha- The Islamic rosary, consisting of 99 beads, although some may vary.

Sunnah- In Arabic, "the well-worn path." This is a record of the customary practices of the Prophet Muhammad, especially his ideas on Islamic law.

Surah- In Arabic, this means "chapter." The Qu'ran consists of 115 *surahs,* or chapters.

Syedna- A prefix to a name worthy of the highest honor and respect in Islam.

Tariq- In Arabic, this means "The Dark Star." This is also the title of one of the chapters in the *Qu'ran*.

Tawaf- The obligatory ritual of circumambulating the House of God, (*Kaa'bah*), seven times.

Thali- A large silver platter which is placed on the ground and is used for eating meals, as a group, around it.

Topees- "Skullcaps."

Tubla- An Indian-Pakistani percussion instrument.

Ummah- This is an important term in Islam. It means "unity," or in the Prophet's time, a strong community of Muslim people.

Umrah- "Small Pilgrimage." This is in contrast to the major pilgrimage, called *Hajj*, which is one of the five Pillars of Islam.

Zakat- One of the five Pillars of Islam. Zakat is a percentage of a Muslim's income which is taxed and given to help the poor. In this day, this tax is usually given to the mosque to which he/she belongs.

Zaqqum- The Qu'ran defines this as a terrible tree in Hell bearing foul-smelling fruit. Its flowers are the heads of demons. The inhabitants of Hell are said to eat from this plant, which burns them.

Zindabad!- "Long Live!"

Zum-Zum Water- (Zamzam) The well of water which Ismail and Hajjar found on the run between the hills of *Safi* and *Marwa*. This well is now a part of the Grand Mosque in Mecca and is considered holy water. It is said to have special healing properties. Pilgrims usually drink this water during *Hajj* and *Umrah*.

Acknowledgments

The author wishes to thank his family without whose guidance, generosity, dedication, and love for their son this publication would have never been possible.

Special thanks to Elizabeth.

Special thanks also go to Peter and Sean of World-Wide Connections for the difficult task of designing the diagrams to Books Three and Four from hand-drawings provided by the author.

Please visit *First Amendment Press* online at www.fapic.com If you would like to send us your comments by e-mail, please e-mail us at fapic@msn.com.

FAPIC Order Form: (Orders may also be placed online).

Please rush the following books:

Noble McCloud, A Novel **By Harvey Havel**
Quantity?_____@ US $25.00 each (Shipping and Handling included).

The Imam, A Novel **by Harvey Havel**
Quantity?_____@ US $25.00 each (Shipping and Handling included).

International Maritime Health and Problems of Seafarers
By Dr. Mohammad Zakaria
Quantity?_____@ US $35.00 each (Shipping and Handling included).

(NJ Residents please add 6% Sales Tax)

Name:_____
Address:_____
_____
City:_____State:_____
Zip Code:_____
Email:_____

Make check or money order payable to:

First Amendment Press Int'l Co.
38 East Ridgewood Avenue
PMB 217
Ridgewood, NJ, 07450-3808

First Amendment Press International Company
uncut. unedited. quality literature

Official Entry Form
For a Chance to Win
Vacations to Egypt or New York City, USA

Please Check One Box Only:

☐ Yes! Please enter me in the drawing to win a 2-Person, 10-Day Vacation Tour and Cruise of *Egypt! (Cairo, Aswan, Kom Ombo, Edfu, and Luxor)*

☐ Yes! Please enter me in the drawing to win a 2-Person, 10-day Vacation Tour of *New York City, USA!*

Please provide the following information about yourself.
(All fields are required!)

Name:_____

Address:_____

_____

City:_____ State:_____ Province:_____

Country:_____ Postal Zip Code:_____

Telephone Number: (Country Code and City Code if outside the United States):

Day Time:_____ Evenings:_____

Email Address:_____

I understand that this Official Entry Form entitles me to One entry in a random drawing to win vacation packages either to Egypt or New York City, USA. If I am selected to receive a vacation package to either location as a result of this random drawing, then I, the Contestant, and my travel companion must abide by and agree to the terms and conditions that will be given to us at the time of selection.

Signature:_____ Date:_____

Please send this form by **MAY 1, 2001** to:
The Imam Vacation Contest, 38 East Ridgewood Avenue, PMB 156,
Ridgewood, NJ, 07450-3808, U.S.A.